aiseal Mór was born into a rich tradition of Irish storytelling and music. As a child he learned to play the brass-strung harp, carrying on a long family tradition. He spent several years collecting stories, songs and music of the Celtic lands during many visits to Ireland, Scotland and Brittany. He has a degree in performing arts from the University of Western Sydney and has worked as an actor, a teacher and as a musician.

Also by Caiseal Mór

The Wellspring Trilogy:
The Well of Yearning
The Well of the Goddess
The Well of Many Blessings

The Wanderers Series:
The Circle and the Cross
The Song of the Earth
The Water of Life

The Watchers Trilogy:
The Meeting of the Waters
The King of Sleep
The Raven Game

The Tilecutter's Penny
Scratches in the Margin
The Moon on the Lake
Carolan's Concerto

For Children
The Harp at Midnight

THE
WELL
OF
MANY
BLESSINGS

BOOK THREE OF THE WELLSPRING TRILOGY

CAISEAL MÓR

POCKET
BOOKS

LONDON · NEW YORK · SYDNEY · TORONTO

First published in Great Britain by Pocket Books, 2005
An imprint of Simon & Schuster UK Ltd
A Viacom Company

1 3 5 7 9 10 8 6 4 2

Simon & Schuster UK Ltd
Africa House
64–78 Kingsway
London WC2B 6AH

www.simonsays.co.uk

Simon & Schuster Australia
Sydney

A CIP catalogue record for this book is available from the British Library

ISBN 0 7434 6857 0
EAN 9780743468572

Typeset by SX Composing DTP, Rayleigh, Essex
Printed and bound in Great Britain by
Cox & Wyman Ltd, Reading, Berkshire

AcknowLedgements

s ever my heartfelt thanks go to my literary agent, Selwa Anthony. With her help I've been able to continue pursuing this passion I've acquired for storytelling. Thanks again to Julia Stiles who has edited every one of my novels since she was Commissioning Editor at Random House Australia in 1994. She's been such an encouragement to me over the years that I really don't think I would have been able to achieve so much without her.

I'd also like to thank all the folk at Simon & Schuster U.K. especially Kate Lyall-Grant who takes care of my novels at Pocket Books.

Of course I'd like to extend my gratitude to all the readers who enjoy my novels and to those who e-mail me or visit my website (www.caiseal.net). It's great to receive so much mail from so many readers. For those who haven't seen my web-page it's the place to find out publication dates and availability of the music I've composed to accompany this trilogy. I look forward to hearing your comments on my work.

This is the last instalment of the tale which started back in 1994 with 'The Circle and the Cross'. It's been a long time coming.

Many Blessings,
Caiseal Mór
Maleny, July 2004

For those readers who haven't visited my website the URL is; www.caiseal.net

Drop me a line if you feel like discussing this novel. My e-mail address is; harp@caiseal.net

If you wish to write to the author, Caiseal Mór may be contacted at the following e-mail address:
harp@caiseal.net

For information about other books and music by Caiseal Mór, please visit his website at:
www.caiseal.net

The Compact Disc of music composed and recorded by Caiseal Mór to accompany *The Wellspring Trilogy* may be ordered through amazon.co.uk or visit his website www.caiseal.net for details.

Pronunciation Guide: The Well of Many Blessings.

Aenghus	ah-noos
Anamchara	ah-num-kara
An Té a bhi agus atá	un chay a vee agus ah-taw
Aoife	eef-ah
Aon Dé	ohn-jay
Aontacht	ohn-tahkt
Áilleacht	Ah-lee-akt
Banba	bahn-va
Ban Righ	bahn-ree
Becc Mac Dé	beg mac jay
Bláni	Blah-nee
Boann	boh-an
Borumh	boh-roo
Branach	bran-akt
Brehon	breh-in
Bride	bree-dah
Caer Narffon	Car-nar-von
Caitlin	kotch-lin
Caoimhin	kay-vin
Cathlinn	kot-len
Cenn Maenach	ken mee-nahk
Cruitne	krit-nee
Curragh	koo-rah
Cymru	kim-roo
Dair Eolas	jayr olas
Dearg Uila	deruk-hoola
Derbáil	der-vahl
Draoi	dree
Dulogue	doo-loge
Dun Righ	dun-ree
Dun Sidhe	dun-shee

Eagla	ah-glah
Eber Finn	ayber-finn
Eirinn	ay-rin
Eoghanacht	yo-an-akt
Eolaí	yo-lee
Éremon	ay-ra-mon
Eterscél	ay-ta-shkayl
Eriu	ay-ree-oo
Fánaí	faw-nee
Feinach	fay-nach
Feni	fee-ni
Flidais	flee-daysh
Fodhla	foh-lah
Gaillimh	gahl-iv
Geas	geesh
Gusán Gelt	gooh-sawn-gelit
Inisfail	inish-fahl
Inis Mór	inish-mor
Isleen	ish-leen
Leabhar Fál	lebar-fawl
Leoghaire	leeh-ree
Lochlann	lok-lan
Lom Dubh	lom-doov
Mallacht	mal-ahkt
Maolán	mwee-lawn
Marcán	mahk-awn
Míl	meel
Moher	mo-er
Molaise	mohl-aysh
Morcán	mork-awn
Morrigán	moh-ree-gawn
Muirdeach	mew-ah-juk
Nathair	nah-hair
Nathairaí	nah-hair-ree

Neart	nart
Oidche	eeh-ha
Ollamh	oh-lahv
Órán	ooh-rawn
Ortha	ort-ah
Rián Ronán Og	ree-awn-roh-nawn-oge
Ruathar	roo-hahr
Samhain Oidhe	sah-win-eeh-ha
Samhna	sawv-nah
Sárán	saw-rawn
Scathach	skah-hah
Sciathan Cog	skee-ah-han-koge
Scodán	skoh-dawn
Segais	sha-gaysh
Sen Erainn	shen-ay-rin
Sianan	shan-nan
Sidhe	shee
Síla	shee-lah
Slua	slah
Sotar	soh-tah
Srón	shrohn
Tairngire	tah-eerun-gee-ree
Tigern Og	tee-gern-oge
Tóla	tooh-lah
Tóraí	toh-ree
Tuatha-De-Danaan	tooh-ah-hah-jay-dah-nahn

to the killibegs

castle lanfranc

lough gur

wexford

Ireland according to Binney.

The Well of Many Blessings

The three strongest forces in this world are the force of water, the force of fire and the force of hatred. Yet one who wields the first two guided by the force of love may be a one to be reckoned with.

The Normans came from across the water bearing fire and the force of hate to Ireland so that our people fled before their savage onslaught and few warriors of the Gael remained who would willingly stand against the foe. Thirty years after the foreigners first set foot on Irish soil, John Lackland, brother of Richard Lionheart, was crowned King of England at Westminster.

By then nearly half the folk of this blesséd island found themselves bowed down under the cruel lordship of the Normans. Yet there were many parts of the country in the west and the north where no foreigners dared set foot for fear of what might befall them. Trust me when I tell you that in those days there were worse things as could happen to a knight than ambush by brigands.

Would you mind not scratching yourself so vigorously! What's wrong with you – are my fleas bothering you? You've come back for the last part of my tale, so have the decency to refrain from all that itching – it's distracting me no end.

I'm glad there's not much left to say, I can tell you. I'm bloody tired. And a little cantankerous.

Did you hear me? Stop that! I'm not sitting here for the good of my health! You wanted a bloody story and you're going to bloody well get one! And you'll like it! Understand?

Now be a dear and take a ferret in your lap to keep you warm. There's nothing so warming as a ferret in your lap. When you get to my age it's the best that may be hoped for. Put your feet up. Take the weight off your prejudices for a while and button your bloody lips.

Now where was I? Oh, yes. There were worse things than ambush in those days. Rumours reached the ears of every Norman that there were dæmons who dwelled in the wild woods. Whisper was, there were monsters that fed on the flesh of mortals and delighted to play tricks to confound travellers. And one tale in particular concerned the Queen of the Night.

She wasn't merely a story spread to instil terror in the Normans. Aoife was real enough. She was a scheming witch if ever there was one. And she had a heart as black as a raven's tail feathers. I should know. I met her.

That's right, I encountered the Queen of the Night and survived. And it's the tale I'll finish for you tonight. You've listened to two evenings' worth of storytelling. Spend another night with me and I'll reveal what became of Robert FitzWilliam. I'll speak of his father William and of the good Culdee people of the Killibegs.

I'll tell you about King Caoimhin and the hosts of the Sen Erainn. You'll hear what became of Sianan and Mawn, Lochie and Isleen, Alan and Mirim, Derbaíl and Clemens, Lom Dubh and Sciathan Cog.

I'll speak once more of Frighteners and Enticers. They are the spirits which feed from our fear and love and who lead us on, if we let them, to all sorts of misadventures in the mortal world. I've told you of them before. But since there are few folk alive today who have any knowledge of them, I'll briefly mention something of their nature to jolt your memory.

Consider the cows. A good farmer keeps his milkers happy. He sleeps them in a warm part of the house or in a byre of their own if he's wealthy. Each day he takes them out into the fields where the lushest grass is growing. Lush grass makes for sweet, satisfying milk.

A good farmer keeps a watch over his cows to make sure no harm comes to them from wolves or cattle thieves. And when their udders are bulging with milk he relieves the discomfort by draining out every last drop.

In the same way Frighteners and Enticers keep an eye on us. Mortal folk are no more than cattle to the feeder spirits. Every day they lead us into the fields of desire or disquiet to feed us up with fear or infatuation. Then at night they make sure we're bedded down all snug and safe. They'll bait us with dreams and nightmares while we rest, but they prefer that no real harm ever come to us.

Like cattle we're largely unaware our keepers have only the daily milking in mind. They milk us for the soul-light that fires up our existence. That's the purest food of all for them. It's the sweetest nectar.

As I've told you before there are two tribes of these beings which feed on the light of the soul. One tribe are called the Áilleacht. Then there are those known as the Eagla. The first tribe are Enticers and the second are Frighteners.

The unenlightened among the mortal kind refer to these spirits as angels and dæmons. I have to laugh at that. Those titles couldn't be more misleading. Such simple names deny the true nature of these feeders. They're neither good nor evil. They just are.

I admit they employ tactics which may seem either benevolent or malevolent according to their purpose. But don't get it into your head that they serve Satan. They serve themselves.

3

Don't mistake their apparent gifts for manna from Heaven. Any boon they bestow will surely pass away soon enough and thus is entirely valueless.

It's the nature of Enticers to draw their nourishment from the soul-light kindled by infatuation and the like. They present themselves as beautiful, compassionate, alluring beings. Folk find them irresistibly attractive. So it's often assumed the Enticers must be servants of God. But they're not the pure angelic forms they appear to be. That's just the adornment they take on to inspire awe, obsession, worship and love. For those are the emotions they feed on.

Frighteners, on the other hand, feast on fear, anger, insecurity and apprehension. They rarely present themselves as pretty creatures. They want us to tremble. So they appear as ugly, threatening, intimidating, uncouth or ghastly. I suppose that's how they earned a reputation for being minions of Satan.

But I urge you not to think of them in such simplistic terms. The world is a far more complicated place than it may at first appear. The holiest of saints is as much a slave to these two tribes as the rest of us.

So the Church fathers can't be entirely blamed for creating a doctrine based on fear and enticement. That's how they came to believe Hell is a place of torment and Heaven a realm of eternal pleasures. Which is only part of the story. Most men of the cloth are merely dancing to a tune played for them by the feeding spirits.

I met a man once who knew no fear. I tell you true – terror did not dwell in his heart. I can see you don't believe me. But you'll hear about him tonight as I reveal the last part of my story.

His name was Guy d'Alville. He was a Norman. He was a bastard. And through no fault but my own, I fell in love with him.

You may ask how he came to be free from fear. I'll tell you, my dear. A man who has no fear is almost certainly suffering from the lack of love in his life. While a man who wields the forces of water and fire yet is guided by the force of love, may be a one to be reckoned with.

THAT BLOODY LION

T here was a Norman knight called Lanfranc de Courcy. I spoke of him the first night you sat by my fireside. He was a good-hearted man and as chivalrous a soul as you were likely to find dressed in a mail coat in those days. Well, Lanfranc had left the Killibegs after he'd finished escorting Mirim and her husband there. Then, with his foot soldiers following him, he'd set off for his home.

Good Lanfranc sat leaning against a tree near his campfire listening intently to the various calls of the woodland night. His warriors were still going about their business, unsaddling horses, cooking meals before they prepared to take their rest for the night. Lanfranc had chosen this spot on a ridge overlooking the valley so the sentries would be easily able to spot anyone approaching the camp.

Nevertheless Lanfranc knew he wouldn't be able to relax this night. In general he was not a superstitious man. But events of the last week had put him on edge. And this was Samhain Oidche, the eve of All Hallows Day. He'd lived in Ireland long enough to have heard many unnerving tales about this festival. And he had a fair notion of what lay in store for any fool who dared to travel abroad on this night.

That's why he was still dressed in his mail coat with his sword and helm nearby at the ready. He wasn't willing to take any chances. If the denizens of the Otherworld decided to attack his company, he would be prepared to deal with them.

Stephen, his ever-loyal sergeant-at-arms, carefully stepped over the roots of the tree as he brought a bowl of broth and an ale-skin to his lord.

'I don't like it,' he said. 'It's too quiet.'

Lanfranc put a finger to his lips to silence the warrior but Stephen took no notice.

'Perhaps it was a mistake to attack those Redcaps at the ford,' he continued. 'We've been dragging that damned catapult all day long and we've barely put three miles between us and the Killibegs.'

He offered the ale-skin to Lanfranc. The Norman snatched it crossly.

'I told you to be quiet! There may be Redcaps about.'

Stephen knelt down so he could speak in a lower tone. It wasn't the Redcaps he was concerned about, it was the soldiers of their small company – he didn't want them to overhear the conversation.

'The men are unsettled,' the sergeant whispered. 'They're unhappy. They're frightened. They're saying we shouldn't have attracted the attention of the Redcap dæmons. What if the devils have followed us all day waiting to deal their revenge?'

His eyes darted furtively this way and that, quickly scanning the dark woods nearby.

'At least it's stopped raining,' Lanfranc replied as he took the ale-skin, uncorked it and put the vessel to his mouth.

Just then a frightening and terrible thing happened.

A great roar not unlike that of a mighty lion tore across the night, rumbling through the bowels of every man who heard it. The broth was dropped to the ground and Stephen was on his feet in a flash, sword drawn and eyes wide with fright.

Lanfranc threw the ale-skin aside, retrieved his blade and

stood close to the tree in readiness for an attack. The rest of the company were also standing ready, silent and tense.

The roar faded into the distance. The Normans breathed a little easier but didn't slack their guard for a second. No one said a word until Lanfranc gave a loud curse.

'It's that bloody lion! It's found me at last. I'm going to have to fight the bugger.'

'Good luck,' Stephen said quickly. 'Better you than me.'

'There's no call for such insolence!' the lord shot back. 'In case you hadn't noticed, we're all in this together.'

He'd just finished saying those words when another mighty roar rent the night air in two. The great rumble of it rattled the little rings of iron on Lanfranc's mail coat. And it was more than enough to test the resolve of the warriors.

Hardly had the echoes of the roar died away when Lanfranc's men set about frantically saddling their horses and packing up their gear. Clearly they were not going to stay in this forest tonight.

'You must stop them!' the knight told his sergeant. 'They'll listen to you.'

'Are you joking? I'm with them.'

Stephen placed a friendly, if overfamiliar, hand on his lord's shoulder. 'It was all well and good to ride down those Redcaps in the broad daylight, but it's midnight now. The forest is full of dæmons. What sort of a fool would make camp here on this night of all nights? I for one won't feel safe till we're home within our own motte and bailey.'

'Are you a coward, man?'

'I'm careful,' Stephen retorted. 'And I've already seen enough trouble for one lifetime. When I signed on with you I expected a quiet life in the countryside of Ireland. I thought this would be an easy job that wouldn't tax my nerves or my patience too much.'

He glanced over at his men. A few had already saddled up and were nearly ready to set off.

'If you don't come along with us now, I'll have to leave you behind.'

'You wouldn't do that!'

Stephen shook his head. 'I have to consider it. Can't you see we're surrounded? For all we know the Redcaps could be ready to pounce at any moment. There's a lion in the woods waiting to pick us off one by one. And all of us heard the rumours at the Killibegs about that immortal dæmon Aoife. I don't want to be caught up in a fight against such devilry.'

Just then one of the lookouts approached and bowed quickly. 'My lord. A great company of knights is passing through the valley. They're travelling by torchlight.'

'Knights?' Lanfranc hissed.

'Are they Redcaps?' the sergeant cut in.

'No, my lord. They're black Hospitallers.'

'Tell the warriors to assemble their horses and ready the catapult for the road,' Lanfranc commanded. 'How many are there?'

'Three hundred or more,' the lookout replied. 'There's a hundred men-at-arms and two hundred archers at the very least as well.'

'There's a dozen of us.' The knight looked sharply at Stephen. 'That makes the odds somewhat unfavourable.'

The sergeant bowed his head in shame as the lookout departed to issue his lord's orders.

'Ride with me,' Lanfranc begged. 'We'll take on the Knights of the Hospital together and we'll win.'

'What quarrel do we have with the Hospital?'

'None. But I fear they are going to attack the Killibegs. You heard what was said in the council hall. There are good folk there who do not deserve to die. We have a catapult in our possession. I'm sure we could cause a bit of a stir with that.'

You may recall the first night of my tale-telling. I spoke to you then of the council meeting at the Killibegs. At that gathering news came in that the Knights of the Hospital had landed at Wexford town intent on driving war before their whips.

We knew our settlement was a prime target for their wrath. We Culdees were the last of all folk in Ireland to openly declare our heretical doctrines. So we all expected we'd be the first to taste the wrath of the Hospital.

A smile slowly formed on Stephen's lips as he considered the proposal.

'You've still got your mind on that woman called Mirim, haven't you? You think she'll look favourably on you if you come to her rescue. Have you forgotten she has a husband? She's not going to look at you.'

'I'm merely hoping to perform my duty as a knight.' Lanfranc looked affronted. 'I must stand up for the weak and be a champion to the poor. The people of the Killibegs don't have a chance against three hundred Knights of the Hospital. We must go to their aid.'

'It's not our quarrel.'

'It soon will be. How long will it be before this land is overrun with Normans? And how long before the Hospital claims this country for its own? I for one do not want to be bowing down to those black bastards. I'm a lord in my own right, appointed by King John. He charged me with the protection of his subjects. And that includes the people of the Killibegs.'

'What about the lion?'

Lanfranc leaned in closer to whisper. 'If we go off chasing the Hospitallers the men will soon forget the lion. Order the men to mount. We'll send them along the road back to the Killibegs. You and I are going to get a closer look at those black knights.'

Stephen's eyes twinkled with excitement.

'I suppose if we're on the move there's less likelihood the Redcaps will find us.'

'Indeed.'

'Then let's be off!'

They were a fine pair those two. Lanfranc was a knight of the old ways. He'd been brought up with the word *chivalry* scribed upon his forehead, if you take my meaning. His sergeant, Stephen, was a good man too. And together they were an almost unstoppable force.

Almost.

Every year before Samhain the Culdees of the community of the Killibegs took to a wintering home for the duration of the cold season. If my memory serves me well, that year was the last in which our people gathered in an exposed place where any wandering stranger or mystic could come upon us unannounced.

Old Father Clemens chose the ancient hilltop rath. He had it in his mind that the chieftains of the north-west who were to be our guests would feel more at home within such a fine fortification.

I've described the place to you before but I think it's worthwhile telling you again what it was like within the Rath of the Killibegs. I'm sure you weren't listening the first time I told you. So pay attention this time. It's essential you understand the layout of the fortification if you're to follow my tale.

Some Norman lord had chosen this steep hill surrounded on three sides by sheer rocky walls for the site of his castle. He'd never completed the work, though he'd come close. For some unknown reason he'd abandoned it some years prior to my tale. Perhaps he'd had enough of the brigands who roamed the land picking off Norman warriors one by one. Perhaps he argued with his Irish wife and simply left the place unattended when he went home to England. Mayhap he went off to the crusades and perished without a trace.

These are all my own private speculations. The most likely reason he left this place was the incessant and relentless rain. Ireland is a beautiful land, as I'm sure you'll agree, but it would be a paradise indeed if the rain would cease once in a while.

I've heard tell it was the hardest thing for many Normans to endure and may have been the reason only a relatively small number of the foreigners ever remained in this country. If this is so then the bad weather was certainly a blessing in disguise. An impenetrable and eternally damp disguise, it's true, but a blessing nevertheless.

The whole fortification dominated the surrounding countryside. Its well-built stone walls were in fine condition. At the bottom of the hill there was a wagon path which led up to a small stone gatehouse. A guard tower stood above the gates, enclosing them so that anyone entering the rath had to pass directly under the gaze of the defenders. This tower faced east a good fifty paces down the hill from the main entrance to the rath.

The guard tower was as tall as a tree with solid walls, three paces thick. On either side of the tower two walls encased a paved stone path which led up the hill to the inner gate. These walls were five paces thick with battlements exactly the same as the walls which surrounded the very summit of the rath. The stone path led all the way up to the main walls of the enclosure. This entrance path was cunningly designed so archers could stand upon the walls to harass anyone who entered the lower gatehouse without leave.

At the upper gate the Norman lord had installed two wide square towers three floors high on either side of the path. Between them a large main gatehouse, two floors high, afforded entry into the rath.

Within the walls of Rath Killibegs stood a large Norman-style hall. It was a masterpiece of the stonemason's craft. The two short sides of the rectangular building measured fifty paces and the two long sides could be paced out at sixty.

It was a hall but in time of siege it was designed to be a keep. It was a last line of defence. The great hall was an impregnable, self-sufficient safe house, as long as the supplies held out. And supplies of food, fuel and weapons were kept in the dry cellars.

These chambers lay beneath the Norman basement of the keep. The ancient dry cellars were large enough to store all the produce of the community for the year. They were spacious and by the ingenuity of their construction remained at an even cool temperature all year round.

Water could be had from an abundant well in the lowest part of the cellars. The bucket fell into a dark open space which was the cavern of an underground lough deep within the Earth. The water was sweet and pure all year round. I've even known the occasional freshwater fish to be hauled out from the blackness on a line baited with bread.

When we of the Killibegs broke our wandering at the rath that year we found the cellars well stocked. There was butter, cheese and wine in good quantity. Most of these provisions had been left behind by the Norman lord when he abandoned the rath. The cheese and butter were kept in excellent condition in the temperate cellars.

All the food had been granted to our people by the chieftains of the district but old Clemens, our spiritual leader, shared it out to those in need. He wasn't stingy either. Yet there was still enough there to see us through this winter at least. If there were any of us left by then.

Solid timber fuel as well as turf enough to heat the whole keep for the winter. Raw, undyed linen cloth had been bundled up in one small room, enough to make summer cloaks for a hundred folk.

There were shields, various pieces of armour, arrows and a hundred leather jerkins stacked neatly in another chamber. Tigern Og, the old chieftain of the north, had long been using this room to store his own clan's weaponry. They had proud possession of a quantity of axes that had been captured from Viking raiders some two or three hundred years earlier.

Before sunset most of those axes were being taken up to a stone house above ground in readiness for distribution to the defenders. Clemens had thanked God for those axes when he found out about them, for our people were not armed. We were travelling folk with no space in our baggage train for such items of war.

There were a few other items abandoned by the Norman lord which were invaluable to us. Two small chambers were each filled with a huge barrel. And both were full to the top with precious lamp oil. Another dozen smaller barrels also held oil. There was enough there to keep the lamps of the rath burning for ten years. Lard for cooking was stored in a small sealed vat within a smaller room.

Above the dry cellars there was a Norman basement which was used in time of siege as a stables for horses and a byre for cattle and other animals. A wide stone stair led down from the basement to the cellars, and wooden stairs led up to a wide timber platform upon which was set a support for ropes and pulleys so larger items could be hauled up from below. Supplies for the day would have been laid out on the wide platform then carried by servants up another flight of wooden stairs. From there two great doors opened into the floor of the hall, wide enough to allow five servants to walk abreast. When closed the doors became part of the floor of the main meeting hall.

There was enough room there to seat a hundred people or more around the central hearth. Lesser cooking fires were set into fireplaces in the north and south walls of the hall with narrow chimneys to let out the smoke. A great timber chimney lined with copper funnelled out smoke from the central hearth through the second and third floors to the roof. The second floor consisted entirely of chambers where servants and family of the Norman knight would have slept.

The top floor had a chapel and housed the private rooms of the lord, and this was where the visiting chieftains were quartered. When we had arrived we'd found abandoned wall hangings rolled and stacked on this floor and Clemens had ordered them to be arranged to cover the cold stone walls.

Above the third floor was the roof battlement. Archers could be positioned here to overlook the entire rath. The surrounding countryside could be seen from that vantage spot. On a clear day, which I admit was rare, you could have probably glimpsed the silvery shimmer of the sea to the west.

There were other smaller buildings within the walls of the rath. There were circular thatched Gaelic homes as well as square Norman outhouses, barns and accommodation for warriors. Some of the older thatch needed repair, but for the most part the place was habitable and a great contrast to the life we'd been living out in the open since the previous snowmelt.

A pair of heavy double doors were set into the ground near the main gate. These doors allowed easy access to the dry cellars under the hall whenever produce was being brought in from outside. They were in poor repair because they'd been exposed to wind and weather without much maintenance. Those doors were the weakest part of the defences. If the enemy breached the walls or the gatehouses those doors could be easily broken open. And of course the stairs beneath led directly to the cellars beneath the great hall. Once the enemy had control of the cellars the fight would be as good as over.

The steep rocks which enclosed the hill on three sides meant there was only one approach to the interior of the fortification. Through the gatehouses. And they were going to be heavily defended.

As midnight on Samhain Eve approached, final preparations were being made for the defence of the Killibegs. Sentries had been posted at intervals around the walls and atop the battlements above the hall. The towers and the inner gatehouse were crowded with archers. Perhaps a dozen of them carried Norman crossbows, though they had precious few bolts for them. The remainder carried a mixture of war bows and hunting bows. The archers were all lightly armoured. None wore any mail. So if the enemy managed to bring down a hail of missiles there would certainly be a slaughter on the battlements.

The small gatehouse was manned by a select group of young archers numbering twelve in all. Their purpose was to act as watchmen as much as to harangue the enemy. But they were also the lure in a simple defensive strategy. When the enemy had made the hard climb up the hill to the small gatehouse, these archers were to retreat along the walls, giving arrows all the way. Their withdrawal was intended to lure the enemy into an act of imprudence that would cost them dearly.

The outer wooden gates were not strong. The timbers would not withstand a determined assault from the axes of the enemy. But any assailant would then have to run the gauntlet up the stone path to the main gate, with arrows, rocks and other missiles falling down in a great rain of fury. The toll from such a hasty attack would surely be enormous.

The inner gate was much sturdier and reinforced by great stacks of timber and carts. It would not be so easy to breach. Of course these defences would only be effective against the Norman Hospitallers of Bishop Ollo.

If it was the Redcaps who fell upon Rath Killibegs first, there would be no stopping them. They wouldn't fall to arrows or stones. They'd simply pluck them out and charge on. If Aoife's host fell upon the Culdees there would be little hope of survival for any of my people.

16

All around the settlement torches were being extinguished and warriors began putting on their fighting gear. Those who were too sick or too old to take part in the battle were being led down to the underground storage chambers where they'd be able to sit out the siege in relative safety, sealed within a few rooms cut deep into the rock.

Now it's a strange thing, you might think, that fires were being put out all around the Killibegs. For at that time of year the nights may turn mighty cold. But it was Samhain Eve. On this night in ancient times all across Ireland the fires had been put out to be lit again from the central Need-Fire at midnight. In those parts of the country still held in Gaelic hands the tradition lived on, though there was no longer a central fire lit on the hill of Tara. Instead each clan or community lit their own Need-Fire, their chieftain bestowing the sparks of life upon those under his care.

Amongst my people, the Culdees of the Killibegs, the fires were not put out until late in the evening. The time between sunset and the midnight hour was usually set aside for revels, drinking, dancing, cavorting and feasting. But at midnight the merry-making ceased, the fires were extinguished and everyone returned to their own homes or retreated beneath the shelter of a friendly roof. At dawn the new Need-Fire was lit by the leaders of the community. Just as the sun rose over the horizon the sparks of that fire were distributed to the people who would immediately cook a breakfast meal.

This year was different of course. All festivities had been abandoned because of the imminent attack. It was the only occasion I know of when such action was ever taken. Folk still talk about it. It was referred to long after as the evening there was no feast for the feast of Samhain. We called it the Night of the Empty Bellies.

Before the lights went out Gusán Gelt sat by the fire in the smallest stone building at the Killibegs, rubbing the stubble on the end of his chin as he considered his next move carefully. Gusán was a brigand, you may recall. He and his clan had been harassing Lanfranc ever since the Norman had strayed into their territory and begun constructing his castle.

He was a tough fellow, our Gusán. He was used to living rough among the woodlands where his dark green clothes gave him a measure of invisibility to those who rarely walked forest paths.

Lanfranc had captured him after a rather pitiful attempt to ambush the Norman and his retinue. But the Norman had gained a grudging respect for the brigand and in the end had released him to stand by the Culdees in their time of need.

Now Gusán wasn't a bad fighter for a brigand. His knowledge of the three skills of the warrior was well rounded. He practised the Sword Dance every day. He was a fine storyteller. But the warrior skill he was renowned for was his talent at the Brandubh. I've spoken of the Brandubh before, though not in much detail. It was a game of skill and tactics played upon a board seven squares by seven. It's a simple enough pastime but I won't explain it any further here. We don't have a board in front of us so the rules would be meaningless to you. Caoimhin has written extensively about the Brandubh. If you want to know more, refer to one of his works – either the Watchers or the Wanderers.

Well, it so happened that when he had been released by Lanfranc, Gusán had presented himself to Father Clemens, the leader of the Culdees. He had told the old priest he was off to raise his own people to the defence of the Killibegs. But Clemens had urged him to stay.

'Every blade we have with us tonight will count for something. By the time you've raised your folk, I fear this battle will be well and truly over.'

The truth is Clemens had an important task in mind for Gusán. The old priest had no idea the brigand was such a fine fighter. You'd never have guessed it from his attire. Clemens assumed that our Gusán was nothing but a lowly soul born of the tribes of travelling brigands who roamed Ireland in those days.

That just goes to show you what a terrible handicap a prejudice can be. For if Clemens had been able to see past his own petty judgements of the untidy brigand clothes and the dirty unshaven face of an alleged thief, things might have turned out very differently for the old priest.

It wasn't usually like our Clemens or any of the Culdees to judge a man harshly on his appearances. That's not what I'm saying at all. It's just that once a man has a reputation for stealing, folk tend to notice the worst things about him.

But I'm jumping ahead of myself again. Clemens knew a crucial piece of information that our brigand couldn't have guessed. So he knew it would have been a waste of time for Gusán to raise his people. He had another job in mind for the brigand.

'I want you to guard the prisoner,' the old man told the brigand.

He meant John Toothache, the Norman foot soldier who'd been sent by Bishop Ollo of the Hospitallers to follow Caoimhin. I told you all about him the first night you came to me for a story. Toothache had been commanded to retrieve the books Caoimhin was carrying. He'd been sanctioned to employ murder if necessary to achieve that end. And he'd been given the means to do it.

Ollo had entrusted the foot soldier with a small pellet of black resinous poison concealed within a silver crucifix. And as things turned out, Toothache had his chance to use the poison. He slipped it into the sacramental wine just before Caoimhin took the first sip.

When I saw the lad collapse and heard someone declare he'd been poisoned I let my temper get the better of me. I swung the cup round at Toothache, knocking him off his feet and relieving him of the troublesome tooth that was the source of his nickname.

Of course Toothache had been dragged out and locked up straight afterwards, so I didn't see him again after that. But a profound change had come over him with the loss of his tooth.

The terrible ache that had plagued him for years was banished. The scowl that had been permanently etched into his face had disappeared. Where one cheek had been drawn up with pain so that his right eye was buried in a deep squint, there was now a self-satisfied grin. And he no longer referred to himself as 'he' or 'him' as had been his habit.

John Toothache was a large man, as tall as an oak and as broad as a horse. But the air of menace that had been evident in him before I knocked out his tooth was gone. He accepted his imprisonment quite willingly and was very careful to be polite to his hosts no matter how much they scorned him.

That's how he came to be seated opposite his guard, Gusán Gelt, that Samhain. But it wasn't the reason he was chuckling to himself.

'What are you laughing at?' the brigand snapped.

'That move you just made,' the Norman replied as he pointed to the Brandubh board. 'Very foolish.'

Gusán sat forward and stared at the board with a deep frown as he struggled to see what the foreigner was talking about. He wasn't entirely happy with the task he'd been allotted. The Norman hadn't washed in a month at least. His stench was unbearable. But that was the way with those stinking Normans before we Irish taught them the value of a good scrubbing.

'Are you sure you understand the rules of this game?' Gusán asked.

'All the pieces moves along the rows just like the rook in chess. The ravens are black. The Gaels are white. The ravens have to capture the High-King of the Gaels. The High-King

20

of the Gaels has to escape to one of the four corners of the board.'

'The sanctuaries,' Gusán reminded him.

'The ravens, that's you, have to surround the High-King on four sides. All the other pieces merely have to be surrounded on two sides to be taken.'

Toothache paused.

'It's your move.'

Gusán looked back at the board. He couldn't believe this foreigner had only just been introduced to the game. His understanding of the tactics of play was remarkable. He glanced up at Toothache and noticed he was again smiling broadly.

'What are you so chuffed about?' the brigand demanded. 'You've failed to murder the one you were sent to kill. You've been captured by your enemies. And it's highly unlikely you'll escape from this settlement with your life.'

'He lived?' the Norman asked.

'The poison made him very ill. But there was a skilled healer here who managed to leech it out of him before it took hold. She saved his life. And she may have saved yours too. If Caoimhin had died you would most certainly have followed on after him very quickly.'

The foreigner smiled more broadly. 'It's your move.'

'I know it is! I'm taking my time. I refuse to be rushed.'

Gusán took a deep breath to concentrate. But the smiling opponent put him off.

'What are you so happy about?' Gusán bellowed.

'I've decided to change my name. I won't be known as Toothache any more. From now on I'm to be known as plain old John.'

'Well then, plain old John, would you kindly shut up? You're putting me off my game.'

'The pain is gone,' John stated with utter joy. 'I'm free. And I'm going to make up for all the awful things I've ever done in my life. I was driven to those foul deeds by the terrible ache in my jaw. But that's all behind me now.'

'Be quiet!'

'I didn't want to be a warrior, you know. I was pressed into service against my will. I just wanted to raise cows for a living. That's what I used to dream of when I was a boy. Cows. I love cows. They're such gentle creatures.'

'Shut up!'

'I love their eyes. Cows have the most beautiful eyes. When you look into those dark pearls you can see right into their souls. And they're so intelligent too!'

'That's enough! Are you trying to distract me from my game?'

'I am not! What sort of a man do you take me for?'

Gusán hummed darkly under his breath but didn't answer the question.'Do you want to play Brandubh or not?'

'Of course I do! I was just telling you about my ambitions for when this is all over.'

The brigand shook his head in disbelief. 'You'll be lucky to get out of here alive.'

'But the boy didn't die! Surely they won't hang me. I'm a good man really. And I've turned over a new page in my life. I won't be a bad fellow any more.'

'There are three hundred knights of the Hospital headed this way intent on putting every heretic in the Killibegs to the sword. There are less than two hundred folk within this rath who are capable of offering any resistance.'

He sat forward before he went on.

'If that weren't bad enough, there's a rumour flying about that Aoife, Queen of the Night, intends to send a host of Redcaps here to wipe out the Culdees in her bid to become a goddess.'

'That's true,' John nodded. 'That's what she told me and Guy d'Alville.'

22

'You sound like you've spoken with Aoife herself!' Gusán gasped in disbelief.

'I have. She laid on a feast for me and Guy. She's not a bad sort for a dæmon. What a bloody palace! You've never seen anything like it!'

'Do you know what's going to happen when her Redcaps overrun this fortification?' Gusán hissed.

'It won't be very pleasant,' the Norman guessed with a hint of distaste in his expression.

'It will be a bloody slaughter! And do you think the Redcaps will take the time to sort out which mortals are their friends and which are their enemies? They'll just put us all to the sword. That includes you. So let's see you smile now!'

John shrugged, then he allowed his smile to return.

'I don't like the Redcaps,' he confided. 'They don't die easily. You have to hit them just the right way so you strike off their heads with one blow. If you don't get the head clean off they'll come back and have at you again.'

He thought for a moment.

'Of course you can always set them on fire. That'll do the trick.'

'What's that?' Gusán shot back, unsure whether he'd heard correctly. 'Did you say something about fire?'

'I'm sure it was Aoife who mentioned it.' John put a finger to his chin in thought. 'Maybe it was that talking crow. In any case I'm certain that's one of the ways the Redcaps may be dealt with. Set fire to them. They're terrified of fires.'

'Are you sure?'

'I'm fairly certain.' The Norman looked back to the Brandubh board. 'It's your move.'

Gusán returned his attention to the game for a moment. Then he snatched up the sword he'd been given.

'I'll be back in a little while. I've got to talk to Clemens. I'm trusting you to stay here. Don't try to escape. Do you understand?'

'Where would I go?'

'That's right.' The brigand nodded. 'The Culdees would kill you if they saw you'd got away. Just stay here till I return. I think I may have come up with a way to free us both from this little prison and give us something useful to do.'

'What's that?'

'Don't worry about all that. Just wait here for now. If all goes well you may end up tending cows in your old age.'

'That would be a fine thing. I'll wait for you. Don't worry.'

Gusán got up then and left the house. But of course he pushed the heavy bolt back across the door once he was outside. He wasn't going to take any chances trusting the word of a foreigner.

All around the settlement those fires that weren't essential in the preparation of the defences were being extinguished. Gusán started to run. This was one Samhain Eve when the fires must not be put out. Fire could turn out to be the element which saved them all. He had to find Father Clemens right away.

At that very same moment Mirim was also searching for the leader of our community. And she had a similar thought on her mind. She hurried from stable to hall and from house to wall calling out for him.

At last she found the old priest at the gate with Lord William FitzWilliam. The pair were talking heatedly but as she approached they both fell silent and bowed their heads as if they were ashamed to be showing such emotion.

'Why are the fires being put out?' the desert woman demanded. 'I've been told no lights are to be allowed tonight and no fires to warm the wounded or the infirm.'

24

'That is so.' Clemens ignored the sharp, impolite tone of her words. 'It is Samhain Eve. Our traditions demand this of us.'

'Traditions?' Mirim mocked, losing her temper even though she had promised herself she wouldn't. 'You'd threaten the lives and health of your people for a stupid tradition?'

As I'm sure you are aware, fire is life in the cold lands of the north as much as water is life in a desert place. Now it's true that Mirim was from a far-off desert land. Her people had their own customs which I'm sure she would have been loathe to abandon if pressured. But I can also understand her concerns.

Fire is light. Fire is warmth. Fire is life. And fire is hope also. We mortals all have an ancient connection with this element which touches each of us to the very core, regardless of clan, language or homeland.

Clemens, however, was not going to be swayed by such arguments.

'I've just convinced William here that extinguishing the fires is for the best. I don't want to have to go through all that again with you.'

'You cannot leave your people without heat and light,' Mirim pressed. 'You know Aoife is planning to gain control of the Need-Fires of Ireland. Are you simply going to allow her to take what she wants without a fight?'

Well of course Father Clemens wasn't about to get into an argument about Aoife's intentions. Yet he could see the desert woman was determined to have her say. So with a shrug of resignation he explained to her, as he had just done to William, why he'd taken the decision to put out the fires of Killibegs.

You see, my dear, in those days the Culdee folk believed tradition was an important link with one's ancestors. Some of our customs, it must be said, were strange, impractical, even downright dangerous. The cheese-rolling race at the Cliffs of Moher spring to mind. Thank goodness no one takes part in that spectacle any more.

The extinguishing of the Need-Fire on Samhain Eve had its origins in the dim dark past of our people, in the days when the Gaels first arrived in Ireland. In those ancient times the fires were put out as an act of faith. Folk allowed the hearth to grow cold at the very start of the snow season then placed their trust in their chieftains and the Druids to reignite the flames. A small spark may start a great blaze, they used to say. And they were right.

The resulting new fire would be kept alive all year until the next Samhain Eve, providing a real link to every hearth in the land. A strong sense of community grew from this. For, even though the traveller might be far from home, he could look into the flames of any hearth and know it was in a very real sense the same fire that burned in his own house and by which he cooked his meals.

Sometimes it was this knowledge alone which prevented great slaughter in time of war. How can any warrior shed the blood of someone with whom they share the hearth flames?

In the days since the coming of the Normans the ritual of the lighting of the Need-Fire had begun to fall into disuse. But this was only because the great royal hill of Tara was in Norman hands. The foreigners had outlawed the practice under pressure from the clergy of Rome.

Only among the rebellious Culdees was the Need-Fire taken seriously any more. I'm sad to say that even in those days the ceremony was fading, as were the numbers of our people in Ireland.

We had been declared heretics. Our practices were outlawed. Our people were put to the sword. Our cattle were stolen. Our holy books were burned. Our leaders were imprisoned, hanged or tied to the stake to be set alight in a hideous parody of the ritual kindling of the sacred flames.

Clemens's decision to extinguish the fires of the Killibegs that night might have been seen by some as foolish. But I can understand why he was clinging to this ancient way. It was in defiance of the Hospitallers he'd heard were marching north from Wexford.

'If we are heretics, then let us live and die as heretics. We will not abandon our ways because some foreigner has decided to threaten us. As for Aoife, we certainly won't bow down to her in fear. That's just what she wants.'

'I don't understand,' Mirim replied in frustration.

'Aoife is driven on by a terrible pair of spirits,' Clemens told her with great patience. 'One is a Frightener and the other is an Enticer. If we allow our faith in tradition to lapse simply because we are frightened, then at least one of her spirits will feast heartily. We will conduct ourselves as we always have done on Samhain Eve. The lights will be put out. Then as the dawn sun rises the Need-Fire will be rekindled.'

'And what if the Redcaps or the Hospitallers overrun this settlement?' Mirim retorted. 'What happens if the battle is lost for the want of some heat and light on the battlements?'

'Every year we face the same threat,' the old priest declared. 'Every year there is a chance the Need-Fire will not be lit or that disaster may strike in the hours between midnight and dawn. This year the danger will be a little more palpable. That is all.'

'How can you say that?' the desert woman scoffed. 'This isn't a silly game you're playing! You're talking about the lives of your people.'

Just then Gusán approached at a jog.

'Father,' he panted, 'I must speak with you.'

'In a moment, my son.'

Clemens turned back to Mirim. 'Your task has been allotted to you. It is most important that the oil and other supplies stored in the underground chambers are protected. Your husband is preparing to enter those corridors to lend his hand in the defence of the entrance. There is not much time. I beseech you to go to him and lend your hand where it may do some good. You are wasting your time trying to convince me to change my mind.'

'This can't wait, Father,' Gusán cut in.

'It will have to!' the priest snapped. 'Can't you see I'm involved in a private discussion?'

But the brigand wasn't going to be put off.

'Father, you must stop the people from putting out the fires. Fire may be the only chance we have of survival this night.'

Clemens held up his shaking hand, barely withholding his rage.

'That is enough!' he bellowed. 'I have made my decision! The traditions of our ancestors will be maintained. The fires will be extinguished! And anyone who says another word against it will be expelled from this rath to fend for themselves in the cold among the enemies of our people.'

'But Father,' Gusán insisted.

'I've told you that is enough! Doesn't anyone respect the word of the father of this community any more? You are all outsiders. How can you possibly understand what it means to us to keep faith with our ways? How can you even guess what it's like to travel as nomads through the land, relying on water, air, earth and fire for our very survival? How can you possibly comprehend what it is to be a Culdee?'

He turned to William.

'Even you, gentle hermit, have only shared this life with us for three winters. How can you truly understand what our customs mean to us?'

'I think I do, Father,' old Will nodded. 'It shall be as you command. The fires must be put out.'

'No,' Gusán cut in.

'No?' Clemens screamed, turning red as he stepped closer to the brigand. 'How dare you question me? You will leave this community immediately if you want to carry on like that? Do you understand?'

'Who'd guard the prisoner if you sent me away?'

Suddenly the colour drained from Clemens's face.

'Who's guarding him now?' he enquired in a low angry tone.

'I left him locked up in the prison house.'

'Then you'd better go back to him! If you can't perform the duties which have been assigned to you, how do you expect any of us to survive this night? Your foolish actions may have already cost the life of one of my people! Go back to your prisoner and stay with him until you are relieved of your duty.'

'But Father,' the brigand tried once more.

'You fool! You'd better pray that Norman hasn't tricked you into leaving him alone so he could escape. If he harms a hair on the head of any Culdee, you'll answer for it.'

Suddenly it struck Gusán that perhaps John Toothache had tricked him. The brigand swallowed hard.

'Well, what are you waiting for?' Clemens demanded. 'Go back to the prisoner. If he's escaped, let me know immediately. Then prepare for a cold night out there among the Redcaps and the ravens. For you will not be welcome within this fortification any longer.'

Gusán bowed. 'Yes, Father.'

Then he was off back to the prison house cursing his own stupidity.

It was a few moments before the old priest regained his composure. When he'd managed to calm his temper he looked up at Mirim. Then he spoke as if he'd never been interrupted by Gusán at all.

'Everything which happens in this world, no matter how terrible, dangerous or uncomfortable it may seem, must, and always will, turn out for the best. That is the deeper truth of the Need-Fire. If we lose faith in that simple truth there will be panic. If we panic there will be disaster.'

He paused to make sure she understood.

'Most years the ceremony merely involves some minor

discomfort during the darkest, coldest part of the night. This year there will be more than the usual discomfort and quite a deal of danger. But we will see it through as we have always done. The fires *will* be put out. If I were to allow otherwise my people would lose hope.'

'You must do what you believe is best,' old Will conceded.

'Yes I must!' Clemens barked, almost losing his temper again. 'You both speak about this as if I had a choice in the matter. Well I don't! There has never been a instance when the fires were not rekindled. My people know that. They trust me as their leader. They trust in God and they do not question His will.'

'You're starting to sound like a Benedictine!' William said. 'I thought the Culdees shunned the way of the fanatic.'

'You have been among us for three winters, William FitzWilliam,' Clemens replied through gritted teeth. 'If, in that time, you have not seen how different I behave from the Benedictines, then you have been walking round with your eyes closed.'

'Father,' Mirim began, but Clemens held up his hand again to stop her from wasting her breath.

'If this decision is not to your liking then no one will object to your departure. Go now and leave us to make our own destiny. But if you would throw in your lot with us then you will abide by the traditions of our folk. And you will take your commands from me.'

William would probably have raised an objection then but he could see the old priest was determined to silence all debate.

'In military matters I will always defer to you,' Clemens stated. 'However, this is a matter of the spirit. If we should survive this coming fight yet have bartered away all our spiritual treasures, it will be a hollow victory. And I for one would not wish to continue living amongst a people who have no spirit.'

Lord William bowed his head in acceptance. When he lifted his gaze again he spoke solemnly.

'Perhaps we might turn this situation to our advantage. It's just possible the enemy will not attempt to face us down in the dark.'

Clemens smiled.

'We are both old men. You have fought many battles. I have fostered many souls. You and I both understand that the folk of the Killibegs are not professional fighters. We have a hundred warriors who serve the three chieftains. Maybe there are another twenty people who have seen battle or can hold a sword.'

He looked to Mirim, drawing her into the conversation again.

'We three know there is little hope our folk can defeat the Redcaps in open battle. But if we can hold them off until dawn, Aoife's plan to be worshipped as a goddess may be delayed a little.'

'What of the Hospitallers?' Mirim asked.

'We cannot defeat them,' Clemens laughed. 'They will march over us and trample us into the ground.'

He shook his head as if to clear his thoughts.

'Do you not understand? This night my people are going to make their last stand. Our time is ended. The foreigners have come upon us and they will not allow us to dwell alongside them. They fear our simple doctrines. They call us heretics. But most importantly of all they covet our homelands and our cattle.'

'Then disperse,' the desert woman pleaded. 'Take your people to safety far away from here. Hide yourselves. Live on to fight again.'

'There is no sense in that. Ireland is a small place. Where do you think we'd hide ourselves? The foreigners would catch us soon enough. I'd rather make my last stand on ground of my

31

own choosing than to be cornered, weak, hungry and broken in some dank cave or on some open desolate bog.'

He straightened his back as he noticed his wife Derbáil approaching the gates. There was a fire in his eyes, Mirim thought. But the desert woman doubted whether that would be enough to keep his people warm.

'The last days have come upon us,' the old man declared. 'We will not slowly fade from the world as so many others have done. We will vanish.'

'It is time,' Derbáil stated. 'The midnight hour is upon us. The last of the flames is to be put out. Come back to the hall and finish this discussion with the chieftains. The time for talk is nearly over. It's time for action.'

The old priest took his wife fondly by the hand. As she led him off to gather the chieftains he spoke to her loudly enough so William and Mirim could hear.

'They're just concerned about what's going to become of us. They're worried we won't have any fires to keep us through the night.'

Derbáil laughed.

'The brightest spark in the hearth is doomed to become ash. What's the sense in pretending we can turn the course of nature on its head? If we're doomed to die this night, a few hearth fires aren't going to make the difference. But if the fires are not extinguished, an ancient tradition will be cast aside. I'd rather be a cold corpse than a Culdee who has abandoned the customs of her ancestors.'

'You see?' the old priest called back to them. 'To be alive without traditions is not really to be alive at all. One who lacks faith is never far from fear. Who would want to live like that?'

'Not I,' Derbáil confirmed with dramatic emphasis.

At that the two of them passed out of earshot.

'My instincts tell me there will be terrible trouble because of this,' Mirim confided.

William nodded. 'There will surely be strife tonight, of that there can be no doubt. I had hoped to stack timber near the gate and set fire to it should the enemy breach the defences. But the stubborn old bugger wouldn't have it. He has brought all the fuel wood that had been stored within the rath into the great hall. He has strictly forbidden any of the people of the Killibegs to light any flames.'

Mirim hissed though her teeth to release some of her pent-up frustration. Old Will shrugged his shoulders in despair.

'He's proud,' the lord said. 'All his people are the same. They've already collected most of the flint and steel in the settlement. He wants to ensure no one is able to start any unauthorised blazes.'

Then the old lord lowered his voice as he dangled a small leather bag in front of Mirim.

'It is up to you and I then. I have this kindling box. Do you have one?'

She nodded.

'Then give it to me quickly,' Will whispered.

'Why?' she asked, suspicious of his intentions.

'So that when Clemens sends a warrior to collect your tinderbox you can honestly say you don't have one. I'll make sure it's returned to you when you need it.'

Mirim hesitated. She couldn't think of any reason why she shouldn't trust William. After all, she'd heard him *argue* against extinguishing the fires. So she removed her little brass box from the pouch which hung at her side.

'Are you certain this is the best thing for us to do?'

'Absolutely,' the old lord told her with a finality that rang of the terrible things to come. 'Tell no one about what has passed between us. As far as I know, yours and mine are the only two kindling boxes left in the Killibegs. They must remain our secret.'

Mirim nodded.

'Promise me,' he pressed.

'I promise I will say nothing of this.'

With that Lord William took the tinderbox from her hand and tossed it in the air a little to gauge its weight.

'Take care. When the time is right I'll send you this box with a messenger.'

Then he turned sharply on his heel. Mirim stood for a few seconds watching him go.

After a short while she swallowed, hardening her resolve, then went off to find her husband to tell him what had happened.

The Epicurean Emperor

Gusán was back at the prison house as quick as his feet would carry him. He slipped off the bolt he'd laid across the door. And it was a great relief to him the bolt was still in place. It didn't mean Toothache was still about, though.

The fire was still burning in the small central hearth and the same three candles lit the tiny chamber. The Brandubh board was sitting where they'd left it. But there was no sign of the prisoner.

'Damn that Toothache!' Gusán hissed under his breath.

No sooner had he said that than a pile of furs near the fire stirred as the Norman foot soldier stuck his head out from under them.

'I told you I'm not going to answer to Toothache any longer. My name is John. You don't hear me going round referring to you as a pain in the arse, which you are, by the way. Your name is Gusán Gelt. And I'd never dream of calling you anything else.'

'What are you doing under those covers?' the brigand snapped.

'I'm keeping warm.' The Norman sat up to stretch. 'I reckon there's a snowfall coming on. I've always been very sensitive to the cold weather. I can feel it in my bones.'

'It's too early in the year for snow.'

Gusán took off his cloak and laid it on the floor by the fire.

35

It was then he realised there was certainly a shivering chill in the air as there often is before a heavy snowfall.

'It's your move,' John told him.

The brigand settled down to look at the game, trying to recall what strategy he'd had in mind when they'd started this match.

'It's going to be a bloody blizzard.' John shivered, pulling the furs around him. 'I'm glad we're not going to be out in it tonight.'

'I told you it's too early for snow. The air is chilled, I'll grant you that. But if it snows tonight I'll eat my cloak.'

Just then the door swung open and a warrior looked in and barked a command.

'Put those bloody lights out! It's midnight. All fires are to be doused. The candles too.'

Gusán stared at the warrior in slack-jawed disbelief. Around the shoulder of the fellow's cloak lay a sprinkling of tiny flakes of white.

'Is that snow?' the brigand asked.

The warrior nodded.

'As if things weren't bad enough. Now it looks like winter has come unnaturally early. I'll wager it's Aoife's doing. It looks like we're in for a blizzard and all!'

Then the warrior slammed the door shut and was gone. John was already pouring water from a skin over the fire. It hissed steam and smoke so the two of them would have choked if he'd carried on.

'What are you doing?' Gusán gasped, shocked that John was extinguishing their only source of warmth on a night such as this.

'I'm putting out the fire as I was told.'

'Don't be a fool!'

The brigand reached over to blow out two of the three candles. Then he carefully positioned the third where its light

36

would not show through cracks in the door. He poked at the fire with the iron until the flames died away but he made sure the coals were still quite bright.

'I suppose you won't be able to boil it without a fire,' John commented. 'I imagine it'll be quite tough.'

'What the devil are you talking about?'

'Your cloak. You'll have to chew it down raw. You said you'd eat it if it snowed tonight. Good job we've a couple of ale-skins here to wash it down with.'

'Shut up.'

'It's your move.'

'I know it's my move. Shut up. As if it's not bad enough that I'm stuck here guarding you this night when I should be out on the battlements! I don't want to hear your smart-arse commentary. Is that clear?'

'It is.'

The brigand turned his attention back to the gaming board. He stared at it for a long while before he made a very tentative move. As soon as he'd made it John shifted one of his pieces into a gap left in Gusán's raven pieces.

'You really should watch those holes in your defence,' the Norman advised. 'Another foolish mistake like that could cost you the game.'

'I thought you said you'd never played the Brandubh before?'

'I've only just learned it tonight.'

'Well you seem to have an unusual talent for one who claims to be a novice.'

'So when do we make *our* move?' the Norman asked.

'What are you talking about?'

'When do we get ready to do our bit? What have you got planned for us? We can't sit here all night freezing our backsides off at the Brandubh. When do we set about saving the people of the Killibegs from the ravages of the Redcaps? *When do we make our move?*

37

Gusán frowned. 'Who said anything about "we" or "us"?'

'Well you can't be expected to kindle a great fire all by yourself, can you? And I've got a lot of work to do if I'm going to make up for my old life. So it stands to reason that I'd be helping you. Doesn't it?'

The brigand grunted as John went on.

'That woman who knocked my tooth out did me a great service. She liberated me from the tyranny of my toothache. You don't think I'd abandon her and her people after that, do you?'

'You're not going anywhere,' Gusán replied tersely. 'You're a prisoner and it's my job to make sure you stay a prisoner.'

'Do you really think either of us will do any good waiting here till the Redcaps burst in to cut us into tiny pieces?'

'Of course not!' the brigand snapped.

'Then I'll help you.'

'How do you know what I've got in mind?'

'You went off to the old priest to convince him to keep the fires burning when I told you the Redcaps might be defeated by fire. But the old man wouldn't listen to you. He has his heart set on putting all the flames out.'

'How did you know that?'

'I'm not an idiot! A warrior just came to the door to tell us to douse the candles and the hearth!'

'I don't know whether I should trust you,' Gusán grumbled under his breath.

'Two heads are better than one,' John noted. 'Two pair of hands will get the job done in half the time.'

The Norman leaned forward to get Gusán's attention.

'I'll help you save these good folk from the Redcaps. I promise,' he whispered. 'Think of it as my penance for all the ills I've done over the years. And for that young lad's life I very nearly stole away.'

The brigand breathed in heavily through his teeth to show he wasn't entirely convinced.

38

'Look,' John went on. 'I had a grand time in Aoife's palace and all, but I've no mind to be her servant. She's a hard mistress. I saw how she treats them that blunder when they're on her business. She's got a terrible temper.'

'You're a Norman. How do I know you're not going to turn on me? How do I know you won't run on after your master, Bishop Ollo, as soon as the Redcaps have been defeated? How do I know I can trust you?'

'Bishop Ollo is the bastard who pressed me into service in the first place. If it weren't for him I'd never have left home. I could have been tending cows right now. Instead I'm stuck in this little room with you, the Brandubh board and but one candle between us to keep us warm with a blizzardy blanket about to descend.'

'You can't help me,' Gusán stated firmly. 'You're a prisoner. You'll stay here.'

'If you have a plan to put into action you're going to have to leave me here unguarded,' the Norman pointed out. 'And what will the old priest say when he finds you've abandoned your watch?'

Gusán touched a palm to his forehead with a light thump as he realised the Norman was right.

'If I'm helping you at your task then at least you'll be able to keep an eye on me.'

The brigand could see he had no real choice in the matter. His hands were tied, as it were, which just proves the old saying that a guard is a prisoner to his duty.

'Give me your word you won't try to escape,' he pressed.

'I give you my solemn vow: I will not attempt to escape.'

He reached out and touched Gusán on the boot to get his attention.

'But you must make me a vow in return. When this is over, if by some miracle we survive, I want you to promise you'll ask the elders of this community to pardon me. I want you to tell them that all I've ever wanted to do was to tend cows.'

Gusán nodded.

'I promise.'

'Then you'd better tell me what you have planned,' John smiled. 'I've got a few ideas of my own.'

Mirim found Alan putting the finishing touches to a storage chamber beneath the great hall to be used as a shelter. All those folk too old or infirm to help with the defence of the rath were to be billeted here in the hope they'd be overlooked by the enemy.

The Norman lord who'd originally constructed this fortification well understood the need to prepare stores against the threat of a siege. Beneath the hall a broad tunnel extended all the way to a set of stones stairs which emerged near the main gate. At intervals along the length of this main tunnel were nine smaller corridors, each of which led to three small rooms.

Fifteen of these tiny chambers were filled with grain, ale, tallow, butter or wool which had been brought by my people. Two particularly cool, dry rooms were kept as treasure houses for our cheese. In that place the solid curds could age without attracting too much moisture.

Another held a dozen barrels of lamp oil abandoned by the lord of the rath. The story I heard was that the Norman who'd built the place gave up his claim to this territory when he'd been driven back to Wexford by hostile Gaelic brigands. After he'd departed he'd only taken what he could carry. I don't know how much of that was true. All I can tell you is that eighteen chambers of twenty-seven were in use.

In total this left nine small rooms dry and empty. It was one of these rooms that was being prepared as a refuge for those who could not take part in the fighting. Near the front gate of the rath, where the stone stairs emerged, stood a little outhouse covering the double wooden doors that led to the storage rooms. This little building was being demolished by a dozen Culdees with axes and large post hammers.

The plan was to cover the entrance completely so the enemy could find no trace of it whatsoever. Within the hall the same efforts were being made to conceal the entrance to the storage rooms from that end.

Few folk held any hope that the fortress could withstand a prolonged assault. These measures were being employed so that at least a few people, the infirm and the old, might escape the terrible slaughter which was sure to come.

As Mirim entered through the main door to the hall she sensed that everyone else in the rath understood the hopelessness of their situation. There was no hope reflected in the eyes of the defenders.

Some were shaking hands solemnly before they parted to go to the battlements. Others went about their work with an air of futility. There were no tears. But there was an overpowering sadness in the air.

She wondered whether she was the only person at the Killibegs who had not come to the immediate conclusion that defeat was inevitable. As she scrutinised the folk within the hall she realised these people had already accepted their fate.

They were ready to die. They had made their peace with the world. And sure enough, to our Culdee way of thinking, death is not such a terrible thing really. So it's no great matter to face one's own end with a certain degree of acceptance.

That doesn't mean that Culdees have no regrets when it comes time to pass on. We are no different from any other folk. A painful death is just as frightening to me as it probably is to you. To be parted from loved ones is a hard thing to bear.

Mirim's heart began to race. She didn't want to die here. She didn't want Alan to perish here either, defending a fortification and a group of people who meant little to them. Her people lived in the far-off Oasis of Shali. And she was determined to see them again.

As she watched her husband nailing down one of the double doors in the floor, three warriors entered the hall bearing buckets full of water. Alan saw them too. He quickly arose to pick up three great candles from the hearth. He lit them from the hearth fire then carried them to where he was working.

The three men with buckets stepped close to the central hearth. Then each of them in turn doused the flames with water. In moments the hall was full of hissing smoke billowing toward the ceiling. Only the dim flame of the three candles remained to light the hall.

'This is madness!' Mirim declared. 'How can we see to work?'

Her husband turned round sharply.

'If we have trouble seeing in the darkness, then the enemy will have the same difficulty.'

He waved to her to come closer. Folk were leaving the hall now. The preparations in this part of the rath were completed. Soon the chieftains would arrive to discuss final strategies and last-ditch plans.

Mirim made her way to where her husband was kneeling. Just as he hammered the last nail into place she reached his side and placed her hand on his head.

'Have the old folk been taken to the storage rooms?' she asked.

'Not yet,' her husband replied as he got to his feet. 'They're going to enter through the doors closer to the gate. Later the stairs will be sealed up but not so securely that those concealed within cannot escape once the danger is passed.'

'I don't want to die here,' she whispered.

'You won't die here,' he assured her. 'And neither will I.'

Mirim frowned. How could he be so sure?

'Clemens has requested that you and I retreat to the storage cellars to help the folk who would shelter there. If the enemy do break in we are to defend the underground chambers with our lives.'

Mirim gasped in shock.

'Don't worry,' Alan soothed as he put an arm about her shoulders. 'The enemy won't have a chance to discover the entrances.'

'I thought Clemens wanted us to help with the defence of the rath. I thought he wanted us to stand up on the battlements. Why is he sending us down into the safest part of the fortification?'

'I spoke with Clemens,' Alan admitted. 'He and his wife were here just a few minutes ago. I pleaded with him that you be allowed to take shelter with the others in the storage rooms. He told me he would only allow that if I joined you. He told me he was entrusting the survival of these folk into our hands. How could I refuse?'

'You couldn't.' She looked at him sadly. 'Clemens knows there will be a great slaughter here tonight.'

'He knows,' Alan nodded. 'He told me he was sorry he'd convinced us to stay.'

'What changed his mind? Only a few hours ago he was confident the people of the Killibegs had a fighting chance.'

'He has received confirmation that a force of three hundred knights is on the march from Wexford. They will arrive before dawn.'

'I was just speaking with him! Why didn't he tell me this?'

Her husband shrugged as if to say he didn't know the answer to that question.

'The Culdees must flee this place. The odds are too greatly stacked against them. What is the use of standing to fight when the result will be almost certain death?'

'Death is not what worries Clemens,' Alan sighed. 'He and

his Culdees aren't afraid to face the end of their lives. They don't even believe there is any such thing as death.'

'What?'

'He told me that his own conviction is that the soul lives on after the body dies. He assured me all his people who perished this night would be born again into new bodies and new lives.'

'I understand now why the Church names them heretics,' Mirim acknowledged.

But let me tell you, my dear, it was not always so with the Church of Rome. Some doctrines labelled as heresy nowadays were not always shunned. There was a time when all Christians accepted as firm fact that the soul passes on into a new incarnation upon death. I can see you don't believe me. So I'll give an account of it to you as it was given to me.

Long ago, three hundred and twenty-five years or so after the crucifixion of Christ, there lived a Roman emperor by the name of Constantine. He was a lively lad our Con. He loved nothing better than to while away the afternoons after his Imperial labours were done indulging his favourite pastime.

Con was what Romans politely termed an Epicurean. I'd call him a drunken letch. Anyway, the Epicureans were a strain of philosophers who believed that life was short, brutal and full of sorrow. So the best remedy for this endless round of suffering was to attend feasts.

You understand that when the Epicureans spoke of feasting they weren't necessarily talking about food, wine or dancing, though I'm sure they found time for those pursuits also. They loved euphemism as much as anything else. All that pretty talk of feasting masked the fact that these gentle philosophers were engaged in unrestrained orgies of a lewd and sensual nature.

Our Constantine had a reputation for laying a good table, if you take my meaning. Folk flocked to the palace every afternoon to drink their fill and tickle one another's ticklish parts. It was generally all over by sunset when even disrespectable

44

Romans went home to sleep off the wine. If you're going to embark on euphemistic feasting adventures every night of the week, you need to pace yourself.

So, as you might imagine, Constantine was a fairly happy man. Life was pretty sweet for him. There he was, seated upon the throne of the largest empire the world had ever known. He only worked a few hours each morning. He spent the afternoon expounding Epicurean philosophy to the noble ladies of the far-flung provinces. These ladies, by the way, were only in town because he'd summoned their husbands to his court under dubious pretences.

When he'd finished his feasting and the sun had gone down, he went to bed. There was only one cloud on his horizon. There was only one annoying problem he hadn't been able to deal with in all the years he'd been on the throne of Rome.

The Christians.

Of course they didn't approve of his daily orgies. Even in those days most Christians had a reputation for prudishness. Indeed, they were very harsh critics of the libidinous behaviour indulged in by most of the inhabitants of the great city. But they kept their harshest criticism for those who clung to the pagan traditions of the capital.

Previous emperors had all been bothered by Christians. And every ruler had had his own unique way of dealing with them. Some had set huge bonfires of Christians. Others had poisoned their water or buried them alive. Nero was famous for having fed all the Christians in Rome to the lions. But there simply weren't enough predatory cats in the whole empire to put an end to this bothersome cult.

By the time Constantine had butchered his way to the highest rank in the western world, there were many more Christians about than ever before. For a long time after Nero official policy had been to ignore them and hope they'd go away.

Well they didn't. In fact, by the time Constantine sampled his first Epicurean delights there were many Christian senators. There were Christians in every walk of life. They held high-ranking military posts. They were governors and judges. Even the emperor's mother had converted to Christianity.

Where was the problem with all that? Wouldn't it have been easy enough to go on ignoring them?

No it wouldn't. You see, the central tenet of the early Christian faith was reincarnation. That is to say that early Christians before the reign of Constantine believed that when their body passed on from this world their soul would be reborn into another. Body, that is.

Now there was a fundamental problem with this doctrine as far as the emperor was concerned. The harshest penalty available to the law keepers of any empire is death. But if you have a population who don't believe death is such a bad thing, you have a bubbling cauldron of unrest just waiting to boil over. If folk aren't particularly worried when you threaten to put them to the sword, you haven't exactly got a great deal of leverage.

As more and more Christians began to speak out against the excesses of the Constantine he simply dished out the same punishment to them as he'd always dished out to trouble-makers. He put them to death. Not surprisingly, considering their strong views regarding the transmigration of the soul, that didn't seem to deter the Christians at all. In fact it stirred them to greater acts of civil disobedience.

Con tried everything. He burned them alive. He buried them alive. He roasted them on spits. He had them torn apart by wild boars. He threw them into deep holes full of adders. He had them publicly disembowelled.

Nothing seemed to put the Christians off their seditious talk and rebellious assemblies. They went smiling to their executions, treating the whole exercise like some sort of garden party.

The family of the condemned man used to spread out a feast before the scaffold. They'd invite the executioner and the guards to join in a final toast to the victim then distribute alms to the audience.

But that wasn't the worst of it. Constantine soon learned one very unsettling thing about the Christians. And it had the potential to bring down the Empire. They believed every one of their number who had been put to death by the emperor had become a martyr.

A martyr is entitled to sit at the right hand of God and to mete out punishment to his or her tormentors. A martyr is a saint. A martyr is considered the very best sort of Christian. Martyrs go straight to Heaven and escape the endless round of birth and death. They're instantly free from the burden of reincarnation.

So instead of persuading folk to abandon the Christian faith, the executions were actually contributing to the explosion of its popularity. In Heaven there were limitless pleasures to be had. In Heaven the music was sweet, there was no taxation, no disease and, above all, no Epicurean emperors.

All the while rumours of rebellion were growing louder and louder. Constantine realised he had to act. He agonised over what he could do to stem the influence of the Christians. He considered using the legions to wipe them off the face of the Earth. That is, until he found out that a little more than half the soldiers of his legions were Christian.

In the end the Christians forced his hand. A rival emperor marched on Rome. He was a pagan renowned for his dinner parties. And he wasn't happy about the way the Christians had taken over all the well-paid jobs in Rome. With a few fierce legions at his back he was determined to succeed where Constantine had failed.

The two emperors faced each other off at a place called the Milvan Bridge. Constantine knew he didn't stand a chance. All the pagan aristocracy of Rome had thrown their support behind the upstart. And the Christians stayed home in droves, refusing to back either man in battle.

It was Con's mother who made the suggestion that would change the emperor's life. She advised him to pray to the Christian God. She told him to beg forgiveness for his past sins and to offer his life in service to the Lord of Heaven. If he truly repented of his licentious ways, she urged him, God would surely come to his aid and the battle would be his. But he had to promise that all persecution of Christians would end. He had to promise that Christianity would become the state religion of Rome.

By the Blessed Boat Hooks of Saint Finbar, our Con was in a desperate state. He didn't want to die because he didn't believe in reincarnation at all. So he was afraid.

That's why he knelt down in the mud on the banks of the river beside the Milvan Bridge and prayed. He stayed there all through the night promising God this and assuring Him of that. Until at last, just as the sun rose, the Christian God sent a reply.

High up in the clouds a symbol appeared backlit by the red morning sun. It was the sign by which Christians identified themselves. It was the first two letters of Christ's name written in Greek. It was called the Chi Rho. And as Con looked on in awe, for he recognised the sign immediately, he heard a mighty voice boom out through the heavens.

'By this sign you shall conquer.'

That was enough for our Con. Before you could say, 'Perhaps I should have got a bit more sleep, I've got a big day ahead of me,' Constantine had ordered the Chi Rho to be painted on the shields of every soldier in his army. He had banners adorned with the Christian symbol. It's said he even had one of his butchers hack the sign into his own chest then rub it with charcoal to outline the letters in his own flesh for all time.

Funnily enough, God must have appreciated that last little touch of Epicurean excess. The Christian legions flocked to Con's freshly adorned banners. As everyone knows, he won the Battle of the Milvan Bridge just as the Christian God had promised. But as is the case with most folk who enter into bargains with deities, Constantine later had a change of heart.

Once Rome was safely in his hands again he had second thoughts about his promise to make Christianity the state religion of the Empire. But what could he do? He'd given his word to his mother and she was a formidable old biddy by all accounts.

One fine morning as he finished work and was wondering how he'd spend the afternoon, an answer came to him. It was so simple he couldn't believe he hadn't thought of it earlier. The best way to get the Christians out of his hair was to grant them exactly what they wanted. He *would* make Christianity the only acceptable faith in the Empire. But he'd do it on his own terms.

So he called a great council of all the world's Christian bishops at Nicea, a place renowned for its lack of proximity to Rome. He told the gathering he wanted to standardise the religion so there would be no more dissenters in the Empire. Of course what he really intended was to impose his own rules on the poor bishops and their flocks.

As soon as he had them all locked in the same room he brought in his soldiers. Then he warned the bishops that unless they accepted his interpretation of the Christian doctrine they would be tortured and imprisoned for life. Then he'd go ahead and appoint his own clergy to rule the Christians. So it was hardly a surprise to anyone when almost all the bishops agreed to accept Con's rules.

First there was to be no more talk of reincarnation. Everyone gets one life and that's it. Second, the Church would teach that after death all sinners who broke the laws of Rome would be relegated to Hell where the Devil would punish them in fire and damnation for the rest of eternity. This was a new idea but it caught on.

Third, only those who followed the doctrines of the one true Holy Catholic and Apostolic Church and were loyal Roman citizens would be allowed entry into Heaven. I suppose it conferred an air of exclusivity on the Christian faith in the same way Roman citizenship had done in the old days.

Any Christians who spoke against these changes were to be classed as heretics. Heretics would be either crucified or burned at the stake. Their lands, homes and treasures would be seized and their families bonded into slavery. Any bishop who dissented would be treated the same way, only with more torture and ill treatment thrown in before a brutal, bloody public execution.

The Gospels would be cut back to four. The other thirty or so books venerated by the Christians were declared to be heretical. As was any mention of reincarnation. Roman holy days of the pagan calendar were to be Christianised so that the old gods of Rome weren't too offended by the sudden change.

Con wasn't entirely certain whether it was wise to get old Apollo off side. He'd been looking after Rome for quite a while in one form or another. So the rituals of the old Roman gods were to be carried over to the new state religion. And the emperor would appoint the high-priest of the Church as had been done in pagan Rome. The Pontifex Maximus would be the chief priest but he'd be known as the bishop of all the bishops. He would be the Pope.

Only those aspects of Christian practice and belief which served the empire would be retained. Everything else would become anathema.

A new symbol was instituted to represent this hybrid doctrine. Gone was the quaint sigil made up of the first two letters of Christ's name. It was replaced by a more sinister sign.

The sign of the Cross. This was the very instrument that had been used to execute Christ.

As an instrument of torture it would continue to be employed for three hundred years in dealing with heretics. The Cross would remind all Christians what fate awaited those who strayed from the path set down for them by Rome.

Well it just so happened that Roman soldiers never made it as far as Ireland. So the legions couldn't enforce Constantine's edicts here. Many heretics fled to this land searching for peace far from the tyranny of the emperor and his pontifex.

The Culdees took their teaching from those early refugees. Our people never accepted all that ballyhooley about the eternal ravages of Hell. So Clemens wasn't frightened of death as so many others in Christendom had grown to be.

He wasn't a brave man, mind you. He had simply accepted his fate. And that's what Alan was on about.

Mirim stood by watching her husband as he finished work on the door to the underground storage chambers. One door was left open but she did not know for what purpose. Only a short time passed before the chieftains entered the hall, followed by Lord William, Derbáil and Clemens.

'It's time for you to be about the tasks I have assigned you,' the old priest told them. 'We war-leaders have much to discuss and we don't want to be distracted by your clever arguments.'

Alan and Mirim both bowed but neither of them moved. That's when Clemens let his temper get the better of him.

'Go now! I am losing my patience with you. This battle will be fought according to the ways of our people, not yours. I appreciate your concern but you are wasting valuable time.'

The two of them bowed again and made for the door. As they reached it Mirim called back.

'Good luck. May God go with you.'

'We will need more than luck if we're to survive the coming onslaught,' Clemens told her. 'May God also be with you. If

51

you complete the task I've set to you, my people will give you their thanks.'

Then he kneeled down to blow out the three candles. That done, Mirim heard the old priest addressing the chieftains.

'Is all in readiness?' he asked.

But that was all she heard. Alan grabbed her sleeve to drag her out the door.

'Come on. We've still got a lot of work to do.'

The Lights Go Out

n the depths of the storage chambers the two Welsh monks Overton and Lewyn were busy settling folk into the room where they'd be sheltering from the attack. There were two old women and four men all about the same age. Each of them had a terrible cough which they'd picked up from the damp stones of the Killibegs.

A pregnant woman and five children had already been sent off, with a warrior to escort them, to the people of Tigern Og who lived to the north. It was hoped those folk would send as many of their warriors as possible to the fight as soon as they got the news. So there were no young folk in the rath at all by that stage.

The two monks went about their work by candlelight, making sure their charges were warm and dry. Overton had a large pot of broth he'd brought down from the hall and he was doling it out with a great smile on his pudgy face.

'Will you have some soup, brother?' he asked Lewyn.

'Don't you ever think of anything but your stomach?' the other monk shot back. 'Here we are about to be cut to pieces by marauding dæmons from out of the very mouth of Hell and all you can do is stir the broth pot.'

'Food always calms me down. I find every difficulty so much easier to bear on a full stomach.'

'It's a perfect example of your utter refusal to accept the

reality of the day-to-day experience we call life. Your attitude to food is a reflection of your weak philosophical position. You claim that this world we witness is merely a manifestation of an implied but unsubstantiated common experience. That is your contention, is it not?'

'It is.'

'You've stated to me time and time again your belief that we're all sharing this dream as if it were by common consent?'

'Indeed.'

'Did it cross your mind for a moment that by utilising food to grant you some consolation from your fears and troubles you might be also be withdrawing from the world?'

'It has.'

'Then tell me, how can you justify blatant escapism in the face of such a potential disaster? How can you tell me that withdrawing into a little world of make-believe is a positive response to the fact that many folk are likely to lose their lives here tonight? Have you no compassion? Have you no empathy? Don't you feel any twinge of guilt for indulging in such selfish behaviour.'

Overton thought for a moment. Then he replied honestly.

'No.'

'You have no conscience!'

'What's the use of panicking?' Overton asked. 'Our lives are in God's hands.'

Lewyn squinted. 'I've got you!'

'What do you mean?'

'All this while you've been arguing that free will is the overwhelming force in everyone's life.'

'That's right. You've understood my argument perfectly.'

'Well you can't argue that we each create the world moment by moment then suddenly say our lives are in the hands of God. I smell a contradiction.'

'It's not a contradiction, you simple-minded Welsh goat!

54

You've simply misunderstood my personal definition of God. That's all. The fault is with you. Not me. And since you are ignorant of the truth you are blameless.'

'I'm only ignorant of what I don't know!' Lewyn grumbled.

'That's exactly my point.'

The two of them could have gone on like that all night. There was nothing either of them loved more than to engage in philosophical banter regarding the meaning, origins and nature of existence.

But their conversation was cut short by Mirim and Alan who appeared at the entrance to the passageway.

'You haven't doused your lamps and candles,' Alan cut in.

Both monks turned to him with surprise.

'And how would we see what we're doing down here in the depths of the Earth if we did?' Lewyn asked.

'Clemens has ordered all the flames to be put out,' Mirim told him.

The rest of the corridors were already dark. Even in ordinary circumstances only folk under special sanction were allowed torches in that part of the storage tunnels. These torches were short and carved of bog oak that had been repeatedly dipped in hot tallow until a ball of the flammable substance had formed on the end.

Only the finest tallow was used for these torches. They were designed so that they would not shed sparks or spit. You see, besides all the other supplies I've already listed for you, there were also barrels of highly flammable lamp oil. These had already been removed from their storage chambers and stacked in the corridors by a team of folk who'd since returned to the walls.

'We'll seal you in,' Alan informed the monks.

'What?' Overton squeaked. 'You can't do that. We'll suffocate.'

'No you won't,' Mirim laughed. 'There are narrow ventilation shafts running down from the buildings above.'

'If we seal you in and cover the entrance you'll have a better chance of survival,' Alan said. 'The enemy will not guess you're hiding here and you'll be able to keep your candles lit. Just don't mention it to the old man after the battle. I don't think I want to have to face down his ire ever again.'

'What about you?' Lewyn asked.

'We're to stand guard out here in the main tunnel. If the enemy does manage to break in we'll hold them off as long as we can,' Mirim stated.

'If they get this far they'll probably assume we were assigned to guard the supplies,' her husband added. 'With luck they won't even take the time to look for hidden doorways.'

'You're ready to sacrifice your lives?' Overton asked.

Both Alan and Mirim nodded.

Overton turned to his companion monk. 'You see. That's what I'm talking about! Our lives are in God's hands.'

'I do wish you'd learn when to keep quiet,' Lewyn sighed. 'There's a time and a place for everything.'

'What better time to debate the nature of existence? It seems some of us might be about to discover the truth for certain.'

'Seal us in,' Lewyn said to Alan. 'I can put up with his wild ranting. But you don't deserve to be subjected to it for the rest of the night.'

'Very well,' the knight replied with a laugh.

Then he and his wife began stacking doors, boxes, barrels and empty earthenware jugs against the door to conceal the whereabouts of the two monks and their sick elderly charges.

Bishop Ollo was a bastard. This should not surprise you. He was a Norman, after all, and with a few rare exceptions the

Normans are a race of bastards. Indeed, before the coming of these invaders to Ireland the worst possible insult available to the humble Gaelic speaker was, 'you foreign person of questionable parentage'.

I'm sure you'd agree it's much more to the point to accuse a miscreant of being descended from the Normans. Saves breath. Wastes no words. And it inspires unmatched outrage if delivered with appropriate gravity. Say it once for me.

Bastard son of a Norman.

You have to admit it has a certain poetry to it.

The other immediately noticeable thing about Ollo was that he was overweight. Far too fat for a man of God, in my humble opinion. I've known a great many fat folk in my time. Owing to the nature of the deprivations brought upon this land by the Normans, not many of them were Irish of course. But I've known a fair number nevertheless.

Now, by and large, if you'll pardon the expression, most fat people are a mix of good and bad, light-hearted or light-fingered, fair-minded or fairly awful. I'm not saying that thin people are any better or any worse than fat. I'm not implying that just because a fellow is stoutly apportioned he is prone to be either a bishop or a bastard.

But in Ollo's case his overweightedness was a direct result of his insatiable greed. Ollo was a lover of fine food laid out in vast quantities. Indeed, even foul food was fine with him as long as it was in vast quantities. And since the rules of his chosen vocation did not condone expression of his more carnal Epicurean passions, he threw the full weight of his indulgence into gluttony.

Now, there are those who hold there is no real sinfulness involved when it comes to overstimulation of the culinary muscles. But I'm not one of them.

I know there are some folk who can eat no more than a handful of grain yet they put on weight straight away. But there are also people who are not inclined to work very hard for their bread. They often end up hauling an extra chariot around behind them, if you take my meaning. Ollo was one of these folk, though he weighed as much as three.

Being a well-born Norman bishop he was surrounded by servants, hangers-on and assorted sycophants, all of whom were inclined toward a toadying disposition. Our bishop had a violent, often deadly temper. And he certainly wasn't inclined toward mercy, compassion, level-headedness or any other condition he considered to be weak and, in his opinion, effeminate.

Of course Ollo had discovered the secret to not only being a bishop but remaining a bishop. He was totally and utterly unpredictable. You see, my dear, most high-ranking clergy who are generous, kind, humble and compassionate end up being treated with contempt by their servants.

Ollo was a sly bugger. He liked to keep people on their toes. Therefore he was constantly being pandered to by all and sundry. Now if there's one thing a toady hanger-on soon learns about the toad he's hanging on to, it's how to keep the bloated tadpole pacified. Ollo wasn't the kind to respond favourably to empty compliments or insincere praise. In fact he'd had a chamberlain burned at the stake for an offhand comment about the fine quality of the Episcopal bedchamber silks. Which should be a warning to you. The clergy are very sensitive about their bedchamber arrangements.

Ollo's descent into gluttony was inevitable. His servants were eager to please their master. None of them wanted to end up suffering a slow tortuous demise. So they cheerfully and relentlessly indulged him his passion for food.

The funny thing is that not one of them realised the old bishop had become too rotund in the belly parts to manage even simple tasks without help. They were so frightened of his temper that it never dawned on any of them that he'd become extremely vulnerable.

The clues were all there if they'd been able to read them. The cut of Ollo's tunic could have clothed three men. No horse had been foaled that could carry him more than three Roman miles. He rarely walked anywhere except on short jaunts. And his dark reputation was certainly caused at least in part by an incurable case of indigestion.

There were rumours he'd had disobedient servants cooked up for his dinner guests. Yes, Ollo was said to be an avid consumer of man-flesh. Even other Normans shuddered to hear his name. That tells you what sort of a bastard he was.

And what had brought him to Ireland? Besides food, there was one other thing that fascinated Ollo in an unnatural fashion. That was magic. Yes, you heard me right. Bishop Ollo was said to be a dabbler in the occult disciplines.

I've told you what I think of dabblers. I don't like them and I don't condone dabbling at all, at all. But no matter how low an opinion I might have of Ollo, I have to say one thing for certain. I think he may have been more than a dabbler.

He came to Ireland in search of books. Manuscripts of magic. Tomes of trouble. Samplings of spell-craft. And he'd heard the community of the Killibegs had one of the finest collections in the country.

Two hundred knights of the Hospital were gathered to his banner. Another hundred knights of no particular affiliation put on the black livery and swore oaths to the order at the promise of plunder. Then there were a hundred men-at-arms to back them up and two hundred archers.

The whole force had landed at Wexford town three days after Caoimhin and his teacher had arrived. Now the archers, men-at-arms and all three hundred black knights were marching with all speed toward the settlement of the Killibegs.

Ollo sat proud on his horse as he brought the creature to a halt. He raised his hand to let his warriors know they should take a short rest also. Then he summoned his chamberlain.

'Fetch me a fresh beast,' he bellowed. 'This one's had it.'

As he spoke the poor animal staggered forward a few steps before its front legs buckled under the weight. It gave out a tremendous groan as the last life-breath left its body. Ollo put one hand up to steady his red bishop's mitre as he deftly stepped out of the saddle at the very moment the animal crumpled. He'd done this many times before.

Once he was off its back the beast toppled over on to its side with a crunch. It was dead of exhaustion and overexertion before it even hit the ground.

'Don't waste that,' the bishop commanded. 'There's still enough meat on the creature to make a fine stew.'

'Yes, your Grace,' the chamberlain bowed as he clicked his fingers at the gathered underlings.

They scampered about collecting knives and butchering tools from their saddlebags then commenced sharpening them. The chamberlain already had a huge travelling stool unfolded for his master. The bishop took his seat without so much as a sidewards glance at the servant.

'I'll watch.' Ollo pointed at the carcass. 'The troops may rest until I'm ready to move on.'

The chamberlain bowed and was about to get on with his duties when the bishop turned his head sharply to him.

'Tell me, Francis. What hour of the night is it?'

'It's Roland, your Grace.'

The bishop frowned. 'What is?'

'I am, your Grace.'

Ollo shrugged.

'You're an honest man and no mistake. Many a man wouldn't have dared to contradict me. What happened to Francis?'

'You had him pulled apart by four horses.'

'That's right! I remember now. He fell asleep on duty.'

'He collapsed while carrying your Grace up on to the battlement wall of Wexford.'

60

The bishop shot a displeased glance at the chamberlain.

'You want to watch your mouth, young man. Or you'll go the same way.'

'Your Grace is too kind,' the chamberlain bowed. 'A quick death would be too good for me. I am undeserving of your blesséd thoughtlessness.'

Ollo snarled. 'Don't bloody forget it either.'

The bishop pulled his black Benedictine cowl around his neck against the cold air. Then he recalled he'd asked a question.

'What hour is it?' he bellowed.

The butchers were already slicing into the steaming horse flesh, making their cuts and separating the various pieces to be hung on hooks in the meat wagon.

'It is just coming up to midnight, your Grace,' Roland replied courteously. 'Would your Grace care to have his tent erected and a fire prepared for the roasting of that delicious-looking beast of burden?'

'No. We're only stopping long enough to butcher that animal and saddle me a new one. We've a way to go before the dawn. I've a mind to reach the Killibegs before sun-up and to launch our attack from the east to blind the enemy.'

'Your Grace,' the chamberlain piped up cautiously, 'the knights have been riding since sunrise this morning. It's been a very long day. Don't you think it would be best to allow them a little longer to rest? Your servants have faired even worse. We've all been awake since last night without a wink of sleep.'

'How dare you!' the bishop screamed and a stream of spittle sprayed the chamberlain. 'Do you want to taste the rack? Are you begging to be sundered head from neck by the axeman?'

'No, your Grace.'

'Then keep silent.'

'Yes, your Grace.'

61

'Bring me a jug,' Ollo demanded. 'And my travelling commode.'

The chamberlain rolled his eyes toward heaven, offering up a silent prayer that Ollo would fall off his dying steed next time and be crushed under his own weight. The thought was so satisfying that a grin spread across his lips.

'What are you smiling about?' Ollo shrieked.

'I'm merely happy to be of service to you.'

It wasn't the first time Roland had been caught indulging in such thoughts.

The chamberlain had no sooner gone off to attend his errands than the bishop heard a great flapping of wings. At first he was a little concerned that one of the Devil's minions had come to take his soul. A man of his ilk lives in constant expectation of such an encounter.

But when he saw it was merely a large raven he relaxed again. As Ollo breathed easier the bird landed in front of him with feathers spread wide.

'I am at your command, your Grace.' The raven bowed his head and stepped back to put his weight on to one leg.

'You're a dæmon, Sciathan Cog,' the bishop snapped. 'Don't ever forget that. You're nothing but a filthy dæmon from the deepest pits of Hell.'

The bird cackled mockingly. 'And you're fat. Watch your tongue or I'll rip it out and feed it to a nest of hungry fledglings. If you want my help you'll treat me with the respect I deserve. The success or failure of your enterprise rests with me. Don't forget it.'

'I'm a bloody bishop!' Ollo barked. 'No one speaks to me like that!'

'Don't soil yourself. I don't care if you're the Pope himself. Either you speak to me with some respect or I'll arrange for those precious books to fall into the hands of some other feckless adventurer. There's plenty who'd pay handsomely for any one of those manuscripts and I've agreed to deliver them all to you for a small fee. So mark my words.'

The bishop sat forward as if he was about to reach out, grab the bird and strangle him. Sciathan Cog watched warily, ready to jump out of the way. But he needn't have bothered. In the next instant the bishop let out a tremendously loud and prolonged fart the like of which few folk have ever heard erupt from the backside of any living creature.

The raven laughed, or as near to a laugh as he could manage considering the stench that accompanied the eruption. Then he turned his attention to the horse that was being slaughtered. The bird hopped closer and the butchers scattered, superstitiously crossing themselves as they departed.

Sciathan Cog daintily pecked at the steaming meat a few times. Then he selected a choice cut that was just the right size to swallow in one gulp. He picked it up, threw his head back and the strip was gone as he gurgled in the back of his throat with pleasure.

'There's nothing so sweet as freshly exhausted horse flesh,' he sighed when it was gone. 'Another one of yours?'

Ollo nodded.

'You are a dæmon. You may even be one of Satan's own imps for all I know. But you have promised to provide me with a service. Do you have the information I seek?'

The raven clicked his beak excitedly. 'You'll have the Killibegs within your grasp. By this time tomorrow night we'll both be feasting on the entrails of heretics.'

'Indeed,' Ollo drawled. 'Where are these heretics to be found?'

'In three hours your force will come to the place. Follow the valley till you reach a small river. Keep to the shallows while you follow it downstream. When you come to a ford over the river you'll see a ruined wall on the right-hand bank. The path which passes along that wall will lead you to the Killibegs within a few short minutes.'

'And they have the books I'm searching for?'

'Of course they do! The real question is whether you're prepared to keep your part of the bargain?'

'I am a man of God!' Ollo protested in affected outrage. 'Do you really believe I'm capable of deceit?'

'Of course I do, you silly fat, flatulent old bastard. Why do you think I asked you? All you mortals are alike. You think you're all so bloody perfect. Well listen to me. You're nothing but another foreigner with a high opinion of yourself. Don't forget, Lord Bishop, that all you mortals, good or bad, end up on my dinner plate.'

'You'd best pray you don't end up on mine. I can't recall whether I've ever tasted the flesh of raven before. I'm sure I must have, though it didn't leave a lasting impression.'

Sciathan Cog hopped closer to eye the bishop with a dark threatening glare.

'Be careful, mortal! You have no idea who or what you're dealing with here. You can't just cook me up for your supper. For a start I'm immune to death. I cannot be killed. I will never decay.'

'Everything falls into decay,' the bishop corrected him. 'Everything. You can no more escape death than any of us. I don't care if you are one of the Devil's own offspring. Everything must die.'

That was the moment when Sciathan Cog lost his patience with the bishop. The raven let fly with a torrent of abuse and foul language which would take me the rest of the evening to relate, even if I had the inclination. Suffice to say that once he'd finished calling the old clergyman every name he could think of, Sciathan Cog needed a short rest to catch his breath. Then he went on to boast about the Quicken Brew.

Now there are some things a fat bishop famous for gluttony should never be told. And the story of the Quicken Brew is one of them. As the tale went on, Ollo realised that here was a way to recapture his youth and indulge his passions forever. His eyes lit up with excitement.

At last, when Sciathan Cog had finished venting and was somewhat calmed, Ollo asked a few discreet questions.

'I'm sorry to have upset you so,' he began, tentatively. 'I had no intention of riling you. I've heard many tales of a magical brew that could heal all ills and restore youthfulness forever. Where might one find such a potion? Do the people of the Killibegs know the secret? Are there any among their number who have attained immortality?'

The raven cocked his head to one side to take a closer look at the old bishop. He clicked his beak before he spoke.

'For a clergyman, you seem to be very accepting of my story. Your kind usually pour derision on any notions of the Quicken Brew.'

'I am not so green as some of my brethren,' Ollo shrugged. 'I have a wide experience of the world. I've read everything to be had on the subject of immortality. It is one of my fondest ambitions to attain to everlasting life. That's why I became a priest in the first place. I heard that eternal life was the reward of every good Christian.'

He coughed with embarrassment.

'Of course I understand the truth nowadays. That was just a story to lure men to the priesthood. I was very impressionable in my youth.'

'There is one at the Killibegs who knows the secret of the Quicken Brew,' Sciathan Cog told him. 'Her name is Sianan. She is the Abbess of Dun Gur.'

'A Christian?'

'You would probably call her a heretic. She has the knowledge to make the Brew. In fact she may even be carrying some of it about her person.'

'Is she the only immortal at the Killibegs?'

65

'As far as I know,' the bird shrugged, or as close to a shrug as a raven can approximate.

'Then I shall go there and enquire of her.'

'There must be no survivors,' the raven reminded him. 'That was our bargain.'

'No survivors,' the bishop nodded. 'Except the immortal called Sianan of course. There's surely no way to kill an immortal.'

'Don't be daft! Of course you can kill immortals!'

If he'd had teeth the raven would have bitten his tongue.

'I knew it!' Ollo exclaimed, clapping his hands together. 'Everything must die. You'd best be careful, my dear black-feathered one. Soon enough I'll discover what it takes to put an end to your life. And then we'll have an equal footing.'

'May you rot until your flesh is unpalatable even to the carrion kind,' the raven answered.

Then he spread his wings wide and leaped into the air. As he soared above, catching the breeze, Sciathan Cog glanced back down behind him. The bishop was already climbing the mounting stairs in readiness to jump aboard another unfortunate beast. And in that glance alone the raven could plainly see that his story of the Quicken Brew had set old Ollo's mind aflame with ambition. Sciathan Cog laughed as he soared on the gathering blizzard wind.

CHIVALRY

Don't talk to me about chivalry. I've heard that word before. It's nothing but a fancy term for elitist, demeaning attitudes with which the Normans delude themselves. Folk who claim to be chivalrous are usually either bullies trying to justify their bad behaviour or fools wandering through the world with horse blinkers to shield them.

I never met a Norman, except Robert FitzWilliam and his father, and Lanfranc too, of course, who even approached the ideals of chivalry in their treatment of others. The truth is the Normans didn't really start to understand the finer points of chivalry until two decades after my tale takes place. It took us that long to teach them how to behave in civilised company. They still get it wrong sometimes, though these days it's more a result of blundering than a hard-headed hatred for all living things.

The idea of chivalry didn't originate in the courts of France or England. I know the troubadours would like you to think it all started with their patrons. Well it didn't. The concept of chivalry was an Irish one from the very beginning. And I'll tell you all about it.

In the ancient days when the Gaels first landed in Ireland they already had a warrior tradition among their people. Aspiring fighters used to seek out an apprenticeship with some great war-leader or other. These war-leaders roamed the countryside round, training their students in the art of battle and generally making a nuisance of themselves.

Occasionally they took things too far and the king was forced to intervene to calm things down. But on the whole these bands of wandering warriors made sure the coastline was free of invaders and that disputes didn't escalate into war.

It was a very effective means of allowing youthful exuberance to find full expression without actually killing anyone. These bands were known as the Fian and they had strict rules governing them.

I won't go into all the details now. I'm sure you've realised I detest rules. It's enough to say that there were three skills accorded to a warrior. And each had to be mastered by any traveller on the warrior path.

The first was mastery of the Brandubh board. The second was mastery of a weapon through the Sword Dance. Warriors in those days could choose between the blade, the bow or the spear. The axe wasn't considered a polite weapon. Only the heathen foreigners ever carried them. The third skill essential to a warrior was music or storytelling.

Now it has to be said that in those days it wasn't enough to be able to beat your rival in a game of Brandubh, then cut off his head with a masterful stroke from your broadsword.

If you were a warrior you had to able to entertain your enemies as well. Don't snigger. It's true. Now it's obvious why a warrior would need to understand the strategies of the battlefield and the Brandubh is fine way to learn such things. Every warrior must be able to wield a weapon effectively, so the second skill is easily accounted for. But why study storytelling and music?

That's simple. We have a saying. Never give a sword to a man who cannot dance. Only one who really knows the joyous things in life such as dancing can truly wield the tools of death even-handedly, respectfully and judiciously. Only one who is able to put himself in the shoes of his enemy should be entrusted with a weapon.

And it is through the mastery of music and storytelling that a warrior learns about the finer things in life. Music touches the soul. It is the quiet discipline.

Whether a warrior be woman or man there is a certain destructive energy involved and invoked when wielding a sword. This is necessary to the occupation of a warrior. But it can become a detrimental force in a warrior's life if it is not balanced with some creative focus.

Such is the role of music in life of a warrior. Music calms the temper. It cools the destructive passions of anger, outrage and the like. It fosters passion for love, nurturing and fun.

As for storytelling. Well it served two purposes. Not all warriors were inclined toward the study of a musical instrument such as the harp. Those who had little affinity for music were encouraged to pursue the art of storytelling.

Now the storyteller in the old days was considered a valuable member of the community. Stories were shared to pass the long cold winter nights. If a community had a good storyteller in their midst they were more likely to get on well together without many disputes.

But stories also held the precedents at law for our people. When a Brehon judge was asked to present a prosecution against an individual he had to quote a story as justification for the charge. The same if the Brehon was acting in defence.

Brehons were a specialist rank of the Druid class and few folk were ever selected to follow that path. But many warriors took up tale-telling for pretty much the same reasons as the judges.

Stories are, and I pray always will be, the way we Irish judge right from wrong. The stories of old are our guides through life. A warrior who knows the old tales is unlikely to break with tradition or the law.

A warrior who understands how to tell stories will have the respect of his peers. In time of trouble they will rally to him without question simply because they like him. And a warrior who can tell a good story is less likely to have to fight, because a warrior who knows how to make people laugh will rarely get into any serious sort of a scrap. None will think such a one to be arrogant. Warriors who retain the joy in their lives are rarely greedy, lazy or aggressive. They tend to be firm, assertive, confident and dependable. Warriors who know how to laugh at themselves always attain the victory. No matter what befalls them they are able to find something worthy to take away from every situation.

In the ancient days of the Fian the training of a warrior was formalised. The schooling of fighters was taken very seriously. No man or woman would have been entrusted with a blade unless they had first mastered the Brandubh and the arts of storytelling or music.

So it was that the war-leaders of the Fian bands selected potential warriors from among those young folk most gifted at Brandubh, music or storytelling. Physical prowess was not considered a necessary attribute for a warrior.

The Normans have things arse-on-their-head. They select their knights according to two criteria. Bloodline and brawn. The first-born son of a Norman nobleman is doomed to walk the warrior path. Whether or not he's competent with the blade he must take it up. Whether he has a pound of wit or less than a pinch of intelligence, he's going to be measured for a mail coat on his sixteenth birthday.

Once he's got a suit of armour, a sword and a shield, he's sent off to war to learn all about it in the thick of the fighting. If he's blessed with any luck, or brains, he might survive long enough to learn a little about how to conduct himself in battle. But for the most part the intelligent ones don't last long. They're the ones who spend too much time questioning the whys and wherefores. It's the tough, aggressive Norman youths who live into their twenties and end up becoming the war-leaders of their people later in life.

If you bear in mind that wits are not valued among the Norman warrior class, it's a wonder of creation they've managed to spread their influence over such a wide area. England wasn't their only conquest. They also have a kingdom in Sicily.

Father Clemens, the leader of the community of Killibegs, explained it to me this way. He knew all the old tales and he was a mighty storyteller himself. He was a fine Brandubh player and in his young days, before he took the cloth, he'd been a warrior.

He told me that the profession of a warrior is like that of a fisherman. When a fisherman is young he learns many skills. Before he can take a boat out on his own he must have a knowledge of the wind and tides. He must learn respect for the ocean currents and moods. He must be able to discern what waters are dangerous and when. Then he has to be able to interpret the signs in the sky to navigate his way to where the fishes are waiting. Then he must be able to find his way home.

When those skills are mastered the fisherman has to learn the mending and making of nets. He has to work as part of a team, taking orders from the master of the boat who has had many years experience. A good fisherman will listen well to the words of the master.

In time a fisherman may be considered worthy to command his own team of fishermen or perhaps even a fleet of boats. But such an achievement takes many years to realise. Along the way any number of accidents, mishaps or chance encounters could end the life or cripple the body of a fisherman. It doesn't take much.

So an aspiring fisherman should not be thrust into the thick of it too quickly. If he is, he will surely place his own life and those of his companions in dire danger. The tools of his trade

– net, boathook, oar, rope and dirk – may all save his life at one time or another. So they must be taken care of and treated with respect.

Warriors used to think of their trade in much the same way.

It used to be said in the ancient days of Ireland that a warrior should possess three qualities: discipline, persistence and compassion. Be known for three attributes: respect, courage and humility. Possess three weapons: reputation, wits and an eye for detail. And have three responsibilities: truth, honour and love.

There are three obstacles which may be the downfall of a warrior. Envy brought about by greed, hatred brought about by anger, and distrust brought about by fear. A true warrior will have three regrets: the use of the sword, the wielding of the spear and the notching of the arrow to the bow.

But if a warrior should remain true there are three certain rewards which will be granted to him. A full cup, a full belly and a house full of friends. What more can you ask from life? What else is worth aspiring to?

But the coming of the Normans changed all that. Now anyone can call himself a knight as long as he has noble blood, a bag of gold to spend on accoutrements and a good nag or two to carry him from place to place.

All it took was for them to win a few unbalanced battles in which they outnumbered their opponents three to one. After that the Irish warriors looked on the foreigners with awe. That's how the Normans have spread a fashion for greed and arrogance among the fighting folk of the Gael.

It's not what I call the warrior path. All this Norman rubbish about mystical quests and rescuing damsels in distress has nothing to do with being a true warrior. You can't go round calling other people infidels simply because they've found a different way to worship God. Cutting down forests to make spears, bows, arrows and shields isn't chivalrous. And if you think challenging ugly giants to feats of arms is a knightly pastime, then you're wrong.

That's not chivalry. That's just interfering in other people's lives for the benefit of one's own entertainment or to add a bit of bulk to one's purse. But that's what the bloody Normans call chivalry. Bough-splitting bastards. They have no respect for anything or anyone. They're more trouble than they're worth.

Now that I've vented a little of my spleen upon the bark-stripping Normans I have a confession to make. They weren't all as I've painted them. In the days when the events of my story unfolded there were a few foreigners who admired the ways of the Irish. Some of them even adopted a few of our customs.

William FitzWilliam wasn't born in this land but he had a deep respect for our way of life and our way of looking at the world. He employed Irish warriors in his retinue. And when he went to the Holy Land to fight in the Battle of Hattin, all his company were native Irish.

Along the way he couldn't help but learn something of the Gaelic attitude and approach to war. And he gained a great respect for the doctrines of respect, honour and decency I have just outlined to you.

He insisted that his two sons, both born in Ireland, learn the art of the Brandubh. He set them to studying music and storytelling. And long before either of his young lads ever picked up a blade he made sure they had at least a basic understanding of their duties and responsibilities in bearing arms.

One of his boys, Robert, took up the Brandubh with

enthusiasm. He wasn't much of a musician, our Rob, but he loved listening to stories. And as he got older and more confident he gained renown as a storyteller himself.

His younger brother was a thorny rose of another odour entirely. Rufus grew into an arrogant, greedy, self-centred youth with a penchant for swagger and a talent for keeping the spark of a grudge burning in his heart like a hot coal in the fireplace.

Not surprising then that he was rumoured to have attempted to force himself on one of the young Irish lassies of his father's estate. Less surprising that he tried to usurp Robert's rightful place as heir to the family fortunes while his elder brother was away in the Holy Land offering his sword to God.

Rufus was one of those nasty Norman lads who think they can go on all their lives bullying and bragging without lifting a finger to help anyone along the way. He was a lazy layabout. The closest thing he ever had to an ambition involved robbery, murder and other unsavoury acts perpetrated upon the defenceless inhabitants of his father's estates.

Whenever his wicked plots collapsed, which was frequently, he never hesitated to blame others. Indeed, it was not difficult to become the subject of one of his grudges.

Rufus was a rude, unpredictable, temperamental type of lad who lacked conscience or any sense of right or wrong. And I can tell you why. Though he learned the rules of the Brandubh as his father had commanded him, he never really took to the game at all.

Rufus had an abiding dislike of anything Irish. He had a silly notion in his head that because the Normans had defeated our people in battle, Gaelic culture must therefore be inferior in every way.

As for storytelling and music, he shunned them also. Music wasn't a strong point in the FitzWilliam family in any case. But Rufus showed not the slightest aptitude for it. And though he loved to brag, he couldn't bear to listen to a word anyone else had to say. He always had to be the centre of attention.

Unfortunately for him he considered himself a fine example of the warrior class. Of course that was a load of old fish-mongers. I've heard he was as inept with the sword as he was in the bedchamber. In the end he committed a terrible murder then set about stealing the FitzWilliam estates for himself. But that's another tale and I'm straying again from my own story.

Caoimhin wrote all about Rufus FitzWilliam and the young life of his elder brother Robert in the manuscript he called *The Tilecutter's Penny*. Read that. It will tell you more or less what happened to Rufus as a result of his arrogance.

He had the bloodline and the brawn I spoke about earlier so he was fairly typical of his people. But it has always been a mystery to me how William FitzWilliam could have fathered such a son or how two brothers could have been any more different from one another.

On the other hand Robert was weaned on a strange mix of Norman and Irish ways. While he understood he was ennobled by his birth, he also knew that the advantages of nobility were balanced by the responsibilities. He respected all those qualities a Gaelic warrior was taught were the mainstay of his profession. But he was a Norman at heart, and he was also imbued with the culture of his own people.

That's where he got all his ridiculous notions about chivalry. I don't know how he got the idea into his head that it was chivalrous to undertake a quest. I don't know who would have taught him that women are defenceless, empty-headed temptresses who only seek to steal a young knight's virtue. I can't say for certain why he became enamoured of the dream of serving God as a Knight of the Temple. But I'm sure all these misguided beliefs had root in the Norman side of him which was for a great part of his life the predominant aspect of his character.

So when he was given a quest to undertake by Aoife, Queen of the Night, he embarked upon it willingly. He never questioned for a moment whether this woman might be some dæmon from the dark places. After all, to his way of thinking all women had a touch of the dæmon about them.

He didn't consider whether or not it was right to take on a task that involved the murder of another creature. In his mind he was the perfect knight. He could do no ill. God was his guide. And God wouldn't lead him into sin. He truly believed he was free from the stain of guilt.

Now it's all well and good to believe you're incorruptible if you've spent forty years locked away in a cell learning how to levitate. Such saintly folk are entitled to be a little cocky. But Robert really wasn't such a holy man, though he longed to be.

The truth is he simply wasn't cut from the right cloth to be a saint. He came from a long line of warriors. He was a fine fighter himself when it came to it.

I don't wish to criticise him. Robert was a good-hearted soul for a Norman. But he was a very confused young man. The ideals of chivalry were the major cause of this confusion. So even when he'd cut off the head of Flidais he didn't realise that he might have done a terrible thing.

Flidais was one of the ancient immortal ones who had dwelled in Ireland in the days before the coming of our Gaelic ancestors. At some time in the dim, distant past she had been declared Goddess of the Hunt. It was her duty to oversee all aspects of the work of hunting. This was in the days before the hunt was a mere sport indulged by the nobility. In those times the very survival of the people depended upon the ability of its hunters to bring in game for the table in times when the crops failed or the snow had lain too long upon the ground.

When the hunters desired a good kill they prayed to Flidais. They offered thanks to her after the success of their endeavour. And she ensured they had enough food for their table but only as much as they needed and no more. Part of her responsibility was to ensure the hunters didn't allow their greed to get the better of them.

Now, there is only one certain way to slay an immortal. That is to cut the head clean off the intended victim with one mighty stroke. Failure to do this in one stroke can prove a messy and rather difficult affair. Those who've tasted the Quicken Brew heal quickly and completely from all wounds, except decapitation.

Flidais represented the ancient ones of Ireland. Aoife, on the other hand, was quite a deal younger than the Huntress. When she'd taken the Quicken Brew Flidais was already thousands of winters on this Earth.

It would be fair to say Flidais did not like the way Aoife was promoting herself as a new goddess. She saw this young upstart as a threat to her and the other ancient goddesses. And she wasn't wrong there.

In those days the worship and veneration of the Old Ones was already on the wane. Few folk today even remember Boann, Goddess of the Cows, or Cathlinn, Goddess of the Cats. Aoife got it into her head to replace all of them in much the same way the Christians had replaced all the old gods with their one God, Aon Dé.

So Flidais did the only thing she could. She began to spread rebellion in the Otherworld. When I say rebellion I really mean resistance. But Aoife saw it as rebellion. And when she got wind of the plan to overthrow her she acted decisively and ruthlessly.

Aoife learned from her spies that Flidais planned to cut her down in her own hall at the feast to celebrate Samhain Eve and her ascension to the throne of a goddess. So with the help of a Frightener spirit named Órán which dwelled in Robert's sword, she lured the young Fitzwilliam into the Otherworld.

Órán was a tricksy old bugger himself. He saw a great opportunity in supporting Aoife's ambitions. He struck a bargain with her that Robert would become her consort if he completed the quest she set for him. In this role Robert was destined to become the new High-King of Ireland, an office vacated since the arrival of the Normans thirty or so years earlier. Órán saw the potential there for his own feeding from the fear of Robert's subjects and the terror the High-King could spread across the world with his marauding hosts.

The Frightener reasoned that it was a short step from the High-Kingship of Ireland to the thrones of England or France. With those kingdoms in Robert's grasp Órán would have almost limitless opportunities to feed and become stronger.

Of course Robert was oblivious to all this. He'd withdrawn to the rear of the feasting hall after he'd murdered Flidais. And that's where I take up my tale of him once he'd sheathed his sword wherein dwelled the Frightener.

His fine white tunic was spattered with the blood of Flidais and it was as he sat in a corner to watch the proceedings that he first noticed this. He took off his helm and placed it by his side to examine the stains closely.

As he placed his helm on the floor, though, he was distracted. At that moment Aoife declared all rebels would die as Flidais had done. Robert watched some folk leaving the hall to hurry to their homes in fear. He noticed others rejoicing that Aoife had triumphed.

Then he heard his own name being chanted as if he were a hero.

'Ro-bert! Ro-bert!' the crowd intoned, giving equal emphasis to each syllable of his name.

Aoife was standing before him, dressed in her green gown. Her eyes were bright like emerald fire. Her long red hair shone as if it had been washed in the very essence of rubies. And the Queen of the Night was smiling.

'Arise Sir Robert,' she commanded. 'You have done your queen and your country a great service this night. You have quashed a rebellion which might have seen my blood spilled in this hall against all the customs of hospitality. You have ensured I will attain the rank of goddess tonight. And you have carved yourself a place by my side as my consort, my husband and the High-King of Ireland.'

'Was it not against the laws of hospitality for me to cut down Flidais?' Robert asked as he dragged himself wearily to his feet.

Aoife was taken aback. No one ever dared speak to her like that.

'You are not one of these people,' she explained with great tolerance. 'You are mortal. There is no offence in what you have done. And none shall ever dare accuse you of any. You will be High-King.'

'I don't want to be High-King.'

Aoife's expression turned from jubilation to anger in a flash. Her eyes still burned with emerald fire but the jewels were red hot with rage.

'How dare you question me?' she spat.

'I wasn't questioning you. I was merely telling you I have no wish to become High-King.'

The Queen of the Night quietly fumed, struggling not to let her temper get the better of her. Then she raised her hand in the air and barked an order to all who could hear.

'Leave us alone!'

Suddenly the hall was full of murmurs and shuffles as the assembled feasters departed through the nearest door. Some stopped by to bow silently to Aoife. Others touched the hem of her gown with their lips. A few thought twice about speaking to her but did not say a word.

In amongst all this movement both Aoife and Robert remained perfectly still, staring into each other's eyes with a quiet intensity. It was several long minutes before the hall was almost entirely cleared.

At the last three figures remained standing close by, trying to get their queen's attention. But Aoife did not grant it to them for a long while. She was intent on staring at this knight to the exclusion of all else.

'My lady?' one of the three stragglers coughed.

'What is it, Lochie?' she snapped.

'Isleen and I were wondering what you'd like us to do.'

'Do?'

'Yes. We're ready to do as you command in exchange for our freedom. And we're very grateful you granted us our old selves back for the evening. It was wonderful to have two legs again. It was simply magnificent to be able to shed the horrible worm bodies that have been our prisons for so long.'

'Simply magnificent,' Isleen echoed.

Aoife turned to them. She eyed Isleen first, then Lochie. And when she was done with him she turned her attention to the third figure who stood with them.

'What about you, Lom Dubh?' she asked. 'What's it like to have your old self back? How does it feel to walk around in your manly form again?'

'It is very nice, my darling sister,' he told her with a bow. 'I'd almost forgotten what it's like to be bound to the Earth. A couple of times I've stretched out my arms ready to take flight, only to find my raven feathers are no more. I couldn't be happier. It was a fine gift you granted me tonight.'

'I want to put all enmity behind us,' Aoife told him. 'I know we haven't always seen eye to eye. I know you have at times held a very low opinion of me. But I want to make it up to you for all the mistakes I've made in the past. I want to be a goddess who is revered for her nurturing, even-handed nature.'

'Well you couldn't do any worse than old Danu,' Lom Dubh assured her. 'As long as you stay awake you'll be one step ahead of her.'

Lochie and Isleen both sucked in a sharp breath at the

mention of the Goddess Danu. It was she who had imposed this punishment on all three of them.

'Is it wise to invoke her name?' Lochie ventured. 'After all, she is still a goddess.'

'Her time is finished!' the queen declared in triumph. 'I have come to replace her. One day I shall be the Goddess of the Flowing Waters. I will take all of her former titles. Danu slumbers. Aoife has awakened.'

'What would you have us do?' Isleen asked, anxious that Danu's name was being bandied about so freely.

'You will go directly to the settlement of the Killibegs. I have some havoc for you to perform. Wait there out of sight in your ugly worm form. When the time is right you will receive instructions from Lom Dubh. I have a tunnel for you to dig. Don't take any notice of Sciathan Cog, mind.'

'But Aoife, he is our brother also,' Lom reminded her. 'Can you not find it in your heart to forgive him?'

'He has done the unthinkable. First of all he presented that incompetent Norman, Guy d'Alville, to me. What a waste of my valuable time he turned out to be. Now Sciathan Cog, who was known in the old days as Sárán, has betrayed me.'

'How?'

'He has aligned himself with another Norman. A bishop of the Christians. Sárán thinks he can beat me at this game. But I was always the better player of the Brandubh. I always defeated him. His strategies are as shallow as his loyalty.'

'Sárán was always headstrong and selfish,' Lom agreed. 'But surely you can put his past misdeeds behind you.'

'Sárán was always a fool,' Isleen commented. 'He is greedy and arrogant. It suits him well to be off with the Normans.'

'Bloody branch-breakers!' Lochie added. 'She's right. One thing I'll say for my darling Isleen, her summary of a person's character is always accurate. She has an eye for these matters.'

'Sciathan Cog is a traitor,' Aoife said. 'And he is no less a traitor than Flidais was. Yet he is my brother. So I will be merciful to him. He will not die a traitor's death. But neither will I free him from Danu's curse. He will remain in the form of an ugly raven for as long as it pleases me to keep him thus.'

'It is only fitting,' Lochie shrugged, and he was glad to be able to move his shoulders thus after all those years trapped in the body of a worm.

'He is our brother,' Lom Dubh said again. 'Would it not be better to forgive him as you would have us forgive you?'

'It's too late for that.' The queen shook her head. 'We've wasted enough breath discussing that one. I have work for you to do. Go to the Killibegs. Fly over the settlement in your raven form. Then return to report to me on the fortifications and the resolve of the poor folk who are trapped within that place.'

Lom Dubh bowed. He had just straightened up when Robert spoke.

'Spare them,' he begged. 'They do not deserve to die.'

Aoife laughed.

'You are speaking out of turn, good knight.'

'I will not bow down to a goddess who so ruthlessly throws away the lives of innocent people. I will defy you. And so will everyone who lives in this land. You will not be a goddess with the blood of the Culdees on your hands.'

Lochie and Isleen stepped back together, expecting Aoife to explode with rage. But she smiled.

'He's a better choice than that other Norman,' Isleen conceded. 'I hope you won't have too much trouble keeping him in check.'

The queen stepped closer to Robert to touch his hair.

'He won't be any trouble at all,' she assured the Nathair. 'I haven't explained the entire strategy to anyone else but Lom Dubh. How could he, or you for that matter, possibly guess what I have planned for this evening?'

Lochie frowned with confusion. 'We are to attack the Killibegs on your orders? Is that not correct?'

'You will do nothing until you receive instructions from me or from my loyal brother Lom Dubh. Do you understand? When the word comes to you there will be no mistaking what I require you to do. Until then keep out of sight and observe what takes place. But under no circumstances are you to involve yourselves in proceedings without my express command.'

'Yes, my lady,' Lochie bowed.

Isleen also bowed her head as she added, 'Thank you for your forgiveness. And thank you for this wonderful evening. I haven't felt so excited for many, many winters. I'd almost forgotten what it is to walk on two legs or to hold a cup in my hands.'

'Soon enough you will have forgotten what it is to be a Nathair worm,' Aoife assured her. 'If you keep to my orders.'

She waved them towards the door.

'Now go to your tasks.'

With a final bow of thanks the three of them were gone. Then Aoife turned her attention to Robert. She walked along the table of food selecting an apple for herself and another for her guest.

'You have misjudged me,' the queen said as she threw the apple to Robert. 'I admit that it was my original intention to send a force of Redcaps to attack the Killibegs. I wanted to send a message of fear to the people of Ireland. Then it would have been a simple matter to call off the ravages of the Redcaps and the Nathairaí while people bowed down to me in thanks.'

'But they are innocent folk,' Robert protested. 'They are good people. They don't deserve to die.'

'As it happens, circumstance has led me to believe you are right.'

'Then they're safe?'

'Not entirely. It is likely a terrible scourge will come upon them this night.'

She moved over to where he was standing. Then she offered her hand.

'Walk with me,' she commanded gently. 'It's time we talked together.'

Robert took her hand after a slight hesitation. With the other she lovingly brushed the hair back away from his face.

'You remind me of someone I knew long, long ago,' she sighed. 'He was a handsome young man. He would've done anything for me. But I chose to take a long sleep rather than spend the eternal summers by his side.'

'What happened to him?' Robert enquired.

'He's still about,' she laughed. 'I haven't seen him in many, many years. But I'm sure he's still about.'

'You miss him greatly,' the knight observed.

'Now and then. I don't know why I've brought him to mind at this moment. Perhaps it is something in the way you defy me. I like that.'

She brushed her hand against his cheek.

'We're going to get along quite nicely, I think. Quite nicely.'

'Not if the people of the Killibegs are to be sacrificed to you,' Robert replied sharply.

'Then they shall not be.'

While Robert was off fulfilling quests and Lanfranc was liberating his catapult I was busy making a bloody fool of myself. I told you last night about my run-in with a bag of herbs which, when mixed with butter in the right proportion, constituted a love potion.

I'd cooked it up with Caoimhin in mind. You see, it was my intention to draw him to me as quickly as possible. I wasn't the only unmarried woman at the Killibegs, you know. And a few of the others had already expressed a passing interest in this lad who'd come over from Glastonbury.

I was certain I'd seen Sianan ogling him across the great hall. So I had resorted to a potion that had been given to me by my old friend Ortha with whom I'd escaped the nunnery.

The love philtre worked a treat too, I can tell you. Caoimhin fell head over heels in love with me as soon as the potion began to digest within him. The trouble is that no sooner had it taken effect than Sianan dragged him away to the Otherworld with her. She was looking for some well he'd glimpsed in one of his visions.

Bloody typical and no surprises there. One thing I can be certain of when it comes to matters of love is that if anything can go wrong for me, it most certainly will. So, determined not to let my little fish off the hook, as it were, I followed on after Sianan and Caoimhin.

That's right. I threw caution to the wind and traipsed after them into the Otherworld with only a skin full of tainted broth to keep me from the ravages of hunger. And what was the broth tainted with? Nothing but the remnants of Ortha's love philtre.

I've called myself an eedyit ever since as a daily penance. And as I told you last night this bad situation was bound to get much worse. The nature of a love potion is that it will not work until it has begun to digest.

If you were to sup some now and give it a little time to digest, the first suitable person you set eyes on would become the object of your adoration. You won't be tasting the love potion. I've only a small portion left and I've a singular purpose in mind for it.

As it happened I drank the love broth in a moment of

hunger and so set a terrible enchantment in motion. I could have been lucky and looked on Caoimhin once the broth started to break down in my belly. Then we would have been utterly besotted with one another and everyone would have lived happily ever after. But it wasn't Caoimhin I looked at.

It was Guy.

Eedyit. That's what I am.

It just so happened Guy wasn't having a particularly good evening either. To start with he'd been turned into an oak by Aoife in a fit of pique after he'd failed to fulfil some silly quest she'd set him. She was always setting quests for potential suitors. Some women are like that.

Well, due to a bungled enchantment cast by a talentless jongleur, Guy managed to escape his jail of timber and branches. And I'm sure it was his time as a tree that changed a few things about him. Though his great-grandfather reckoned it was me.

If you recall, after Guy was set free from Aoife he stumbled across a Frightener spirit who'd been dwelling in a sword owned by his great-grandfather. That's right. Both Robert and Guy had ancestral spirits attached to their families which sought to bring both of them to power and prestige in the world.

It just so happened that Eterscél, the Frightener who'd attached himself to Guy's great-grandfather, had high hopes for the young Guy d'Alville. He even renamed him Guy Stronghold. It was probably more to avoid confusion than anything else. And for that reason I'll refer to the younger Guy d'Alville as Stronghold from now on. The older Guy will still be Guy.

D'Alville, I mean.

Do you follow me? I do hope this isn't too confusing. You can just imagine how I felt at the time. All these intense emotions rushing through me. Infatuation. Adoration. Dare I say that I experienced more than a little twinge of lust whenever I spied Stronghold out of the corner of my eye?

Here I am, a woman of ninety, and I still flush when I think about it. I'll never get over it, you know. Never. Well maybe not.

So Old Guy set about instructing Stronghold in the ways of chivalry. He and Eterscél had come to the conclusion that Stronghold would make a fine High-King of Ireland. But Old Guy knew the Irish wouldn't accept a Norman who wasn't possessed of the basic manners required of a ruler.

As an aside, I have always marvelled at the fact that Guy and Robert were rivals in every respect from the very moment they met. There was some tussle in the Holy Land over the Ark of the Covenant, I've been told, which kicked off their feud. Then both of them ended up fighting over the same satchel of books. They both fell into Aoife's web. And both were touted as a possible High-King of Ireland. I'm fascinated by details such as these. They're what makes life interesting.

So there's where we all stood just before midnight on Samhain Eve. That is to say, we stood under the intertwining oaks trees which marked the way into the forests of the Otherworld.

I was never happier than at that moment. I'd escaped the strange Land of Dreams without any discernable damage to my reputation or my wits. Of course that just goes to show how wrong I can be about myself on occasion. Beside me stood the man of my deepest desire; the knight of my passions; the object of my lusting loins. Guy Stronghold. Pardon me. The thing about a love potion is it never wears off. I still go all mushy when I think about him.

That's why I have to keep reminding myself what an utter bastard he was. He was the lowest of the low, an awful man with alluring eyes and the most wonderful laugh. Not that he laughed that much. But when he did it was a delight to hear.

I think I might talk about something else for a minute or

two. I seem to be getting distracted. I'll tell you something of what Stronghold's great-grandfather had to say about chivalry.

The Old Guy d'Alville was a rugged individual who'd seen war, famine, pestilence and death galloping their war steeds across the Earth in full measure. He'd witnessed bloody intrigues at the Norman court. He'd been a party to murderous plots to rid the realm of traitors and usurpers. But through all that dirty work he'd managed to retain his dignity. You see, Old Guy was an old-fashioned fellow. He believed that integrity and truth count for more in the world than wealth and power.

He was wrong of course. But bless him, his heart was in the right place. The truth is that wealth and power aren't that bad. If you can manage to value truth and integrity whilst wielding wealth and power then you've done well and congratulations and all that.

What I'm trying to say is that if you aspire to the High-Kingship of Ireland you've got to be ready to deal with all the resultant trouble that comes your way. For a start, there's jealousy. As soon as you're proclaimed ruler of Ireland every man and his ferret think they can do a better job than you.

Everyone has some petty criticism to contribute and before you can shout, 'Keep the bloody noise down in the throne room!', they're all contributing their own views on your reign so far. It's only one short step from that to open rebellion, civil strife and a rift with the Church over a minor detail of dogma and practice.

That's usually followed by excommunication. Then comes the execution of your first wife and her lover or lovers as the case may be. After that there's the endless family recriminations on the part of her bloodline which can drag on for centuries.

In the meantime the chancellor has been tithing himself a neat little nest egg from the royal coffers. But nobody flits an eyelid until it's discovered he's drinking better ale than even the king can afford. That's when things start to get really bother-some.

I haven't even mentioned the eventual dynastic struggles that are sure to erupt once there are two sons who claim parentage from the royal line. Usually one of them is a bastard fathered to a serving woman and much loved by the people.

Of course his younger brother is the son of the first, now deceased, queen. So there's some doubt to his claim to the throne. Before the sheets on their father's death bed have even been changed they're raising warriors ready to face each other down.

I won't even mention the day-to-day struggle of keeping a kingdom running. What with foreign invaders landing every day of the week, dissent with the clergy over the dating of Easter, raising taxes and organising extravagant feasts, a king has very little time for the fine things in life.

Just consider the constant threat of plague which arises in the world these days. A single instance of the black death can cripple a landowner's ability to pay his taxes to the treasury. Serfs aren't cheap, you know. And they're not as easy to find as they used to be. You can't just sail off to England and pick up a boatload of slaves like you used to be able to do in the good old days.

It only takes a minor outbreak of pestilence to bring famine on the country. Famine leads to invasion. Invasion leads to even more folk like the Normans coming here.

No wonder the last High-King of Ireland spent his days going round checking the armpits of his subjects for pustules.

When you consider all these likely hellish scenarios you have to ask yourself a question. Who'd want to be a king these days? The answer is a surprising number of foolish folk, that's who.

And Guy Stronghold would have counted himself among

them before his magical transformation into a tree. The change had a profound effect on him. Even if it did take a little while for that profound effect to show up.

It was after we crossed back into the waking world, it was. I'll never forget it. Guy Stronghold went straight over to a bare patch of ground among the grass. He stood there in silence for a few moments, his arms spread wide to the sky. All the while his great-grandfather kept talking to him about the responsibilities and troubles likely to befall a king.

Then Stronghold wriggled his fingers, mimicking the fluttering leaves of a great oak.

'Hush for a while, Great-Grandfather,' he whispered. 'I just want to feel the breeze in my branches.'

You could have knocked the old man over with a pair of pigeon feathers. He was so astounded he didn't know what to say. Stronghold, on the other hand, breathed deeply, taking in the cool night air. His chest heaved as he stared skyward into the clouds.

'Are you ill?' I asked.

'I've never felt better.' Stronghold turned his attention to me. 'At last we're free of the Otherworld and its dæmonic enchantments.'

He smiled broadly like an idiot. But what a smile it was. I sigh to think of it even now.

'I was a tree this night,' he confided.

'I beg your pardon?' I was seriously worried he might have injured his head at some point or overexerted himself carrying me through the woods. He went on to explain.

'Earlier this evening I stood here on this patch of ground as a mighty oak. I knew the soft moist soil between my roots. I tasted the sweet life-giving sap within my bough. I was a perch for ravens and a hiding place for a band of entertainers. I watched helplessly as Robert FitzWilliam stole away the treasures I'd intended would change my fortunes.'

'Sit down, boy,' Old Guy suggested. 'Perhaps you should rest a while before we press on to the Killibegs.'

'I don't need a seat,' Stronghold laughed. 'Aoife, Queen of the Night, changed me into a tree. I was an oak and this was the place where my roots were nestled in the warm earth. How can any man who has tasted such a marvellous experience ever yearn for anything else?'

'You'll be the High-King of Ireland,' his great-grandfather reminded him.

'I can still feel the breeze tossing my leaves,' Stronghold sighed with his eyes closed lightly. 'I don't want to be High-King of Ireland. I just want to be an oak tree.'

That was about all the old man could take. He grabbed his descendant by the shoulders and shook him hard.

'Now listen here!' he bellowed. 'I've made an arrangement with Eterscél. He's agreed to allow me to go on living if I can make a king out of you. And you'll bloody well be the king even if I have beat it into you.'

'I don't want to be king,' Stronghold repeated. 'I just want to be free.'

'Watch your mouth, my lad. I've been set the task of teaching you about chivalry. And I promise you that if you don't put yourself to learning the manners that befit a monarch I'll thrash you with the back of my riding crop until the leather discolours. I want my life back!'

The old man stepped back from his great-grandson and breathed deeply, trying to restrain his hands from unseemly violence. When he'd managed to calm himself a little he went on.

'I've been a bloody prisoner in the Otherworld for longer than I can recall. And I've got a lot of living to catch up on. I'm not going to let you spoil my one last opportunity to taste the fruits of life.'

The old knight put a hand to his brow as he struggled to find the words.

'Look, son, you've got a lovely woman here who thinks the world of you. She loves you, though I'm at a loss to understand what it is she sees in you. I concede that you're smart. You've got some skill with a blade and you know how to dress. Simple yet impressive. You've got style and character. I'd even be willing to wager you've got a sense of humour under all that bluster.'

Stronghold turned to face me.

'Do you really love me?' he asked.

I nodded.

'Say it.'

'Guy Stronghold,' I whispered, 'I love you.'

Now, even though I was in the depths of delusion brought on by the love potion I could see the change that came over Stronghold's face when I spoke those words. His smile deepened.

'No one's ever said that to me before,' he confided, ignoring his great-grandfather. 'Except under torture. But that doesn't really count, does it?'

I shook my head in agreement.

In that instant Eterscél stepped out of the forest. He was a strange looking creature dressed all in purple with a green shirt under his tunic. His hair was silvery white and his skin was a deathly pale. Spirits of the frightening kind are known for their extravagant forms.

'Was that a touch of fear I sensed in you, Stronghold?' the Frightener enquired in his deep resonant voice.

Young Guy laughed. 'It wasn't fright. I think it was delight.'

The Frightener skimmed across the ground between them so fast his feet didn't touch the ground. Before Stronghold had a chance to react Eterscél was standing right in front of him. The Frightener turned to look at me with contempt then suddenly pushed me aside roughly. I fell on to the grass.

'I don't want anything to get in the way of our plans,'

92

Eterscél barked. 'She's only a means to win the hearts of the Irish to your claim to the High-Kingship. She is nothing. You will not become attached to her.'

'What makes you think I am?' Stronghold asked, and I caught a glimpse of the Guy I'd first encountered at the Killibegs: arrogant and manipulative.

'Your heartbeat jumped,' the Frightener pointed out.

Stronghold averted his eyes so Eterscél could not see too deeply.

'I knew it!' the Frightener exclaimed. 'This is getting out of hand. The girl cannot stay! She's going to ruin everything.'

Stronghold ignored the comment and offered me a hand to help me to my feet. His great-grandfather stepped between them then with a hand on the Frightener's chest to calm him.

'It won't hurt to have her with us,' he soothed. 'And if my great-grandson ends up having feelings for her, then all the better. The people will see he is genuinely in love with her. They'll soften to him. If they soften to him they will not baulk when he commands them to go to war.'

'She'll be nothing but trouble,' the Frightener spat. 'I've seen it a thousand times before. It's always a woman who comes between me and my feasting. I'm a Frightener! Not an Enticer. What use are feelings of love to me? I can't feed on that sort of food.'

'But the deepest fear that any mortal may experience is closely bound up with love,' the old man reminded him in a conspiratorial whisper. 'You should know that. Let it be. You'll see the wisdom of this in time.'

'You'd better be right. Or I'll make you suffer for it.'

Then the Frightener turned his attention to Stronghold again.

'We have a wager, you'll recall. If I can inspire fear in you, even the slightest twinge of fright, I will become the senior partner in this relationship.'

Young Guy nodded. 'That is true. I will not renege on our wager. But for now I am the senior partner. And I am going to the Killibegs to aid in the defence of that settlement. I've had enough of bullying and cruelty. I intend to change my ways.'

'You'll always be Guy d'Alville at heart,' Eterscél scoffed. 'You can't turn around a lifetime of foulness in one evening.'

'My name is Stronghold. Guy d'Alville is dead.'

It's a powerful thing to undergo a change of name. Look what happened to Caoimhin. When he first arrived in Wexford his name was Harold. Not a very inspiring name, you must admit. Few Saxon names *are* since they rarely have a meaning. At the suggestion of his teacher he took an Irish name so the Gaels would find it easier to accept him.

That is often the way in a strange land. It is sometimes better to adopt the customs of those folk who are the majority than it is to cling to old symbols of class and culture. Why is this so? I'll tell you. Most mortals, for good or ill, are intimidated by that which they don't understand. If you have anything about you that marks you as different from the herd, you'll end up attracting attention to yourself. Now and then the attention might be pleasant but for the most part you'll find yourself under attack.

It wasn't always that way in Ireland. Time was when a man was honoured for those qualities which set him apart from the crowd. Time was when names were considered an important clue to a man's character. In the old days, before the coming of the Christians and the Normans, the Gaels honoured names.

In those times folk reckoned a name was more than just an empty, random label. You see, your name is a magical spell. When you hear it spoken the very depths of your soul awakens to the call. It is how you identify yourself in this life.

Now it so happens that amongst the Normans, the Saxons and the other barbarian peoples of this earth, a child is given a name at birth. That name is the one they will carry for the rest of their days. Amongst the Saxons any man who changed his name could be executed. Only the King of the English had the power to change a name. For he owned the name of each of his subjects.

Unless a man earns himself a nickname he will always answer to the name his parents gave him at birth. Even nicknames aren't usually that pleasant. Amongst the Saxons nicknames are a form of ridicule.

I knew a Saxon man once who was known simply as Nuck. He'd been called that name all his life. He'd forgotten whatever it was his parents had originally called him. Of course in the beginning he'd been known as Feckless Nuck. Over time it got shortened to Nuck. And how, you might ask, did he earn this distinctive nickname?

The fact is he had a very short neck. Indeed, when I first met him I marvelled at the way his head seemed to join seamlessly with his shoulders. Now obviously this was the result of an unfortunate birth or an accident of some kind. But in typical Saxon fashion his peers had come up with an obscene name to ridicule his condition. That's the English for you.

Thus Feckless Nuck spent his life withstanding mockery, abuse and downright prejudice. Folk assumed that simply because he had a short neck and an amusing nickname he must, by rights, be stupid.

Of course he wasn't. And he proved that shortly after he became King John's chancellor and had most of his childhood acquaintances burned at the stake for heresy. I've heard it said that if he hadn't been branded with Nuck he might never have set out to obtain power and revenge by attaining the highest office in the land.

That tale only goes to prove the power of a name.

In the Gaelic-speaking parts of Ireland and Alba there has always been a different approach to naming. We follow an ancient tradition, the origins of which are lost in the fog of antiquity. At birth a child was merely referred to as he or she. Within seven days a name would be found for the baby.

The surest way to discover an infant's name is to ask a Seer. Failing that, ask another little child, preferably a sibling of the babe. At the seventh birthday the child used to be given the opportunity to choose their own name and discard the one it had carried for the first part of its life.

We Gaels once held to the understanding that every life is divided into stages of seven years. At each stage it was considered right and proper to select a new name to carry you through the next part of life. So a man of seventy years may have taken on nine names in his lifetime, each appropriate to the stage of life he was about to embark upon. And where did these names come from?

They were granted in dreams.

Even in my youth folk were already beginning to listen less and less to their dreams. Nowadays few people take their night visions seriously. But I have always held that the dreaming world is the real place where we dwell. This waking world is more of a dream. It is not real. It is as insubstantial as a rippling reflection on the face of a pool.

As I was saying, names are powerful spells which hold our identity and express our own vision of ourselves. So when young Guy accepted the new name of Stronghold a very strange and profound transformation took place.

All that bitterness, hatred, burning vengeance and cruelty that was attached to Guy d'Alville was banished. Stronghold had no history. Stronghold was a new man. Stronghold was a clean slate, a freshly ploughed field, a newly forged blade, a reinvigorated soul. Stronghold didn't have to carry on in the same way as Guy d'Alville had. He was free.

In those minutes as Stronghold stood with his arms wide like an oak, the former Guy d'Alville died. He passed away from this life as surely as if he'd had his head cut off his shoulders and stuck on a pole for all to see.

In his place Stronghold was born. And Stronghold was all that the young Guy d'Alville was not. Stronghold was a generous, kind, courageous and honest man. He shunned grudges and cultivated reconciliation.

And I don't want you to think I'm saying all this just because I'd taken a love potion and was filled full of foolish notions about the man. My foolish notions had nothing to do with the situation. He genuinely had changed.

'It's time we made our way to the Killibegs,' Stronghold told Eterscél. 'I'm impatient to present my services to those people. They'll need all the help they can get on this night. You and I will defeat the Redcaps and the Hospitallers together.'

The Frightener narrowed his eyes and searched the knight's face.

'I'm beginning to wonder whether it was a good idea for me to latch on to you the way I have. I hope you're not going to be as much trouble as your great-grandsire was.'

'I'll do my duty,' Stronghold smiled. 'I'm a knight. It is my lot to protect the weak and uphold the defence of those who are persecuted. You're a Frightener spirit. So let's see you do some frightening. You could start with putting the fear of God into the enemy.'

'I could start by frightening you!'

Suddenly Stronghold was alone. We'd all vanished from his view. Nearby in the woods a creature of immense size was stalking through the underbrush. The knight sighed, shaking his head as he stared skywards in exasperation.

In the next instant the air was torn apart by the mighty roar of a ferocious lion. Guy's heart raced with anticipation as his hand searched for the hilt of his sword. But the blade was gone. He was defenceless and alone and a great beast of the feline species had caught his scent on the wind.

Stronghold took a deep breath, held it for a moment and then laughed.

In a flash the night was transformed. Old Guy was shaking his great-grandson by the shoulders.

'What's the matter, boy?'

Stronghold laughed again as Eterscél pushed the old man aside.

'You weren't scared, were you? Even though you were all alone with a lion and no sword to slay it with, you didn't even shudder.'

'There are no lions in Ireland,' Stronghold smiled. 'You'll have to do better than that if you want to scare this knight.'

'You can count on me,' Eterscél retorted. 'I'll find your weakness. Mark my words you will buckle under to fear before long or my name isn't Eterscél.'

Then the Frightener stepped back to whisper a few words to Old Guy.

'By the way, I know you said you were going to teach him all about chivalry but don't you think you might have taken it a bit far?'

'I'm not responsible for this change. He just suddenly started talking sense. Don't worry. I'm sure it's for the best. I'm certain he'll make a perfect High-King.'

'For your sake he'd better,' the Frightener warned. 'He'd better.'

ḥERETICS

T he sad thing about both Robert and Stronghold was that they were indoctrinated with certain beliefs which they never thought to question. Then again, not many of the Normans ever thought very much about anything, so perhaps I should be a little less harsh on the two of them.

If you reckon the change that came over young Guy was remarkable, consider Robert FitzWilliam for a moment. Our Robert was an intelligent, well-rounded and gentle soul. But when he first went off to the Holy Land to fight he hadn't really any idea of the world at all.

When the Church fathers told him that the Muslim invaders were infidel barbarians who regularly roasted children at their hearths for supper, Robert swallowed the lie. When he heard rumours of the vicious tortures to be endured by any who were captured by the Saracens, Robert shuddered and believed.

He wasn't the only one. Most Christian knights had a case of the shakes either on board ship to the Holy Land or some time after they landed. And for most of them the strangeness of the country added to their sense of foreboding.

The sad thing is that almost everything the crusader knights were told about the Saracens was utterly untrue. In fact the crusades were, as I've already told you, an elaborate sham invented to rid the kingdoms of the west of the worst of their brigands and thieves.

The Saracens were in fact a wonderfully wise people who valued learning and piously held to their beliefs, come what may. They didn't sack Jerusalem as we'd all been told. They didn't even seize the city. It had been in their hands for five hundred years before the crusaders blundered along. Our knights have been stuck there for a hundred years or so. All the while they've been bogged down in a silly conflict with a people who could teach them more than a thing or two about most subjects.

Take for example a few aspects of life in the Norman lands which have been affected by the knowledge of the Saracens. The lute came from the Holy Land where it is known as the oud. The musical scales which the Normans now claim to be their own were imported to Rouen from the east along with the instruments themselves.

Norman physicians regularly travel to Jerusalem, Baghdad, Alexandria and other cities of the east to study the ways of medicine. The Saracens are much more knowledgeable in such matters and they have a long tradition of medical practices which are far in advance of anything available in the west.

Spices. Where would we be without spices? I'll tell you. We'd be supping on bland boiled mutton or boring old bacon. Pepper is a godsend and any man who says otherwise deserves to have his tongue cut out for failing to use it in copious quantities.

Ginger is my favourite. It stings the mouth a little, I'll admit. But don't the best things in life always leave a bit of you tingling and numb?

I could go on listing the many wonderful things the Saracens have given us over the years since our folk first went off to the Holy Land intent on murdering as many of them as possible. But I believe you may be starting to see my point. The whole adventure of the crusades was a fabrication to distract folks at home and to unify Christendom at a time when the Holy

Roman Catholic and Apostolic Church was falling apart at the seams.

There's nothing like an evil foreign enemy to unite dissenters to a common cause and distract them from the real problems they're facing. And by the Bléssed White Pebbles of Saint Finbar there were dissenters everywhere before the crusades. The Church fathers liked to call them heretics.

I've already told you that the Culdees of the Killibegs were considered heretics. Across the water in England, France and Germany there were many other heretics as well. Some of them upheld the most shocking customs and beliefs.

The Quarto-Decimans were condemned by Rome because they insisted on keeping the Feast of the Holy Week, which the Saxons call Easter, on the fourteenth day of the first month of the year. That was March in the old Roman calendar.

It was an evil practice, as I'm sure you'll agree. But I'm not certain they deserved to be burned at the stake in their hundreds just because they didn't see eye to eye with the Pope in matters of the calendar.

The Artotyrites were persecuted because they offered both bread and cheese as a sacrament. This alone surely has all the hallmarks of the Devil's intervention. However, that wasn't the end of their heresy.

They also admitted women to the priesthood. And for that the Artotyrites were hunted down and murdered in their thousands until dairy products were expunged forever from the rituals of the Church. It goes without saying that ordained women of the Artotyritian persuasion were unceremoniously defrocked wherever they were encountered.

The Montanists believed their leader, Montanus, had been privy to revelations not vouchsafed to any of the Apostles. Whatever those revelations might have entailed was sadly lost forever when his followers were completely wiped from the face of the Earth by the zealous monks of the Holy Inquisition.

There were other heresies besides these. The Agn Stæ recognised the God of the Roman Church as the creator of all things but argued that he didn't know when the Day of Judgement would take place. For this they were sentenced to be drawn and quartered before they were burned alive. I'm sure God himself, being vengeful, would have punished them in this manner had not the agents of the Roman Church beat him to it.

The Collyridians offered sweet honey cakes to the Virgin Mary. I shouldn't have to explain to you the inherent evil involved in that particular ritual. Honey cakes are the daily bread of sinners and of sinfulness. At least the Pope felt compelled to declare they were. That perhaps explains the popularity of such confections in Ireland.

The Melchizedechians claimed the only true Messiah was a shadowy individual who called himself Melchizedek. Depending on who you speak to he may, or may not, have already visited the Earth to redeem mankind long before Christ was born. But in any case he had recently revealed himself in order to be hailed by the faithful.

He and his followers were eventually forcibly evicted from their plush villa south of Rome and crucified at regular intervals along the road to the capital. If only he hadn't insisted on entertaining his largely female priesthood with orgies of cheese and honey cakes on the fourteenth day of the first month.

I could go on. The list is extensive. There were so many religious dissidents preaching in the streets in those days, the poor Pope must have been shaking in his silk-lined, purple velvet shoes.

With all the different stories flying about concerning who was or who wasn't holy it's no wonder fellows like Robert and young Guy ended up changing the direction of their lives. All that theological correctness can't have been healthy for anyone.

The strange thing is that Guy Stronghold, who arrived in Ireland bearing a contempt for our people, should have so completely changed his mind. I suppose that goes to show you how mysterious is the soul-voyage.

I told you about the soul-voyage. I'm sure I did. Our word for it is Imramma. It's an expression which refers to the journey we all take through life and beyond. I like to equate it with a voyage undertaken on an ocean-going ship.

The ship is this body we are born into. We spend a lot of our childhood years learning to navigate this body-ship through the sea of existence. Along the way our soul is enticed by stories of exotic ports or far-off ambitions. And as soon as we get the chance we set sail on our own to reach those ports of call.

For some of us those places we voyage toward may be the desire to learn a craft or become the master of a trade. For others the destinations may have more to do with attaining wealth or fame or power, or likely all three.

Others may only be interested in sailing alongside a beloved one throughout this life. A goodly number of us set about populating our ship with children in the hope they'll crew it when we're too old to sail on alone.

And like any sea voyage the soul journey may be disrupted by unforeseen circumstances. Wind and tides must be taken into account. Sometimes it's better to ride out a storm in some safe harbour. At other times the risk of wreck is worth the rewards waiting at the next port of call.

Sails may tear and rigging will wear out along the way. The timbers of our vessel will need to be cleaned, maintained and kept free of barnacles. Reefs and rocks, icebergs and sandbars must be avoided.

Pirates will occasionally appear on the horizon, so be prepared for them. And most of all, don't forget to keep an eye out for sea monsters. Then when the working life of your vessel is ended you will be able to retire her to the ship's graveyard without any regrets, ready to take up the helm as master of a new boat.

That's if you haven't sailed off the edge of the world, of course.

I hope you understand what I'm on about. It'd be a terrible shame if you didn't. It was talk like that which earned the Culdees the reputation for heresy. Stories of our ways attracted all sorts of mystic adventurers to Ireland in those days. But as I've said before: To go to Rome will avail you not, yet cost you endless pain. The answer you seek in Rome, you find at home or seek in vain.

Robert and Stronghold both came here to this land seeking for something. Stronghold probably didn't know it except in the very depths of his soul. I suppose he thought he'd only come here in search of plunder and vengeance.

But Robert had grown up in Ireland. He'd been born on his father's estates here. He was almost as Irish as we were. That's why he came back to these shores looking for the answers to the mysteries of his soul.

His yearning was to find a way to be himself. He wanted to be able to sail the boat of his soul through waters of his own choosing and not be restricted by the edicts of the self-proclaimed harbourmasters of this world.

He already knew that everything he'd been told about the Saracens had been a bucket full of boiled badger bollocks. He'd guessed that most of what he'd heard about the heretics probably weighed about the same.

And he suspected that much of what he'd come to believe about the Faerie folk, the creatures known as dæmons, and the reputed Satanic origins of their kind, was untrue. So it's no wonder he left the sea lanes of the Church to explore the unchartered waters of the Otherworld.

In truth if you think carefully on everything I've told you these last few nights you'll realise why the Pope was so eager to have the ideals of the Culdees suppressed. If life is a soul-voyage and we are free to travel wheresoever we will, what role does Rome play in the lives of mortals?

If we may simply change ship when one is washed up in a storm or runs aground, why abide by the charts of the Church? There is a whole wide world out there waiting to be explored. Don't restrict yourself to sailing those oceans marked out on dusty outdated maps.

Be bold. Look to the horizon. Sail on to adventure and do not fear. No matter what you do or where you go you cannot be separated from God. For God is the ocean and the wind and the sky.

That's the gist of my favourite Culdee blessing.

> May Sea calm before your bowsprit.
> May Earth firm your mooring.
> May Sky lift your spirit.
> And may the Wind of good fortune carry you home.

The Dark Twins

B ack to the story. I told you last night about how Caoimhin had been wandering in the Otherworld and had become separated from Oat-Beer the red Sotar dog and Sianan. I told you how he was taken prisoner by a company of rebel Redcaps then released when they realised he was no threat to them.

Next our Caoimhin did an uncharacteristic thing. After reading a section of a treatise on enchantments which he'd discovered in his book satchel, he thought he'd have a crack at magic himself.

Caoimhin cast a sigil.

And the sign he made for himself was aimed at saving the people of the Killibegs. What he didn't understand was that such enchantments rarely, if ever, follow an expected course. I'm not saying that sigil magic is ineffective. The results are always exactly as one desired them to be. It's the way those results are produced which varies wildly.

So the first thing that happened after Caoimhin cast his sigil was that another enchantment was broken. Nearby where he'd been seated in the forest of the Otherworld two warriors of the Sen Erainn had been placed under bonds of magic to take the form of wooden idols.

It was Aoife's doing. She loved transforming folk into different forms and leaving them that way. And that's how

Srón and Scodán would have stayed if it hadn't been for Caoimhin. Of course they were very grateful to him and insisted he accompany them to find the Well of Many Blessings to help them complete their mission.

It seemed to them our young Benedictine must have been a Draoi master if not a Druid indeed. Well it so happened, as you'll recall if you'd been listening, that Caoimhin ended up being responsible for freeing the entire host of the Sen Erainn from a similar curse.

Thus, to his dismay, Caoimhin found himself proclaimed their king. Of course a king of the Sen Erainn is not the same thing as a king of any other folk. The Sen Erainn are fisher folk from the islands off the west coast of Ireland. They'd lived without kings for nearly three thousand years.

Caoimhin had proved himself a wise practitioner of the Draoi-craft and they were grateful to him. They granted him armour and fine clothes, even a beautiful war-helm to go with his title. But the chieftains of the Sen Erainn weren't about to start taking orders from him. The title and function of king was a purely honorary one.

He was told to select his war council, which he did. He chose Srón, for whom he started to develop quite an attraction. You see, the love potion I gave him had been nullified after he tasted the waters of the well. He also named Scodán and Becc mac Dé, the old War-Druid of the Sen Erainn.

But he'd also called on Mallacht of the Redcaps who had been imprisoned by Aoife in the form of a stone well-head. Now that Mallacht had been freed he was eager to bring war to the doorstep of the Queen of the Night.

There was one other player in this little drama at the Well of Many Blessings. When Robert FitzWilliam sliced the head off the Goddess Flidais all the spells she had ever cast, all the enchantments she had ever sung, all the Draoi-craft she had ever woven was annulled.

Many folk were freed from her will. But only one of them concerns us. His name was Mawn. And once upon a time he had been chosen to take up the life of a Fánaí, the keeper of his people's law and lore.

Along with his companion, Sianan, he'd agreed to take the Quicken Brew. The Druids of their day before the coming of Patricius had discerned a great threat to the culture of the Gaels. They feared that the doctrines of Christ would destroy the old ways of the Irish.

So they came up with a plan to preserve the lore with two travellers, two Wanderers, who would live as immortals, thus acting as guardians of our culture. But as with all good plans it did not take much for this one to go astray.

Sianan and Mawn were separated at a great battle in Alba not long after they had been granted the Quicken Brew. And they had never set eyes on one another again except in dreams.

Flidais had got her hands on Mawn not long after the battle. She found him wandering about the battlefield in a daze with a fine harp on his shoulder. She offered to take care of him but he politely refused. And that's one thing I'd advise you not to do with a goddess. Whatever you do, don't refuse her.

Flidais was upset that Mawn wasn't interested in becoming her paramour. So she imprisoned him at the bottom of the Well of Many Blessings. Every once and a while she'd return to see whether he'd changed his mind. But Mawn was a loyal soul. He never forgot Sianan and always asked after her. So he stayed in the well for a long, long time.

Now that he was free and had heard word from Caoimhin about Sianan, he was keen to find his way to the Killibegs to make contact with her. Indeed the whole nine hundred warriors of the Sen Erainn were on the march along the same road I had taken out of the forest.

They couldn't have been too far behind us. But you must remember it takes a lot longer to move a host of warriors along a road than it does for three travellers to traverse it. Scouts had to be sent out ahead and behind to keep an eye out for hostile Redcaps.

The baggage train of any army always moves slowly. In this case the small Sen Erainn packhorses were more sure-footed than most so they moved faster than would be expected. But the going was still very slow.

Caoimhin found himself beginning to fume with frustration. He knew everything depended upon reaching the Killibegs as soon as possible. If Aoife's force made it there first, there would be a terrible slaughter.

Nevertheless he was forced to calm his impatience. But it didn't stop him setting a cracking pace which even the strongest among the Sen Erainn found difficult to match. Only Srón and Mawn managed to stay close to him.

At length they came to the bridge where I'd met Old Guy d'Alville. By that time they were so far ahead of the Sen Erainn hosts, Mawn and Srón persuaded Caoimhin to take a short rest.

That was when our lad Caoimhin asked Mawn all about himself. The Wanderer played a tune upon the ancient harp he carried and then he told his story. I won't repeat it here. Enough to say that the tale Mawn told that night was the basis for Caoimhin's account of the Wanderers which he later wrote down in a manuscript.

He expanded upon the story somewhat and I'm sure he took liberties with the truth. Besides which I know there were many details Caoimhin simply got wrong. But that's how it was with him. He often romanticised our Gaelic ways. He was certainly starry-eyed when it came to Draoi-craft and the like.

Nevertheless his rendering of Mawn and Sianan's lives is worth a look at. If you ignore the inconsistencies he's not a bad storyteller, our Caoimhin. Read it and judge for yourself.

By the time the hosts of the Sen Erainn arrived at the bridge

Caoimhin had already decided to write Mawn's story down. He was fascinated by the premise that anyone could simply drink a cup of the Quicken Brew and be granted immortality. It was unbelievable to him.

If only he'd known that Sianan had slipped *him* a cup of the Brew to save him from dying of the poison. I told you all about that on the first night of our story.

'Immortality of the body is a heathen belief,' he told Mawn. 'Surely you can't expect me to accept that you have been alive for over seven hundred years.'

'You saw me imprisoned on the bottom of the pool,' Mawn shrugged. 'How do you think I managed that without drowning?'

'It was some sort of a trick.'

'How long have you been wandering in the Otherworld?'

'A few hours.'

'And in that time you've seen over nine hundred beings transformed from lumps of wood or stone into living, breathing creatures. Yet you cannot accept the idea of immortality granted by the Quicken Brew.'

'I was brought up a Christian. I was taught that such things are dæmonic. Such enchantments are the work of Satan.'

'You cast a spell,' Srón cut in. 'You drew a sigil. That's what freed Scodán and me.'

'That was different,' Caoimhin protested. 'I was just playing around with something I'd read in a book.'

'Do you have a knife?' Mawn asked the warrior woman.

'I do.'

In a flash Srón had unsheathed her long, broad-bladed fishing dirk. She flipped it around in her hand so she held it by the blade to offer the hilt to Mawn. He took it carefully. Then he held the knife up to the moonlight to examine the workmanship.

'That's a fine blade.'

'It's for gutting fish. It's very sharp. So be careful.'

Mawn smiled. Then without warning he slashed the knife across his hand. The blade cut straight down to the bone and blood immediately gushed out all over the bridge.

Mawn calmly wiped the blood off the blade on to his tunic. Then he handed the knife back to Srón.

'Forgive me,' he said to her, clutching his bloody hand in obvious agony.

'What are you doing?' Caoimhin gasped. 'Have you gone mad?'

'I'm proving something to you,' Mawn answered calmly.

No sooner had he finished speaking than he held up the slashed palm. Before Caoimhin's and Srón's unbelieving eyes the wound ceased bleeding. The flesh on either side of the slash began to knit together again. Strand by strand of muscle closed tight. Then the skin covered over the gash.

In less time than it takes to accuse a man of trickery the wound was gone. There wasn't so much as a scar to show where the knife had cut Mawn's hand.

'Now do you believe me when I tell you I'm immortal?' the Fánaí asked. 'Now do you believe in the Quicken Brew?'

While Mawn was presenting his credentials to Caoimhin, Lom Dubh had transformed back into the form of a raven. He soared up over the forests of the Otherworld and, being an old hand at this sort of thing, crossed into the waking world without so much as a sneeze to upset his passage.

He squinted his raven eyes against the cold Samhain air and scanned the ground below, searching for the slightest movement on the road to the Killibegs. And as you'd know if ever you'd looked through raven eyes, there isn't much that escapes the attention of these carrion birds.

Not surprising then that he spotted our little party making its way to the Culdee settlement. He took note of our number and the fact that we were travelling with a Frightener spirit. Then he circled a few times to make sure he hadn't missed anything before he flew on.

Lom Dubh was turning circles in the air above the Killibegs a very short while later. He scouted out the defences, taking careful note that all the fires had been put out and the warriors were standing at the walls ready to fend off an attack. Snow was falling steadily, though the clouds hardly seemed to be able to support such activity.

Satisfied that he'd seen all there was to see he swung around in a huge arc to head back to where Aoife was waiting to hear his report. It was just then he caught a glimpse of lights in the distance.

The wind suddenly began to rise. The bright moonlight that had lit the world earlier in the evening was now only a dim memory. So the flickering torches of Ollo's knights on the march stood out starkly in the valley. They'd already reached the stream Sciathan Cog had advised them to follow.

Lom Dubh immediately understood their plan. His first thought was to fly back to Aoife. It was essential that she know the Hospitaller force was much closer than she had anticipated. By following the valley rather than the path they had cut hours off their journey. The battle Aoife had hoped to take place at dawn would surely be joined much sooner than that.

He tilted his left wing down slightly to bring his body round in a sharp turn to head back to Aoife's hall. At that moment something came flying through the air and struck him hard on the side of the head.

Lom Dubh was so stunned that he tumbled crest over tail feather, plummeting toward the Earth. Beak over claw he rolled until he finally managed to shake himself, spread his wings again and put an end to his reckless descent. Then he shook his head, tasted blood in his mouth and realised he'd been attacked by another bird.

The thought had barely formed in his mind when another sharp blow struck him in the gut. This time his assailant had attacked him from below. Lom Dubh rolled over several times with his wings tucked tightly to his body.

All of a sudden he spread them again to drag himself out of the spin. As he straightened out to flap his wings hard he caught a glimpse of a black shape flitting by his field of vision.

His eyes widened with wonder. Then he frowned. If his assailant was another raven there was only one bird that could possibly be. The injury he'd received to his head by the first blow was already healing. For Lom was one of those who had tasted the Quicken Brew.

He soared on the up-draught of a strong breeze until he reached a point where he had to bring his wings down hard in a flap or begin to fall. Then he saw the black bird again. This time he was certain who it was.

Immediately Lom Dubh rolled into a cloud to disappear from sight for a while. He'd guessed the path along which his adversary was flying so he tried to parallel him as closely as possible. When he emerged suddenly from the cloud his luck had held out.

There ahead of him, ducking and weaving through the night sky, was his attacker. Lom Dubh flapped his wings harder as he dived down toward the enemy, picking up speed so that his strike would have the maximum effect.

Then in a swift, sure attack he threw the full weight of his body into the assault. The other bird shrieked in surprise. He hadn't expected Lom would fight back. The enemy tucked his wings under him to fall into another cloud. Lom Dubh tasted blood on his beak.

It was raven blood.

In the next second he'd soared up high above the clouds again where he could have a clear view of all below him. But there was no sign of the other raven. Lom was beginning to worry. Why had he been attacked? What treachery was afoot here? How could one raven strike at another so viciously?

There was only one answer to all those questions. And the answer came when the assailant emerged from the clouds far below. Lom Dubh had sharp vision, even for a raven. Though the other bird was a long way off, Lom recognised him immediately. He screeched the name of his brother in the raven language so that every bird of any breed also heard the call.

'Sciathan Cog!' he cawed.

Then he resorted to the speech of the Gaels to call his brother by his man-name.

'Sárán!'

The other bird twisted about in the sky, rolling over briefly on to his back to get a glimpse of Lom's whereabouts. Even at this great distance Lom Dubh could see the delight in the eye of his twin brother.

He knew his brother must be desperate. Whatever had inspired this attack, there was genuine ruthless malice in the way it had been carried out. Lom remembered those torches in the distance and Aoife's comment that Sárán had given his loyalty to a Christian bishop. And the answer came to him.

'So be it!' he cackled. 'If you want a fight you shall have it!'

Lom Dubh pulled his wings back behind him and dived directly down to where his brother was dipping and weaving in the night sky. I don't know if you've ever witnessed an aerial battle between two of these birds but it is an awesome sight.

Such mastery of the air they have. Such ferocious energy focused on the object of their hatred.

Once again Lom struck a blow with his beak. And once again he tasted blood. But it wasn't his own. Sciathan Cog was retreating now with a wild cawing over his shoulder as he flew.

Lom had him on the run and he wasn't about to let him go either. What was Sárán thinking? Did he imagine he could kill Lom Dubh? Weren't they both immortals? Whatever the truth, Lom had determined he was going to teach his brother a lesson he wouldn't soon forget.

Sárán suddenly looped head over tail and in the next flash he was flying behind his brother, screeching out insults.

'You moth-eaten excuse for a crow! You call that flying? I've seen a cow falling off a cliff do a better job of it. You don't even know what's up and what's down!'

Lom clicked his beak in frustration, executed the same loop his brother had performed, then was flying behind Sciathan Cog again.

'You're a disgrace to those black feathers,' Sárán cried back at him as Lom moved into position close to his brother's tail.

But he soon stopped his pernicious squarking when Lom reached out to pluck a large tail feather from his backside. That's when the screaming really began.

'You black-hearted bastard!' Sciathan Cog shrieked. 'You'll regret that!'

Once again Sárán dived down lower to the ground and in the next instant he'd entered the forest at the head height of a man. With consummate skill he wove his way between the tall oaks and the twisted yews, Lom still close behind mirroring every move he made.

Sciathan Cog used all the tricks he'd ever learned to lose the other bird. He dodged this way, rolled that way and pulled away from disastrous collisions at the very last breath. But still Lom Dubh clung to him as if he'd been attached with a leather strap.

'You won't escape me!' Lom cried out triumphantly. 'I'll wear you out, you mange-ridden pigeon!'

Sciathan Cog laughed and that was all Lom could hear: his brother's mocking caws on the wind. Something boiled over in Lom Dubh at that moment. All the countless years he'd been imprisoned in this raven body had been only just bearable. But this night he'd had enough.

'It was your fault we were punished like this!' he screamed. 'You! You stupid, murderous, self-centred, black-hearted bird.'

Sciathan Cog laughed.

'You're the very essence of evil!' Lom cawed. 'I wish Danu had put you to the sword instead of leaving you here to torment me! I'd gladly live another span in this ugly form in exchange for the pleasure of watching you die a slow, lonely, painful death!'

Sárán screeched as he dodged a huge birch then suddenly he found a gap in the branches overhead and shot out into the sky. Lom didn't let up. He followed as closely as ever. And now that he didn't have to watch for trees he was free to snap at his brother's tail again.

'If I'm evil then you're plain stupid!' Sciathan Cog screeched.

He rolled again away down into the valley below that part of the forest. He was headed toward the army of Bishop Ollo. But Lom didn't give a fermented fig about them. All his concentration was on Sciathan Cog.

'Wait till Aoife hears about your treachery!' Lom cried out. 'She won't let you get away with it. You've betrayed her too many times. If you think it's hard being trapped in the form of a raven, wait till you've spent a thousand years stuck in the body of a gnarled old oak.'

Sárán laughed again. 'Aoife won't find out! Because you won't tell her.'

'Yes I will! It's time you paid for all the evil you've done. If it wasn't for you I would never have been trapped in this raven form for these countless years. It's all your fault.'

'Catch me if you can!' Sárán dived closer to the ground in a deliberately provocative move designed to challenge his brother's skill.

'I'll catch you, you bastard!' Lom promised. 'I'll catch you!'

The next thing Lom Dubh knew he'd been struck hard in the chest by something. The impact knocked the wind out of him. He couldn't move his left wing. In a flash he was tumbling earthward out of control.

He struck the ground with a great thump that punched what remaining breath he had right out of his body. Before he could so much as roll over in the grass rough leather-gloved hands had a firm hold of him.

The crossbow quarrel was torn out of him with such force that he swooned and would have lost consciousness but for the fact that he glimpsed his brother preening himself on the grass nearby.

'What's going on?' Lom managed to gasp.

His brother laughed again as Lom was thrown into a cage too small for one of his kind. It was a few moments before he'd caught enough breath to raise his head. When he did, Sciathan Cog was standing close to the cage.

Behind him was a large man dressed in the black robes of the Benedictines but wearing a red bishop's mitre. A terrible stench caught Lom's nostrils. He had to retreat to the corner of the cage to escape it. But it did him no good. He couldn't seem to get away from the stink.

'What is that awful smell?' he managed to caw.

'That is your host,' Sciathan Cog replied. 'Allow me to introduce you to Bishop Ollo.'

Sárán hopped closer to the cage and stuck his beak through the finely wrought iron bars.

'Let's see you catch me now,' he smirked, or as close to a smirk as a raven can manage.

'It's your fault I was put into this raven form,' his brother managed to mutter as he shook the blood out of his eyes. 'It's all your doing. And I'll never forgive you.'

A thick swirling mass of snow such as one might expect to see once in ten winters was descending upon the Killibegs. It was strange. It was dramatic. And it was all that Aoife's doing.

I hate snow. I make no secret of it. There's much I despise about the stuff but the worst thing is the way it creeps up on you when you least expect it. It makes my blood boil when I hear some fool say, 'It looks like snow clouds up there, I hope we get some'. Which is just as well because with boiling blood in my veins I probably don't suffer from the cold as much as some folk.

Don't argue with me. Snow is awful. It gets in your hair. It sticks to your boots. It's cold, wet and slippery. The moment it starts to melt it turns lethal. If the cold and damp of it don't kill you, then you're just as likely to slip over and break your bloody neck in it. I don't know why some people find the stuff so alluring.

Wait till you get to my age. You'll know what I'm on about. In those days I was still young. My bones didn't mind being frozen. But I was suffering from the effects of a love potion. Even something as awful as snow can look beautiful when you're in love.

I know. I was an eedyit through and through.

As it happened Old Guy, Stronghold and myself made it to the fortification of the Killibegs just as the worst of the snow begin to fall and the wind started to pick up. Eterscél had withdrawn back into the sword at Stronghold's side. He wasn't keen to be seen by the Culdee folk who would have recognised him for what he was and likely been unwelcoming.

The closer we came to the gate the thicker the snow fell. The wind was whistling around the walls in a great chorus of wailing sighs. I'd heard the word blizzard before. But I'd never witnessed such a weather spectacle as this.

I was scared, I can tell you. Even a mild winter can spell the death of the old and infirm, but snow falling in barrel-loads hints at a wider disaster. Even healthy folk starve when there's no game to be had. Cows stop giving milk. Hens stop laying eggs. All manner of creatures simply curl up in the bushes and die.

I clung tightly to Stronghold's arm as we made our way up the path to the main gates. I had my head in my cloak to keep the flakes out of my face. Of course I peeped out now and then to look ahead of me. I knew it was Samhain Eve and I guessed that the midnight hour had passed. So I didn't expect there would be any fires burning.

Nevertheless I began to wonder whether the fortification had been abandoned. Then a terrible thought struck me. What if the Redcaps had already attacked the Killibegs? What if the battle was over?

We must have got to within a dozen paces of the gatehouse when the sentry challenged us.

'It's Binney!' I called out. 'I've brought two warriors to aid in the defence.'

The guard stepped out from the gatehouse to peer at me with suspicion. I recognised Martin the Breton immediately. He was the fellow who had travelled with Sianan. It was his dog that was called Oat-Beer.

'Show your face!'

I threw the cloak away from my head. His eyes widened with surprise.

'How did you get out?' he gasped.

'It's a long story. Martin, will you take us to Father Clemens?'

'Who's that with you?'

'Two knights. They're Normans but they wish to lend a hand to us in our time of need.'

'What are their names?' Martin asked with suspicion.

'My name is Guy d'Alville,' the old knight declared proudly. 'And this is my great-grandson. His name is Stronghold.'

'*Great*-grandson?' the warrior stuttered in disbelief. 'I don't know if you'll be much help to us, old man. Can you lift a sword?'

'I can raise one high enough to strike your fool head off,' came the reply. 'So I'd imagine I might have a chance against a real warrior.'

It was at that moment Martin recognised the younger Guy. You see, Martin had been a warrior mercenary in the service of young d'Alville. That is until Guy had lost his temper with him over some trivial matter and condemned him to die with Sianan in the well-house at Dun Gur when the Nathairaí emerged.

You may recall that he and Sianan had escaped. So our Martin didn't really expect his former lord to look too kindly on him. After all, the Breton was a deserter, an escaped criminal and a condemned man. Any one of those things will get you hanged under Norman law.

'That one there is Guy d'Alville!' the Breton exclaimed. 'I'd know him anywhere. I used to be his sergeant-at-arms!'

'That seems like a long time ago,' Stronghold said. 'I have undergone a change for the better.'

Martin's eyes narrowed. 'The only change for the better as far as Guy d'Alville is concerned would have to involve a violent death and a hasty burial.'

'You certainly seem to have made a terrible impression among your soldiery,' Old Guy noted under his breath so only his great-grandson could hear. 'That will have to change.'

'I know I was harsh with you,' Stronghold answered, ignoring the old man. 'But I hope you'll find it in your heart to forgive me.'

'What did you say?'

Martin slapped his hand against his ear.

'The snow must have affected my hearing. I thought I heard Guy d'Alville asking for my forgiveness.'

'Please let us in!' I urged, cutting across him.

'I don't think he's going to be welcome here,' the Breton stated with confidence. 'Not after the terrible ruckus he caused last time he was here. He stole the holy books of this community.'

'Martin,' I pleaded. 'We're freezing! We've been traipsing through the Otherworld this night. I've brought these two in to help us. Will you take us to Father Clemens? Let him decide what's to be done.'

The warrior thought about that for a second.

'Very well. But you will all stay close to me and no treachery. I'll have bowmen following with arrows notched at the ready to strike any of you down the instant there's the slightest sign of trouble.'

With that, Martin waved us through and led the way into the fortification. I was stunned at what I saw when we walked through the gate. There were warriors everywhere, draped with cloaks, huddling together in pairs and groups to keep warm. They didn't look like they could stop a determined attack. And I got the overwhelming impression they knew it too.

Stronghold kept his arm around me as we marched to the great hall. Everyone looked up to stare. And it must have caused a few tongues to wag when folk realised it was me hanging off the arm of the rude Norman who'd stolen their holy books.

At last we came to the door of the hall. Martin held up a hand to stop us going any further.

'Wait here. I'll tell the old man you've come. I don't want you bursting in on his meeting with the chieftains.'

He disappeared into the hall and closed the door behind him, leaving us in the howling wind. He wasn't gone long before I realised there were people gathered all about us in a wide circle. They'd come to get a better look.

Tómas, the young lad who was the favourite son of Father Clemens, approached me dressed in a mail coat that dragged on the snow behind him. He had a bow across his back and a dozen arrows in a quiver by his side.

'Is that you Binney?' he asked.

I lifted my cloak from my head to show him my face.

'It's me. What are you doing here? I thought all the children were being sent off to the clan-hold of Tigern Og.'

'I'm a man now. I'm a warrior. And we'll need every available fighter at the walls tonight.'

Then the lad noticed the Norman I was leaning against.

'What are you doing with that bastard?'

Old Guy d'Alville leaned close to whisper to his great-grandson.

'You seem to have made a lasting impression on the peasants as well. Doesn't anybody like you?'

Suddenly there was a terrible shout from within the hall. I couldn't hear the words but I recognised the voice. It was Clemens. In the next second the door flung open and the old priest stepped out into the falling snow. His eyes fell on Tómas first.

'What the bloody hell do you think you're doing, lad?' he bellowed. 'Get back to your place on the wall!'

I'd seen the old priest in a temper before but never anything like this. His face was bright red and his eyes were bulging white with rage.

'Please Father,' I began, but I didn't get a chance to say anything more.

'Don't "Please Father" me!' he screamed. 'Where the hell have you been?'

'I followed Sianan and Caoimhin into the Otherworld,' I explained.

There was a general chorus of shock and sharp intakes of breath all around. Clemens suddenly realised that an open brawl would be terrible for morale. He stepped past me and raised his hands to the sky, waving everyone off.

'There's nothing to see here!' he shouted. 'Go back to your posts! You have work to do! This rath must be defended. Who's going to do that if you lot are standing round listening in on discussions which really aren't any of your business?'

People started moving off to their assigned positions again as Clemens stepped closer to me.

'What do you think you're doing bringing that bastard here?'

He shoved his thumb at Stronghold as Old Guy whispered into his great-grandson's ear again.

'Even the clergy seem to have a poor opinion of you. You have a talent for upsetting people, my boy.'

Then Clemens noticed that Stronghold had his arm around me.

'What in the name of Saint Michael's Vomity Beard is *he* doing with his arm about you like that?' the old priest fumed.

A few folk turned round to listen for my reply. Clemens grabbed me by the sleeve and dragged me into the hall. Then he pointed at the other two.

'You'd better get your scrawny Norman arses in here as well.'

As soon as the door was shut behind us Clemens turned on me.

'I want to hear some answers, young woman!'

'This old knight is Guy d'Alville,' I explained. 'He's young Guy's great-grandfather and he's been held captive by Aoife in the Otherworld for a long, long time.'

Old Guy bowed politely. 'An honour to make your acquaintance, sir.'

Clemens pointed his finger at the old man.

'You watch yourself. As far as I'm concerned you're just another one of those worthless Norman bastards. In a few hours we'll be slicing your lot up as they try to storm the walls. And right at this moment I can't see any good reason why we shouldn't start with you and your patrilineal namesake.'

'My dear fellow, I quite understand how you must feel,' old Guy protested. 'But all this bluster isn't going to get us anywhere, is it?'

'Don't take that bloody patronising tone with me!' the old priest shot back. 'You may be some sort of a lord where you come from. You may have castles and titles. Folks might bow and scrape to you when you're at home.'

Clemens stuck a bony finger in the old knight's chest.

'But you're on my turf now! So keep your mouth shut or I'll have your throat slit and your body parts exhibited on the battlements as a warning to your brethren.'

'Father!' I cut in.

'I don't have time to be dealing with this problem right now,' Clemens went on, ignoring me. 'I've got my hands full trying to find some way out of this mess. As it stands I don't expect many of my people will see the dawn. I'm not going to waste any more energy on you lot. What are you doing here with my daughter?'

'I've come to offer my services,' Stronghold replied. 'I have repented of my ways. I wish to help your people.'

The old priest was speechless for a few moments. But Clemens was never at a loss for words for more than a breath or two.

'I don't believe you.'

'It's true,' Old Guy interrupted. 'By chance he stumbled across me in the Otherworld. I've convinced him of the error of his ways. I'm trying to teach him how to be chivalrous and kind.'

'This is unbelievable!' Clemens laughed mockingly.

Then he turned to me again.

'How did you get involved with them?'

I quickly told the story about how I'd encountered Old Guy at the bridge. Then I went on to tell about young Guy's arrival. And that's where I strayed from the truth a little. I didn't want Clemens to know anything about the Frightener spirit. That wouldn't have made him very happy at all.

He didn't really need to know about Eterscél. Did he? I mean to say, in the long run I probably saved him a great deal of worry. I just said that Old Guy had convinced his great-grandson that he'd been a bad lad and he should make amends for his awful past behaviour.

Clemens wasn't entirely convinced of course. But he didn't have time to be asking too many questions. On the other hand he couldn't really afford to reject any sword that was offered to the cause of the Killibegs.

Then he noticed I was standing even closer to Stronghold.

'You didn't answer me!' he bellowed. 'I asked you a question outside. What in the name of Saint Finbar's Holy Boat is that bastard doing standing with his arms clasped about you?'

'I love him, Father,' I explained rather indelicately.

Well that shut the old boy up, I can tell you. He couldn't even mutter any words of confusion or dismay. After a few moments he simply leaned against the wall and stared at me, wide-eyed and woe-begotten.

'Are you all right, Father?' I asked.

That must have stirred him from shock.

'Where did I go wrong? I tried to raise you as a good Culdee lass. But at every opportunity you're off flirting with some foreigner. It's your mother's fault!'

He turned to look me directly in the eye.

'What happened to that young Benedictine scribe? What was his name?'

'Caoimhin.'

125

'Yes, that's what he's called. What happened to Caoimhin?'

'I don't know, Father. He ran off with Sianan into the Otherworld and I lost track of them.'

'I thought you were interested in him,' Clemens said through gritted teeth.

'That was before I'd really got to know Stronghold.'

The old priest squinted his eyes to show he didn't believe me. Then he leaned closer to sniff my breath.

'Poke out your tongue. Have you been drinking?'

I shook my head and did as I was told. He grabbed my tongue, nearly ripping it out by the roots.

'What's that green stain in your mouth?'

'I don't know,' I shrugged.

But the old priest understood me well enough. He could see I was lying. I knew what had caused the stain. It was the residue of Ortha's love philtre. The old priest turned to Stronghold.

'Have you taken advantage of her?'

The knight shook his head in protest.

'No!'

'Just wait till this business is finished,' he hissed at me. 'You'd better pray that Aoife's Redcaps break into this fortress and tear you into tiny shreds. Because if they don't, I'm certainly going to.'

He stepped closer to speak into my ear so no one else could hear.

'I know the symptoms of a love potion when I see it!'

That's when Clemens decided what he was going to do with the two Normans.

'You're all going down to the storage rooms to defend them from attack. You'll find another pair of foreigners down there. Alan de Harcourt will give you your orders and you will report to him. You will remain in that place until I command you to leave.'

'I'm not going to stand guard over the grain and tallow of

your people,' Old Guy replied. 'I'm a seasoned fighter. I'll face the enemy alongside you.'

Clemens told him to shut up. It was all well and good to be talking about facing down the enemy. But the truth was that even if the Culdees of the Killibegs survived this night and defeated the fierce foes arrayed against them, there was still a greater challenge to face.

The winter. And if the early snowfall this night was anything to go by, it was going to be the hardest one in living memory. The battle might be won but should the stores be lost there would be general famine amongst the people of the Killibegs. If that happened, it would be better they were all cut down in the fight.

'We'll do as you ask,' Stronghold promised. 'The stores will be safe.'

'Go then. The doors are about to be closed above ground near the main gate. Guards are to be posted soon to prevent anyone entering through that way. When all is ready the entrance to those stairs will be sealed and hidden from view.'

The two Normans turned around to leave.

'I'll go with them,' I volunteered.

'That would be best,' the old priest agreed. 'At least if you're sealed within a deep underground chamber I won't be worried about what mischief you could be getting yourself into. It will be your duty to spread the true tale of what happened here this night. Do you understand?'

It was in that moment I realised Clemens didn't expect to survive this fight. Nor indeed did he expect many of the Culdee folk to live. There was a resignation in his expression I'd never seen before. I hugged the old man close to me as I tried to hold back the tears.

'I'm sorry I let you down, Father.'

'You'll be sorry if you don't get your arse out that door and down into the storage rooms. I'll teach you the true meaning of

THE WELL OF MANY BLESSINGS

sorry if you don't bugger off and let me get back to planning the defence of this rath.'

Then he pushed me away. I knew with a certainty I'd never experienced before that he and I would never meet him again in this life. I stepped away from the old man with tears in my eyes.

'By the way, I have one last question,' Clemens added as Stronghold opened the door just enough to let the snow blow in. 'What happened to the holy books of the Killibegs? What did you do with the Orchard?'

Stronghold looked directly into the old priest's eyes.

'You'll be happy to learn that Robert FitzWilliam retrieved them from my possession just after sunset this evening.'

At the mention of his son's name Lord William strode forward to where he could better see Stronghold's face lit by the dim moonlight.

'And where is Robert now?' he asked under his breath.

'He wandered off into the Otherworld. I know not what paths he walked after I last saw him.'

With that we went to report to our post in the underground chambers of the storage rooms.

And it's a fortunate thing we left the hall when we did. The snow was already banking against the sides of the buildings and the walls in great drifts. If we had dallied there with Father Clemens another few minutes we might not have made it into the underground stores at all. The warriors were just about to seal the double wooden doors shut when we reported to them.

Martin was in charge of the operation. He was anxious to get the work done as quickly as possible. So he opened only one door to allow us to enter. All I could see was the first few steps leading down into the cellar. The Breton told me there were thirty and that the stairs were steep.

'Be careful. There are no lights in the settlement tonight. It's Clemens' orders.'

Then he held my hand until I stood on the top step before he asked me a question.

'Is it true you've been in the Otherworld?'

'Yes.'

'Did you see Oat-Beer and Sianan?'

'No.'

'They will be all right, won't they?' Martin pressed.

'I'm sure that if I were a red Sotar dog running around in the Land of Dreams I couldn't have a better companion than Sianan. She'll take good care of him.'

'I hope I see them again.'

'You will,' I assured him. 'You will.'

IMMORTALS

That reminds me, I haven't told you what became of Sianan and Oat-Beer. Or should I say Tóraí Tairngire? That was the name he adopted for himself after the mystical waters of the Well of Many Blessings had worked their enchantment on him. I told you last night all about how he was transformed from a red-haired dog into a red-headed man.

He went from four legs to two in a matter of moments just from taking a sip of those waters. Indeed, that wasn't the only gift he'd been granted. For when he'd been drinking from the pool he met Flidais. And she told him he'd have the gift of Seership for as long as he remained in the Otherworld.

She also informed him that he wouldn't always remain in the form of a man. The very instant he crossed over back into the waking world he would be transformed back into a dog, whether he liked it or not.

As it happened, by the time he and Sianan had made their way back along the path to where the gate to the waking world stood, he was good and ready to be a dog again. You see, although he'd wondered all his life what it would be like to be a man, and he was initially overjoyed to find himself in that form, the experience hadn't entirely lived up to his expectations.

For a start he soon found that Sianan wasn't very happy when he emptied his bladder against a tree right in front of her. He hadn't seen anything wrong with that. He'd been doing it all his life and no two-leg had ever complained about it. Of course she explained that men don't usually do that sort of thing in public unless they're trying to make some sort of statement.

Then he'd been rushing about sniffing at the air in his own inimitable doggy way. He could sense Sianan wasn't comfortable with that either. There were lots of other little things he felt shy about. And he couldn't manage to scratch himself like he used to when the need arose, which was quite frustrating.

He soon enough realised that two-legged folk don't regard dogs the same way as dogs regard two-legged folk. Indeed, he discovered that very few two-legs had any respect for dogs at all. Naturally he was shocked to find out that many of them held cats in higher esteem!

So after they'd left the feasting hall of Aoife, the two of them made their way as quickly as they could to the forest gateway. They'd witnessed the death of Flidais at the hands of Robert FitzWilliam and both of them were heavy of heart at what they'd seen.

By that time Tóraí was eager to leave the Otherworld. So he set a cracking pace as he led Sianan along narrow paths that twisted their way through the great forest. In a remarkably short time they came to the place where the road joined their path. A little way ahead they could see the forest gate. Beyond that lay the land of mortals and the Rath of the Killibegs.

It was as they reached the road that Sianan called a halt and sat down on the massive root of an ancient gnarled oak. She threw back the raven-feather cloak that had been the costume she had stolen from the jester called Feverfew. She was sweating and she was tired.

'Stop!' she begged. 'I must rest.'

'We must not dally!' Tóraí told her. 'I'm eager to return to my old self. I've had enough of walking about on two legs.'

Sianan ignored him. She sat back against the tree, panting

heavily. But the truth was she was in no hurry to see Tóraí turned back into a dog. She'd grown to like him just the way he was.

'Are you sure this is what you want?' she ventured. 'Are you certain you wouldn't rather stay here in the Otherworld and remain as a man?'

'I was born a dog,' he laughed. 'I am used to being a dog. Why would I desire to be a man?'

'You are a fine man. I like you this way.'

Tóraí squinted and sniffed the air around her in his red Sotar way.

'You think I'm too good to be a dog! You think I'd be better off as a man because men are better than dogs!'

He laughed with derision.

'I don't believe it! You actually believe you're better than me because you walk about on two legs and other animals have four. You people are intolerable!'

'That's not what I meant!'

'Yes it is! All your kind are the same. You think you're the pinnacle of creation. You see yourselves as above all the other creatures.'

He sat down on a root nearby.

'That's why you don't want to be the Queen of the Raven-kind. You think you're too good to take on the form of an animal or a bird.'

'That's not true!'

But, my dear, there *was* an element of truth in what he'd said. You may recall that at the feasting hall the Morrigán, Queen of the Raven-kind, had made an unusual offer to Sianan. You see, the Morrigán is an office which may be held by any immortal woman. Sorcha the Druid had reigned as queen for three hundred years short of three thousand. Her time was coming to an end. At the next Samhain she was due to step down. And she needed a willing replacement. So she'd asked Sianan.

There was a good reason why Sorcha had asked the abbess. No other woman of the immortal kind was likely to want to take on the duties of the office. They all knew what was required of the Morrigán.

The Queen of the Ravens was expected to oversee an endless string of petty quarrels which inevitably led to bloodshed. Then there were the brawls, fights, disputes and temper tantrums which always ended in death or injury. Not to mention the pitched battles and wars which were her responsibility to watch.

The Morrigán was a chief among the immortal kind. Her position was a very ancient one. And her objective was simple: to keep the numbers of mortals down to manageable levels.

Now, you might say that sounds like a terrible thing. But try to look at the situation from their point of view. Immortals have to put up with our utterly foolish, selfish, destructive ways. They have to live with the consequences when one of us short-sightedly decides to obliterate a forest to feed his hearth fire.

They have to put up with the stench our kind spread through the land. They have to witness the destruction we cause and the distress we spread to the rest of creation. For we, who live such brief lives, think nothing of the future beyond our own individual span of years. Whereas the immortals will always be here. Some of them were here on Earth long before our ancestors ever emerged. And many of them will be here when we have turned to dust and are no more than a vague memory.

Long ago when they understood what manner of beast we were the immortals proposed two solutions. The first answer they came up with was very effective for a long time.

The Ever-Living Ones took us under their wings. They selected certain members of mortal society and educated them in the care of the Earth. They taught these chosen ones that we are all the Guardians of the Garden and granted them amazing experiences of the Otherworld beyond the waking state they knew. These spiritually enlightened folk then went on to guide their kinfolk through the world. It was the aim of such mortals to teach our kind how to live without leaving any trace of our existence.

Walk gently in the world. That's what they taught our ancestors. Do not take more than you need. Plant three trees whenever you are compelled to cut one down. Do not kill any animal that will not be consumed as a sacred meal. Use every part of the carcass. And offer thanks to the spirits of the wild wood creatures who give their lives that we may live.

For a long time the mortal kind listened to this wisdom. And so it came to pass that the immortal kind, seeing that all was good on the face of the Earth, withdrew from us. That was when the trouble began.

For, as I said, mortals are short-sighted. I have heard it said that things first went awry when an old mortal man was forced to stay behind when his kinfolk travelled on to new hunting grounds. He'd been injured in a fight with a bear or some other large creature. He wasn't expected to live.

They left him a bag of wheat or some such grain and bid him farewell, expecting to find his bones there when they returned next season. But the old man did not eat any of the grain. He spent the last of his strength planting it in neat rows and then he died.

When his people returned the next year they found the wheat ready to harvest and they thanked the old man for his gift from beyond the grave. In a very short while those folk had settled into a farming life, living off the harvest of their planted crops.

Now I'm sure you understand that the farming life is radically different from that of the nomad. Permanent shelters require sturdy timber construction. Animals need to be harnessed to help the farmer in his endeavours.

Before long this group of mortals were cutting down the

forests for fuel, clearing the woods to create grazing land and splitting timber to build houses. Their corner of the garden of Earth was devastated.

Soon enough the fish were all gone from the nearby river. Instead it was filled with stinking wastes. The deer were all hunted out from the mountainside. Their hides were made into clothes.

That's when the immortals stepped in again. They'd been awakened from their slumber and they could see the farming life would spread through the mortal kind like a disease. They feared the way of the plough would lead to other worse crimes against the soil of the Earth.

I don't know about that but I know they were right about the lure of the cultivated field. Peoples everywhere left the forests to take up the planting of crops and the domestication of animals. They exploited the land for their food, shelter and clothing. And they grew fat.

Try to see it from the immortals' point of view. They're generally happy with a lot less than we are. They are patient and wise. They understand that whatever you take from the Earth must be paid for. They recognise that what mortals call riches and wealth is really nothing more than dust and dry autumn leaves.

So they could foresee disaster was going to strike. As the mortal kind were able to feed their children better and keep them warm through the winter with reliable stores of grain and meat, their numbers grew. Before long there were more mortals alive than there had ever been before. The immortals began to feel crowded. A few of them tried to reason with the mortals. But it was to no avail.

That's when the Old Ones instituted the first wars. Yes, it was the Ever-Living kind who first stirred up jealousy, envy, rage and murder among our peoples. And they did it to keep our numbers down.

In Ireland it was the Morrigán's duty to ensure enough wars, battles and smaller conflicts were regularly fought so the population of the mortals in the land never became too great. By the end of Sorcha's reign this job was already proving to be too much for one raven-queen to handle. The mortal kind were breeding too quickly.

Of course there were always those among the immortals who questioned the wisdom of pursuing a policy of stirring up war. For war had brought even more devastation to the Earth as it became an acceptable practice among our ancestors. In their all-consuming desire to be masters over other creatures, mortals had invented more elaborate ways of killing one another.

And all of these methods required vast numbers of trees to be cut down for ships, shields and siege engines. War had become an efficient way of culling the mortal population. But the cost for the Earth had become too great to bear.

Many among the immortals had by now decided to withdraw to sleep until our people had finished wiping themselves out. I'm sure no immortal woman would have willingly taken up the office of Morrigán by the time Sorcha was ready to retire.

Only Sianan was different. She was a youngster compared to others of her kind. And she'd lived apart from the influences of the immortals. That's why Sorcha asked her to take on the mantle of queen. Of course she also knew Sianan didn't really understand what duties it involved.

So as Sianan leaned back against the tree trunk she thought hard on Tóraí's accusation. She didn't like to admit that perhaps she thought of animals as lesser beings, but she was starting to understand perhaps he was right.

She turned her head so her face was pressed up against the bark. Then she sighed deeply with contentment to feel the bark and her skin so close together. Her eyes opened and she yawned.

But what she saw as she opened her eyes killed that yawn dead, I can tell you. Right beside her on the tree trunk there was a great bulge that seemed out of place, almost what you'd call unnatural. And the shape of this bulge was exactly that of the face of a man screaming wide-eyed in agony.

Sianan was on her feet in a second, stepping back from the oak without looking where she was planting her feet. As she retreated she kicked something made of iron. It rattled along the ground for a few paces but the abbess didn't take any notice.

Her eyes were fixed on the man-face in the tree. Tóraí was at her side in a flash.

'What is it?'

She pointed. He sniffed then bent down to pick up the rusty iron helm she'd kicked over in her haste.

'It's a Norman helm. It must be a hundred years old.'

Sianan knelt down to brush the leaves and forest detritus away from a fine kite shield of a very old design. It was Tóraí who lifted it up. Underneath lay a sword rusted into the iron mountings of its cracked leather scabbard.

'What is all this?' Sianan asked, knowing her Seer companion would only need to concentrate his thoughts to discover the answer.

This was the gift Tóraí had been granted by Flidais when he drank from the Well of Many Blessings. He could not discern the future as some Seers could do. All that was open to him was the present and to some extent the past.

'He was travelling this road on his way home.' Tóraí touched the brow of the helm. 'He and sixteen of his men-at-arms were ambushed by Redcaps. His companions were slaughtered in a hail of arrows. He was confronted by Aoife, Queen of the Night. He thought she was a dæmon and he told her so. She turned him into a tree.'

'How did you find all that out?'

'I asked him with my thoughts. He's still got his wits about him.'

'Find out his name.'

There was a considerable pause during which Tóraí closed his eyes tightly and frowned. At last he opened them again and shook his head with deep sadness.

'He doesn't remember.'

Let that be a lesson to you. If, by awful chance, you find yourself wandering in the Otherworld, remember always to be polite to those you meet there. Aoife is by no means the only inhabitant of that place who will do you harm if you're not courteous.

There are some who'll give you a lot worse trouble than her. So mark I've warned you and don't ever say I didn't.

'Let's go,' Sianan whispered as she clasped her companion's arm. 'I don't want to stay here any longer.'

Tóraí shrugged and stepped off into the middle of the road. But Sianan didn't move.

'What are you waiting for?' he asked as he turned back.

'If I were to decide to take on the duties of the Morrigán it would be contrary to my oath to preserve the lore and law of my people. It simply goes against all I've ever believed in to abandon my own culture in favour of some silly adventure.'

'What are you talking about?' Tóraí laughed. 'Aren't you an immortal?'

'Yes.'

'Don't you know what the Morrigán does? Don't you realise the role she plays in this world? Are all you two-legs stupid?'

That last comment was a bit unfair but in truth Tóraí was coming to terms with the fact that two-legged folk don't really consider the other inhabitants of this Earth to be their equals. I'd have thought that was bloody obvious, but there you go. And he was quite offended by the whole thing, as you would be if you were not of the two-legged kind yourself.

Sianan shrugged.

'I'm sure I don't know the duties of the Morrigán. Except that she oversees the battlefield and cleans up the slain.'

Tóraí beckoned her on. 'I'll tell you then.'

And as they walked together back towards the Killibegs he revealed to her more or less the same story I told you earlier about the significance of the Morrigán and her duties in the realm of mortals.

In that manner they passed the time until at last they reached the gateway under the two intertwining oaks trees beyond which lay the waking world. Sianan stopped and grabbed Tóraí by the sleeve to prevent him going any further.

'Where did you learn all this?' she asked him.

'Every dog knows the tale of the immortal ones and the duties of the Morrigán. The cats know it and all the beasts of the forest. The cows know it and all the enslaved creatures of the farmyard.'

Sianan swallowed hard. 'Yet we who walk on two legs do not.'

'That is because your kind place yourselves in opposition to the rest of creation. Your kind are a threat to the survival and happiness of all other creatures that walk the Earth. And that includes those which fly above or swim around as much as those who are rooted in its soil.'

Sianan hung her head in shame. She couldn't believe she'd lived for over seven hundred and fifty summers and yet she did not have as much wisdom as this one soul.

'Don't be so hard on yourself.' Tóraí put an affectionate hand on her shoulder. 'You can't know everything. Life is a journey. Let's get on with ours.'

Her heart was filled with respect for him as she looked up into his deep dog-like eyes. Truly he was a man who could teach her much about the world. And if she were to take on the duties of the Morrigán she would need someone beside her such as him. He was loyal, he was wise in his own way and, despite her foolishness, he was still her loyal friend.

'Don't cross back into the world of mortals,' she suddenly begged him.

He frowned. 'But I belong there. I was born there. I am a dog not a man. I can't deny my true nature any longer. I've learned much walking about in the shape of a two-legs. But I already feel like my shoulders are bowed down with responsibility and my feet drag with a sense of duty. If it's like this after a few hours as a man, what will it be like after a few years?'

Sianan smiled and nodded understandingly. Then she took his hand at her shoulder and squeezed it tightly.

'It has been wonderful to have this opportunity to speak with you as an equal,' she told him. 'But I do miss Oat-Beer.'

Then she leaned closer to kiss him on the cheek.

'So do I!' he agreed. 'So do I!'

As Sianan stepped through the gateway the tingling sensation of crossing between the worlds shuddered through her body. The ground was covered in snow and a mighty wind whipped up the flakes so that she had to brush them away from her eyes.

'Where did this blizzard come from?'

'It's Aoife's doing!' Tóraí called from the other side of the gateway.

'Come on then, my friend,' Sianan beckoned.

He laughed for joy as he leaped over the threshold, glad to be free of his two-legged form at last. But as he landed on the other side a most unexpected and disturbing thing happened.

Nothing.

Tóraí stood in his man form on the mortal side of the gate

waiting for the change to take place. With every breath he took, a little more sweat formed around his brow, a little more fear filled his eye. His face was bathed in snowflakes. His red hair sprinkled with white.

'Why haven't I been restored to my dog self?' he shrieked. 'What's the matter? What's happening?'

He turned to face Sianan and rounded on her with an awful accusation.

'You have put a curse on me!'

'Not me!' she protested. 'I wouldn't dream of doing such a thing.'

But the truth is she had done something of the sort. Even though Sianan was a wise woman with many years experience, there were still one or two facts about the world she hadn't quite grasped. The most important being that as soon as you make a wish, no matter how small, you set the wheels in motion for it to come true. Whether Sianan could see it or not, she had caused Tóraí to remain in this form because of the one selfish moment in which she'd longed for a companion to see her through the long days of the future.

That's why we Culdees have a saying. Make sure what you wish for is what you really want, because if you're not careful you will most certainly receive it.

Neither Sianan nor Tóraí had the opportunity to reflect on this turn of events, however. Just at that moment a terrible cry rumbled across the Earth. It was the unmistakeable roar of a lion. Well, it was unmistakeably a lion to anyone who'd never encountered one before or to anyone who had ever been scared of facing one.

I have heard the rumour that Richard de Clare, the first Norman to invade Ireland with any success, had a mating pair of lions in his possession. But that was thirty years or so before the events of my tale. Frankly, I've always had my doubts about that lion. I can find no evidence whatsoever for its existence and certainly no corroborating witnesses. That doesn't mean it didn't exist. It just means it only existed in the poor suffering minds of those feeble-brained lunatics who imagined it.

'We should get moving,' Sianan said.

Tóraí stepped close to her. 'T-That sounded like a lion.'

'How would you know what a lion sounds like?'

'My mother always warned me to look out for them when I was a pup. She was very talented at imitating the calls of other animals.'

He turned to face Sianan with a tear in his eye.

'If I am going to stay in this form I'd like us to be friends. I'm sorry if anything I said has upset you.'

'Let's get back to the rath. I'm going to call down Danu to intervene on behalf of the people of the Killibegs. It's our only hope now. Perhaps Danu will consent to changing you back to your dog form if your heart is still set on it.'

'Perhaps she will!' he echoed with enthusiasm. 'Let's be off.'

Neither of them were dressed for the extreme cold. Sianan had left the Killibegs expecting to be back within a few hours. Her cloak was of fine wool but it wasn't thick enough to keep out a cutting wind with a snowfall at its back.

Tóraí was suffering too. He was dressed well enough for a cold human, I suppose. His cloak was very fine and his clothes were also of the highest quality. They had been a gift from Flidais. But he was used to wearing a coat of long red dog hairs. Walking about in a pink skin wasn't at all to his liking. His fingers soon enough turned blue from the chill and his nose was bright crimson. To cap it off his teeth knocked together in uncontrollable bursts of chattering.

By the time they'd gone as far as the stream the surface of the water had frozen over. A cow had become trapped in the ice and frozen to death half out of the water. The freeze must have happened both unexpectedly and incredibly quickly.

The further they walked the worse the snow-storm became,

until at last they were making hardly any headway against the wind and sleet. So they took the decision to shelter by the wall at the far side of the bridge.

'Is it still Samhain?' Tóraí asked.

Sianan did not understanding the question.

'Is it possible we could have lost track of time in the Otherworld?' he pressed. 'I've heard that folks can stray in that land for a hundred years and not realise the time has passed. It seems to me like we've come back in the midst of winter. But we left on Samhain Eve. I've never heard of weather like this at this time of year.'

The abbess thought about what he'd said for a moment. It was the only answer to this strange situation.

'You must be right,' she gasped, all hope deserting her. 'We must have strayed away too long.'

She stood up to look around her.

'The snow is getting heavier. We must push on to the rath. At least we'll be able to shelter there.'

With that they were off again struggling against the wind, the icy path and the blinding snow.

The Young Seal-King

hree chieftains of the north-west had come to the Killibegs to spend the feast of Samhain among our people.

The first and arguably the most famous of the three was Tigern Og of Connachta. Tigern was already an old man in those days. He was a legendary figure, famed for his exploits in the wars against the Norman invaders. You may think it strange that his name means the young lord but he'd carried it around since he'd been elected chieftain by his people when he was barely eighteen summers on this Earth. And there was more than a touch of vanity in the way he clung to it in his latter years.

He was a large man who had obviously overindulged in the finer things of life. His muscle had all but turned to fat and he was balding with grey hair where there was any. Tigern had an air of impending death about him. He coughed constantly and he walked with a pronounced limp from an old war wound to the left thigh.

It was his face that was most terrible to look upon. The skin had broken out in seeping sores. I'm told they were brought about by an awful malediction some disgruntled poet had placed upon him. There's a warning for you! If you engage the services of a storyteller or a poet, you'd better not underpay him for his work. Everyone knows such folk have short tempers when it comes to being cheated.

144

Mind you, Tigern was renowned as a tight-fisted bugger with a terrible temper. So he probably deserved to be afflicted with a weeping pustule or two for all the trouble he'd caused professional bards down the years.

The next chieftain who'd come to the defence of the Killibegs was Rián Rónán Og of Muirdeach. He was a man from the west whose tribal lands bordered those of Tigern Og. The holy Isle of Inis Muirdeach was the birthplace of his ancestors.

His people had graciously granted that island to the blessed Saint Molaise generations earlier so his family had lived along the coast ever since then. They were proud of their ancestry and of their connections to the saint of their island.

Now, the clans who called Tigern Og their chieftain had always been rivals to these folk. They didn't like having to live alongside them and there were often little quarrels, which sometimes exploded into full-blown squabbles, between various members of their respective families.

Under the rule of Rónán the kinfolk of the Muirdeach had continued to resist the advancing Normans. Tigern Og, however, had settled a peace with the foreigners. This had been a bone of contention between the two men. That's why Clemens had brought them together that Samhain. He'd hoped to settle their differences over a few barrels of fine mead.

There was another thing about Rónán that might interest you. His name meant the Young Seal-King. His kinfolk held that he was descended from a seal-woman of the Otherworld who'd seduced his grandfather. There were fine folds of skin between his fingers and toes like those of a seal. I saw his hands so I can vouch for the membranes between his fingers. He was thirty years old or thereabouts and happily wed to a woman of dark wet eyes who never spoke a word to anyone. It was thought by many that she was a seal-woman herself.

Then last of all the chieftains there was Morcán. His reputation for ferocity was unequalled among the Gaelic chieftains

of the north-west. They'd called him the warhorse, for that is
what his name meant. He was a warrior indeed. Even in his
decline, as he was in those days, he was a stronger man than
many half his age. He was renowned for his battle fury and a
sword arm that could strike a man in two with a clean sweep of
the blade.

He'd been the first among the three to encounter the
Normans and he'd fought them relentlessly for twenty-five
years. In all that time no foreigner had successfully held any
territory his people called their own.

However, in the end the constant war had wounded his soul.
He'd grown sick to the stomach of fighting. So, understand-
ably in my humble opinion, he had been the first chieftain to
make a treaty with the Normans. For five years he'd had no
other dealings with the foreigners except with regards to the
purchase of wine which he was famous for being able to
consume in vast quantities.

This treaty was why his people had taken to calling him
Marcán behind his back. One syllable may make all the
difference in the Gaelic language. The adjustment of this one
nicknamed him 'Packhorse'. Of course the meaning was
broader than that. His kinfolk were really calling him a slave.
Which in many respects he was. He had become a slave to the
drink and grown to rely on his trade with the foreigners. I don't
think he would have been able to face life without their wine at
his table.

I think you will understand from these short descriptions of
their characters why the three chieftains did not get on well
with one another. Indeed, it was surprising they'd not fallen
into open war long ago. I reckon it was simply that Tigern and
Morcán were old men. They didn't want to face the younger
Rónán in open battle. So I suppose that's why they all managed
to keep the peace.

As I said, Clemens had brought Tigern and Rónán together

to settle some of their differences. Morcán had heard about the meeting and insisted on being invited too in case the others were hatching a nest of plots against him.

I can't blame them for distrusting one another or holding malicious suspicions about each other's motives. The coming of the Normans had turned Ireland topsy-turvy.

War brings with it many other ills. Famine, destruction, theft and pestilence are but a few of the troubles that will visit a country ravaged by conflict. Worse by far than these, however, were the fashions the foreigners introduced to our country.

I'm not just talking about hairstyles or the cut of the tunic. I'm also talking about attitudes and morals. These three men had each been ardent enemies of the Normans at one time or another. Nevertheless, they had adopted many of the Norman ways.

So it must have been quite a shock for the three chiefs to find themselves trapped within a rath which was about to become besieged by a force of Normans. Outwardly each one of them deplored the threat to the Culdees of the Killibegs. But in private with their chancellors, the three chieftains were desperate to extricate themselves from this fight.

None of them wanted to be known for standing up to the foreigners. Such a position would only attract severe retributions of one kind or another. Morcán stood to lose his precious trade in wine. Both he and Tigern would have to pay reparations for the breaking of their treaties. But it was Rónán who had the most to lose from engaging in a fight in support of the Killibegs. For he had never entered into a treaty with the enemy. Tigern and Morcán would be reprimanded for their actions then quickly forgiven. But Rónán and his kinfolk would likely be made an example of. If the Normans destroyed the Culdees of the Killibegs they would certainly wipe out the folk of the Muirdeach as well.

That is why, after much heated argument, Tigern Og and Morcán decided to depart the Killibegs after the fires were extinguished. Both men claimed that the large Norman force marching toward the rath was also a threat to their own lands and kinfolk. They had a duty to return home to raise their kin for war.

Of course you and I both know that's not what they intended to do at all. They were going to slither back to their nests and pretend they'd known nothing about the Culdees of the Killibegs at all.

They took thirty warriors each with them. And the lack of sixty men-at-arms was a sore blow to Clemens. He couldn't stop them leaving of course. What could he do? Ask them to leave their own kin and cattle undefended?

I swear to you now that sixty warriors could have changed the course of events that night. If they'd stayed and stood to the defence of the rath things would have been altogether different for everyone concerned.

All honour to Rián Rónán Og who remained behind with his bodyguard. I'll never forget those twenty archers and ten warriors who'd accompanied him. And as long as I have breath in my body I'll sing their praises. For I'm the last one left who remembers their heroism.

Tigern left his store of axes. So I suppose he should be thanked for that contribution. But the flower of the Gaelic chieftains was disgraced that evening when the forces of Tigern and Morcán departed the rath for their homes under the cover of darkness in the driving snow.

Lord William FitzWilliam watched them go as he stood upon the battlements. Long after they'd marched away he stayed there staring out into the cold bleak night hoping they might change their minds and return, praying they would have to come back to seek shelter from the storm.

The old knight wrapped his cloak about him closely to stop

the edges flapping in the wind. He'd chosen an axe from the store of weapons Tigern Og had left behind. It was an ancient instrument of war but it was all that was suited to him.

He was used to carrying a sword. And not just any sword either. He had carried Órán. Now that blade was with his son and no one knew what had become of Robert.

The old man allowed his teeth to chatter in the cold, knowing that no one would hear them. He paced up and down along the battlements overlooking the gate, searching the darkness for any sign of the approaching enemy.

Old Will was a veteran of many battles. He was famed for his valour in a fight and his cool head in a crisis. But there was something about him most folk didn't know. Lord William had strong instincts and they were rarely ever wrong.

As he looked out down the hill towards where the stream was shrouded by the snowy night he felt a trembling in the pit of his stomach. It was that same sense he always had just before a battle when the enemy were about to hove into view.

This instinct had saved him many times. He'd never been surprised in battle. Yet this night he desperately wanted to believe his intuition was wrong. He stopped pacing to concentrate all his attention on the place where he guessed the path wound its way up the hill.

The intense snowfall had buried it entirely from view. The shadowy night had swallowed all other trace of its existence. Even so, something caught the old man's eye and he heard a noise on the battlements. It was the sound of an archer's hard-soled leather boots pounding against the stones. There were voices raised too.

'Someone's coming,' Will muttered half to himself, half to the warrior standing further along the battlements. 'It's a watchman from the small gatehouse.'

In the distance on the slopes of the hill he glimpsed a movement. He wasn't sure what he'd seen at first. Was it a glint of steel or the flicker of a torch? He cursed the howling wind that muffled sounds and concealed the noise of the approaching enemy.

Then Lord William saw an orange flicker. Suddenly, before he'd even had a chance to call out, a long line of flaming torches appeared as if they'd popped up from beneath the snow. There must have been a hundred of them at least. And as soon as one rank appeared another materialised behind them.

'The enemy are upon us!' the watchman archer cried out before Will could speak. 'It's the Redcaps!'

Clemens was at the lord's side almost in an instant. William removed his helm which restricted the movement of his head. The black coif which cushioned his head against the helm was instantly dotted with white flakes of snow.

'How many are there?' Clemens shouted above the wind.

'Too many,' the old lord noted with more than a hint of hopelessness.

'Three hundred. Maybe more,' the archer cried as he scuttled along the wall to where they stood.

'Are you sure they're Redcaps? Could they be Knights of the Hospital?' Clemens demanded.

Old Will squinted, brushing the snowflakes out of his eyes as he shielded them.

'I can't see any horses yet. But in this weather the knights may well have dismounted their horses. It would be a hard ride up the slope and it would not be any advantage for them to bring their mounts.'

The archer was bending over, panting from the exertion of the run.

'Can you see any banners?' the old priest asked him

'No,' he managed to gasp.

As they spoke another rank of torches appeared as a second great company of warriors stepped out of the shadows. There

were as many marching in that company as there were in the
first.

'Six hundred at least,' Old Will informed the priest.

'Is that a third company behind them?' Clemens asked.

And sure enough as he asked the question another column
appeared arrayed slightly to the left flank of the first two. The
warriors were marching steadily forward as if nothing could
stop them, as if the snow and the wind were no impediment
whatsoever to their progress.

'Every one of them has a cap of red upon his head,' the
archer declared, having caught his breath. 'They carry long
sickles. They are not Norman warriors.'

Unexpectedly the companies of fighters halted at what
William estimated to be a distance of about a thousand paces
from the smaller gate. With this much ground between them
and the poor visibility, the old warrior could not make out
the manner of their dress or the style of their weaponry for
himself.

'Damn this snowfall!' he cursed under his breath.

'Aoife has brought this blizzard down upon us,' Clemens
reminded him. 'I fear these are her warriors come to attack us
hard against the storm front.'

'You must be right.' Old Will's heart sank.

The old warrior had noticed their battle array. No Norman
army had formed ranks in that manner since long before the
invention of the crossbow. These folk were closely packed in
companies which exposed them to high casualties from a rain
of missiles, especially crossbow bolts.

They were either ignorant of the effect arrows could have on
such a closely formed company or they weren't in the slightest
bit concerned. In other words, the force arrayed before them
was unlikely to consist of mortal beings.

'We are facing the Redcaps,' the lord nodded to Clemens.

'Then I'll call for Tigern Og's battleaxes,' the old priest

replied. 'At least we'll have a chance of taking off a few heads before this night is ended.

'Is everything in readiness within the keep?' Will asked.

'It is.'

'Are you still convinced that your way is the best?'

'I am.'

'Then I will stand beside you to the last. We've come through too much together. I will not desert you when you need me most.'

Clemens took Old Will's hand.

'Though you are a Norman you have been a true friend to all of us. You have the spirit of a Culdee and the heart of a Gael.'

'Thank you. Does this mean you won't be calling me a bloody mystic behind my back any more?'

'Who told you I said that?' Clemens sputtered in outrage.

'Everyone.'

'Well there's so many of you bloody foreigners wandering round Ireland searching for your souls and an answer to your spiritual questions. How was I to know you'd be any different?'

William smiled broadly. 'Don't worry, I didn't take it to heart.'

Then the two of them threw their arms about each other and embraced.

'My wife is waiting for us in the hall,' Clemens said at last. 'I will go to her and await you there.'

'When it is time I will lead them to you. Have the door ready so I don't have a hard job of it. Until the time is right I'll go to the north tower to await the assault. I'll get a better view from there. I'll send messengers to you with tidings as the enemy advances.'

Clemens nodded and turned toward the stairs which led down from the battlements. One last thought struck him.

'No needless bravery! No foolish acts of self-sacrifice. Just

152

get the Redcaps into the hall where we can deal with as many of them as possible. Do you understand?'

Lord William did not hear. His mind was filled with thoughts of his son, Robert. He was saddened he would not have a chance to see him one last time.

With his brother, Lom Dubh, safely caged up by Bishop Ollo, Sciathan Cog was free to go about spreading a bit of his own mischief. He was a bitter old bird, that one. I can't say whether he'd learned anything at all from the countless seasons he'd spent in the form of a raven, other than how to make trouble.

Danu had turned his brother and him to the shape of carrion birds to make up for the murder of two ravens in the long-ago past. Their tale makes up part of the story of the Watchers which Caoimhin had from Lom Dubh. I won't go into the details of it. Therein lies an entire tale-cycle in manuscript.

Now Lom had always had a reputation for being a good-hearted individual with no real malice in him at all. Until he became a raven of course. That changed everything. It brought out the worst in him. Greed, grudging and grumbling became his hallmarks.

So you can imagine what effect the raven feathers had on his twin! Sárán was a selfish fool with a mean streak as wide as a river. And that was long before he took to the wing. After he was imprisoned in the form of a black raven he just got worse. And as time went by I think he'd harboured so many grudges his soul was fairly weighed down by them.

It would be no exaggeration to say the raven punishment had sent him completely and utterly mad. Not just unbalanced. Quite insane. Indeed dangerously so. He saw every other being as his enemy. He judged every soul as his rival. And he plotted the discomfort of as many folk as possible, whether they be winged, finned or legged.

So as he swooped down over the place where the two oak trees overlooked the gateway to the Otherworld he was mighty pleased with himself. He was about to embark on the finest piece of disruptive, devilish and downright dirty mayhem he'd ever aspired to.

When he came to rest after flying directly from Ollo's army he landed with his wings wide upon the bare patch of ground where Guy had stood as an oak. He dug his claws into the soil there as he wondered what could have happened to the knight Aoife had turned into a tree.

He had no way of knowing Mugwort the jester had inadvertently freed the Norman from his enchantment while dabbling with the sigils. But I told you that tale last night so I won't repeat it.

There was no hint in the grass or upon the cold dark disturbed soil which might offer some clue about the fate of Guy. So Sciathan Cog had to content himself as he waited for Queen Aoife to arrive. As he knew she would.

I'll give him this much. He was a wily, cunning old bird. He could see to the heart of mortal and immortal alike. If only he'd turned that skill to more productive purposes.

Sure enough, he didn't have to wait long for the Queen of the Night to make her appearance. He heard her approaching long before his sharp raven sight could see her. The hum of the hurrying hive sang the song of her arrival. The buzzing of bees was the melody of her approach.

In a very short while Sciathan Cog glimpsed the cloud of little insects. They were soaring up over the forest headed directly for the place where she'd agreed to meet Lom Dubh.

The raven's heart beat fast as he prepared himself for the great deception. It was one thing to pull the wool over the eyes of some mortal Norman with more body fat than brains. It was quite another to attempt to deceive those of the immortal kind. And it was a bold move to try to mislead Aoife, his sister.

Before he'd managed to quell his doubts the swarm was swirling about between the two gate-trees. In less time than it takes to draw two breaths a pair of dark forms began emerging from the frantic spiralling cloud of bees. The first figure fell to the grass upon his knees.

This fellow was a knight, dressed in a knee-length mail coat and a helm of unusual design. The headgear had a long shining iron beak which reminded Sciathan Cog of his own. He was dressed in a white surcoat in the fashion of the Templars. But the stranger held a sword which the raven immediately knew contained a Frightener spirit.

He didn't need to see this knight's face. He knew from what his raven scouts had told him that this was Robert FitzWilliam, the man Aoife had chosen as her consort, the man who had replaced Guy d'Alville.

'Greetings, my lord,' the raven bowed, or as close to a bow as a carrion bird can manage.

As he spoke Aoife emerged from the bees and the swarm dissipated into the air as if it had never been.

'What news, Lom Dubh?' she asked, brushing the fine locks of tousled red hair from her face. 'Where are the Normans? What of the defences of the Killibegs?'

Sciathan Cog would have smiled had his long beak allowed such a gesture. Aoife had convinced herself of his identity without any effort on his part at all.

'The Rath of the Killibegs is defended by only a few hundred. They are determined but their spirits have wavered with the snowfall. It will be an easy matter to walk over them.'

'And the Normans?'

'They're a short distance away. Three hundred is their number, plus a hundred or so other combatants – archers and the like. But their commander is also losing heart. This blizzard is not to his liking. The Normans do not fight in winter.'

'You promised me they'd fight!' the queen snapped. 'You told me that stupid brother of yours had convinced the fat bishop to come here. You assured me Sciathan Cog had no idea you knew about my intentions and that he would lead them on no matter what.'

The raven paused for a moment as he tried to take in what he'd just heard. Treachery was one of his favourite pastimes but he didn't like to be the brunt of it himself.

'Sciathan Cog has been placed in a cage,' he lied. 'The bishop took a strong to dislike to him. The Normans intend to murder him if they can. He is no longer of any consequence.'

'My poor brother,' Aoife sighed. Then she laughed. 'He bloody well deserves it too! After all the mischief he's spread about the place over the centuries it's about time he got a dose of his own medicine. I'll bet you're not unhappy about his demise.'

Sciathan Cog paused again. He would have bit down on his tongue if he'd had any teeth. But he managed to control himself.

'He's only getting what he's earned,' the raven agreed.

Robert rose to his feet when he heard those words. Then he lifted the beaked helm from his face so he could look more closely at the raven.

'You're voice is full of malice, brother bird,' he stated. 'I had no idea you held your brother in such contempt.'

Sciathan Cog swallowed hard. He wasn't sure how this mortal could have possibly seen through his ruse. No one had ever been able to tell him and Lom Dubh apart, not even their mother. He recalled the last words his brother had said to him before he abandoned him to the cage.

'Is it not his fault I was placed in this awful raven form? Is it not his doing that I am condemned to spend eternity feeding from the rotting carcasses of the battlefield? I have no thought for him. May he suffer as I have. Indeed, he will soon be free of his carrion form so it can be said that he is being shown great mercy.'

'He is your brother,' the knight said. 'Have you no fear for his safety? Have you no concern?'

'None!'

'I've never seen this side of you before.' Robert looked bemused.

Sciathan Cog breathed a sharp anxious sniff of air. He had no idea his brother and Robert had known one another.

'Every one of us has some bitterness in us, dear Robert,' the raven told him, thinking quickly. 'In me it lies just beneath the surface, waiting to bubble up and burst.'

'You used to say that even a one such as Sciathan Cog has some hope of redemption. I can't believe you would have so completely changed your mind.'

'That shows how little you've understood me! You are a mere mortal after all.'

Robert narrowed his eyes with suspicion. Then he reached inside his mail coat and withdrew a rosary which hung about his neck.

'Do you remember this? I promised it to you as a gift. It is the Rosary of the Venetian Merchant-King.'

Sciathan Cog swallowed hard.

'Of course I remember it. And a very fine present it will make. But can we wait until after the battle to exchange such pleasantries? I can't wear it about my neck while I'm flying about as a raven. When I have my man-form back again I'll put it on and wear it with dignity.'

Aoife laughed and Sciathan Cog immediately turned his head sharply to her.

'Did I say something amusing?'

'I was just thinking about how miffed our brother will be

157

when he discovers I've transformed you back into a man and left him in the feathered state.'

'I'm sure he'll be most upset,' Cog mumbled, stifling his rage. 'If he lives that long.'

'If you won't wear my rosary then let me tell you the story of it,' Robert cut in. 'I know you were eager to hear it.'

'Very well,' Sciathan Cog sighed.

'Will this take long?' Aoife asked impatiently.

'Not long. And it's a fine tale.'

'Go on then.'

'I rescued a merchant from the sack of the city of Acre when I was there during the crusade. He was so grateful he offered me anything that was within his power to give. I could've married his daughter, the most beautiful woman in the whole of Venice. I would've inherited all the merchant's gold and been a wealthy man if I had. But I foolishly declined his offer. However, the merchant wouldn't let my deeds go unrewarded. He insisted on giving me some gift to honour my courage and chivalry. I told him that during the hard fight to save him my rosary had broken and the beads had all been scattered and lost.'

Robert paused to observe the raven carefully.

'So the merchant removed these beads from his own neck. They're worth a fortune by any standards, yet that means little to me for I am sworn to poverty and my oaths prevent me from looking on the rosary as anything more than a companion to my prayers.'

'That's not such a good story,' Aoife declared. 'You've got a touch of the arrogant about you, don't you?'

'I'm sorry to have wasted your time with my trifling tale,' the knight replied, bowing his head.

But all the while his eyes never left those of the raven. And his mouth turned up ever so slightly at the corners in a knowing smile. If you recall the earlier part of my tale you'll know why. Robert had already repudiated this story to Lom Dubh. He'd told the raven what a load of bollocks it was. And surely Lom would have remembered. He concluded of course that this was not Lom at all, but Sciathan Cog his twin.

The queen grunted loudly with frustration.

'I suppose I'll have to do something about those bloody Normans. I don't want the Redcaps involved in the fight against the Culdees if I can help it. It's much better we pit the foreigners against the Killibegs and let the Redcaps come to their rescue.'

In that moment Robert understood her plan. All along he and the folk of the Killibegs had assumed she intended to send her own warriors against them. But it was in fact her intention to use the Redcaps as an intervening force.

That was her strategy, indeed it was. You see, Aoife wanted to be treated like a goddess. She wanted folk to bow down and worship her as they had done to Danu in the past. If her Redcaps were involved in the attack against the Killibegs, people wouldn't have been too keen to venerate her for they knew she was Queen of the Redcaps.

But if her warriors came to the rescue of the poor folk of the Culdee faith they would surely be thankful to her. She intended to deal with the Nathairaí by transforming them back into their two-legged form. She wanted the common people to believe she'd saved them from both menaces.

Once our Aoife had the gratitude of the Irish she planned to plant her own man, Robert, on the throne of Ireland. He, of course, would insist that everyone in the land pay homage to her.

In a very short while her Enticer spirit, the one which lived inside her, would grow strong feeding off the adoration of the masses. Once in a while she'd unleash some terror to keep her Frightener happy too. And in time she'd grow to become the greatest goddess the land had ever known.

Aoife turned to Robert.

'You have completed the quest I set for you. Are you ready for another?'

'I am,' the knight bowed.

'You will lead an army of mortal knights who owe allegiance to me,' she commanded. 'You will join forces with the Normans of Ollo and fall upon the Killibegs. But take care to wear your helm so it covers your face. I don't want the Culdees recognising you. If you're going to be High-King we don't want folk knowing what part you had in this battle.'

'I thought I was to lead your Redcaps,' Robert protested.

'You will,' she cooed. 'Once the Normans are within the walls of the rath, I'll send the Redcaps to you. You'll throw off your helm and take command of them. I should not have to explain that the Normans are to be slaughtered to a man. Show them no quarter whatsoever.'

Robert immediately recognised the opportunity to deliver the people of the Killibegs from Ollo and his Hospitallers. And it was all he could do to keep a straight face thinking about it. Who'd have thought it'd be the Redcaps coming to the rescue of the defenders of the rath?

'What of the Culdees?' he asked.

'They are of no consequence. I leave it to your discretion as to how many will live or die. But make a good job of the Norman attack. It should be a bloody affair. Show no mercy to the Culdees until the Redcaps arrive. I want this to be a fight that is remembered for generations to come.'

'But where are these knights who are loyal to you? How long will it take to gather them?'

'They are already gathered,' Aoife laughed. 'They are all around us and behind us. They are the oak-knights of the Otherworld.'

She raised her hands to the sky and with a great shout cried out three words.

'I release you!'

The snow ceased to fall at that instant and the wind dropped away. The leaves of the trees stopped their constant rustling. The branches stilled their creaking groans. And then the forest suddenly came to life.

Oak-Knights

Now, if you'd been listening to my tale the last two evenings you'd know it had long been Aoife's amusement to capture stray knights who wandered close to her abode. A few like old Guy d'Alville had been put to work within the Realm of Dreams guarding bridges or standing sentinel over important wells.

But the vast majority had been turned into oak trees or the like, as had young Guy Stronghold. Why did she do this? I have a theory. Indulge me for a moment.

Aoife was an immortal. And as I've already told you the immortals aren't generally too tolerant of the ways of mortals. But when it comes to the Normans they are downright hostile.

To the Ever-Living Ones the Normans are also known as the bough-splitters, the bark-strippers, the branch-slicers and the like. Now it's true the foreigners didn't really get around to invading Ireland until at least thirty years before the events of my story took place.

But they'd been around in one form or another for hundreds of years. The Normans used to be known as the Norsemen or the North-men. And under those names they'd been coming to Ireland in longships for five hundred years at least.

Their hearts, if they had any, were set on plundering the rich monasteries and wealthy lordships of this land. Their hands were set on cutting the forests to build their towns and castles and more bloody longships.

There were no towns in Ireland before the coming of the Viking Norse. We had no need of permanent settlements in those days. Everyone lived like the Culdees of the Killibegs until the North-men changed our ways.

A hundred years before my tale takes place the Normans, who were direct descendants of the Viking Norse, started arriving here again after a lapse of a hundred summers or so. They came in dribs and drabs, drawn by legends of wondrous mountains of gold and plunder to be had.

Savage tribespeople of the Saxon folk came with them, but even they in all their uncouth barbarity never matched the wanton destructiveness of the Normans. The English were no equal for the people of Normandy, that's for certain.

Well of course it wasn't long before Aoife and her kind began playing tricks on the strangers. Anyone who's fool enough to cut a forest down is going to be called to account one day. The woodland spirits exact a terrible price for the slaughter of their trees.

Some Normans simply ended up quickly dead, which isn't a bad end really when you consider the alternatives. At least if you're reduced to nourishment for the trees your pain is finished swiftly. But Aoife wasn't the kind to let anyone get away with murdering her beloved forests.

It suited her sense of humour as much as her sense of justice to turn the Norman knights she encountered into the very objects they'd entered the woods to destroy. That's why you'll notice, even to this day, the trees will seem to tremble if you enter the forest bearing an axe. Mark my words, a great many of them will have no doubt about your intentions. That's how they got there themselves.

So when Aoife raised her arms to the sky and declared her words of release, a most wondrous thing happened which fairly took Robert's breath away. Even Sciathan Cog was stupefied, and you can be sure he'd seen a thing or two in his time.

The whole forest began to hum. Then the hum became a rumble. The rumble changed to a sigh and that sigh rose into a loud rolling thunder which coursed through the ground beneath their feet, shaking the soil and everything which stood on or in it.

Suddenly the two great oaks which stood entwined above the gate to the forest began to flail their branches about wildly. Bark and bough the pair were twisting as if in great agony. Then, as abruptly as that had begun, the oaks transformed into two Norman knights wearing old-fashioned coats of mail.

They were pushing against each other with their hands clasped together when the spell was broken. But they didn't immediately realise what had happened to them. Robert gasped. Sciathan Cog shrieked. And then the two knights turned to face Aoife.

Both men were dressed in tattered cloaks and tunics weathered by age and the elements. Their mail coats were rust red; the leather of their belts, boots and pouches was cracked and split. Their faces were unwashed; their hair and beards were grey, overgrown and knotted. Both men had the wild eyes of madmen, not to mention rotted teeth, blackened by the years.

'Where am I?' the first asked. 'What is this place?'

'You are standing at the edge of the Otherworld,' the queen informed them. 'You are a tree.'

The first knight looked down at his body, stretched his arms out in front of him and took a tentative step.

'I'm no tree. I'm a bloody knight.'

'Of course you are,' Aoife soothed. 'And I have turned you into one.'

'Who are you?' the second knight asked with suspicion.

'I'm called Aoife. I am the Queen of the Night.'

Straightaway both men sank to their knees with their heads bowed and eyes averted.

'We'll do anything you want!' the first knight vowed.

'Anything,' the second agreed.

'Just don't turn me into a tree again.'

'Nor me.'

'Every bone in my body aches from standing there these last hundred winters.'

'Every bone.'

'My ears ring with the sound of sap coursing up from the roots to my trunk.'

'They ring,' the second affirmed.

'My head echoes with the ghostly whispering language of the woodland.'

'Echoes.'

Aoife held up her hand to calm them.

'If you serve me well I will free you from this bond.'

'We will serve you,' they promised in unison.

'I want you to follow Robert FitzWilliam into battle. Do as he commands. And if this battle goes well for him you will walk the rest of your days as men.'

As Aoife spoke the entire forest melted away. Hundreds of warrior-knights in Norman mail coats came wandering out from between the sparse remaining trees. As they reached the spot where the two oaks had stood they also fell to their knees in obeisance to their queen.

'Swear to me that you will be loyal and serve me well,' she declared so all could hear. 'If you do this, and you fight well this night, I will release you forever more from the enchantments of your oakness.'

'We swear! You are our queen and we will do whatever you will.'

Aoife turned to Robert with a self-satisfied grin.

'There you have them. They are your army now. Take them

165

to meet with the force Bishop Ollo has brought. Command him in the strongest terms to submit to you and to hand his warriors over into your keeping for the duration of the battle.'

'He will not do so willingly. He is a Benedictine and his warriors are Hospitallers. They will not acquiesce to a Templar such as myself.'

'Then slay him,' Aoife shrugged.

'And if his knights will still not submit?'

'Slay the bloody lot of them as well.'

'As you command,' Robert bowed.

But he glanced out of the corner of his eye at the raven who had claimed to be Lom Dubh. Sciathan Cog felt Robert's gaze upon him and it made him most uncomfortable.

'I'll fly ahead to scout the exact place where the Hospitallers are presently located,' the raven volunteered. 'As soon as I've found them I'll let you know.'

With those words Sciathan Cog spread his wings wide and was off. But of course he had no intention of doing as he'd promised. He was off to warn Bishop Ollo to be ready to strike down Robert FitzWilliam at the first opportunity. He didn't want this young upstart interfering with his plans.

'March away with your knights then, Robert,' the queen commanded. 'I am counting on you to make a good job of this attack.'

She turned to the oak-knights. 'Go to battle for me! Show no mercy! Give no quarter! You will rage over the soil like a mighty firestorm! Nothing will remain standing in your wake and no one will live. All life will be extinguished. All hope will be drowned in an ocean of blood!'

The Normans cheered with one terrible voice that shook the ground as the thunder of their transformation had done earlier. They raised their rusty swords and shields. They waved their tattered banners and wrapped their threadbare cloaks about themselves, ready to march off.

Then Robert drew his blade and the Frightener spirit known as Órán surrounded the young FitzWilliam in a bright blue luminescence, making him seem like he himself was of the Otherworld. Which I suppose he was by that stage, for he had seemingly become taken with all the glamour and the artistry of Aoife.

The Normans formed ranks seven abreast. The clatter of their antiquated arms filled the air. Their boots may have been cracked and brittle, their weapons may have been blunted by the years, and the colours of their clothing may have become as faded as their memories of mortal life; but their hearts were stout, and eager for this fight. Their eyes were bright again with anticipation. Their voices rose together in a marching song from the old days. And if you had seen them when they set off on their march through the swirling snow you would have scarce believed your eyes.

For though their weapons were rusted and their lances rotten, they were a thousand strong. And they were the largest gathering of foreign knights to have ever marched out of the forests of the Otherworld into the world of mortals.

Say what you will about the Normans. They are bastards to a man, I will not disagree with you on that. But even if they are reduced to a tatty band of ill-equipped, underfed and ragged toothless warriors, they walk proudly when they march to war.

And so they might. These men knew they were descended from warriors. They were the fruit of war, ripened on the trees of slaughter. I shudder to think of them even now and there's seventy years have passed since their dreadful march.

As they passed her each one saluted Aoife in his own way. Some flourished their swords. Others lowered pennants or bowed their heads. Many raised their axes high to whoop with delight at a chance to earn freedom in this manner, as befits a warrior.

It took a long while for them to pass, even spread out in

ranks of seven. When the last had gone on toward his doom Aoife spread her arms wide and looked up to the heavens.

'Let's see you stop me now, Danu of the Flowing Waters! By sunrise my dreams will have been attained and I will have replaced you in the minds and hearts of the Gaelic people. Shudder in your sleep, Danu! Shiver as the worst of your nightmares comes into being with a vengeance!'

You see, my dear, Aoife had planned very well for this night. To begin with she'd thought simply of employing the Redcaps to spread havoc and fear throughout the land. But when she had discovered there was a force of Norman soldiers on its way to attack the Killibegs heretics, she'd changed her mind.

She was a clever one, that Aoife. She was a masterful strategist. And the mark of a masterful strategist is the ability to adapt one's plans to changing circumstances as smoothly as if that had been their intention all along.

Of course it goes without saying that each and every one of those oak-knights was probably going to end up dead by the dawn. She couldn't afford to have any of them survive to cause her more trouble. But she considered their lives to be a worthwhile investment in the future. She'd always known they'd come in handy one day.

Now all that was left for her to do was to raise the Redcaps for war. When they were ready to march Aoife would sit back and watch Robert ride at their head to the rescue of the Killibegs. She would rid the land of the Normans and earn the gratitude of all the Gaels with one stroke.

I don't blame her for being a little smug. I'd have probably had an air of self-congratulation about me if I'd been in her position. But it doesn't do to be smug when you're aspiring to be a goddess. Few folk admire those who indulge in the smugger aspects of gloating.

That's what smugness boils down to, you know. It's just another form of gloating. I'm sure I've warned you about gloating, my dear. Don't be a gloater. Gloaters are the most friendless of all folk. And smug gloaters are the worst of them all. Smug gloaters shouldn't aspire to the status of deity. They really shouldn't.

By the time Sianan and Tóraí had found their way along the path to the Killibegs it must have been about two hours after midnight. The going was slow and exhausting in the blizzard. Once or twice Sianan had to remind herself that the people of the settlement probably depended on her for their very survival. If she hadn't she might not have been able to keep on going.

In those days she was one of the few skilled exponents of the Draoi-craft still walking these lands. She knew of none other who might have been able to call down the great Goddess Danu with the Draoi-songs of the old ones. That was the only hope now for the Killibegs in her opinion. Danu's intervention alone could save the Culdees from certain death.

In the back of her mind she sensed there just wouldn't be enough time for her to wake Danu and stop Aoife. But she wasn't about to give up so she pushed that thought away completely.

Well, as if she didn't have enough on her mind there was yet another thing nagging at her. She was having trouble keeping her thoughts clear. Have you ever had a melody running through your head? One you can't seem to get rid of?

That's what Sianan was suffering from. It was a song from her youth. And it was one Mawn used to sing to her. In the end she started to sing it under her breath in the hope she'd be able to clear it from her mind if she stopped fighting it.

'Mine is the sea, yours the bright blue sky. A silent plea softly fills my eye. All my words, all speech, all my prayers beseech; these things I have learned.'

She paused in her song to catch her breath. Then she took it up again in time with her footsteps.

'The rose she sleeps and the garden's bare. New snow lies deep on the doorstep there. But winter's breath will not taste of death. This thing I have learned.'

She had to really search her memory for the last verse.

'For the honey is sweet and the tree grows strong and we will meet, pray it won't be long. You'll dance with me on the rolling sea. This thing I have learned.'

'That's a pretty tune!' Tóraí complimented her. 'Where have I heard it before?'

'You wouldn't know it. It's from my childhood. I haven't heard anyone sing that since Mawn hummed it to me long, long ago.'

The blinding snow had blanketed the world in a white wrapping. Visibility was limited to no more than ten or twenty paces ahead. So the two of them caught the scent of trouble long before they saw any hint of it.

'I smell smoke on the wind.' Tóraí sniffed this way and that.

Sianan imitated his sniffing and her eyes widened.

'It's the odour of burning torches dipped in tallow!'

That told her there was danger ahead. She knew Clemens well enough to realise he wouldn't have had any torch alight on this night. This was the smell of the enemy's lights. She was just about to tell Tóraí to keep his voice down when a dozen warriors stepped out of the darkness, bearing lighted rushes and long-handled sickles. They wore hats of red and their faces were painted with strange dotted spiral designs.

'Redcaps!' shrieked Tóraí.

He turned this way and that, searching frantically for an escape route. But all paths were cut off. Suddenly they were tightly circled by warriors who lowered their sickles to hem them in. Sianan placed a hand on her companion's chest to calm him.

'All is not lost. Stay calm and follow my lead. Do not resist or try to escape for they will surely kill you without hesitation.'

Of course Sianan had little to fear from Redcaps herself. She was an immortal. There wasn't much harm they could do to her unless they took her head off. And that was unlikely. Redcaps may have had a reputation for unmatched brutality but they rarely dispatched one of the immortal kind from this world lest the same fate be visited on them in the future.

Sickles were brought in closer as one of the strange warriors quickly searched the prisoners. No words were spoken between captor and captive. There was no need.

The blunt outer edge of a sickle was pushed hard against Sianan's shoulder to urge her on.

'Don't worry,' Sianan whispered and immediately felt a hard shove at her back to warn her to be quiet.

As I said she wasn't worried for her own safety. Sianan was concerned for Tóraí. He may have been shape-changed into a two-legs but he was still a mortal being subject to death, wounding and maiming. She was determined he would not suffer for her foolishness.

They were marched through the parting ranks of many warriors. More torches appeared in the darkness, flickering furiously in the high wind. Sianan could make out two companies of warriors and both comprised three hundred sickle-bearers.

At last they came to a group of warriors standing apart from the rest. Seven banners of blue flapped wildly about them, barely held down by the standard-bearers in the gale. A shout went up as the small group turned around. Clearly these were the war-leaders of the Redcaps for their armour was finer than the rank and file of their host.

One old man stepped forward. He had a bright red cap upon

his head but that did not hide the fact that he was a Druid. It was obvious his head had been shaved in the fashion of all the practitioners of the Draoi. Sianan saw her chance.

She quickly pulled the hood of her cloak away from her head to reveal that she too wore the same style of hair: shaved from ear to ear and around the nape of the neck. As was the custom in those days the old man removed his headgear in salute to a fellow Druid, then held up a hand in blessing.

I know it may be difficult for one such as you who is accustomed to the Norman way of warfare but things were done differently in the time of the Druids. They respected one another even if their peoples or tribes were brought to war. Even if there was enmity between two particular Druids they never lost deep respect for one another.

The Redcap Druid bowed low to Sianan as she was pushed closer to him. When he stood up straight he looked at her searchingly. At last he spoke and his voice was deep and masterful. Here was a man who had learned his craft well. He was a natural storyteller.

'You have come upon us in time of war,' he stated, as if that had not been obvious. 'Are you friend or foe?'

Sianan cast a glance this way and that. She wasn't sure how to answer that question. She hesitated.

'You must understand that we are pressed for time. If you cannot reply we will treat you as the enemy.'

'How can I know whether I have a quarrel with you if I do not know your name?'

It was a simple truth which would certainly buy her some moments to think. As far as she was concerned there was no doubt about who these folk were. They were Aoife's Redcaps.

'My name is Becc Mac Dé,' the old man told her. 'I am a War-Druid of the Slua Sen Erainn and advisor to the King of the Fisher Folk. It would be easier to judge your relationship to us if we also knew your name.'

172

Very polite it all was indeed. That's the way things were in those days. It wasn't considered the right thing to ask a direct question. And fair enough too when a simple misunderstanding could lead to blows.

'I am Sianan, Abbess of Dun Gur. And this is Tóraí Tairngire. He is a Seer and my guide.'

'What is your business on this battlefield?'

'Forgive me. I thought you were Aoife's people. I saw your red caps and assumed you must be the hosts of her warriors.'

'We are not,' the old Druid answered curtly. 'We have come to the aid of the Killibegs at the command of our king.'

He paused for a moment before he went on.

'You have not answered my question. What is your business on this battlefield?'

Sianan explained they were trying to reach the rath where they hoped to help in its defence. Becc Mac Dé informed her they had halted here at the suggestion of their king and his counsellors.

'We do not wish to be mistaken for the enemy in the dark and in the snow. It would be a sad thing if our warriors fell under the arrow rain of the defenders. Our lord the Fisher-King has withdrawn to make a decision about our next move.'

'What would you do?' Sianan asked.

'I would send an envoy to the rath. Alas we have no one among us who would be recognised and thus safe from attack.'

'We'll go,' Sianan offered. 'I'll be recognised immediately. I'm well known to the people of the Killibegs.'

'You must wait to ask the Fisher-King,' Becc Mac Dé smiled. 'I know he will be relieved to hear there is one who can perform this task.'

Of course Sianan had no idea that the king the old man was referring to was Caoimhin himself. Nor could she have guessed that Mawn was with him and he had his harp slung over his shoulder in its otter-skin case. How could she have guessed? It was the least likely of all possibilities.

As it happened both Mawn and Caoimhin had withdrawn only a short distance from the bulk of the warriors to discuss the situation. Our Caoimhin had been landed with the responsibility of giving the order either to advance into possible danger or to stand ground in the worsening blizzard.

They had a single torch between them, Mawn and he. But it offered neither sufficient heat nor light. The flame was buffeted by the wind so that it was at risk of being extinguished at any moment.

'What will I do?' Caoimhin asked his new-found companion. 'I've never fought a battle before. Why are they leaving this decision up to me?'

'It is an old Druid-trick,' Mawn replied. 'Becc Mac Dé is frightened to make a mistake. He doesn't know which way to turn or what to do. He has never fought a battle either.'

'But he's a War-Druid!'

Mawn explained that just because a Druid had chosen to specialise in the crafting of war, it didn't necessarily follow that he had ever engaged in a battle. Becc mac Dé was eager for Caoimhin to make a decision so that if a disaster ensued the blame would not be laid at his feet.

'But that's dishonest!' Caoimhin declared with distaste. 'Is that why they pronounced me Fisher-King?'

'In part.'

Mawn went on to enlighten his new friend about the practicalities of leading a huge war party such as this. They had not been to war in generations, so none of these warriors had ever raised a sickle in self-defence. Their war leaders and chieftains had no experience of conflict either. All they had to go on was the learning that had been passed down to them through the generations. It was likely there would be a great loss of life among these untried troops and everyone in command knew it.

That's why, when Caoimhin had appeared, the chieftains had breathed a collective sigh of relief. With him in charge, their own reputations were safe, for how would they retain the respect of their people if they were responsible for a disaster on the battlefield?

Now, I admit that at first glance this attitude might seem very self-serving. And I'm sure that one or two of the chieftains of the Sen Erainn probably suffered from a touch of that affliction. But Becc Mac Dé wasn't one of them. He was a wise old soul who had survived many winters and witnessed many threats to the survival of his people. His leadership was essential to their continued survival.

You see, war isn't the only disaster that might befall the fisher folk. Their lives were fragile by any measure. The old Druid had devoted his life to them. So although he did not like having to pass responsibility on to Caoimhin he knew it was the only way to preserve his position as Druid chieftain and thus ensure the continued existence of his kinfolk in the long term.

Of course the old man had no intention of embarking upon some foolhardy attack or risky strategy. He'd told Caoimhin to go off and make a decision but the truth was Becc Mac Dé would make the decisions and Caoimhin would believe they were his own.

Naturally Mawn didn't mention anything about that to Caoimhin. So our lad was very concerned that if he made the wrong decision he could be responsible for the deaths of many warriors.

'No matter what I do, too many of these folk will die needlessly tonight.'

'That is the responsibility of a king,' Mawn said. 'If only more war leaders thought as carefully on the consequences of their actions perhaps there would be less suffering in the world.'

'I wonder what Gobann would do?' Caoimhin sighed.

That got Mawn's attention, I can tell you. He wanted to know straightaway where Caoimhin had conjured the name of his old teacher who had perished in battle over seven hundred years before.

Well, our lad told his friend where he'd met the Druid and what Gobann had taught him. All the while Mawn stared directly into Caoimhin's eyes, searching for clues as to the truth of what he was being told.

Caoimhin recounted every detail he could recall about the Druid. He described his hair, the way it was shaved in the same manner as Sianan, Clemens and Mawn himself. He described the way Gobann would often appear as if out of the very air. He related some of the wise sayings the Druid had passed on to him. And then he recalled something very important indeed. It was a riddle-poem. So he recited it just as Gobann had.

'Tend the fire of loving. Call upon the flames of joy. Sweep the hearth with songs. Stir the coals of memory. Hear the ocean's song. And the dark sea swell. Drink the cold wave spray. Taste the water in the well.

'Bless the stones of waiting. Bless the stones of certainty. Bless the bread of friendship and the sands of the centuries. The mouth of a saint tells the world as it should be. The lonely heart of grieving will mourn eternally. An eye of compassion watches over Earth and sea. The lively heart of giving will sing eternally.

'I tend the fire of loving. I call upon the flames of joy. I sweep the hearth with songs. I stir the coals of memory.'

'That's a fine riddle,' Mawn nodded. 'Do you know the answer?'

Caoimhin was about to tell him that he had a fair idea what the riddle-poem was all about when a figure approached them bearing a torch. The strange thing was this flame did not flicker in the wind. It was as steady as candlelight in a cupboard.

The figure halted a dozen paces away with his torch held high. The man's face was concealed by shadow but he had long brown matted hair shaved across the forehead in the style of the Culdees. His beard and moustache were twisted into knotted strands. He wore boots of red doeskin cut to an unusual design with pointed toes and straps that held them tight to his calves.

His trousers were cut from cloth of a once-bright pattern. Time and weather had greyed the colour out of them and they were patched about the knees. Over these he wore a tunic of dark brown. Under the tunic was a shirt of grey linen, the sleeves of which were tied at the wrists. Over all this he wore a black cloak which shimmered with a sheen like raven feathers.

'Who goes there?' Caoimhin called out into the night.

But he'd known the moment he glimpsed those clothes who was standing there in the snow. The flame of the torch burned suddenly brighter. Orange it glowed, then yellow, until at last it settled down to a pure white luminescence which reflected against the snow and was so bright neither Mawn nor Caoimhin could look directly at it.

'Who are you?' Mawn demanded. 'What business have you here?'

The figure stepped forward and drew the hood from his face.

'Gobann!' Caoimhin exclaimed. 'Why all the mystery?'

'I like to make an entrance,' the Druid shrugged.

'I am so glad to see you! We need your help.'

'Gobann,' Mawn repeated, awestruck by the appearance of his teacher. 'How is this possible? I was with you when you passed from this world. I thought you were dead.'

The Druid approached them, leaning heavily on his staff. As he got closer he noticed the harp case which sat on the snow beside Mawn.

'Is that her? Have you managed to keep her safe all these years?'

'It is she,' Mawn nodded.

Gobann smiled broadly.

'It is a wonderful thing to see you both again. A great joy has filled my heart and I am grateful.'

Mawn stepped tentatively closer to embrace his old friend, as though he half expected to find that Gobann was little more than a ghost. So he was surprised to discover the Druid was as solid as any mortal. He smelled of the forest and of the wood smoke of the campfire. His raven-feather cloak was warm, musty and imbued with sweat.

'How can this be?' Mawn asked again. 'You were dead.'

'There is no death!' the Druid laughed. 'What you imagine to be death is simply a stage we go through. You will never know that transition from one life to the next. And now neither will I.'

'What do you mean?'

'Have you not guessed?' Gobann smiled. 'Do you have no idea what has come to pass?'

Mawn shook his head.

'That one is my student now.' The Druid gestured at Caoimhin with the point of his staff. 'He came to me searching for truth and for the answer to the riddles of his heart. And he's got a lot more than he bargained for.'

'I didn't seek you out,' Caoimhin protested. 'We chanced upon one another.'

Gobann laughed again.

'There is no such thing in this world or the Other as chance or coincidence. Only those who are lazy, incompetent or unadventurous believe in fortune. I was waiting for you to come home so I could begin my own journey anew.'

'I don't understand you,' Caoimhin replied, shaking his head.

'There was a woman once,' the Druid began. 'Her name was Síla.'

Gobann and Síla had been sworn to the Druid path. They

had taken their duties so seriously that they had not had enough opportunity to live out their lives together in love, peace and friendship.

'When I fell at the battle of Dun Righ we were parted from one another. Now we have both returned in new skins to live out our lives together as we deserve. She is my one true love. She is all my heart. And this is *our* time now.'

'Who is this woman?' Mawn asked. 'What name has she taken in this lifetime?'

'She calls herself Binney. But she knows nothing of the past we shared. Indeed, if you would but consider this for a moment, even I am unaware of who I really am.'

Caoimhin frowned deeply. 'I don't understand. I don't know what you're talking about.'

'Of course you don't, my boy,' the Druid smiled.

Then he stepped closer to raise his torch high. The wind immediately dropped and the snow ceased to fall. Even the cold bite in the air had the edge taken off it. Then Gobann whispered, for there was no need to raise his voice any longer.

'Tend the fire of loving. Call upon the flames of joy. Sweep the hearth with songs. Stir the coals of memory. Hear the ocean's song. And the dark sea swell. Drink the cold wave spray. Taste the water in the well.'

'It's about being a Druid,' Caoimhin said. 'That riddle-poem is about me.'

Gobann nodded.

'I'll take good care of him,' Mawn promised as his suspicions were confirmed. 'I mean I'll take good care of you. I'll make sure no harm comes to you. You will have your time with Binney.'

'I wouldn't worry about that too much,' the Druid shrugged. 'Sianan gave the lad a draught of the Quicken Brew. No harm will come to him. It's Binney I'm worried about.'

'Then I will protect her from all harm,' Mawn assured his teacher. 'Come what may, I'll watch over her for you.'

'What is going on here?' Caoimhin asked. 'I'm getting a sickly feeling in my stomach. Are you telling me that Gobann and I are the same person? Are you saying that Sianan gave me the potion of immortality?'

He shook his head and looked away.

'I don't believe in such things! I'm a Christian. Such talk is devilry. It can't be true. How can he be me? It doesn't make sense.'

Nevertheless it was true, as you'd know if you've been listening attentively to my tale. For every tradition has two aspects to it. Every religious doctrine likewise has two facets. There is the literal interpretation based on the scriptures which Caoimhin had been indoctrinated with at the monastery of Glastonbury.

And then there is the esoteric side of the story which can only be known through practical experience of the deeper mysteries.

As each of us moves through this life and our consecutive lives, our point of view may change. Indeed there's not much sense in this whole existence if your point of view remains the same. We start off concentrating on attaining food, shelter and clothing. This state is known to the wise as the stage of *possessing*.

Eventually we move on from this when we begin to understand that it is more rewarding for our soul when we behave within certain ethical constraints. This is the stage where we respect and adhere to rules. It is the stage when we read and interpret scripture as literal truth. In this phase of life we are focused on *doing* the right things and living what we are told is appropriate.

Finally, if we have attained enough experience of life and the world, we will come to understand that even when one is following the rules one may lapse into sin. It is intention that counts at that stage.

Only then may one understand that merely *being* is enough. Since we are not separate from the mystery but one with it, there is no good nor evil. The One desires only to observe itself in a mirror, as it were.

And in desiring to observe itself the One had to become the many. We are the mirror and the many. Yet we are the One also. When you come to that knowledge you will no longer need rules. You will behave with perfect love because you will know that you and everything you perceive is perfect love. For the One is that love and the One is all.

Forgive me. I have lapsed into a sermon on the beliefs of the Culdees. As if it weren't bad enough that I'm filling your head full of Frighteners, Enticers, Nathairaí, goddesses, Redcaps and ravens!

I don't mean to preach. And I know there are few folk in these times who are willing to hear such heretical words. I'll try to avoid speaking about them for the rest of my tale. It's not as if this is a lesson that can be imparted from mouth to ear. Only first-hand experience teaches the art of *Being* or the way out of *Possessing* into the state of *Doing*.

In some ways my tale could be understood as a fine illustration of these principals at work. For example, there is always transformation in the world and many of the main participants in this story have undergone changes.

Then there is the sigil magic which Mugwort indulged himself in and which Caoimhin used to liberate Srón and Scodán from the enchantments of Aoife. That's typical of the *Doing* stage of awareness. As is Aoife's shape-shifting and other mischief.

But as for Gobann. Well, he would have been ready to take on the *Being* part of existence if it had not been for his attachment to Síla. That's why he kept coming back to live life after life until they were able to meet again and fulfil their desire to be together. This is how it is with some souls.

They get to a certain point and can go no further until the idea of being at one with the One is firmly planted in their experience. When two become one they are living love and that's when they both have the best chance of returning to the One that is the mystery.

Allow me to quote to you from the Gospel of Thomas, the very manuscript which Robert carried in his saddlebags.

Jesus said to them, 'When you make the two into One, and when you make the Inner the same as the Outer, and the Upper like the Lower, and when you make male and female into a single One so that the male will not be male nor the female be female, when you make eyes in place of an eye, a hand in place of a hand, a foot in place of a foot, an image in place of an image, then you will enter the domain of the Father.'

If you've understood these words then well and good. You'll know how Gobann came to be there with Mawn and Caoimhin. But if you haven't understood what I've told you, don't let it bother you too much. Think of it all as the mad ramblings of a silly old woman if you like. I won't be offended in the least.

Now, as I was saying before we took that little diversion from the main track, Caoimhin could grasp what he was being told but he couldn't quite accept it. He'd been brought up in the literal tradition of the Christian doctrine. And the literal tradition of any faith allows for only a very narrow interpretation of the scriptures.

Esoteric concepts are not only avoided by literalists but also condemned as dangerous. Which they most certainly are without the benefit of a full, well-rounded understanding. Now it just so happened that while Gobann understood through experience the concept of the One, he wasn't quite ready to fall into oneness with the One.

He still had a little way to go before he would be able to let go completely of everything he'd formerly perceived to be the truth. That's why his soul had returned in Caoimhin's form. And perhaps that's why Síla had returned in my body. Or so I'm led to believe.

I must confess I have no recollection of any past life as a Druid. That doesn't mean it didn't happen. It just means it's a little difficult for me to comprehend. Never mind.

'You are me?' Caoimhin asked the Druid.

'That is true, my boy. I am you.'

Caoimhin shook his head.

'This is no time to be foundering on the rocky outcrops of such obtuse concepts,' Gobann told him. 'You have a duty to the folk of the Killibegs, to the Sen Erainn and to yourself. A great deal of responsibility has been laid at your feet. You must consider your actions carefully and go forward with wisdom.'

'What would you do? If you were me, which you've said you are, what would be the action you'd take?'

'A good question!' Mawn exclaimed. 'He's very bright!'

'Thank you,' both Gobann and Caoimhin replied in exactly the same breath. But it was the Druid who answered the question.

'If I were you, which of course I am, I would withdraw the hosts of the Sen Erainn around behind the rath to either side. Then I'd take a small force into the fortress to aid in the defence and make sure Binney is safe.'

'Then what?'

'When the enemy is about to breach the walls, bring the Sen Erainn out from behind the hill at some prearranged signal. They'll encircle the foe in the old movement known as the Hammer and the Anvil.'

'Brilliant!' Mawn exclaimed.

'Thank you,' both the new king and the Druid replied in the same moment. Again it was Gobann who continued speaking.

'In that way not only do you ensure the safety of Binney, who is most important to me, but you also give the chieftains of the Sen Erainn the opportunity to take command of their own hosting. If the plan succeeds they will be praised for their leadership. If it fails they will be able to lay the blame at your feet, along with the responsibility for any resulting massacre of their own folk.'

'I'll do it!' Caoimhin declared loudly, as if a great weight had been lifted from his shoulders. Which it had.

'But you're going to have to forget that woman you've latched on to,' the Druid added. 'You know the one I'm talking about. Srón of the Sen Erainn. She'll just distract you from Binney. I don't want you wasting time with her.'

Caoimhin blushed.

'I don't know what you mean.'

'Yes you do! I've seen the way you both look at each other. I know what you've got in mind! Well I won't have it! Do you hear? I've waited a long time for this opportunity and I won't allow it to be spoiled by a distraction. You won't interfere with the attainment of my desires.'

'My desires,' Caoimhin corrected him. 'How can I interfere with the attainment of my own desires?'

'Believe me,' Gobann shot back, 'I've done it myself a thousand times before.'

'We don't have time to discuss this now,' Mawn cut in. He grabbed Caoimhin's sleeve to get his attention. 'Let's take your decision to the chieftains of the Sen Erainn. I'm sure they'll be relieved to hear what you've come up with.'

'It was me that presented the solution!' Gobann said. 'And don't you forget it. You owe me a debt of gratitude for all the help I've given you. Do you think it was a pleasant task leading you on from one place to another across the length and breadth of Ireland? Do you think it was an easy thing to listen to all that endless palaver from those two Saxon monks?'

'But you are me. And I am you. How could it have been a difficult task for you if it was not difficult for me?'

'You'll understand one day, my lad.'

'Not if I'm relying on you to explain it to me!' Caoimhin laughed.

'How dare you?' the Druid exploded. 'Don't think you can fool me with all your pretty philosophical prattle. You can't outdo me in that arena. I'm a master of it.'

'Thank you!' Caoimhin snapped back sarcastically. 'At last you accord me the title of master. Perhaps I'm a Druid after all!'

'Perhaps you are!'

'Well it takes one to know one!'

Gobann grunted as he realised Caoimhin was having a joke at his expense. But before he had a chance to say another word a scent caught in his nostrils. He turned his head to sniff at the wind.

'There's someone coming!' he whispered. 'I must be off.'

Then he pointed his staff at Caoimhin as he spoke one last warning.

'Leave that Srón alone. It's Binney you're after.'

A moment later he disappeared completely from view as if he'd never been and his slow steady torch went with him. No sooner had the light vanished than the snow began to fall again and the wind picked up. It was suddenly chilly once more and Caoimhin wrapped his cloak about him.

'It's Binney *you're* after,' he hissed, determined to get the last word and not realising that he couldn't help but do that in this instance.

Just as he spoke Srón appeared trudging through the snow. She was carrying a torch high above her head so she wouldn't lose her footing on the uneven ground.

'There's someone here who wishes to speak with you,' she called out. 'She says it's urgent. And the chieftains are awaiting your command. You must return.'

'We'll come now,' Mawn answered.

Then he came close to Caoimhin and put a hand on his shoulder.

'Gobann was my teacher,' he said with tender fondness. 'You are Gobann. But you are also Caoimhin. You must do what is best for you. If you would listen I have a piece of advice for you. Do not cling to old ideas or desires. Live for the now, not the what might be.'

Caoimhin nodded then pushed past his new friend to meet Srón. Mawn couldn't be certain in the dark but he was fairly certain the Fisher-King was blushing deeply.

'We're going to war,' Caoimhin told the warrior-woman.

Srón smiled broadly back at him before she turned to call into the night.

'Let the warriors take up the chant! The Sen Erainn are marching to battle!'

WANDERERS MEET

Gusán and John, formerly known as Toothache, both heard the great war cry of the warriors amassed on the hillside. People of the Killibegs were shouting back at the strangers but their words were indecipherable amidst the rush of blizzard wind and the din of battle horns.

The two men looked at one another and silently agreed they had to act soon. The enemy would be upon the Culdee folk before too long. There would be no time to act once the foreigners had breached the defences of the rath.

'Can I trust you?' Gusán asked his prisoner.

'You can,' John replied solemnly. 'If that's Bishop Ollo's army out there, I'm in deep trouble. He'll personally disembowel me for failing in my mission. That's if I'm not cut down by his knights first.'

'And if it's the Redcaps, we're both in trouble. If we sit here we'll be slaughtered.'

Before either of them spoke another word the door to the prison house swung open and one of Rónán's warriors stuck his head in. He looked directly at the two of them.

'Have you got a light in here?'

Without waiting for an answer he stormed across the room to where the candle was concealed behind a barrel. With a savage kick he knocked the light over.

'Clemens ordered all lights to be extinguished!' the warrior shouted.

'What's that awful din out there?' Gusán cut in.

'It's the enemy sure enough. There's too many of them to count. We don't stand a chance.'

'Are they Normans or Redcaps?' John asked.

'They certainly aren't like any Norman knights I've ever seen. It seems Aoife's Redcaps have come upon us. There won't be anything left for the Normans to pick over.

'We're trapped here in this rath,' he said before he left again. 'But you must not light any flames until dawn. Do you understand?'

The two men didn't have a chance to agree to his demand. He was gone, leaving the door open to the snow.

'I have a flint and steel,' Gusán declared. 'All is not lost.'

Without another word Gusán and John were off toward the double doors which led to the cellar storerooms. It wasn't easy finding the spot behind the gates where the doors should have been. The darkness and the swirling snow conspired to confuse them both.

'The doors have disappeared!' Gusán shouted above the wind as he scrabbled about in the snow searching for any sign of them.

'They must be here!'

Out on the slopes of the hill the enemy warriors were rattling their sickles against their shields as they sang in one rhythmic chorus of threat. The warriors of the Killibegs stood around the battlements, no more than dark shapes with spears, axes and bows at the ready.

Gusán heard William give the command for the archers to hold steady. There would have been no sense in loosing their arrows in this wind. Not that arrows would have been any good against the Redcaps anyway. Nothing but a beheading would stop one of their kind for long, though a heavy rain of arrows might slow their advance for a little while.

188

'We must hurry!' John cried. 'We must find a way down to the stores of lamp oil.'

The terrible snow storm obscured the two of them digging away to remove the covering which concealed the cellar doors. Not that anyone was looking back in that direction anyway. All eyes were on the mass of warriors slowly making their way up the slope toward the rath.

A great cry rose up from the warriors standing at the wall just as Gusán found one of the iron rings that were set into the doors. But the doors had been covered over with soil. It was going to be a hard job to uncover them.

'Wait here!' he called to John over the whining cry of the wind. 'I'll be back in a little while. Don't move.'

With those words he was off into the night. John heard the war trumpets of the enemy and he prayed he wouldn't have to face the Redcaps again.

That was the moment John realised he was unarmed.

'I'm not going to face the Redcaps without a cold steel blade in my hand,' he muttered to himself.

Then he was off to search for a weapon among the buildings of the rath. It wasn't long before he encountered a Gaelic warrior who yelled some warning at him in his own language. But John couldn't make out the words, though he spoke Irish well enough. The stranger pointed to a stone building near the prison house. So John headed in that direction.

Exhausted from his fight with the snow and the wind the Norman finally made it to the door of the stone building, pushed it open and to his amazement he saw a hundred gleaming axes standing neatly on racks.

As he stood there marvelling at the array of weapons two Gaels pushed past him into the room. They loaded one another's arms with the axes then they made their way to the door again.

'Don't just stand there!' one of them snarled. 'We have to get these weapons up to the battlements. The Redcaps are upon us. These axes are our only hope.'

'Why didn't Clemens issue them earlier?'

'We were expecting the Normans to come upon us first. We could have held them off with arrows.'

Then he was gone.

John took a few moments to choose a particularly sharp weapon with a broad bearded blade. Now when I say bearded I don't mean the axe had hair on the chin. These were Viking weapons. They came from an arsenal of weapons captured from the Norse invaders two hundred years earlier. They belonged to the treasury of Tigern Og and they were honour booty. That is to say, they had been kept in pristine condition as a matter of honour to show the world what the ancestors of Tigern Og had achieved in defeating the Norse.

And where was the best place to keep such weapons? In the storage rooms of the Killibegs, of course. So it was to the great good fortune of the Culdees that one chamber beneath the hall held an armoury.

The weapons were called bearded blades because the shape of the blade swept back in a curve so that it looked like a warrior in profile. He had a long pointed beard at the bottom and a conical helm on the head.

The axe John chose also had a rudimentary outline of an eye on either side of the blade and the scratched profile of a nose. It was a sharp blade too. The Norman ran his finger along the edge and, to his surprise, it cut him deeply.

'That'll do nicely.' John picked another for the brigand and was off back to the cellar doors.

As it happened he didn't have a hard job finding the spot where they'd been clearing snow. Gusán was already there with a shovel clearing away the soil, snow and other debris that had been piled on top of the doors.

'Where the bloody hell were you?' the brigand shouted when

he spotted his prisoner. 'I thought you'd buggered off and left me.'

'I buggered off to find us some weapons.' The Norman held up the two axes.

'Good thinking. Now pick up a shovel and help me clear this rubble.'

Sianan looked on Caoimhin with wonder. He was dressed in a warrior's garb. His hair was no longer honey coloured. It had grown long and matted and it stuck out from beneath the helm he wore. It seemed to be light brown.

A long straggly beard grew on his chin. His fingernails had transformed into sharp yet rounded claws like those of an animal. His eyes were unearthly large and bluer than they had been.

'What happened to you?' Sianan gasped when she saw him.

'I fell into the Well of Many Blessings. It cured me of the love potion.'

'And how did you come to be named king of these people?'

'That's a long story,' he shrugged. 'And it's better left to another time.'

Caoimhin held out a hand to her. 'Come with me. I have someone here who'd like to reacquaint himself with you.'

But before he had taken her hand Sianan heard a familiar song.

'Grey is the dawn; red the morning sun; black the raven's scorn, but the day will come. When the clouds are gone I will sing your song. This thing I have learned. For the honey is sweet and the tree grows strong and we will meet, pray it won't be long. You'll dance with me on the rolling sea. This thing I have learned.'

Of course even if he hadn't been singing that song she would have recognised him immediately. It's true that seven hundred and fifty winters had gone by since they'd last looked on one another's faces. But true friends always know one another even at the first meeting, so the saying goes.

The years had been so long since they had spoken together they hardly knew what to say.

'I will leave you,' Caoimhin bowed. 'I have the duties of a king to attend to.'

And then he was gone.

'Caoimhin brought me to you,' Mawn said as they stood a few paces apart, staring at each other in wonder.

'Caoimhin is our old teacher. He has taken a new form in this life.'

'I know,' Mawn nodded. 'I have just spoken with Gobann.'

Sianan looked at the great bag of otter skin which was slung over her left shoulder.

'Is that his harp?'

'It is.'

'I would dearly love to hear you play her once this terrible business is settled.'

Then Sianan threw her arms about her fellow Fánaí and hugged him close.

'I have dreamed about this day,' she told him. 'I have prayed with all my heart and soul for our happy meeting. I have shed oceans of tears for the loss of you and I had all but given up hope of ever seeing you again.'

Mawn couldn't speak. He was choked by emotion. Instead he held her close and shut his eyes. And truth to tell, for the first time in many, many years he felt safe and warm despite the raging snowstorm and the threat of battle.

'We have not the time nor the leisure for our own joy just now,' Sianan said. 'These folk are about to march into war and we must aid them if we can. I am going up to the rath to help with the defences. Come with me.'

'I will. For I have promised to take care of one called Binney who is up there in the Killibegs. Gobann wants me to keep her safe.'

Sianan smiled.

'She is Síla,' she whispered.

'I know.'

While they had been speaking Caoimhin had explained his plan to the chieftains of the Sen Erainn. And they had endorsed his strategy whole-heartedly. A band of fifty were chosen to accompany Caoimhin up the hill to the rath where they would aid in the defences on that side of the wall. The remainder of the Slua Sen Erainn would take up positions on either side of the fortress out of view of any approaching enemy.

Nothing So Unnerving

U p on the battlements of the north tower Lord William FitzWilliam leaned heavily on his war axe as if it were a staff. He wasn't feeling up to this fight. He'd never enjoyed warfare, though he'd seen plenty of it. It was just one of those things that had to be endured, like famine and pestilence.

You may stock up on grain against the famine. You may study the wisdom of the apothecary against the advent of pestilence. But no matter how much you work for peace, war is inevitable in a world where folk put their own selfish desires ahead of the good of their fellow creatures.

That was what set the Culdees apart from the Normans and even from many of our own Irish folk. We did not seek to engage in warfare. We did not encourage it. We did not nurture it. But now that it had come upon us we were determined to face it as we would any other trial of life.

William thought he'd put the warrior life behind him when he came to the Killibegs. Peace had been what he'd most desired from life. Now, at the last, it seemed as if it was to be denied him.

But isn't that the way? The more we avoid the lessons of life the more life thrusts those lessons under our very noses. You can run from those things you haven't overcome but you can never entirely escape them.

Lord Will was an old man, you understand. He was a wise fellow too. But he hadn't yet fully grasped the lesson of his life. That's why he was forced to engage in battle one last time.

I had no idea then as I do now what it must have been like for him that night. I'm ninety winters on this Earth. I know what it is to shiver with the cold. I know what it is to have it seep into your very bones and swell your joints.

You don't catch me standing around on the battlements at Samhain. Not a chance. And that night was a hard, cruel, snowy eve when the wind whipped up a frenzied howling that would have shook the dead if they'd been fool enough to be abroad at all.

So the old lord wasn't at all comfortable in his aged body, I can affirm that for certain. He must have been suffering immensely. Nevertheless he was a stalwart old soul, our Will. I never heard him complain, no matter how badly I'd burned the porridge oats.

Apart from the terrible pain in his muscles and bones there was also an awful sadness in his heart. In fact, as he stood there on the battlements the thought crossed his mind that perhaps he should throw it all in and desert his post.

Yes. Lord Will considered leaving his Culdee friends to go off into the wilds to search for his son. Because his thoughts were driven by love for Robert I can forgive him.

As he stood looking out at the ranks of red-capped warriors his mind drifted back to the greatest battle he'd ever witnessed. It had taken place at Hattin in the Holy Land and it had been a bloody slaughter.

On that battlefield the crusader army had been decimated by the forces of the Saracen commander Saladin. As the memory of that conflict flooded back to him he recited the opening lines of his own version of the tale of the battle. He'd told it many times since he'd returned from the Holy Land.

'There is nothing so unnerving as the breathless trembling silence that strangles all sound in the anxious hour before battle. There are those who say, "What folly is fighting!" or "How wasteful is war!" but the Earth, our mother, passes no judgement on her children. She silently watches our petty strife and at day's end she gathers up the slain to her bosom once again.'

Old Lord William lifted the axe and laid over his shoulder. In his heart he was readying himself for the last fight of his life and the pain he was likely to suffer before the end.

'Pain is a liar,' he reminded himself.

That's what we Culdees used to say when it seemed that things weren't going that well for us. In our tradition pain is not real. It is just the body giving out a warning that something is either threatening the health and wellbeing of the flesh or that something is drastically out of balance.

Often when pain strikes it isn't really such a terrible thing, even though it may seem like the end of the world to the recipient of it. Take Toothache for example. He'd allowed the pain of his rotten tooth to rule every aspect of his life. He'd become grumpy, sullen, violent, angry and destructive. That's not to mention rude, bullying, ruthless and grammatically distracted.

However, the very moment the pain was removed, his entire attitude changed. Suddenly he was filled with remorse for all his awful actions. And the truth is, the difference between his pain and the relief of his pain was a simple act. You may recall what it was.

I knocked his rotten tooth out.

Let me put it another way. If you're healthy and happy and your life is going along exactly according to plan, then the slightest upset to your joy can seem like a terrible disaster. A runny nose will ruin the rapture, as my people used to say.

Now I think about it, it's clear to me what a lot of silly sayings we have.

We mortals tend to overreact to difficulties in our lives. A small headache can make a wedding feast unbearable. A brush with stingy nettles can put an end to a roll in the hay. Yet these mishaps are really minor discomforts. Of course I might add that depends on where the stingy nettles have stung you and what you were doing while you were rolling in the hay.

Pain is a liar. Don't trust it. Listen well to its warnings but don't be ruled by it. If you are a slave to pain your whole life will become nothing but a loathsome lurch from one agony to another. Learn to put up with discomfort. Don't place too much importance on it.

Enjoy as much of your life as you possibly can. You never know when you'll find yourself standing on a battlement running your thumb across an axe blade to test how sharp it is and wondering whether you'll ever see the sun again.

Old Lord Will clasped his hands in front of him, the axe in between both, and offered up a prayer.

'Lord of all, let the end be swift.'

That was about as elaborate as any prayer he'd ever offered up. Even though his stories could drag on for days, he was a man of few words when it came to speaking with God.

Below, on the hillside, his attention was drawn to the movement of the many torches.

'At last,' he sighed, and his words were steaming clouds of breath billowing from his lips.

However, to his surprise the enemy split their companies. One marched off to the left around behind the rath and another went off to the right. A third group much smaller than the others headed straight up the path toward the lower gate with banners furled as a sign of parley. The old man put a hand to his brow to shield his eyes from the wind.

He could hardly believe what he was looking at. William

sensed a trap or a trick. He swallowed hard and readied himself to meet his doom.

'Lord of all,' he repeated. 'Let the end be swift.'

Inside the storage rooms we were all huddled together around one candle. Despite Clemens's ruling that we were not to have any lights, the blackness had proved too daunting for any of us to endure.

It is strange, is it not? There were at least four folk present who had experienced the worst life had to offer. Mirim and Alan had trudged from the Holy Land to Ireland. Stronghold had fought many battles and relentlessly pursued the life of a warrior. Old Guy had been a prisoner in the Otherworld.

Yet none of them was happy to sit there in the dark. And the tiny fragile flickering of a candle had been enough to give them all hope. The five of us huddled there round that candle as if it were some holy relic. I held my palms out before it to collect what little heat it offered.

The storage cellars were not only dark, they were cold. But at least they were perfectly dry. For that I was very thankful. These chambers were ancient. They'd been here long before the Norman buildings. Normans always construct their fortifications using straight lines squared off to sharp corners. But the corridor beneath the rath twisted about like a serpent. Indeed, in the dark I could almost imagine that this had once been the home of some Nathairaí couple like Lochie and Isleen.

Perhaps it had been. I will never know. Certainly the tunnels were very old. The only part of this underground maze that was devised by a Norman would have been the doors to each branching corridor. These were of heavy oak bound with iron so that no axeman could have hacked away at them without great effort. They were next to impenetrable.

I thought we'd be safe there. I thought it would take more than a few Redcaps to break their way in. And if it were more than a few we were doomed anyway. I shivered at the thought of those devils rushing down the steep stair into the chambers.

My Stronghold noticed me shaking so he put an arm about me. His great-grandfather smiled when he saw that.

'We'll be all right, Binney.' Stronghold's voice echoed in the chambers, driving out the shadows of ghosts long dead. 'There are two knights here. Alan and I will keep you ladies safe.'

'I'm a bloody knight too!' Old Guy grunted.

'I have a plan,' Alan piped up. 'I think we should go out to meet the enemy with the other warriors I don't like the idea of skulking here in the dark shivering with fear.'

'I'm shivering with the cold,' Stronghold shot back. 'Not with fear.'

Alan shook his head at this blatant display of Norman pride. If only he'd known Stronghold was telling the truth. He had no fear whatsoever.

'Have you seen anything of Eterscél?' his great-grandfather asked.

Stronghold shook his head.

'Not since we approached the rath.'

'Who is Eterscél?' Mirim enquired.

'He's a Frightener spirit who dwells within Stronghold's sword,' I replied without thinking that a little discretion might have been appropriate under the circumstances.

'You have a poor reputation, Guy d'Alville,' Mirim noted. 'If you consort with dæmons perhaps that reputation is well founded. I don't know how you came to be here among us or how you ended up worming your way into the affections of young Binney, but I promise you won't get away with any tricks while my eye is on you.'

Stronghold looked away from her in shame. In his former life he had been a complete and utter bastard.

'He's not called Guy d'Alville any more,' I cut in. 'His name is Stronghold and he's turned a new page in the book of his life. The vellum is clean and he's going to write words of valour, dignity, honour and chivalry across it. He may have been an insufferable tyrant in the past but everyone may change.'

'A fox cannot change the colour of its tail,' Alan said. 'A hedgehog is known by its quills. A blooded dog is a danger to young children. You will face punishment one day for your crimes, Guy d'Alville.'

'You're wrong!' I shouted.

Even in those days I felt very strongly that everyone should be judged fairly and given the opportunity to make amends for their misbehaviour. I'm more convinced of it now after living these last years under the so-called law of the Normans.

You see, my dear, in those days we Irish still maintained our own system of law. It was called the Feinach. And it wasn't based on a regime of punishment or imprisonment in recompense for crimes. It was based on fines. Everyone had an honour price in those days. Indeed this concept may be undergoing a revival among the Normans. Some of them these days see our laws as much more humane and fair. I'll tell you how it works.

A bishop, for example, is worth twelve cows. If anyone offers insult to the bishop he may call in a blush fine for his embarrassment. That would be equal to his value in cows. If the blush fine is upheld by the Brehon judge the offender must pay it immediately. If he cannot pay then he makes an arrangement to enter into debt to the bishop.

If someone injures or murders the bishop the same rules apply. No one was ever imprisoned for the killing of another in the old days. They were made to pay a fine to the family of the deceased. This fine might be three times the honour price of the person involved if it were outright premeditated murder, or half their price for an accident.

But such fines for murder could also affect one's status within the community and entail a loss of rights until the debt was paid. So a chieftain would be banned from office until the fine was settled. Acceptance of the fine implied remorse. Payment of the fine ensured restoration of all rights.

And as soon as the fine was resolved the guilty party was considered free of any further retribution. Any slurs against an accused who had paid his fine were considered an attack on his honour and so could incur a blush fine. In this way grudges were discouraged.

We Gaels tended to forgive freely those folk who owned up to their crimes, begged absolution and made amends. Those who did not, however, could suffer the harshest penalty under the law. Banishment.

Banishment meant the guilty party was cut off from all society. A banished person could not be offered help, food or even conversation. It was as if they had died and were placed beyond the realm of mortals. Anyone who aided or so much as spoke to a banished person was liable to be placed under banishment as well.

In a community where everyone relied upon each other for survival, banishment was more than a sentence of solitude. In many ways it was a death sentence.

But returning to the storage chambers. I couldn't understand how the foreigners saw the world. In my mind Stronghold was just as entitled as anyone else to change his ways and thus be accorded some respect for having done so. It was as if he was paying his fine for his past misdeeds. Such behaviour merited some respect in my mind.

'How can you expect a man to make amends for his life if you won't let go of your mistrust for him?' I argued.

Perhaps if I had not been drunk with infatuation I wouldn't

have bothered to stand up for him like that. Perhaps I would have been just as damning of Stronghold as Alan and Mirim were.

'I've promised to be a true knight,' Stronghold told them. 'You may not believe me but you must give me a chance to prove my heart is changed.'

'I wish we had the luxury of being able to do so,' Alan told him. 'But our lives may depend on us being vigilant with you. So if you will forgive us for our mistrust, we may perhaps come to forgive you for your misdeeds.'

That was as far as the conversation went. The doors above us suddenly swung open and a voice called down into the chamber. Mirim blew out the candle straightaway, fearing it was Clemens come to check on them.

'The enemy are approaching the gates!' Gusán cried out.

Then he and John, once known as Toothache, carefully made their way down the stairs with axes at the ready.

'We have a plan to deal with the Redcaps!' the brigand called into the darkness. 'Will you help us?'

Five voices replied.

'Aye!'

WATER FROM THE WELL

tronghold told me to stay put in the cellars before he set off. Then he was up the stairs headed toward the main gate of the rath. Alan de Harcourt wasn't far behind him.

Mirim grabbed my hand.

'Don't let him get away with that! We've got as much right to risk our lives as the men do. Have you ever held a blade?'

'Not me.'

'What about a bow?'

Well, I used to go hunting with my brother Eriginas when I was a child. But it's one thing to be waiting in the woods for a stag to cross your path and quite another to be standing at the battlements aiming arrows at the enemy.

'I'm not sure I'd be much use as an archer either.'

'I saw the way you knocked that Toothache fellow with the chalice. Maybe it'd be best if we armed you with the cup of the sacrament.'

I caught the sarcasm in her tone.

'Give me an axe,' I hissed. 'You can't take the heads off Redcaps with a chalice.'

She and I were at the top of the stairs by then. The main gates of the fortress were just swinging open. I was shocked at that I can tell you. I couldn't work out why our warriors were opening the rath to the enemy.

Old Lord Will had run down from the north tower so I called out to him. But his response wasn't as friendly as I might have expected.

'What the bloody hell do you think you're doing?' he bellowed in a rage. 'The Saracens are upon us and you've deserted your assigned post. Get back down there with the camels immediately!'

'Who has come upon us?' I asked as I got close enough to see that his eyes were wild and darting.

'The Saracens are at the gates. But King Caoimhin has come with his host of warriors and they will save us from the ravages of the infidel.'

Mirim caught up with me at that moment. Her husband and Stronghold arrived seconds later, in time to see a company of fifty or so warriors wearing red caps marching up from the lower gate.

As they entered the rath the warriors on the battlements gave a cheer. The strangers waved back and cheered a response.

'What's going on?' I managed to ask the old lord.

'I told you. King Caoimhin has come to our rescue.'

'I'll go to fetch Father Clemens,' I gushed, excitedly. 'Wait till he hears this!'

But Will caught me by the arm and looked me sternly in the eye.

'It's too late for that, my dear. Clemens won't want to be disturbed. He has much work to do and a great weight to bear upon his venerable shoulders in the coming hours.'

He turned his attention back to Caoimhin and let go of my arm.

'These warriors are too few and too late to stem the tide. Even if there were nine thousand of them there wouldn't be enough to beat the Redcaps in open warfare. Whatever happens we must stick by the plan that was agreed on earlier this evening. There can be no certain victory unless we do that.'

'What plan?' I asked. 'What are you talking about?'

'It's up to me,' he muttered to himself, ignoring my question. 'I must decide what to do all alone. There's only one way to deal with the Saracens.'

'What Saracens?' I asked, by now deeply concerned for the state of his mind.

But old Will didn't reply. He was watching intently as the strangers halted. Then the gates swung shut behind them. Five of their number stepped out from the crowd and advanced toward where we were standing. And I have to say I was shocked, surprised and somewhat embarrassed when I saw a somewhat changed Caoimhin leading the way.

I had to rub my eyes, I did. I thought I'd gone mad. But there he was, as large as life and just as lively, dressed in the fine mail and tunic the chieftains of the Sen Erainn had granted him. He showed off the finely carved walking stick that had been a gift from Gobann as he strode towards us. And I suddenly recalled that I'd been quite taken with this handsome young fellow when I'd first met him.

In the next second our eyes met. I knew I was going to be in trouble. I called myself an eedyit out loud, I did.

'What did you say?' Mirim asked.

'Nothing,' I assured her as Caoimhin walked straight up and addressed me first.

'Binney. It's good to see you. I'm so glad you're safe.'

I noticed something odd about him straightaway. First of all, the sparkle he'd had in his eyes when he'd left the Killibegs was all but gone. Second, he was standing very close to a warrior-woman who was also dressed in a fine coat of mail. I noticed the circlet at his brow and wondered what had happened to him.

'This is Srón,' he said 'She's a warrior chieftain of the Sen Erainn.'

'I'm in charge of the bloody walls, young man!' William

rebuked him sharply. 'I make the decisions here now that Clemens and the others have taken up their posts inside the hall! You'll make your bloody report to me.'

'I'm sorry,' Caoimhin said. 'Lord William, I have been elected to the rank of Fisher-King of the hosts of the Sen Erainn. My people number nine hundred and we have come to help you in the defence of this rath.'

I looked at the lad in disbelief. How did he manage to get himself a crown? He couldn't have been gone more than a few hours. But then I'd already forgotten that in those same few hours I'd fallen in love with Guy, gained the friendship of a great-grandfather and abandoned my former feelings for Caoimhin.

'You're welcome, King of the Fisher-Folk,' Will replied. 'And so are all your kith and kin. I must say I'm surprised at your appearance but you could not have come to us at a better time.'

He took the young man in a fatherly embrace and as he did so he whispered into Caoimhin's ear.

'Have you seen my son?'

'No, my lord. I have not.'

'He went off to the Otherworld, some say. I hope he is safe. I fear I'll never see him again.'

'You'll see him,' Tóraí the Seer cut in as he stepped forward. 'Your son is not far from here and the foremost thought in his mind is to find you.'

'Your friend seems very confident,' old Will noted. 'Did you meet him in the Otherworld?'

'No, my lord. This is Tóraí Tairngire.' Sianan stepped forward. 'He left the Killibegs with me to keep me company on the road to the Otherworld. Now we have both returned.'

'Nonsense! I know everyone who dwells at the Killibegs and I've never met this fellow before.'

'His name has changed. And that's not all. For he was

known as Oat-Beer and he wore two more legs than he does now when he departed.'

Martin pushed his way through the assembled warriors who were gathering to witness this curiosity.

'Oat-Beer!' the Breton warrior exclaimed when he'd got a good look at the red-haired stranger. 'It *is* you!'

He threw his arms around the dog-man and hugged him close.

Sianan stepped closer to William so only he and Caoimhin would hear what she had to say.

'There's not much time, my lord. Can you hold off the attackers until I manage to sing my Draoi-songs?'

'How much time do you need?'

'The enchantments must be said just before the sunrise.'

The old man's eyes told her that he doubted they could hold out that long, but he didn't say so.

'We'll hold the walls against the assault as long as we can. Clemens and I have one or two surprises in store for the Redcaps if they get inside the fortress. So we must not give up hope.'

'Eight hundred and fifty of our folk have withdrawn to either side of the hill,' the Fisher-King told him. 'There'll they'll wait until the enemy marches up to the rath in force. As soon as I give the signal they'll come down from either side of the hill to crush them in between the hammer and the anvil.'

'That should buy us some precious time,' the lord answered solemnly. 'But the Saracens are a wily people. We must expect that they'll have a few tricks of their own.'

Sianan and Caoimhin shot a glance at one another

'My lord,' the Fisher-King ventured. 'It's the Redcaps we are fighting, not the Saracens.'

'Don't you think I know that!' Will bellowed. 'I just wish it *was* the Saracens!'

All fell silent then for a few uncomfortable seconds until Sianan cut in to introduce Mawn. That done there were a few other details to be dealt with.

'Where would you have us deploy?' Sianan asked. 'We will stand wherever you wish.'

William told them that the best place for their force was down in the storage cellars. We all protested but he was adamant that the warriors of the Killibegs would man the walls and that all the preparations had been made.

'Your people will be needed to protect our supplies. And you, Sianan, will not be disturbed by the fury of battle if you go underground. I don't doubt you'd appreciate some peace and quiet when you set about trying to summon Danu.'

There was a storm of protest from all sides.

'Srón and I will come to the battlements with you,' Caoimhin insisted. 'We've arranged to give the order for our warriors to attack by the blast of a horn.'

'Any of our people could sound that blast,' William replied. 'You will be better off in the storage chambers with the rest of the foreign folk. This is not your fight. It is for the Culdees to stand up this night in defiance of the forces of Rome and the Redcaps. If we fail you will have enough to worry about with tending to your own survival.'

He was very persuasive, old Will. I'll give him that. Everyone respected him. You couldn't help but do so. He was a living legend. So Caoimhin bowed to him before he spoke.

'The warriors under my command would not have sailed across the ocean from their island, marched down from Gaillimh then endured Aoife's curse if they had no intention of fighting. You would do us a great honour if you'd allow us to stand on the walls with you, side by side as allies.'

He'd come a long way himself, our Caoimhin. When he'd first landed at Wexford town with his teacher he'd been quite a timid lad. Now here he was offering to fight alongside the warriors of Rónán and the Killibegs. And he'd never before lifted a weapon in anger in his entire life.

William knew it too. But the old lord also understood that the eight-hundred and fifty folk of the Sen Erainn who were waiting outside the walls would be invaluable allies when the crunch of armour started in earnest. How could he deny these fifty the opportunity to stand against the foe?

'You speak eloquently, young king.' Will placed a fatherly hand upon his shoulder. 'But you only do so because you have no idea of the danger we will all face tonight. I wouldn't ask any of you to join us. Yet if you decide to lend your sickles to this fight I will not command you to skulk in the cellar out of sight.'

'Thank you,' Caoimhin replied with heartfelt pride.

Will ordered the Sen Erainn to the walls and they gave a great rousing cheer as they held their sickles high. Moments later they were rushing to take up their positions. Will told Caoimhin and Srón to stay by his side for the moment so he could give them last-minute instructions.

'We will also stand with the Sen Erainn,' Alan declared, cutting in.

William turned to face the knight and there was fire in his eyes.

'You will not! I have given you your instructions. Everything depends on you being able to carry them out to the letter. Lives will be saved this way. Do you understand?'

Alan nodded then dropped his eyes away from the old man's gaze shamed that he thought he knew better than this legendary veteran.

'I do.'

'Very well,' William added. 'Then go to your tasks and may Heaven watch over us tonight and in the coming weeks. For even if we gain the victory, that will only be the beginning of our troubles.'

'I will come to the battlements,' Stronghold declared bravely.

But I could see William wasn't going to have any of that.

'Alan de Harcourt has been placed in command of the cellars,' he replied tersely. 'You are under his orders. You have a vital job to do and in the end our future may depend on you.'

'I'm a man of honour!' Stronghold started to say in protest, but he didn't get any further.

'You have yet to prove that to me!' Will shouted. 'If it were not for you my son would still be here with me where he belongs. He is the last thing in this world that I hold dear.'

The lord took a deep breath, struggling to control his rising emotions. But he could not hold back.

'It was you and none other who took my Robert away from me! Where is he now? Until Tóraí told me he was alive, I thought you must have murdered him in a cowardly ambush. You will go down to the cellars and submit yourself to the commands of Alan de Harcourt. I wouldn't trust you to be on the walls behind me with a drawn blade in your hands.'

'But—'

'There will be no but! Your petty vengeance brought you to this land in search of my son. Your arrogance aided Aoife against the Culdees. Your dishonourable behaviour has robbed us of our books. Haven't you done enough?'

'I will do as you command,' Stronghold replied in shame. 'Your anger is just. But there is one thing you should know.'

'What's that?'

'I relinquished the holy books of the Killibegs to your son. I had no choice in the matter. I'm sure if it had not been for Aoife's intervention I would have likely fought with Robert again and again until eventually one of us fell to the sword of the other.'

'Are you certain Robert has the books?'

Stronghold nodded.

'It is my wish to make amends,' the Norman went on. 'So I

will return to the cellars and I will submit to the commands of Alan de Harcourt.'

Stronghold bowed his head low so that his chin pressed against his chest. Then he took me by the hand and together we headed back to the stairs which led down to the storage chambers.

Old Guy d'Alville bowed too. Then without a word he watched his great-grandson walk off with me.

'I'll stand beside you, if you don't mind,' the old knight told William with a mischievous smile. 'I've had quite a bit of practice at fighting during the last hundred years or so.'

'You're welcome,' William said with a smile, recognising a true chivalrous gentleman when he saw one. 'I'd be honoured if you'd stand with me.'

'I'll just be grateful to get away from my silly descendant for a while.' Old Guy grinned.

Sianan approached the lord as soon as we'd gone. She bowed her head out of respect for the old man, then she grabbed him and held him in a tight embrace.

'I saw Robert tonight,' she told him in a low voice.

The old man held her out at arm's length where he could look into her eyes.

'He was at the court of Aoife. Somehow he has become entangled in her web. He murdered Flidais of the Hunt in cold blood and was hailed as a hero for saving Aoife's life. She has him ensnared.'

William's eyes filled with tears, though no expression of sadness showed upon the features of his face. He stared on past Sianan with a stern, tight-lipped acceptance.

'Is he safe?' was all he managed to say.

'I believe he is. Aoife seems to have adopted him.'

William swallowed hard.

'So be it. If he is safe from harm this night then I am happy. It matters not to me whether he has joined the enemy. I have been granted a sense of peace to know that he will likely live to see the dawn.'

The abbess of Dun Gur put a reassuring hand on Lord Will's shoulder before she turned to go to her assigned place in the storage chambers. That's when Caoimhin remembered he had something important to give her.

'Wait!' he called out as he hastily removed the water-skin which hung over his shoulder beside his satchel of books. 'Mawn wasn't the only thing I brought back for you!'

Sianan turned around and he held out the water-skin.

'It is full of water from the Well of Many Blessings. I brought it so that you could heal Alan of his troubled mind. Perhaps if you give him a drink his memory will be restored.'

Sianan took the skin by the shoulder strap. 'Mirim will thank you.' As she weighed it in her hand a smile formed on her lips.

'There's one more thing.' He removed the satchel of books he'd carried ever since the death of his teacher, my brother, Eriginas. 'Will you look after this for me?'

'Yes.'

She stepped back with the two precious burdens to where Mawn was waiting beside Tóraí.

'I'm going to stand with Martin,' the Seer told her. 'It is my place to protect him if I can.'

Sianan dropped the satchel and the water-skin and hugged the dog-man close to her.

'Take care of yourself,' she whispered. 'Don't go indulging in any dog heroics. I will need your help in the coming months if we're going to help the people of the Killibegs.'

Tóraí kissed her tentatively on the cheek then turned to join Martin on the walls.

'I'll take care,' he called back. 'Don't worry about me.'

As Sianan picked up the water-skin Mawn hooked the book satchel across the right shoulder, opposite his harp.

'We'd better go,' he advised. 'The enemy will be upon us soon enough. And there is much for us to do.'

She smiled at him, overjoyed to hear his voice. And although all she wanted was sit down and listen to the tale of his life since they'd parted, she silently led the way to the underground stairs.

Old Will watched them go, thinking it might well be the last time he saw Sianan. He called a silent blessing to her then turned to give his orders to Srón and Caoimhin.

'Your people are to remain on the battlements no matter what else happens. The people of the Killibegs have a strategy in place which will draw the Redcaps into the fortress where they can be dealt with.

'With any luck the enemy won't bother with the warriors on the walls. They'll run straight into the trap that has been set for them.'

Now to the tale of Alan de Harcourt. Circumstance had brought him to a village, south-west of Alexandria in the Holy Land, bearing a book. He'd been a Templar knight who'd got himself lost; not a difficult thing in the featureless desert.

But what was a Templar knight doing out there in that barren place? Why would the Order of the Temple be so interested in a book that it would risk the lives of its knights? I'll tell you.

In those days, and I suppose it is still the case, there was a deadly rivalry between the Knights of the Order of the Temple and those of the Order of the Hospital. To understand this rivalry you have to know something of the changes that were taking place in Christendom around this time.

First of all and most importantly, pilgrims regularly plied their way to the Holy Land to visit the sacred places of the

Bible. This was a relatively new phenomenon. There'd always been pilgrims. What had changed was the vast numbers who were travelling to see the birthplace of Christ and the site of his tomb.

I've already told you something of the origins of the military orders of the Hospital and the Temple. In simple terms they both claimed to have been set up to protect the pilgrims to these places.

The truth is there was a lot more going on than that. All these pilgrims who went to the Holy Land expected to find that the Church of Rome was firmly in control of the sacred places and shrines. But this wasn't the case.

Orthodox Christians of the eastern variety inhabited that part of the world and the doctrines of the Roman Church were hardly known. Now, Orthodox Christians have quite different beliefs from those of the Roman kind.

The Orthodox had preserved the more esoteric doctrines of Christ's teachings, known to some as the Path to Gnosis. I won't go into the details of their faith. I've already mentioned much of it to you since we Culdees shared many of their tenets.

The point is that the Church of Rome wasn't too happy with what these Gnostics were teaching. First and foremost their doctrines were popular among the masses. Many pilgrims returned to their homes profoundly changed by their exposure to the Gnostic ways.

Second, all the Gnostic teachers preached that the way to God was in the hands of the individual. The Roman Church, on the other hand, held that the only way to reach Heaven was to pay obeisance to the priests and hierarchy of the one true Church in Rome.

We Culdees shared the Gnostic understanding in many respects. All esoteric Christians saw the Passion of the Christ as merely a symbolic representation of the abandonment of the material world leading to eventual redemption and eternal life.

214

Jesus used the parable of the house built on sand. Well, he was talking about the five shifting senses which are easily distracted and move from one point of focus to another constantly, like the sands of the desert. Build the house of your being on the sandy senses and it will fall time and time again.

On the other hand, the house built on a foundation of rock does not so easily collapse. That is why we Culdees advocated practices involving meditation, periods of abstinence and solitude and the development of deep consciousness of the One. The first step towards building foundations of rock was always deemed to be abandonment of the self and the never-ending satisfaction of the senses.

The house of Alan's being was founded on the sandy doctrines of the senses enclosed within the flimsy structures taught to him by the Roman church. Perhaps he didn't realise it at the time but he was fated to find a firm rocky place, in a manner of speaking.

When he became lost in the desert he blundered his way through the sand storm to the oasis of Shali. Ironically, those folk who dwelled amidst the sands knew well what it meant to build upon rock. Who better to show him a different way?

Alan drank from the sacred well of that community to slake his thirst. But he did so without asking permission of the woman of the well who watched over the waters of that place. And according to tradition there was a punishment which had to be suffered for that act. His memory was taken away from him. As soon as he tasted the life-giving sweetness of that water everything he ever knew was taken away from him. He could not recall what he was doing in the desert.

Now you might think that this was a terrible thing. But sometimes the greatest gift anyone can give you is to steal something precious away.

Alan couldn't remember his family or friends. He didn't even know his own name. Perhaps that's why the people of the

Shali Oasis called that place the Well of Forgetfulness. Now I don't want you to confuse that well with the one we Culdees call the Well of Forgetfulness. That's another thing entirely.

We believe that upon death each soul drinks from the Well of Forgetfulness. Those waters have much the same effect as the well at Shali. They take all memory of the life that has just been lived away and wash the soul clean so that a new life may be undertaken without taint of trauma or longing for lost love.

The well at Shali had that effect in the material world. So you might say that Alan had been afflicted with a terrible curse. Though if you were to look at it from an esoteric point of view, Alan had been granted a great gift.

You see, he'd been able, through the qualities of the waters of Shali, to release his hold on his understanding of himself. His mind was washed clean of memories and with them his view of the world had been transformed. That's why the well of Shali was venerated as a holy place and watched over by a wise and venerated woman.

If Alan had not tasted those waters he would never have been able to fall in love with Mirim and marry her. He was an honourable man who had sworn his life to the Temple. That meant he had vowed to forever shun the company of women, a most unnatural practice in my opinion.

It's one thing to practice abstinence now and then, or even for prolonged periods, in order to come to some understanding about oneself. But to abstain from the tickling arts for life is plain wrong. In the end the practice of abstinence ends up working against you, as you'd know if you've ever tried it.

Now, our Alan was very happy with his wife and his new life at Shali founded on the rock of true kinship. In fact folks actually called him Shali for they did not know his name any more than he did. But there was still the matter of the book he had in his possession, which he'd been supposed to deliver to the master of the Temple. And there was something else. Alan was curious to know who he was.

Mirim was a wise woman herself. She understood that he could never be completely committed to their life together. One day, sooner or later, he might wake up to recall everything about his former life. Then what would happen? Would he repent at having broken his vows? Would he simply disappear from her life, never to return?

An old hermit visited the oasis some months after Alan appeared there. He could read Latin and he knew the significance of the book immediately. From the orders contained within a letter found on the lost adventurer's person he was able to tell the young knight his name: Alan de Harcourt.

He advised that they set out to find William FitzWilliam who was a trustworthy knight blessed with a compassionate heart. He would be able to help the young Templar sort out the mess he'd got into. Make no mistake, the Temple used to deal viciously with any knights who deserted their duties. And in the view of the order that's just what Alan had done, whether he was aware of his actions or not.

So when he and his wife set off for Acre to find William FitzWilliam and hand the book over to him, Mirim made up her mind she'd discover a way to restore her husband's memory to him. Then he'd be able to make a decision about their life together based on whether or not his vows were more important to him than she was.

As I said to you the night before last when I spoke of the Well of Yearning, Alan and Mirim ended up setting off to Ireland in search of Lord William with William's son Robert to guide them on their way. After many adventures and three years on the road, they'd decided to go off to the Otherworld themselves. They were to have set out in the morning at first light.

So it was a wonderful miraculous occurrence that brought

Caoimhin back from his jaunt in the Land of Dreams bearing a skin full of water drawn from the Well of Many Blessings.

Now Sianan had the water-skin she was eager to hand it over to Mirim. The mystical waters would prove invaluable to them this night. For a start, Alan's affliction could certainly be healed. But any and all who were wounded in the coming fight would have the chance to be healed of their injuries by simply tasting the sweetness contained within that water-skin.

Sianan thanked the stars in the heavens she'd taken Caoimhin with her to the Otherworld, though she'd regretted it at first.

When she, Mawn, Stronghold, Gusán, John and the rest of us were down in the cellars, the warriors of the rath closed the doors above and all light was banished. Then we all listened as the folk above ground covered up the entrance.

A few minutes after the doors were shut sparks started to fly here and there as Gusán, Alan and Sianan struck up the flints from their tinderboxes. Before long a dozen candles and two rush-lights had lit the interior of the main corridor. Everyone gathered round the candles in reverential silence as if they were holy relics that could keep all harm at bay.

'I don't care what that old bugger Clemens says,' Gusán said. 'If I'm going to be stuck down here the rest of the night I want to be able to see.'

Alan looked around at us all and then began to relate the plan the old priest and the chieftains had come up with to save the settlement from the ravages of the Redcaps. It was going to prove a risky business, to be certain. You see, Clemens's idea was to draw the main force of the Redcaps into the great hall. Old Will and a dozen warriors were going to wait by the main gate until the Redcaps were pounding on it to be let in. But the enemy would have to climb the towers before they'd be able to charge into the main part of the fortification.

William and his archers were going to send a volley of arrows into the Redcaps as they entered the rath to enrage them. Then they'd quickly retreat into the great hall where Clemens, his wife and a dozen of their warriors would be waiting to set the next part of the trap.

Once the enemy were inside the hall they'd be led a merry chase down to the basement beneath the hall. As soon as they'd reached the lower floor Clemens and his people were going to set fire to the upper parts of the building, cutting off the Redcaps' escape.

With little hope of retreat through the flames the Redcaps would soon have no other choice but to descend the wooden stairs to the lower floors. The fire would surely send them into a panic, or at least that was what Clemens hoped. Eventually they'd have to make their way into the storage chambers where there would be more surprises waiting for them.

'It's our job to pour the lamp oil over the floors behind the doors at the hall end of the corridor,' Alan told us. 'I'll be standing at the door with an arrow dipped in flaming pitch.'

As soon as the Redcaps appeared in the corridor it was Alan's intention to shoot his arrow, thus setting fire to the floor of the chamber. A narrow space had to be made, only wide enough for one warrior to pass through at a time.

'As the Redcaps are driven through that door we'll strike their heads off one at a time. Now we have much to do. And we must work both quickly and quietly.'

'The Redcaps may be killed by fire,' John said. 'I was among them. I heard they fear it almost as much as they do an axeman swinging his blade at head height.'

'Then you know more about those dæmons than I do,' Alan replied. 'And I'm sure Clemens only had it in his mind to frighten the Redcaps with fire and send them into a panic with the burning. But I pray the flames may prove as deadly as any axe.'

Then he assigned us all to tasks. I was told to help Stronghold, Gusán and John with the spreading of the oil across the floor at the bottom of the stairs which descended from the upper basement level of the hall.

We went about our job rolling barrels out into the corridor beyond. There were thirty of them in all. Ten were laid on their sides with a single axe cut carefully splitting the lid of each so that oil seeped out slowly.

The remainder had the ends smashed in so the precious contents spilled across the cobblestone floor. This left the floor awash with highly flammable oil. And that's when Alan ordered us all out and extinguished the candles that had lit our work.

'Now we must gather every empty barrel and box we can find,' he told us. 'The doorway leading to that corridor has to be narrowed so that only one warrior at a time may pass through it.'

While we were at our task Sianan approached Mirim with the precious water-skin.

'I have something for you. This vessel contains sacred waters from the Well of Many Blessings. They will heal the affliction to Alan's memory.'

Mirim stepped back.

'I hadn't expected this so soon. I thought my husband and I would have some more time together before he was healed.'

'But chance has brought this to you,' Sianan told her. 'And since your lives may be in peril this night, perhaps that is how it is meant to be. For who knows what will befall this settlement before the coming of the dawn?'

Mirim swallowed hard as she reached out to take the skin. It was heavy and she hugged it close to her as she glanced at Alan who was helping stack barrels. Mawn was at his side.

The desert woman looked into Sianan's eyes. 'You have found your soul-friend at last. You must be very happy.'

'I haven't had the opportunity to rejoice as yet,' the abbess told her. 'There's much to do before I'll have that luxury.'

'Thank you for this gift.'

'Thank Caoimhin for it. I was at the well but I did not think to retrieve a measure of the waters for you and your husband. Caoimhin has brought back enough to ensure that all the wounded of the Killibegs may have a chance to be healed.'

'It is strange. I would not have paid any more attention to him than I would to a loose thread on a blanket. And yet he thought to bring this water back with him for my husband. Where would any of us be but for the compassion of strangers?'

Mirim held the water-skin tighter.

'Perhaps I should wait until after the battle to give it to him,' she said, half to herself. 'I don't know what effect it may have on him.'

'It will restore his memory so that he will be truly himself again,' the abbess told her.

'That is what I'm afraid of.'

Mirim smiled at Sianan warmly and kissed her lightly on the cheek.

'Will he know me after he has been restored to himself?' she whispered.

'I cannot tell you,' Sianan replied truthfully.

Mirim smiled once more.

'Again I thank you. Now I must take this to my husband. His thirst must be quenched and I would not deny him this refreshment.'

The abbess watched as Mirim went over to speak to Alan. Though she could not hear what it was they said she saw Alan's eyes light up with joy. He held his wife close to him for a long time and she wrapped her arms about his neck as if she'd never let him go.

When they broke apart Alan noticed Sianan watching them. He bowed to her in thanks. Then he grabbed a candle and took Mirim by the hand to a place within one of the storage rooms where they could be alone.

There Alan carefully removed the skin's stopper and cautiously sniffed at its contents.

'Are you sure this will work?'

'Sianan has told me this water comes from the well we were seeking. Once you have had a mouthful your memories will be yours again. You will know your name and all those things which your mind has turned away from in confusion. The effects of the Well of Forgetting will be lifted and you will be free.'

His face lit up with jubilation as he lifted the neck of the water-skin to his mouth. But as he was about to taste the precious healing liquid he hesitated.

'What if I should remember all my past life, yet forget you?'

'That will not happen, my love.'

'How do you know? Did Sianan tell you?'

'This will bring back to your mind all that is important to you in this life. Am I not important to you?'

'You are more important than anything or anyone,' Alan assured her with a sparkle of emotion welling in his eye. 'You know that.'

'Then how could you possibly forget me?'

His expression brightened again. This time he lifted the neck of the vessel to his mouth and took a deep draught of the liquid.

'Just a mouthful is all you need!' Mirim placed a hand on the water-skin to hold him back.

A few drops spilled around the corners of his mouth as he lowered the skin and replaced the stopper firmly in position. He handed the vessel back to his wife and then stared at her as his eyes cleared of the foggy grey that had clouded them ever since they'd known one another.

His face was flushed with a healthy pink. Even Alan's hair suddenly had a sheen about it that had not ever been evident before. He coughed a little. Then he laughed.

222

'How do you feel?' she asked urgently.

'I don't feel any different than I did before I tasted the water. But my mind has changed, that's for certain. It's a miracle! I know who I am.'

'Who are you?' Mirim asked with trepidation.

'I am Alan de Harcourt. My grandfather carried the standard of Duke William of Normandy at the Battle of Hastings. I have sworn myself to the Order of the Temple. I am a knight.'

The desert woman could not help but urge him on.

'What else?'

'I am twenty-seven years of age. And I am married to the most wonderful woman I have ever known.'

Mirim's eyes filled with tears in that instant. She dropped the water-skin and threw her arms about her husband to hold him close. That's when I passed by the room and saw them. And I thought to myself what a wonderful thing it is to be alive and to taste the waters of the Well of the Goddess, which is what love is.

But at that moment I had no idea Alan had also taken a draught from the Well of Many Blessings.

Sealed in her Chamber

s soon as she'd handed over the water-skin Sianan went off to find a quiet place. She needed somewhere private to prepare herself for her part in the defence of Rath Killibegs.

You see, Sianan had decided to deal with the Queen of the Night herself.

Well there was only one way to do that, my dear. Aoife was an immortal and she was a cunning, powerful, highly skilled one at that. The only way to stop her was to call down the great Goddess Danu. Of course Sianan didn't really know for certain how to do this, but she had in her possession two enchantments which might help.

I suppose I'd best tell you something about old Lady Danu, hadn't I?

In the ancient days before there were ever any mortals on the Earth, Danu and her kind reigned over this world. I don't know where she came from. I don't know who her mother was. And I'll wager even Danu doesn't remember either. So much time has passed since she first appeared.

What I can tell you is that she wandered the Earth ceaselessly searching for a place to call her home. But it wasn't till she came to Ireland that she made up her mind she'd found it.

One of the places she stopped on the way is called the Danemark in her honour; another place she dwelled for a while was on the banks of a river called the Danau by some and the Danube by others. It's in the east on the way to the Holy Land. I've seen that river. It's a wide beautiful expanse of slow moving water and it reminded me of her straightaway. For she is named the Goddess of the Flowing Waters. I can only guess this was because she had a fondness of the rivers, seas and rainy places of this Earth.

Now you know why she loved Ireland so much. There isn't a place on Earth where it rains so often or so much as this country. Indeed, some scholars claim that it is the rain which prevented us Irish from ever conquering any other lands.

I'm sure our ancestors considered the prospects of conquest now and then. But you try picking a fine day to sail across the sea in search of new lands. Every morning they'd stick their heads out the door and mutter, 'Bloody rain' to themselves. Then they'd crawl back under the covers till midafternoon.

On the other side of the coin, though, the relentless precipitation in this country could also be the reason why so many magnificent works of art and music originated here. It's certainly the reason why we are such great storytellers. There's not much else to do if you're rained in for days or even weeks at a time. It may also be why we tend to have large families.

So Danu settled down here quite happy with the endless grey skies and the damp weather because that's the sort of thing that touched her soul. Perhaps she had a measure of the melancholy about her. I don't know.

I've heard that it was she who planted the Quicken Trees and enticed a few of the Fir Bolg and Danaans to join her in immortal pursuits. That's likely quite true. For it would have been awful lonely to be one of the few immortals on this Earth and the only one in Ireland.

That's how the Tuatha De Danaan got their name, you know. She adopted them. She taught their Druids how to look after the land and how to tend the Earth with care. Danu was their mother and their teacher. She was their guide and their protector. So they came to call themselves the people of the Goddess Danu.

Now, all would have gone on well and good and everyone would have been happy in Ireland if the Gaels had never stumbled on this land. My people are Gaels and I'm ashamed to admit that my ancestors drove Danu off to her bedchamber when they arrived here and forced the Danaans to share the country with them.

Danu took to sleeping more and more then. Whereas she'd once been a common sight wandering the cow paths of the west, she started to travel less and slumber more. I suppose she'd become disgruntled with the Gaels in the same way the Danaans eventually did.

Our people had the skill of working iron. And the iron forge is a voracious consumer of timber. So although our folks were not as destructive as the Normans would later be, our coming must have been a shock.

Danu was a goddess. I hear you ask what that means exactly. Well I'll put it this way. A goddess is a woman who has a certain aura of power, majesty and beauty about her. Even a mortal can become a goddess. Indeed, there was a mortal goddess alive in the time when my tale took place.

Her name was Queen Eleanor of Aquitaine. Yes, you heard me right. Queen Eleanor, mother to Richard Lion Hearted and wife of old King Henry, was a goddess. She was worshipped in her day not just for her beauty, which was incomparable, but also for her courage, which was unmatched. Men admired her for her wit, charm, education, ruthlessness and because she attained anything she ever set her mind to.

At the end of her exceptionally long life everyone in Christendom knew her name. Everyone in France knew at least one song about her. And everyone in England claimed to have actually met her. She was a living legend and she will go on to be so, mark my words.

She's a perfect example of a goddess. If you can imagine what Queen Eleanor of Aquitaine might have been like if she'd been immune to death, you'll start to understand what sort of woman our Danu is.

I speak of her in the present tense because she has not succumbed to mortality. She's still out there somewhere, sleeping the sleep of the sleepy or dreaming the dreams of the dreamy. But I'm jumping ahead of myself again.

In the old days the Danaans used to venerate her by singing songs in her honour and throwing magnificent parties to please her at Samhain. But as the summers rolled on Danu got bored with the Danaans and their constant toadying.

Believe me, if you had to put up with people bowing and scraping day in day out through the whole of eternity you'd probably have to end up stifling a few yawns yourself every once in a while.

In the end she granted a few of the Danaan folk the Quicken Brew. Some of them had earned the honour through loyal devotion to their goddess. These folk were given responsibilities that Danu thought befitted them. For example, Bridey was made the Goddess of Fire and Having Fun. There's a great deal of hard work involved in doing that particular job, I can tell you. It might sound like a lark but poor old Bridey was rushed off her feet. Considering how dismal and wet the weather is in this country I'm personally surprised she stuck at it. But she did and her diligence relieved a great deal of the burden from Danu's shoulders.

Boann of the Cows was given responsibility for all matters to do with dairy products and cattle in general. You might think this wasn't a very important job at all. And you'd be right. But it was a terribly time-consuming, frustrating and above all smelly occupation. Boann must have done something to really upset Danu.

The list goes on. But the point is that the Goddess of the

Flowing Waters probably just lost interest in doing the same old job day after day. So she appointed a few other folk to do parts of it for her. And she worked it so that each of them was so busy in their own specific area of responsibility that none of them could ever be a threat to her supremacy.

Danu also instigated the office of Morrigán. I've already told you what duties were assigned to that office. And since there was a terrible possibility that the holder of the title could get it into her head that she was all-powerful and better than the Mother Goddess, Danu appointed a new immortal woman to the position every so often.

Danu also appointed men from among the mortal kind to be gods, but she was always careful not to give the men too much responsibility unless she wanted some specific disaster to take place.

Now, Sianan was a Gael. And among the immortal kind she and Mawn were the youngest of all. She didn't have all that much experience of the world really. She'd certainly never encountered Danu. I don't even think she'd ever met Bridey or Boann in those days. In fact I know she only met the Morrigán for the first time at Aoife's feast.

So she was quite nervous about summoning the Mother of All into her presence. I mean to say, wouldn't you be? I hope so – it's not something to be undertaken lightly.

For a start Danu has always been known for her rather sleepy and forgetful nature. I hope she doesn't mind me saying so. It's not that the Mother of All is slow-witted or dull. No. That's not it at all. She just doesn't really give a festering fig about us mortals any more. So while she's a very sharp-minded soul, she doesn't take that much notice of those things which don't interest her. That is to say – us.

As for her sleepiness, well that isn't really a true account of her at all. She's not really a sleeper as such. It's just that she slumbers longer than any mortal might do. All the Ever-Living

Ones are like that. Their cycles are so much longer than ours. So Danu might be awake for nine hundred years and then slumber as long to recuperate from the exertions of her duties.

It so happens that at the time my tale was taking place it was well known that Danu had slipped into one of her immensely long sleeps. And as everyone who's ever met her will tell you, she doesn't like to be woken up for any old reason.

The last time anyone dared to do that was back in the days when Lochie and Isleen were wandering the land bringing havoc. Look what she did to them! She turned them into nasty, slimy worms. And then she forgot about them. And all because she was miffed at having her sleep disturbed.

So you can understand why Sianan was nervous about calling the old girl up. I would be. There was also the problem that our Sianan didn't actually have the means to summon Danu. However, she'd got two Draoi-enchantment songs that had been written down in one of William's books and miraculously left behind by Guy when he rifled through the collection. The Draoi-songs had the power to put Frighteners and Enticers to sleep and to open the doors to the Otherworld.

The problem was that Sianan didn't know how to raise an awakening spell. I suppose she thought she'd do what she could once she'd returned to the Otherworld. There was another difficulty: Sianan was going to have to. fall into a deep meditative state in which she'd be able to cross to the Otherworld and stir old Danu into action.

Such a deep state requires a quiet calm place where there is little chance of interruption. I'm sure you'd agree that a fortress under siege is not the ideal environment to have to practise such a craft.

Well, Sianan found herself an empty room where the din of preparations wasn't too overpowering. Once she'd decided it was the best place available to her she went back to tell Mawn what she intended to do.

'I need your help. The trouble is that as soon as I start to sing the Draoi-song which lulls the feeding spirits to sleep I won't have much time to find Danu.'

'Why do you need to put the feeders to sleep?'

'So Aoife will be stripped of some of her power.'

'Why would that be a problem?' Mawn asked, confused.

'I'm afraid that Aoife will immediately become aware of what I intend to do. Though she has not attained to the worshipful rank of goddess herself, I'm sure she would be sensitive to those things which goddesses know intuitively.'

'What will she do?'

'She'll try to get to me to stop me. She may send Redcaps or the Nathairaí. So it's up to you to stop them. She may even come looking for me herself.'

'I'll do what I can,' Mawn promised. 'I've had some experience with goddesses myself.'

'You were imprisoned by one for nearly seven hundred years,' Sianan noted dryly. 'I hope you manage to do a better job with Aoife than you did with Flidais.'

'Don't worry, you don't spend seven hundred summers trapped at the bottom of a pool by a petulant huntress without learning a thing or two. I'll be ready if Aoife comes looking for you.'

'Now seal me in this room,' Sianan demanded. 'If she does come down here into the cellars searching for me, we have to make it as difficult as possible for her to reach me. Every moment she can be delayed will tip the balance in our favour.'

Mawn turned to call in help from those of us who were working to narrow the corridor. When he'd done that he turned to take Sianan's hand in his.

'Let's hope we have some time after this is over to make up for all that could have been.'

He raised her hand to his lips and gently kissed the back of it.

'Farewell for now. And give my regards to the Mother of All,' he laughed.

Sianan grabbed a candle, entered the room she'd chosen and closed the door behind her. A few moments later barrels and empty jars were being stacked against the doorway to seal her in. All the while she had that song running through her head which had come to her when she'd been on her way back to the Killibegs with Tóraí.

'Mine is the sea, yours the bright blue sky. A silent plea softly fills my eye. All my words, all speech, all my prayers beseech. These things I have learned.'

OLLO

Old Lord Will took up his position on the battlements beside Martin the Breton who had been assigned as his personal guard. Tóraí Tairngire, who had been known as Oat-Beer, chose to stand with his former master, Martin. And that proved to be a very fortunate turn of events.

William FitzWilliam stared out into the night searching for any sign of the enemy.

'Can you see anything, Martin?' he asked.

'Nothing.'

'I see something,' Tóraí piped up.

Both men squinted into the darkness and spoke together.

'Where? What?'

'I don't see with my two eyes. I see with my one eye.'

'What do you mean?' old Will asked.

'I see what is happening far off. I can see your son.'

'And where is he?'

Tóraí described a great ragtag force of a thousand weary knights in tattered tunics and rusted armour. They were marching with all speed toward the rath and at their head strode Robert FitzWilliam dressed in gleaming mail and carrying the sword named Órán.'

'How do you know it's him? How do you know it's my son?'

'I saw him at Aoife's feast. I'd recognise him anywhere.'

'Who are these warriors he leads?'

'They are old men who have been released from an enchant-ment.'

'Then this force of knights is coming to our rescue?'

Tóraí shook his head.

'They are sworn to the service of Aoife, as is Robert.'

William turned sharply to face the dog-man. Then he looked him up and down with a scowl.

'You must be mistaken,' he growled.

'I am not! It is Robert who leads these warriors on to attack us.'

'He wouldn't. My son is an honourable man.'

'It's true. He is. And even as we speak he is struggling with the weight of the responsibility that has been placed on his shoulders. There are two sides to Robert FitzWilliam and one is in conflict with the other.'

Sure enough Tóraí was right about that. As Robert marched at the head of the oak-knights he was engaging in an inner battle. He had promised Aoife he would lead her troops into the assault against the Killibegs and he had given his word he would also abandon them to be slaughtered at the hands of the Redcaps.

That didn't sit well with him at all and as he trudged through the snow he had to ask himself why he'd so readily agreed to such a thing. Of course he had no idea Aoife had cast an enchantment over him.

It was her Enticer spirit that gave her this ability. Every goddess or aspiring goddess has one. And Aoife had an Enticer that was particularly powerful. So she always got what she wanted.

Well almost always. Robert was beginning to wonder how many of the wishes and desires that had filled his head recently had actually been his own. He was starting to think that perhaps he didn't really want to be a lord at all. Maybe he didn't want a wife and family either.

What if he'd been manipulated by both Aoife and Órán? What if he was simply a tool of their ambitions? As it happened he didn't have any more time to consider such possibilities. For as those questions arose, the torches of Bishop Ollo's Hospitallers appeared a short distance ahead.

The snow eased a little as the oak-knights came to the bridge which crossed the frozen stream near the rath. Ollo's men were leading their horses along the ice toward the bridge just as the oak-warriors were about to cross it.

Robert ordered his force to halt until the bishop had brought up his men. It wasn't long after that one of the black knights was brought to Robert. A short while later Rob was brought before Ollo.

'Who are you?' the bishop bellowed. 'What are you doing here on this night?'

'I've come to attack the Rath of the Killibegs.'

'Under whose orders?.'

'My queen has commanded me.'

The fat old bishop laughed.

'You're a Templar! I can see that by the colour and markings of your tunic.'

'I am.'

'I could have you burned at the stake here and now for crossing paths with me. I could have you cut to pieces for raising an army against the Hospital.

'I know why you've come here.' Ollo peered at him with narrowed eyes. 'You've come for the books.'

Robert touched a hand to the satchel over his shoulder and laughed.

'I'm not after any books.'

'Then what do you want?'

'I've been sent to join forces with you. My queen has commanded me to take charge of your force and to storm the rath.'

This time it was Ollo's turn to laugh.

'You're going to take charge of my force, are you?'

'And you're to release the raven you have in your custody as well,' Robert added. 'He was falsely imprisoned.'

'I've already been warned about you, Robert FitzWilliam,' the bishop told him as his horse kneeled down from exhaustion.

As soon as the beast was on its knees the bishop stepped off. Then the animal rolled over on to its side and expired.

Robert raised an eyebrow as Ollo kicked the poor dead creature and swore.

'You've been sent to put an end to my ambitions,' Ollo said.

'Who told you that?' Robert asked, but he already knew the answer.

Sciathan Cog. Sciathan Cog had been pretending to be Lom Dubh. And Aoife had fallen for the trick.

'Who told you that?' he repeated when the bishop offered no more reply than a smile.

'A little bird told me.'

Robert smiled back but the gesture was obviously insincere.

'If you release the raven I will place my warriors at your disposal.'

'How many?'

'A thousand.'

Now, Ollo was known to be a proud old bastard but he was no fool. He'd already been told where these warriors had come from. Sciathan Cog had flown straight from Aoife to tell him they were coming. And he knew who Aoife was and all. But it didn't worry him one bit.

He was a bit full of himself – fairly typical of the clergy in those days. You see, even though Aoife was a force to be reckoned with, Ollo held her in very low esteem. For despite her alleged power she was still just a woman. And the scriptures say that women are lesser beings than men.

That's if you read the scriptures Emperor Constantine

approved. We both know what a barrel load of badger bollocks they are.

'You will place your warriors under my care immediately,' Ollo declared. 'I will not broker any deals with a Templar who consorts with dæmons.'

Robert laughed again. Then he turned sharply round.

'Lads!' he commanded. 'Slaughter the bloody lot of them!'

A great bloodthirsty cheer rose up as a thousand oak-knights unsheathed their blades, notched arrows to their bows and stepped out across the bridge to do their duty. Ollo's face drained of all colour in an instant. And before a single pair of oak-warrior feet had come within a dozen paces of him he'd held his hand up to call Robert's men to a halt.

'Wait!' he shrieked.

Our Rob smiled.

'Wait!' he repeated calmly.

The oak-warriors halted in their tracks, ready to charge forward at the first hint from their leader.

'Bring me the raven you have caged,' Robert demanded.

Ollo frowned. He looked as though he was about to protest. So Robert shrugged.

'Are you ready for the slaughter, oak-knights of Aoife?'

'Aye!' they bellowed with joyous blood-lust.

'Now where's the raven?'

'Bring out the bird!' the bishop ordered at the top of his lungs.

A cage barely large enough for a hunting hawk was brought out. Crammed within was Lom Dubh, stuffed into in a corner with his claws stretching out between the bars.

'Robert?' Lom Dubh asked. 'Is that you?'

'Let the bird go free,' our Rob demanded.

'Do it yourself!' Ollo spat.

So Robert strode across and flipped the catch which held one side of the cage locked in place. The front side fell open and Lom flopped forward to stagger a few steps.

'They tried to kill me! They poked me with spears. They cut me with axes. And they sliced me with swords. And they laughed at their sport! They could've cut off my head at any moment but they chose to watch me suffer agony and be healed from each awful wound.'

'This is Sciathan Cog's doing,' Rob said.

'He tricked me. He trapped me. That traitor!'

'You're free to go now. Fly back to Aoife and tell her I've taken charge of the Hospitallers.'

As Robert spoke Lom Dubh heard the creak of a drawn bowstring. His sharp raven eyes caught sight of the archer and his wings were wide with a leap before anyone else knew what was happening.

The arrow shaft let loose from the bow like a bolt of feathered lightning. The aim was true, straight for Robert's heart. But our Lom was too quick for the bowman's shaft. He caught the deadly missile with his own body, and before Robert understood what had happened the raven was fluttering wildly on the ground before him, an arrow in his chest.

'Get it out!' Lom Dubh screamed. 'Pluck out the nasty Norman needle!'

Robert leaned over the bird as his own archers drew their bows daring any of Ollo's men to try to strike down their commander while he was tending his black-feathered friend. Rob placed a boot on the raven's body and grasped the arrow firmly.

'I don't want to hurt you.'

'You cannot hurt me. The injury will last no more than a few moments. The pain will pass with the arrow. Pluck it out! It burns like a fire in my chest with the agony of it.'

Rob held the shaft tight in his sweating palms but he could not bring himself to draw the missile out.

'Do it!' Lom Dubh screamed. 'Every moment that you hesitate is agony.'

237

Robert took a deep breath and held it as he pulled the arrow out. It tore through the flesh of the raven, spurting forth blood and gore from the ripped flesh and feathers around the wound. He held it up to inspect it, relieved that the ordeal was over.

Then he noticed a nasty thick black substance on the tip. He touched it with his finger but just as he was examining the oily residue Lom Dubh shrieked again.

'I'm sorry!' Rob hissed.

He leaned close to Lom. Then, before his disbelieving eyes, the wound sealed up, knitted and was gone as if it had never been.

'Thank you,' the raven said quietly.

Robert held the arrow up with the point levelled at the bishop's nose.

'Bowmen!' the Templar bellowed. 'Take up your target! Aim well at Ollo. When I give the order you will strike him down without mercy. His heart shall be your prize. And you'll stick it full of splinters just like this one.'

Thirty bowmen turned their arrow points to the bishop and held their trembling bowstrings steady, waiting for the word. The bishop immediately broke out into a flowing sweat and his face drained to grey.

'I offer you command of these Hospitallers,' Ollo said quickly. 'They are yours to do with as you will. But only if you spare me my life. Kill me and your warriors will have to fight three hundred knights and a hundred men-at-arms before they besiege Rath Killibegs. They'll be battle weary before they even reach the battlefield.'

Robert smiled broadly. He'd got what he wanted.

'It doesn't matter how many times that happens to me,' Lom Dubh noted, 'I never seem to get used to being struck through the heart by an arrow. I don't know what it is exactly. Perhaps it's the internal bleeding or the broken ribs. Maybe it's having the breath knocked out of me. But I can tell you the whole experience is very unpleasant.'

'Go to Aoife with all speed,' Robert told the bird as he snapped the arrow in two and tossed it aside. 'Warn her about your brother and his treachery. Tell her the oak-knights are marching to the Killibegs with the Hospitallers at their side.'

Lom cawed loudly, spread his wings and was gone as soon as Robert had spoken.

The Templar turned and addressed the Hospitallers. 'You are under my orders now. Let's put our differences aside. We have a job to do. Let's do it and divide the spoils afterwards.'

But in the back of his mind he couldn't help wondering what the Grand Master of the Order of the Temple would think of him marching at the head of such an army. The Hospitallers were enemies of the Templars. And the oak-knights were strange enough to be reckoned dæmons by most reasonable folk.

'What about me?' the bishop spat. 'You can't just leave me here.'

'You're coming with us,' Robert assured him. 'And you'll fight alongside your knights in this siege.'

'I've not come here to fight!'

'Then what have you come for?'

Robert guessed the answer before he'd even finished asking the question.

'Books.'

'Yes,' Ollo admitted with a glint of greed in his eye. 'I've come to take the books which the Culdees of the Killibegs have in their possession. They are all heretical works. And I have been charged with retrieving them and milking them of every ounce of worth.'

Robert swallowed hard to think that the very books Ollo was after were hanging at his side in the leather travelling bag Guy had stolen from the Killibegs. But he wasn't about to let the bishop in on that little secret.

'You shall have the books,' Rob promised. 'If you can manage to find them. For I've heard they've been hidden in a place where no man would expect to encounter them.'

Ollo sneered. 'My knights are yours then. As long as you reserve to me the holy books of the Killibegs.'

'As I said, if you can find them they are yours. Now march your men beside mine on the left side of this road and we'll bring our force into position for the attack. I want to launch the assault before dawn so that the dark will mask our numbers and the rising sun will herald our victory.'

'That's a nasty trick!' the bishop noted. 'Perhaps I won't mind marching behind you after all.'

That's how it came to be that Robert FitzWilliam gave the orders to march on, not Ollo. And every step of the way forward he smiled to himself that the old bishop had come so close to attaining the books of the Killibegs without a fight.

That's what he wanted after all. Ollo wasn't so much interested in murdering heretics as attaining magical manuscripts. If Lom Dubh hadn't saved Rob from that arrow the fat bishop would have got them.

Then the bishop surely wouldn't have bothered to attack the Killibegs. Perhaps the whole battle could have been avoided. All these thoughts of what might have been bubbled round in Robert's head as he led his army toward the rath. He didn't know how this was all going to end but he felt a lot better that he seemed to be in control at the moment.

Of course it didn't take long for Bishop Ollo's force of Hospitaller knights to lose heart in the midst of the storm. They'd made only a slow headway along the frozen stream up to the bridge. By the time they'd reached it and been confronted by Robert's warriors, they were exhausted. Now they were closer to the Killibegs and no one could have ignored the evidence that a large company had recently gone on before them. To the experienced scouts among Ollo's warriors the flattened icy mud slush told a tale of its own. It spoke of a force numbering nearly a thousand, though lightly armed and moving quickly. There were dire mutterings amongst the black-robed Hospitallers.

When Ollo heard about the tracks in the snow he sought the opinion of his senior knights. They didn't want to go on. They argued it was madness to be fighting in this weather against a force so large. Clearly the warriors who'd come this way had been called to the defence of the Killibegs. There was no other explanation.

But Ollo was a determined old bastard. He hadn't terminally tortured three warhorses with his weight on this journey only to be turned around at the last.

'You are Knights of the Hospital!' he bellowed at his senior warriors. 'You are unstoppable! Are you going to allow the heathen, heretic Gaels to frighten you by the force of their numbers? Would you back away from a scrap with these lightly armed barbarians?'

But the older knights among his host were convinced they did not have the numbers to undertake such an attack in the falling snow against a well-defended position.

There's no such thing as a simple siege. Even with a large force of warriors in their retinue there would be no easy attack on the Killibegs. The weather was foul. The ground was unfamiliar. And their supplies were limited. If the rath wasn't taken immediately there would be a terrible loss of life to the cold and to starvation.

And none of them expected that the rath would fall easily. It takes more than a weight of numbers to win a fortress. It takes siege engines, catapults and engineers to dig tunnels under the walls. It takes battering rams and warriors with scaling ladders. Ollo had ladders. But that's all he had.

So he sent scouts ahead to report on the defences of the rath. And when those scouts returned the news was grim.

Even in fine weather with the sun at their back such an assault would have been tricky. That's why there had been a rath on that hill for three thousand years. It was a strong defensive position.

Ollo decided then and there he wouldn't pass this news on to Robert. He'd let the Templar lead the assault and hold his own men back to the very last.

'Let them soften up the fortification. Then we'll have the glory.'

Ollo's force massed at the foot of the hill with their knights dismounted. In front of them stood the men-at-arms, numbering some one hundred. In a long line in front of them were placed two hundred or so crossbowmen and archers.

The oak-knights formed up ahead of the Hospitallers. They didn't want to have anything to do with them. And to be sure the black knights weren't too keen on sharing the field with those strange warriors either.

Robert gave the signal to advance according to a strategy he'd handed down to his company commanders. The archers were to take up positions close to the battlements and send a hail of missiles over the walls.

He was no fool, our Rob. His first objective was to protect the Culdees and other inhabitants of the rath. That's why he'd agreed to lead this force. With him in charge of the attack there was more than a slight chance it would fail. All he had to do was ensure the Normans bungled any attempt to storm the rath until the arrival of the Redcaps.

He knew the Norman archers would probably come under a hail of arrows from above and so prove ineffectual against the warriors on the walls. And he understood that his father, William FitzWilliam, would have prepared his warriors for just such an assault by missiles.

There wouldn't be too many defenders exposed upon the battlements or behind who would be likely to fall to the arrows.

While the archers were moving into position, the men-at-arms were charged with placing ladders against the small gatehouse in preparation for scaling the walls. This tactic of siege warfare was always costly. And it was the lowly men-at-arms who always bore the brunt of that cost. Of course the knights held back. They weren't about to risk their lives on such a dangerous endeavour.Robert had seen the scaling ladders employed many times before in countless conflicts. But it had been successful only in a handful of cases. In every instance the loss of life had been terrible.

He tried to put it out of his mind that these Hospitallers and these Norman oak-knights of Aoife would perish needlessly. He tried to convince himself that what he was doing would preserve the lives of the innocent folk of the Killibegs. But he was a man of conscience and there was a secret part of him that wished every one of these warriors in his force well.

The Hospitaller knights had dismounted and given the reins of their horses over to their squires. They were also trudging up the hill. But they halted out of bowshot from the defenders to wait until the lower gatehouse was taken by the men-at-arms.

A few of them were singing bawdy songs as they stood watching the warriors with ladders on their backs make their way up toward the gatehouse. Robert decided to join them. It had been his original intention to bide his time among the banners and the baggage, watching the battle from the rear where he could keep an eye on developments and ensure any success was short-lived. Aoife had also commanded him to stay out of the fight. She wanted him kept safe among the rearguard.

How it irked him to have to loiter round waiting to see what happened next! He'd never been one to lead from the rear. He considered Aoife's orders. Then he decided that, all things considered, it was probably best he stay put.

But the singing Hospitallers had got under his skin. And he was itching to be among them, if only to keep them quiet. So he turned to the half-dozen bodyguards who'd been assigned to watch over him during the fight.

'We're going forward!' he informed them.

The warriors all looked at one another in confusion.

'We've been told to keep you out of the thick of it,' one man protested. 'Aoife commanded us to guard you well and watch the battle from the rear. You're not to be out of our sight for a second.'

'Then you'd better run to keep up with me! I can't fight a siege from back here.'

With that he set off with the six oak-knights following hard on his heels.

'Come back, my lord!' they each cried. 'It's too dangerous! This is folly! Watch for arrows!'

But our Rob paid them no heed. He was determined to give those Hospitallers a piece of his mind about singing filthy songs before the battle. It was unchivalrous in his opinion and it unnerved him that a few of them might have the womenfolk of the Killibegs on their minds.

As he drew up to their company the Hospitallers fell back to let him through. And all the way he ordered them to silence. For the most part they obeyed him, apart from a few who stood close to the front ranks.

These fellows were tough-looking veterans who had obviously seen a few fights in their time. They were being egged on by one very ugly warrior with a scarred face and a gravelled voice. Robert sought him out by the sound of his taunting song until he stood directly behind the brute. Then he reached out to slap a firm hand down upon the Hospitaller's shoulder.

Now it would be true to say that Robert was not a man who usually indulged in thoughts of a prejudiced nature. But you must try to remember that he'd been a member of a military order for some years by that stage. He'd been a Templar. And Knights of the Temple were the sworn enemies of the Hospital. Imagine yourself in Robert's shoes. He's only encountered a very few of the black knights in his time. Guy was one of them.

He'd been filled full of stories about their brutality, their foul treatment of prisoners, their corruption and their arrogance. Some of those stories may have been true, but most of them were exaggerated tales concocted to stir up young Templars to righteous fury against the warrior monks of the rival order.

Something else may have contributed to Robert's outrage. Robert had always believed that anger was a terrible force which should be avoided at all costs. But of course the more you attempt to deny or suppress an emotion the more likely it is to sneak up behind you and bite you hard on the backside. And that's what happened to Robert in the very instant he laid his gloved hand on the Hospitaller.

Years of unexpressed anger, resentment and frustration erupted from his depths. It was as if this warrior before him personified everything that was evil in the world. And Robert wasn't going to let him get away with it.

'Be quiet!' the knight commanded. 'Silence!'

The Hospitaller spun around and flicked Robert's hand from his shoulder and frowned.

'What's the matter with you? We're only singing a song.'

That must have been too much for Robert. Suddenly all the constraints of his life were gone, as if he was a ship cut free from its anchor in a mighty storm. Before the Hospitaller had a chance to raise a hand in his own defence Robert raised his fist and thumped the man in the face.

The warrior fell backwards in a crumpled heap, as much surprised as injured. Then Robert really lost control. While the defenceless fellow lay cowering on the ground our Rob laid into him with fist and boot, screaming his frustration as the warrior refused to fight back.

It took all six of his bodyguard to haul him away from the Hospitaller and it was a good while before Robert had calmed down enough to realise what he'd done. But he didn't have the opportunity to indulge in any shame.

Just then a flaming trail soared into the air to the right flank of his force. It described a graceful arc which ended somewhere on the other side of the walls. His archers were sending flaming arrows into the Killibegs.

'Who gave the order to use fire?' Robert screamed. 'Who gave the order?'

The Hospitallers fell back before his rage, each one unwilling to be the next victim of his displeasure.

'Who commanded that fire be sent into the rath?' he shrieked.

Still no one replied. The warriors just kept their distance, staring with wide eyes at his battle fury.

'It will cease! Or I'll have the skin of every one of you flayed off you while you stand before me.'

I'd have to say that if I'd encountered Rob at that moment I might not have recognised him. But that's the way with anger. If you don't give it expression when it arises in you, then it festers and boils deep within you until one day it simply explodes like barrel of lamp oil that's been put to the torch.

It's something I've never understood about the Normans, and the English too for that matter. They're all prone to holding down the ravages of anger within themselves so that no one knows they suffer from it.

Among our folk anger is spent quickly, often with such intensity that it can scare the wits out of those it's aimed at. But then it's over and done with. Gone. And everyone is free to sit down together to work out a solution to the problem that caused all the trouble in the first place.

Saxons and Normans tend to cling to foolish notions of what is right and proper. I think it's their greatest weakness. Indeed, it's why they so easily lose the respect of our folk. We simply can't take a man seriously who's frightened to express his own outrage. We can't abide anyone who insists on believing they aren't capable of anger or that it's a sin to experience certain intensities of passion.

Everyone is capable of anger, my dear. And don't you let anyone ever try to convince you otherwise. It's just how you choose to express it that makes the difference.

So if Robert had been riled by the Hospitallers' singing he was more so now the archers were shooting flaming arrows into the rath without leave from him. They were a good three hundred paces away along the side of the hill to the right flank. It would be hard going to reach them but he had no choice if he wanted to stop the hail of fire.

It was at moments like those Lom Dubh was wont to appear, just when he was most needed. And, my dear, that's what he did on this occasion. The great raven swooped in close over the Hospitallers, screeching loudly so that it was all the knights could do not to fall back or drop to the ground in fear of him.

He landed a short distance from Robert with a mighty sweep of wings. A few brave souls among the Normans waved their torches at him but Lom wasn't frightened off easily. With talon, tail and wingtip he knocked aside any warrior who got too close to him.

'What do you think you're doing, my lad?' the raven cawed with disgust. 'Have you become one of these heathen? You can't set fire to this rath. If it burns down there won't be any

247

survivors! Would you set fire to the defenders rather than face them eye to eye? That smacks of cowardice! And tell me, what use is the fortification if it's nothing but ashes?'

'Fly to the archers!' Robert cried out. 'I gave no order for fire. You must stop them!'

Lom clicked his beak in reply, then he jumped skyward and was gone. Robert didn't waste a moment. His mind was made up. Even if it should cost him his life he wasn't going to let these Normans break into the Killibegs. He knew the Culdees depended on him for their survival. He could not let them down.

Of course the folk of the Killibegs weren't his only consideration here. His stomach turned to think of what awful crimes Ollo's men might perpetrate if they gained access to the fortification.

And that's to say nothing of Aoife's treacherous plan. She'd sent the oak-knights into battle with the promise they'd win their freedom. But in truth they were doomed. She was ready to sacrifice their lives without the slightest hesitation.

As he was looking across the battlefield to reassess his strategy Lom Dubh returned to his side.

'What sort of a commander are you?' the raven shrieked. 'Can't you even control your own warriors?'

Our Rob didn't take the slightest bit of notice. He was busy in his own mind working out a way to turn the tide of this fight without too much bloodshed.

'What are you doing, young man? I thought you were given a task to perform by your queen. What is keeping you from it?'

'Summon the oak-knights to me,' Robert ordered. 'Muster them across the path. I'm not waiting any longer for this battle to come to us.'

'That's more like it!' Lom shrieked in joy. 'Now we'll have ourselves a fight worth remembering.'

Then he was gone again. By the time he returned the oak-warriors of Aoife were already approaching the Hospitaller position. And the black-clad knights were none too happy about it either. They saw the decrepit state of the weapons, armour and apparel of the oak-knights.

The oak-warriors looked as though they'd stepped out from some story of the Norman conquest of England. Their gear was so ancient you might have thought they'd all posed for the artists who wove the great tapestry of Bayeaux. Their presence unnerved the warrior-monks and set them to muttering about devilry, dæmons and desertion.

'Stand to your ground!' Robert commanded the Hospitallers. 'If one man among you leaves this field I'll have you all cut down by the oak-knights. Do not try me with this. I will not hesitate to give the command and they will not baulk at carrying it out.'

'What are you going to do?' Lom Dubh pressed. 'You can't stand your war host here at the gates waiting for action to come to you. The only thing that will arrive is a hail of Culdee arrows.'

Almost as if Lom had given the order himself with those words, a hail of arrows fell down upon the Normans then. The greater part of the volley fell short but a dozen men were wounded and several killed outright.

'Move your warriors!' the raven insisted. 'They cannot stand here under the hail with bowshot.'

But Robert did not listen. He pushed his way through the Hospitallers until he reached the ranks of the oak-knights. Then he called them in close with a wave of his hand. When they were packed in tightly to listen to him he silently thanked Aoife that the wind had dropped and the snow had ceased.

'Oak-knights! We have a task to perform. Aoife has given you her word that you will be freed from your enchantment if you do her bidding.'

The old Norman knights were silent and sullen.

'Oak-knights. I call on you to follow my commands no matter how strange they may seem to you.'

'You are Aoife's man!' one of them shouted out. 'What choice do we have but to follow you? Any man among us who broke ranks would have little to look forward to but an eternity trapped in the form of a tree.'

'I command Aoife's hosts. But I am not Aoife's man.'

The oak-knights laughed. A thousand derisive voices were raised against Robert. But it was only a short while before they settled down again and one of their number spoke.

'You are a madman if you think you can stand up to her. We can all see it in your eyes. You would dare to go against her wishes!'

'Fool!' the oak-knights called, and, 'Impudent untried boy!' When they'd settled again Robert spoke up.

'You have each stood up to Aoife and been defeated.' The knights hummed agreement. 'That's the way it often is both in this world and the Other. Wherever one man alone stands up to bullying he will risk to be knocked down. But you are a thousand. And there are three hundred Hospitallers here who would back you up with another one hundred of their men-at-arms and two hundred archers.'

'You know not what you ask of us!' called one oak-knight.

'I know that Aoife would sacrifice your lives for her cause. Once you have breached this rath, as you surely will, she plans to send in her Redcaps to finish you all off. Thus she will firm her reputation by saving the Killibegs from the Normans invaders. And in this way she will win the gratitude of the Irish folk and rid herself of you interlopers in one sweep of her hand.'

A wave of outrage passed through the oak-knights. They'd all seen what the Redcaps could do. They didn't have to be told what would become of them if those warriors were set loose on them.

'How do you know this? Who told you of this plan?'

'Aoife commanded me to lead the Redcaps against you. I am to turn against you just as your victory seems sure.'

There was a terrible shout as each oak-knight vented his outrage at her betrayal. Aoife had promised any man among them who survived the battle would be spared the fate of the eternal oakness. Now her words took on a different slant. None of them were intended to survive at all.

'How do we know we can trust you?' one among them called out. 'How do we know you won't betray us?'

'You cannot be certain of that. But what I have told you is the truth and I am offering you an honourable way out. I am offering you an opportunity to face the foe with dignity and to show your defiance to Aoife. If you each stand alone you will be defeated. She is too powerful. But if you will stand together you may be able to face her down. You might just gain your freedom from her enchantment and avoid the slaughter she has planned for you.'

'That's not much of a choice, is it?' the same warrior cried back.

'But at least it's a choice you are free to make. If you are trapped in the form of a tree you will have no say in the matter. If you lose your lives to the Redcaps you will have no choices left to you.'

'What would you have us do?' they asked all at once.

'Let's give Aoife a scare.'

There was an almighty cheer from the oak-knights. This was more than simply an empty gesture of chivalry, it was a rebellion against tyranny.

'If the Redcaps win the field against you this night, do you think Aoife will be any more lenient on the Irish than she has been on you? She will place them under her yoke forever more.'

'What are the Irish to us?' the oak-knights muttered. 'They're no more than savages!'

251

'Yet they did not venture into your forests to cut you down,' Rob reminded them. 'How many of you have fallen to the axe?'

There was a grumbled general agreement.

'If this country had been in the hands of Norman folk, how many of you would be standing here now? How many would be boat-boards and barrels?'

Again there was a grudging acknowledgment that he spoke the truth. There would have been very few of them still alive if the land had been in Norman control.

'You owe a debt of gratitude to the Irish,' he went on, but of course that didn't go down too well.

Even a hundred years trapped in the form of an oak won't heal some men of their prejudices.

'You must summon the will to stand on your own feet and seek vengeance for what was done to you,' Robert continued, appealing to the darker side of the Norman character. 'Vengeance is the key. Only vengeance will thrown open the padlocks of your hearts.'

Wasn't that a clever thing for Robert to say? Devious it was. Out of character, you might argue. I reckon his words pointed to his darker side. And they struck a sweet chord with every oak-warrior, you can be sure.

'Wouldn't you rather fight with what strength you have to foil Aoife's ambitions than to fall to the weapons of her warriors like wheat before the sickle? Are you men? Are you alive?'

'Aye!' they replied, solemnly, as one.

'Then heal yourselves. Let the sword be your salve. And if the Redcaps come, then take their heads off. Think of them as nothing but crimson poppy flowers. Mow them down with your hatred.'

That was enough for the oak-knights. There was pandemonium as they each let fly their own opinions on the situation and spoke out against the Queen of the Night, swearing, cursing and shouting their taunts to her Redcaps.

But as was his habit Lom Dubh flew back in with a great flapping of wings so that the oak-warriors parted to give him room. He'd been listening in of course. Not much escapes his notice when he has a mind to find something out. And he was appalled at what he'd heard.

'You have all sworn oaths to Aoife. Do you Normans have no honour? Are you all cowards?'

'Leave this place, Lom Dubh,' Robert shouted back at him. 'These men will not fight for Aoife. Nor will they help her attain her aspirations at the cost of their own lives. They are not food for carrion.'

'I had such high hopes for you, Robert,' the raven said. 'I thought what a wonderful High-King you'd make. But all you Normans are nothing but bark-splitters and bough-strippers. Your talk is treacherous and your tongues are fickle with the truth.'

'My intentions are true,' the white knight countered. 'It is Aoife who is false. She has offered these men hope where there is none. She has granted them life with one hand yet she would take it away with the other.'

'You saved my life,' Lom pleaded. 'You brought me out of the prison where I had been placed by my brother. How could you do such a thing and yet have such a treacherous heart?'

'My heart is not treacherous. My heart is true.'

'All your life you've sought the honour of a quest. Would you betray the queen who bestowed upon you the quest you so earnestly desired? Would you raise your hand against the woman who has offered to free us all from the bonds of our slavery?'

'My hand is true.'

'You speak of hand, heart and thought,' Lom sobbed. 'But you are our hope. You can help my sister to become a goddess. And when she has attained that status she has promised to free me from this feathered prison wherein I dwell. Aoife and I have nurtured you all your long life. She has watched over you. I have kept you under the protection of my wings. What will you do without us? What will we do without you? You must strive with all your will to do as she commands. You must pass this test!'

'Fly off to Aoife,' Rob demanded. 'And tell her the oak-knights are standing at the foot of the Rath of the Killibegs. They will go no further. If she wants to send her Redcaps to us we will gladly receive them with open arms.'

Then he swallowed hard as he took in everything the raven had just said. Suddenly everything was clear to him. In those few moments the riddle of his life was solved and Lom Dubh had revealed the answer to him.

'I have chosen my destiny,' Rob declared. 'I am done with you and your conniving comrades. Your conspiracy is at an end.'

Lom didn't wait to be told twice. He spread his wings and was off before Robert had even finished speaking. But he called back over his shoulder as he flew.

'You'll live to regret this decision, Robert FitzWilliam. But if I know Aoife, you won't live very long.'

hammer and anvil

om Dubh was hardly out of sight before Robert began to lose heart. Although he'd won over the thousand oak-knights, he hadn't counted on Ollo's further interference.

The bishop appeared mounted on a struggling horse, pushing the poor creature through the crowd of knights.

'What's the delay?' he bellowed as soon as he caught sight of Robert. 'I thought you said your warriors would lead the assault! Why are you all standing round here waiting to be picked off by archers?'

'I'm giving the orders, your Grace,' Robert replied.

'Not any longer!' Ollo decided. 'You've wasted too much precious time. Throw these men into the attack or I'll have my Hospitallers drive them forward at the point of the sword.'

The oak-knights growled as one and began pelting Ollo with snow.

'Call them off!' he demanded. 'I will not tolerate such insolence!'

Robert hesitated. It was clear the oak-knights were ready for a scrap and Ollo had blundered into their path at the wrong moment. In a matter of moments things could turn very nasty indeed.

So it was a great relief to him when he heard the noise of war trumpets. The ringing blast of the horns caught the attention of the oak-knights as well. They immediately stopped venturing their fury on the bishop and turned to Robert for guidance. Of course he was no more the wiser than any of them but he knew he had to act quickly if he wanted to save the situation.

'Form a shield wall!' he ordered.

In moments the entire company of oak-knights began organising themselves into a formation ready to repel attack. Warriors with long spears stood beside those who carried swords. And every man among them held his shield before him so that it overlapped with the man on either side.

Ollo and his horse were ejected from the formation very quickly. Outraged and still cursing the ragged rabble, the bishop rode off as quickly as his overburdened horse could carry him to a spot further down the hill where his Hospitallers were also forming into a defensive square. It was only a few seconds later that the first of the Hospitaller archers ran headlong into the oak-knights and were allowed to seek shelter within their formation. They were shouting about being chased by warriors with sickles and red hats, so naturally Robert immediately feared the worst.

But his oak-knights didn't flinch. They'd probably all realised it would come to this sooner or later. To a man they stiffened their resolve.

Reports about the Redcaps filtered through to Robert in the centre of the square but he didn't want to believe what he was told. He thought that Aoife must have had these troops waiting nearby to fall on the oak-knights at the first opportunity.

Our Rob was desperate to find out which direction the attack was coming from. But locked within the formation he could see nothing. He pushed his way to where some of the archers had crashed into the shield wall in their hasty retreat.

Most of the bowmen had taken up positions at intervals along the front rank where they'd be able to shoot their missiles into the advancing Redcaps but still be able to fall back behind the shields when the fighting turned hand-to-hand.

By the time Robert reached the front he could see the attackers were already running in full flight toward the formation. Their trumpeters were blowing short sharp bursts into their instruments as the wild warriors ran on with sickle or sword raised high.

'Redcaps!' Robert cried out, half in despair, half in utter disappointment.

Then he realised his every word could make the difference between fight or falter for the oak-knights. They were looking to him for guidance, a steady heart and a strong will.

'Stand your ground! Make ready to take heads!'

The archers were shooting into the midst of the enemy now. The Sen Erainn would have been no less than three hundred paces away on the side of the hill. And they were falling, both wounded and dead, to the arrows.

Robert must have noticed that the injured Redcaps didn't stand up again once they fell. He must have seen warriors rolling about on the ground in agony. But in the confusion, fear and fury of the impending fight it simply didn't cross his mind that these warriors could have been anything but immortals.

And even if it had struck him as strange he wouldn't have had a chance to consider the implications. It just didn't strike him as possible that these folk could have been acting in defence of the Killibegs. There was no doubt but that they were Aoife's folk.

Behind him he heard another blast of trumpets and he realised his defensive square was being attacked on both sides. This tactic was known as the hammer and the anvil. It was an attack on two sides that had the potential to hammer the life out of any defence. And in this instance it was doubly effective. For the attackers had suddenly been transformed into defenders.

Such a bold move could easily have cost the Sen Erainn many of their finest warriors. But the oak-knights had been surprised.

It crossed Robert's mind that he could stop the carnage by simply stepping out in front of the line. If he commanded the Redcaps to lay down their arms, they might just do it. But he suspected they would not follow his commands until all the oak-knights had been slaughtered. That's what Aoife would have told them they had to do.

So instead he drew his sword from its scabbard and lowered the beak of his helm down over his face. The very moment Órán was free from the sheath Robert was bathed in an unearthly red glow. Even Robert was taken aback just a little.

'Is that absolutely necessary?' the knight asked the Frightener.

'It's just an added touch to liven things up a bit. Don't you approve?'

'You're scaring my warriors. I don't want them deserting the field in panic.'

'Sorry. Perhaps you're right. I'll tone it down a bit.'

The red glow diminished ever so slightly. But it wasn't enough to settle the oak-knights who saw him. Many tried to step back away in awe at the transformation.

The Sen Erainn directly in front of him screamed with terror. Some threw down their swords or sickles and landed on their knees in the snow to beg for mercy. Others simply pushed their way to either side to avoid coming into contact with this fearful knight of the glowing blade.

Don't forget that Órán was a Frightener. And he wasn't a newcomer to his vocation. He was an old hand at terror. A great semicircle cleared around Robert as he raised his weapon high.

In the next instant the archers pushed their way back through the defensive line and the wall of shields locked behind them. Then spears were levelled to bear the brunt of the attack as Robert braced himself for the impact of the enemy warriors barrelling down on top of him.

The clash was terrible to behold. In the depths of the storage cellars we all plainly heard it. An awful, sickening, gut-wrenching crash was immediately followed by the battle cry of the Sen Erainn: a low short, sharp word that sounded like, 'Huh!'

Then the noise was not so intense but the ring of swords, spears and sickles against armour, shield and flesh was a great gaggle of confusion. I recall that I nearly deserted my post to take a look at what was happening when I heard that great din. But Stronghold held me back. It was too late for us to go back to the walls.

Down on the slopes of the hill Robert had already cut down four of the Sen Erainn. When they did not rise up again he started to wonder what was wrong. These folk were certainly not immortals.

After the initial clash the fight soon degenerated into a desperate push of shield against shield with the occasional spear-thrust or sickle-sweep to take advantage of a gap in the defences.

Robert cleared himself a path through the warriors to his rear, hoping to get a glimpse of the attack that had fallen on the other side of the square. Of course he didn't stand a chance of seeing anything. He was caught up in the press of warriors and soon locked in among their ranks, pressed tight beside his fellow knights.

Trumpets sounded again to front and rear. In a few seconds the great crush of warriors was relieved and there was room to move. Naturally Robert knew what was happening. This was the oldest trick of the battlefield. The enemy had sounded the withdrawal. They were falling back in retreat on both sides of the square. And they were making off in such apparent disorder that the oak-knights would not be able to resist the temptation to follow on after them, jubilant that they had driven their foes into a panic.

'Stand your ground!' Robert shouted. 'Hold your positions! Do not follow them!'

But his voice was lost in the victorious hooting cries of the oak-knights as their tight defensive formation disintegrated like a handful of feathers scattered in the breeze. He shouted. He pleaded. He cursed them till his voice was hoarse from the effort, but there was nothing he could do.

The oak-knights smelled victory in the wind. They'd had a hundred years, some of them, in which to pent up their anger at Aoife. Now the Redcaps seemed to be falling before them like as many trees before the axeman's stroke. And they weren't about to let the enemy escape the field of battle in one piece.

The withdrawal was a masterstroke on the part of the Sen Erainn chieftains. After an awe-inspiring clash of arms they'd managed to call back their warriors in good order with minimal confusion or casualties. The lightly armed, swift-footed Sen Erainn retreated around to either side of the hill, and because they knew the ground, having just crossed it in the dark, and they had left torches stuck in the snow to light the way, they outran the jubilant oak-warriors.

As they retreated they took with them the torches. In no time at all the poor Normans were foundering in the snow, slipping and sliding on the trampled icy ground, weighed down by their armour.

The Sen Erainn were not dressed as heavily as the oak-knights and that had worked to their disadvantage in the initial clash. However, now it was proving to be a great boon for they could retreat unhindered by mail coat and helm.

And most importantly of all, the feigned retreat had split the oak-knight battle formation in two. If only the Normans had stood their ground that night they might have suffered less. So many more of them might have lived to tell the tale of the Redcaps who were not immortal.

So effective was the Sen Erainn strategy that the Normans of that company of one thousand did not return to the field that night or the next morning. Their formation was shattered on the slopes of Rath Killibegs where they had to fight uphill after that.

And to their credit most of them struggled on till either they were mortally wounded or fell down upon the snow in exhaustion and pleaded for quarter. I am told, for I only heard second-hand accounts of that part of the battle, that the Sen Erainn showed great respect for their adversaries and wherever quarter was asked it was immediately granted.

While the thousand oak-warriors were off chasing after the Sen Erainn the archers who had fallen back into the defensive square made a break for the ranks of the Hospitallers. Archers rarely wear much armour, so they also seldom charge off after a retreating enemy. The black knights had readied themselves in battle formation but since they had not been attacked by the Sen Erainn they had offered no assistance.

Robert was left alone on the field among the slain and wounded of both his company and the Sen Erainn. He threw off his helm. All he could hear were the cries of those in pain and the whistling of arrows falling from the battlements and towers above. There were torches scattered about still sputtering with the last sparks of life.

Robert sheathed Órán, picked up a light and decided to do what he could for the injured. He had no thought for himself as usual. It wasn't foolishness on his part, you understand. It was simply that he felt responsible for all this carnage, which to some extent he was.

'These warriors aren't Redcaps,' he mumbled to himself as he went round from one to another, offering them each a sip of water or a few words of encouragement. As for his oak-knights, the wounded amongst their number were just as surprised the enemy had proved to be mortal.

Robert could not have seen Bishop Ollo riding round in front of his knights issuing commands. If he had perhaps he might have protested. The next few minutes were a strange blur for our Rob. He wandered about from warrior to warrior and as he looked on the face of each man, either dead or alive, he began to suffer a terrible weight of guilt.

At last he fell down on his knees before the body of one oak-knight who had fallen backwards with a sickle wound across his throat. The eyes of the gruesome corpse were wide open and the mouth poised as if to speak one final word of parting.

'Thou shalt not kill,' Robert muttered as he crossed himself and bowed his head. 'I should have been the one to fall.'

That's just typical of the Normans, even the decent ones like Rob. They all seem to think they're the very centre of the known world. They think everything revolves around their own desires, mistakes, misfortunes and selfish dreams. It is a profoundly foolish way to look at creation but there's no telling some folk.

'If it be thy will, O Lord, send down a punishment upon me,' he prayed earnestly. 'I will take the blow gladly in penance for my sins. I should not have followed that dæmon-woman. I should not have listened to her.'

Well, you know what happens when you wish for it, don't you, my dear? You'll bloody well get it. And that's what happened to Robert.

Ollo was riding around not far off behind his archers. And

he had the thought to finish our Rob once and for all. So he ordered the bowmen to do a very nasty thing indeed. Before they'd set out from Wexford town that old bugger had distributed a very potent poison to his archers. It was made from the vermilion death-sleep berries of which I'm sure you've heard. Some call it 'whisper from the grave'. Others name it 'soul-beckon'. Whatever you call it you'll know that if the point of an arrow is soaked in the juice of that plant it will bring death to anyone it so much as scratches.

Ollo got his bowmen to dip their arrows. Then he directed them to shoot a rain of missiles down upon the spot where Robert had last been seen before he knelt down. With the poor visibility due to darkness and snow they couldn't be certain it was him kneeling there. Anyway Ollo was determined this fellow of the white tunic wasn't going to leave the battlefield alive.

No sooner had Rob finished his reprehensibly self-indulgent prayer than he noticed a familiar whistling sound coming in from somewhere behind him. He didn't have a chance to turn around before an arrow struck him hard in the left shoulder.

A thumping crunch was all he heard, as if someone had hit him with a heavy mace. He fell forward on to his knees. His vision blurred with tears and he had trouble breathing.

It was a barbed missile with a head the shape of a triangle so it couldn't be withdrawn easily. And the edge had been sharpened so that when it found the gap in the neck of Robert's mail coat it cut deep. Since it had been shot from nearby, the force of the blow was all the more devastating.

Robert FitzWilliam felt a terrible pain in his shoulder and he probably thought his life was ended. That's why he let himself fall forward across the body of the dead oak-knight.

And that's why he spoke a few final words to his God.

'Thank you, Lord. Forgive me. Bring me back to your bosom again.'

Then he closed his eyes without so much as a squeal of pain or a shiver of discomfort. In a very short while the severe cold had lulled him into a death sleep such as few men ever experience and afterwards live to speak of.

REDCAPS

While Robert lay among the slain, Bishop Ollo was rallying his troops. And he was having a very hard time convincing them to advance. You may recall that the men-at-arms had been sent forward with ladders ready to scale the walls of the gatehouse.

They had reached their objective by then and were cowering around the walls trying to avoid the unwanted attention of the archers William had placed on the battlements. Ollo screamed, he bellowed and at last he threatened his warriors.

Men-at-arms aren't trained as highly as knights. They aren't as fanatical as warrior monks. So it's no easy matter to get them to throw their lives away. But you'd expect better of the Knights of the Hospital. And so did Ollo. The truth is that the biting, unseasonal snow, the dark night and the forced march had all taken their toll on the bishop's warriors.

Eventually, though fearing for their mortal souls, the Hospitallers moved slowly forward to take up positions at the foot of the ladders. Ollo went with them, kicking his horse to goad it on until it slipped its footing and broke a leg tumbling over in the snow. He abandoned the poor screaming animal, then paid no more heed to it than he might have an ant trod underfoot in the monastic gardens.

The arrows were raining down now from the walls so Ollo commanded his surviving bowmen to take up positions to the north flank of the lower gate. From there he hoped they might be able to bring down enough arrows on the enemy archers to distract them from the main attack.

The tactic seemed to do the trick. As soon as the Gaelic bowmen on the walls came under attack they concentrated their arrow-fall back on the Norman archers. Ollo's knights were free to scale the walls almost entirely unhindered. So they continued their climb up the hill toward the ladders, a slow march in their heavy mail coats.

Up in the north tower of the rath William FitzWilliam was suffering a deep sense of foreboding. He'd not been able to see clearly everything that had happened between the Sen Erainn and the oak-knights. But he'd heard, as we all had, the awful clash of arms and the sounds of retreat and pursuit which followed on after.

He was glad the snow and the wind had dropped. Now he could just make out what was happening on the battlements of the gatehouse. With rising concern Will watched the bowmen change their focus of attention from the warriors in front of them to the archers at their left.

He was an old warrior himself. He knew this little trick well enough. So he dispatched a messenger down to the gatehouse to order the bowmen to direct their arrows to the advancing enemy. Minutes passed by but it seemed his command had not reached the archers. So William took a difficult decision.

He decided to go down to the gatehouse himself. Once the decision was made he was quick about it. He turned to Caoimhin and Srón.

'You take command here. Soon you will see my bowmen fall back. You will hold firm on this wall. I want you to retain this position no matter what.'

Then he bowed to them both and hurried down the ladder which led into the tower interior. Moments later he was off along the southern battlement as quick as his old legs could carry him. The enemy archers couldn't see him from there so he was unmolested by them on his way to the gate.

Along the way he realised what had become of his orders and his messenger. The man's body lay on the stones below with an arrow through his neck. He'd obviously taken the north wall and been targeted by the enemy.

It was a relatively easy progress down to the gatehouse. At intervals there were steep steps which took old Will down a level along the way until he reached the heavy oak door which led to the tower.

He leaned against it to catch his breath as he looked back along the way he'd come. He suddenly realised it would be no easy matter for him to make his way back to the tower.

'I'm an old fool,' he told himself. 'And I've got myself into some deep trouble now.'

He pushed against the door. But it wouldn't budge. It was bolted from the inside. He banged against it with his fists. When that didn't do the trick he took up the axe he carried and struck it hard into the timber.

In seconds the door opened just enough for an archer to point his bow through the crack. Will ducked aside as the arrow missed him. Then he pushed with all his might against the door, forcing his way into the gatehouse.

As soon as he was inside he grabbed the young bowman by the hair.

'It's me!' he shouted. 'Lord William. 'Get back to your post!'

The young man did as he was told. Will bolted the door behind him again before he went out on to the gatehouse battlements to issue his orders. When he burst out into the cold air he could hardly believe the scene which was presented to him.

From that vantage point he was better able to see what had become of the oak-knights and the Redcaps. As soon as he

267

directed the archers to shoot at the footmen below Will got the sergeant of bowmen to report all he had witnessed of the fight so far.

He searched to the north and south for any sign of the Sen Erainn or their enemies. He could hear the far-off clash of arms but he could not see any signs of battle whatsoever.

Below him the Hospitallers, dressed in their distinctive black livery, were advancing up the path toward the gatehouse, their shields held above them to protect them from bowshot.

It was clear they would soon be scaling the walls. And since there were no warriors on the gatehouse, only bowmen, William had to make the difficult decision whether to abandon this part of the wall and fall back to the rath.

He hesitated as long as he thought he could. Then he waited a little longer. Every arrow shaft that left the battlements meant possibly one less enemy warrior to be dealt with inside the walls.

The Hospitallers were perilously close when Lord Will finally lifted his axe high in the air to give the order. But the words never left his mouth. At the very instant he was about to command the bowmen to retreat an incredible thing happened. It was such an unusual occurrence that Will simply forgot everything else that was on his mind and watched wide-eyed.

It must have been three and a half hours after midnight by then. The clouds had covered the moon entirely for a long while, shrouding the world in darkness. But just then they parted and the silver disk was visible in its full round form hanging high in the northern sky like a great silver penny. The sky transformed to a wild vibrant blue, perhaps coloured by the storm clouds that had brought the blizzard in.

Then the snow started to melt upon the stones of the battlement. Down on the slopes of the hill it seemed as if the grass had started to grow and the flowers of the fields had suddenly bloomed in a miraculous Otherworldly display. That much was Aoife's doing.

The bowmen on the walls looked straight into the face of the moon in wonder as they stopped shooting. The light was so bright they had to shield their eyes. William simply squinted as the silvery rays bathed his face in their soft nurturing light.

He smiled. Then he laughed. Many of the bowmen did the same. Their hearts sang as their spirits rose. Surely this was a miraculous sign from God. Surely the battle was theirs and the fight was ended.

As the hillside was lit up, the carnage of the fight between the Sen Erainn and the oak-knights was revealed in its full horror. Corpses lay strewn in a wide arc around the hill where warriors had fallen in the charge, the clash or the retreat.

The Hospitallers stopped in their tracks, confused, terrified or simply dismayed at the unexpected reappearance of the moonlight and the sudden melting of the snows. Many refused to go on up the hill, though Ollo swore to personally flog every one of them to within an inch of their lives if they did not obey the order to attack.

William must have been the first to notice the long ranks of warriors standing at the foot of the hill behind the Hospitallers. They wore bright red caps identical to those the Sen Erainn had been wearing. But they were a fiercer looking bunch.

Indeed, William had never laid eyes on such a terrifying force of warriors in all his life. There were three hundred of them, he guessed. And that was more than enough immortals to deal with the Normans and overrun Rath Killibegs completely.

One thing came to the old man's mind and one thing alone.

'There is nothing so unnerving as the breathless trembling silence that strangles all sound in the anxious hour before battle. Warriors take up their positions with no words twixt one another. The field is green and ready to accept a generous libation of youthful blood. There are those who say, "What folly is fighting!" or "How wasteful is war!" but the Earth, our mother, passes no judgement on her children. She silently watches our petty strife and at day's end she gathers up the slain to her bosom once again.'

He looked down on the assembled Redcaps with resignation. He realised these were probably the closing moments of his life. Yet with only the slightest hint of regret in his voice he issued a command to the bowmen stationed on the battlements.

'Fall back to the towers! Fall back!'

Bishop Ollo had noticed the Redcap force standing at the rear of his knights. Of course he had no idea who these folk were. But he'd watched the attack of the Sen Erainn. And they were indistinguishable from these warriors. So Ollo prepared to receive their charge. He gave the order for the Hospitallers to fall into a crescent formation known as the horns. This was a favourite move of the Hospitallers. Like many other ideas and skills of that age the horns had been learned from the Saracens. It was a tried and true tactic. The left and right flanks of the company jutted out ahead of the rest of their comrades so they resembled the horns of a bull.

His one hundred men-at-arms were still up at the walls so he sent a knight up the hill to fetch them down. Then he ordered the main force of the formation to hold back in the widest part of the crescent which was also the furthest away from the enemy.

When a foe charged into this formation they tended to be confused by the shape of the company and end up attacking at the centre. Then the flanks encircled them completely in a pincer, which usually ended the hopes of any enemy.

Ollo had employed this tactic on many occasions and it had never failed him. His warriors were confident, well drilled and disciplined, *even if they were tired and reluctant to attack the fortress.* This was the kind of battle they preferred. Out in the open facing their enemies down was better by far than trying to reach an opponent who was skulking behind fortress walls.

They were a force to be reckoned with and they knew it. Besides the which, these Normans didn't have much more than contempt for the naïve Irish of which these Redcaps simply seemed to be the most savage they'd encountered so far.

I can't tell you how unnerved the Hospitallers were at the return of the moon or the melting of the snow. They were all professional warriors. So my best guess is they simply ignored the strangeness of the situation and went about doing their jobs as best they could. They certainly weren't going to break ranks over such mysterious events.

'The works of the Devil must be resisted!' Ollo reassured them. 'Stand firm in the face of evil and you will triumph!'

He was a great one for keeping the warriors' spirits up, our Ollo. He always knew exactly what to say. That is until he saw a woman step out in front of the Redcaps. That left him at a loss for comment, I can tell you.

For this battle Aoife had chosen a very tasteful dark green cloak edged with fine silver embroidery in the pattern of two intricately intertwined serpents. Beneath this she wore a sparkling silver mail tunic that might have been woven out of the moonlight. This reached to her knees. The tunic she wore under that was a very rich burgundy edged again with silver and black in a raven motif.

Her boots were black to the knee and she wore green riding britches where any other woman might have worn a skirt. Her long red hair fell freely about her shoulders and she leaned on the long shaft of a spear.

'A woman?' Ollo finally managed to mumble in shock. 'Is there no end to the barbarity of these heathen Irish?'

LANFRANC

Poor old Ollo was looking at none other than Aoife, the Queen of the Night herself. Of course he had no way of knowing who she was. Even if he had, he probably wouldn't have guessed that her appearance would herald his own spectacular demise.

His knights were already up the hill out of earshot, so the bishop ordered his trumpeter to blow a signal to fall back into defensive positions. The short sharp blasts rang out through the brightly lit night and his knights turned around to look down the hill at Ollo in frustration.

Every one of them grumbled as he abandoned the arduous ascent to the top of the path. At least the going was easier downhill. But the call to fall back had dampened their spirits. They'd all watched impotently as the oak-knights clashed with the enemy. How they'd all itched to get amongst the foes!

Aoife was in no hurry to advance her Redcaps. She was more than happy to let the Norman bishop array his forces in any battle order he wished. There was no way they'd have a chance of beating her host. It took a while for the knights to form into a square. But once they had, they settled into a defensive role and waited patiently for the attack.

Aoife raised her arms in the air then let them drop to her sides. The next thing Ollo noticed was that the Redcaps had set off at a leisurely pace up the hill toward his square. He had to laugh at their audacity. They looked as though they were off on an afternoon stroll through the countryside.

'I'll show them what damage Norman arrows can do to Irish arrogance,' he hissed under his breath.

He gave the order for his archers to dip their arrows in the poison once more. When all was ready they notched them for the attack.

'Ready!' the bishop cried. 'Hold your arrows at the ready!'

The archers shook with the effort to hold back their bowshot. At last, just when it seemed they would not be able to hold on any longer, Ollo gave the command.

'Shoot!'

A forest of deadly missiles sailed across the intervening space as the Redcaps advanced, seemingly undeterred. With awful accuracy the arrows landed all among the enemy, biting deep into their flesh and splitting bone. For a few seconds the whole company of Redcaps halted while those who'd been struck plucked out the darts.

As soon as the arrows had been tossed aside the company set off again as if they'd been struck by little more than snowballs. Ollo frowned, trying to make sense of what he saw. The enemy were three hundred paces away by now and closing with every step.

'Notch arrows!' he commanded, and there was a telling hint of panic in his voice.

His knights were beginning to murmur too. A few stepped back and it looked as though they might all break into a run.

'Stand your ground, you cowardly bastards!' Ollo shrieked. 'The first man among you to run will be roasted up alive for my morning meal!'

Then he turned his attention back to the archers.

'Shoot!'

This time every man among his force watched the arrows fly. Up they went in a graceful trajectory. Then down they fell to strike their targets hard and heavy. The bishop breathed a sigh of relief as the Redcaps halted again. Then he noticed they were once again plucking out arrows from themselves and their comrades. They were much closer now so he could better observe the horrendous wounds the arrows had inflicted. Yet the Redcaps didn't seem to be put off their advance at all.

As soon as the arrows were all removed and tossed aside the company set off again at a steady pace. Ollo swallowed hard. His men faltered. Ollo held them back from retreat by the very force of his will.

'Stand! Stand your ground or you'll find yourselves cowering at the throne of Satan before this night is out. Stand or I'll visit a punishment upon every man among you and your families. Any man who runs while I still have breath in me will suffer torture before I burn him at the stake!'

The Hospitallers knew their man. They'd all seen what this fat bishop was capable of and not a knight among them was willing to be his next victim. Ollo then called the trumpeter to sound a charge. But it wasn't meant for his knights. It was directed at the men-at-arms who'd been waiting at the walls.

Suddenly there was a tremendous cheer as the one hundred who'd been waiting to scale the walls careened down the hill around either side of the square and on to face the Redcaps.

This firmed the hands of the three hundred Hospitaller knights. Any who'd considered retreating earlier now stood their ground, confident the men-at-arms would soften the enemy up before they had to deal with them.

But just as the men-at-arms ran on past the knights, another extraordinary thing happened. Indeed, it was so unexpected that fighters on both sides stopped in their tracks.

Out of nowhere, a huge rock the size of a horse came flying down from above to crash with a huge earth-shattering thump amongst the men-at-arms. Two warriors were crushed into oblivion immediately. Another four were flattened as the rock rolled down the hill a little further.

'What in the name of Heaven was that?' Ollo managed to say.

Out on the road leading up toward the rath Lanfranc de Courcy and his men were already hauling back on the mechanism which wound up their catapult. A great stone that took four men to raise was lifted into place.

Lanfranc himself rode in on his horse as they were ready to let go again.

'That's it!' he cried. 'We hit the bastards!'

His men cheered. They'd been supervising the dragging of this war machine half the night. It was bullocks did the work, but the warriors had a hard job of keeping them to their task.

Lanfranc and his sergeant had followed Ollo's host on horseback as far as the frozen river. From there they'd known for certain that the enemy would not be taking the road. But they'd also ascertained that the Normans were headed for the Killibegs.

So they'd made the decision to bring the catapult in by the road and to ready themselves to dump rocks on the Hospitallers at the first opportunity. It was a bold move and not the least because in taking this stance Lanfranc was taking the side of the Irish against those folk of his own blood.

'Thank God for this moon!' Lanfranc exclaimed. 'We couldn't have asked for a better night!'

'Thank God for this catapult,' Stephen laughed.

'Are you ready to let go again?'

'We're ready. And we're itching for it.'

'Then shoot!'

By the time Ollo realised his company was being assailed by a catapult it was already too late to do very much about it. He couldn't spare any warriors to break off from the main force to deal with the war machine.

Meanwhile his men-at-arms carried on down the hill with less enthusiasm for the fight though they certainly seemed to be running faster. I suppose it gave them some comfort to think they could outrun the falling boulders.

The bishop gave the order for his archers to shoot again but by this time his own men-at-arms were within the fall of the archery. Another boulder came crashing down soon after and this one landed in the very midst of the Redcaps. There must have only been another hundred paces separating the enemy from the charging men-at-arms. The Normans all saw what happened very clearly. After the boulder landed, crushing a couple of the Redcap warriors, their comrades stopped their advance to roll the rock away. The two enemy warriors who'd been squashed under the missile emerged shaking the dust off and laughing with their friends. They'd been scratched and bruised to be sure, but they were essentially unharmed.

That changed the wind for the men-at-arms. Most of them stopped charging toward the enemy and turned to run. The knights began teetering again.

'These are dæmons which may only be defeated by gallant Christian knights!' the bishop declared. 'If you run they will destroy you. If you stand the victory will be yours.'

But the Redcaps kept on coming, heedless of his words. Ollo's knights broke out into a collective sweat, caught between a company made up of what seemed to be the Devil's own minions and a commander who was certainly Satan's bedfellow. Immobilised by fear, they could do nothing but stand and await their doom.

'Who has brought this curse upon us?' Ollo hissed under his breath. 'Who dares to launch a catapult against me?'

Well, he couldn't have guessed it was Lanfranc de Courcy. I don't suppose old Ollo had ever even heard of Lanfranc. But for an unknown, our lad was certainly having an impact, if you'll excuse the pun.

The bishop wasn't going to be put off by falling boulders. He wasn't going to let himself be compromised on the field by a company of devilish dæmons in ridiculous red hats either. These folk were uncivilised barbarians who knew nothing of bedchamber silk. It was his mission to bring them into the fold of the Mother Church so that when he arranged for them to be exterminated they'd have the certainty of a place by the hearth fire in Hell.

'Notch arrows!' he bellowed again and the archers did as they were told, though they knew it was pointless.

'Shoot!'

Off went the hail of missiles soaring over the intervening distance, which by now had diminished to a mere hundred paces from the knights of the Hospital. The men-at-arms were already gone. They'd seen which side their boulders were buttered on and they weren't going to hang around to be spread thinly on the oatcake, if you take my meaning.

The knights watched the arrows strike at their targets. Once again the Redcaps stopped to patiently pull out the offending missiles. And not one of those who was struck, whether through the head, the arms or the chest, evidenced the slightest amount of discomfort.

Ollo was faced with a terrible decision. He knew his warriors would not hold firm against these dæmonic creatures. He could see they'd turn and run and not even their fear of him would be able to prevent it. So he gritted his teeth and prepared to give the order to advance.

I suppose he must have reasoned that at least if they were

running headlong down the hill at the enemy they'd find it harder to turn round to retreat. He told his trumpeter to sound the charge but the man just stared at him in disbelief.

'Sound the bloody charge!'

The poor fellow put the trumpet to his lips and he was so shaky the only noise that came out was a feeble sound like a cow passing wind. But he soon gathered his composure and managed to play a blast of the short tune everyone recognised as the command to charge.

The knights turned to look at their bishop. Most of them were too frightened to set off at this enemy. And none of them wanted to believe their bishop would issue such an insane command.

When the call to charge ended and they hadn't moved Ollo ordered it to be played again. Once more the trumpeter put the instrument to his mouth. This time he was pleased with himself. He had a look on his face when he'd finished which said that trumpet call could well have been his best performance ever. But no one had moved and the Redcaps were steadily trudging ever closer up the hill.

'I'll curse every man among you who doesn't do his duty!' Ollo bellowed. 'I'll take the skinning knife to every mother's son! May the lord strike me down if I don't.'

And of course, true to his nature, the Lord of the Old Testament, the god of fire, brimstone, Earth-drenching floods and pillars of salt answered the invocation. Those knights closest to Ollo stepped back when they saw the boulder sailing down from on high. But Bishop Ollo didn't see it till it was far too late.

The great rock landed directly on top of him, giving him what I suppose was the surprise of his life and utterly obliterating him before the entire company of the Knights Hospitaller. There was nothing left of old Ollo to speak of except for his bright red bishop's mitre. Which is odd really when you think about it. There were so many red caps running round that night.

There was one less now. And I guess Ollo's warriors finally stopped fearing him the moment the life was squeezed out of him. They looked to one another with raised brows, wide eyes and slack jaws. Then, conscious that every moment had suddenly become very precious indeed, they scattered to the four winds, throwing off their armour, weapons, shields and, in more than one instance, soiled underwear as they went.

Dragonfly

By the time William, Old Guy and Martin had made it down the stairs from the battlements the north and south towers were sealed. The small force of Sen Erainn warriors who'd accompanied Caoimhin into the rath and some of Rónán's people also had earlier closed the exits to the walls with stones piled against the doors. This left the Redcaps with one way out of the towers and into the fortress.

They didn't come straightaway. There was a tense wait while those Redcaps who had not been drawn off to pursue the fleeing Hospitallers secured the ladders that had been abandoned against the lower walls. In time one hundred and fifty of Aoife's warriors made it to the top of the battlements where William had been standing earlier with his archers.

It wasn't long before they'd charged along the walls into the north and south towers. Then they made their way down the staircases which snaked through the inside of each tower. They easily smashed down the doors at ground level.

By that time Tóraí was already up on the battlements, passing on the orders from William for the warriors stationed along the walls to stay perfectly still. He didn't want them shooting arrows into the advancing Redcaps.

The Seer reached Caoimhin as William, Old Guy and the dozen archers down in front of the main gate were turning to retreat toward the great hall. Sen Erainn bowmen were notching their arrows to draw the enemy off them. Tóraí arrived as the first arrow flew off.

'Don't shoot! Don't let the Redcaps know you're here!'

But it was too late. Several Redcap warriors were struck with barbed arrows from behind. They each immediately plucked the shafts from their bodies as if they'd been no more than thorns. Then Aoife's warriors were torn between pursuing William and his men or charging up on to the walls to slaughter the Sen Erainn.

William saw the danger straightaway. He commanded the archers who accompanied him to throw all their arrows into an attack on the Redcaps, hoping to enrage them. The ploy worked. The Redcaps fell under a rain of missiles which stung them like as many shards of glass falling from the sky, but which did not of course cause any more long-term discomfort than as many leaves falling in the autumn time.

Most of the Redcaps turned their attention back to William and his warriors. They surged forward as Will and his men retreated into the hall and disappeared from the view of those on the walls. While they were retreating into the hall Tóraí had managed to call off the Sen Erainn bowmen.

But three Redcaps had decided to turn their attention to the warriors up on the walls. Armed with the great sickles for which their folk were famous, the three headed up the main staircase to the battlements.

'Shoot them down!' Caoimhin commanded.

At his order ten arrows struck the first Redcap who started up the stairs. He stopped in his tracks, shafts sticking out of his body at odd angles. For a moment it looked as if he might even topple off the stairs and fall down dead as any mortal would surely have done.

But the warrior did not fall. He recovered his breath after a few seconds. Then, enraged by the terrible pain from the arrow wounds, he screamed a mouth-frothing phrase in his own language.

Whatever he said must have been the most terrible kind of curse for it caused the Sen Erainn warriors to recoil in horror of what was to come. They understood the language of the Redcaps for these folk were their distant cousins.

Only Srón and Scodán stood firm at the top of the stairs, their sickles lowered ready to fend off the attacker. Caoimhin snatched a sickle from one of his warriors and took position behind his two friends. All the while he cried out to the Sen Erainn.

'Stand! Stand behind your king!'

By the time the three Redcaps had got to the top of the stairs the fifty Sen Erainn were chanting as one voice.

'Kay-vin Ree-an! Kay-vin Ree-an!'

Which means 'King Caoimhin' in their tongue.

Our lad heard his name shouted in adulation and it raised a tingling sensation on his skin. When he'd first landed on these shores he'd never expected that he'd end up standing here among these fine folk with them speaking his name as a battle cry. Then again, he'd never imagined he'd be called Caoimhin either. You might recall he'd been known as Harold before he came to Ireland.

He looked around at the determined faces of the warriors as they tightened their ranks, and he was so proud to stand with them that he felt his heart would surely burst. But he had no chance to savour the moment.

The first Redcap up the stairs fell backwards, pushed over by Srón and Scodán working together to set him off balance. He couldn't swing his sickle round freely because of all the arrows sticking out of his body.

'Put some shots into the others!' Caoimhin shouted to his archers, realising that the Redcaps were virtually unable to attack if their bodies were encumbered with arrow shafts.

The bowmen did as they were told but the next Redcap was already swinging his sickle round at Scodán before they'd had a chance to shoot at him. The Sen Erainn warrior expertly parried a blow from the Redcap within the curve of his sickle, but as he was recovering from the attack his foot slipped on the top step.

Scodán fell backwards as his knee collapsed under him. He held the long handle of his weapon high as he teetered and that's what saved him from another sweep of the Redcap weapon. But as he fell he dropped the sickle and it clattered to the ground below, near to where the first Redcap was plucking out the last arrow from his chest.

The second Redcap had a dozen arrows in his body now, so it was an easy matter for Srón to get in close enough to force him back down the narrow stairs. He growled at her viciously then rushed forward with bared teeth so that she fell back a step.

That's when Caoimhin saw his opportunity. With a great swing he brought down his sickle hard upon the Redcap. He hadn't aimed his blow well but the flash of the weapon had caused the enemy warrior to relent in his push slightly. He flinched and turned his head just enough so Caoimhin's sickle struck him on the neck.

The Redcap's throat was cut by the blow and he reeled backward. That was just enough time for Srón to raise her own sickle and bring it down with such force that it finished the job. The Redcap's head rolled off his shoulders and down the stairs past his two comrades.

Then the body fell backwards into the arms of the third Redcap who simply fended off the lifeless corpse, tossing it aside so that it landed on top of Scodán's sickle. Now this third monster stepped forward up the stairs and his voice was fearsome as he came.

His eyes were wild with rage at the death of his comrade and it was plain he intended to have his revenge. This ugly fellow wasn't going to be shoved aside as easily as the other. Though he already had four arrows sticking from his chest he rushed forward, ferocious and unstoppable.

In a flash he'd pushed Srón off her feet with the blunt edge of his sickle. She landed hard against the wall of the battlement, the wind knocked out of her. She lay there struggling to breathe as she helplessly watched what happened next.

Caoimhin was overcome with outrage. Gobann had been right about that much. Our lad was more than a little bit interested in Srón. Well, it doesn't do to allow your emotions to get the better of you in battle. Ask any seasoned warrior about the secret of victory and they'll tell you to keep a cool head at all times. Even the most adept of the fighting kind make mistakes in the heat of the moment. But Caoimhin had never wielded a sickle in anger in his entire life. This was his first battle and his first hand-to-hand scrap.

So when the Redcap stepped back to feign a withdrawal the Fisher-King fell for the ruse. Caoimhin strode forward two steps so that he'd get a better swing at his enemy. And that's when the Redcap let his blade touch the ground in front of him. There was fear on the enemy face as his eyes narrowed to tiny slits of fright.

Caoimhin lifted the sickle high ready to bring it down in a broad sweep and he'd never felt so powerful in all his life. It seemed as if no foe would ever be able to withstand him. He felt invincible.

But just as he was about to bring down the blade he heard Srón struggling to make a noise behind him. She hadn't been able to catch her breath yet but she was desperate to get the Fisher-King's attention. Caoimhin frowned.

And in that very instant he saw the Redcap's expression change from fear into a smile as the warrior raised the blade of his own sickle. The point of the weapon struck Caoimhin's unprotected inner thigh, cutting through his britches and deep into his flesh.

Before Caoimhin even had a chance to express his pain the Redcap withdrew the weapon to swing the handle round and strike his opponent in the face. The Fisher-King stumbled backwards a few steps, but he did not fall. The Redcap screamed with delight though the arrows flew at him and his body fairly bristled with them.

Caoimhin regained his balance just as the enemy swung his great sickle round again. But this time the razor-sharp leading edge of the weapon was sweeping straight at our lad's shoulders.

Only a warrior who has known battle can truly understand how the passing moments transform during a fight. They drag out so that each breath seems to take an age to draw in and another long while to exhale. Every detail of the moment is indelibly etched into the mind of one who witnesses such a distortion of the world and a slowing of the normal state of time.

That strange warrior experience overwhelmed Caoimhin as he leaned back as far as he could to escape the blow. In his desperation he twisted his body slightly to the right, hoping to avoid the sharp slice of the sickle. At this angle the sickle missed his neck but the point cut deep into his chest, slashing through the mail coat as easily as if it had been made of sunflower stalks.

Caoimhin's face was spattered with blood. The Redcap withdrew his weapon expertly then punched his opponent three times hard in the forehead with the blunt edge of the curve.

From that moment Caoimhin knew nothing but pain as his legs turned to curd-water and the life started draining out of him. The moments were slowing even more so that he couldn't understand why he wasn't already lying flat upon the ground. More arrows hit the Redcap and he was set upon from behind by sickle-bearing Sen Erainn. They shouted their battle cry above the noise of the clash of arms. And even their words were drawn out and seemed to be set in a low unfamiliar pitch.

'Kay-vin! Kay-vin!'

The sounds of conflict were becoming ethereal. Every noise was filtered through a thick haze of agony. It was as if he was sitting at the bottom of the pool at the Well of Many Blessings again, struggling to hear what folks were saying on the pebbled shore. Everything was garbled and indistinct.

Then, against his will, his eyes half closed. He felt like a child struggling to stay awake long after bedtime. He couldn't hold himself up. There was no feeling in his legs. He glanced down at his chest and there was a great open gash through the mail coat. Under that the tunic was torn aside and the flesh mangled so much that he could plainly see his own broken ribs. There was blood everywhere: on the ground, on his clothes, on his hands. The battlement beneath his feet was awash with the bloody evidence of his defeat.

He coughed up blood and let go of his sickle. It fell down toward the ground below the battlements where the headless body of a Redcap was sprawled upon its back. Then some great weight seemed to press down upon Caoimhin's shoulders. The irresistible force of it dragged him over the edge of the battlements as he plummeted down, turning head over heels once before he struck the ground.

Srón's sweet face flashed before his eyes. It was painted with horror as she leaned over the battlements to watch him fall. But it was only a glimpse and then his eyes were fixed on the dead Redcap below him.

He smelled the stench of the creature's sweat an instant before his body landed with full force on top of his enemy. The breath was knocked out of him as he coughed again. His mouth was full of blood and phlegm and he knew with certainty he was about to die. Caoimhin summoned the last measure of strength left in his body to roll over on to his back. It took every ounce of determination left in him to do it. But when he lay there looking up he saw Srón's tear-filled face looking down on him from above.

As he watched a single drop of salty sorrow parted company with the corner of her eye. Down it slowly fell toward him, like a sparkling jewel thrown into a lake in offering to the gods. The moments were still passing slow and strange so he was able to keep an eye on the teardrop as it sailed through the air.

As it struck him in the middle of the forehead he smiled one last time, closed his eyes and let go of life. For though he was sorry to leave this world he'd been overcome by an immeasurable sense of peace. In that instant, as the teardrop fell, our Caoimhin knew for certain that someone held him dear to their heart.

And that is probably the most satisfying sensation anyone can ever know.

Now there's a few things you'd know about Caoimhin if you've been bothering to listen to my tale. Our lad had a particular attribute that set him apart from most of his mortal contemporaries. He had a skill with the Sight.

The Sight is as much a blessing as it is a curse to most folk. And so it was with our Caoimhin. For his was the worst kind of Seership. He had visions not only of the present and the past. He also saw what was yet to be.

The way it happened with him was quite different than the manner in which Tóraí Tairngire experienced his visions. All Tóraí had to do was shut his eyes and concentrate on asking the right question. Sometimes he didn't even have to do that! Information just flooded into his thoughts and he occasionally had to sort through it to find what was relevant.

But Caoimhin rarely experienced the Sight so easily. It usually came upon him when he was exhausted or occasionally when he was asleep. Now and then he experienced the Sight in times when he was suffering great anxiety or pain. But Caoimhin could not summon his ability at will.

So it will not surprise you to learn that as soon as our lad the Fisher-King closed his eyes to let his pain take him he fell into the dreaming of a powerful vision. And it was such an all-consuming experience, involving the five senses, that Caoimhin had no idea at first that it was a dream.

The first thing he knew was the feeling of the warm sun on his cheek. He was glad of it after the icy blizzard. He slowly stretched his arms and savoured the wonderful warmth before he opened his eyes.

When he did he had to shield them from the morning sunlight. The sky was blue and the grass all about him was lush and green. He breathed in deeply. The scented flowers of spring sweetened the air the same way honey sweetens bland porridge.

Caoimhin allowed a smile to form on his lips but soon found he was laughing for the joy of the day. He turned his head where he lay. All about him were hundreds of butterflies merrily going about their business, oblivious of him.

'I saw a dragonfly drink a flagon dry,' he whispered to himself, remembering something Eriginas used to say at springtime. 'I saw a butterfly flutter by.'

Caoimhin sat up when he heard the bees, though he couldn't see any in his immediate vicinity. He wasn't fond of the honey-gatherers as he'd been stung a number of times in his youth when he'd been working at the monastery hives.

When he looked around him he forgot any worries about

bees. What he saw took his breath away so that even if he'd wanted to cry out in shock he wouldn't have been able to.

And just what did he see? What had caused him to become so rattled? I'll tell you. It was the Rath of the Killibegs. He was lying on the grass on the top of the rath.

But the battlements, gates and stone houses were in ruins. The buildings were little more than shells. The great hall consisted of only three walls. It had no roof and the floor had collapsed.

Caoimhin was on his feet in a second, his heart pounding in his ears. He searched this way and that for any sign of life or another living being. But there was no one else anywhere on the hilltop. He took a few tentative steps and noticed a great hole in the ground where the doors near the main gate had once opened into the storage chambers. There was smoke coming out of that hole so he made his way over to it.

The stairs led down into the darkness of the cellars. He stood at the top of them for a long while wondering whether he should venture down to see if anyone was there. Then he caught a whiff of what he thought was roasting duck. His stomach growled with hunger and his mouth began to water.

Suddenly he was overcome with the desire to go down into the storage chambers and introduce himself to the cook. He was so captivated by the delicious aroma that he was completely distracted from the strangeness of the circumstances. He tentatively placed a foot on the top step ready to set off down the stairs, but he hesitated.

'What are you waiting for?' a familiar voice called up from the depths. 'Aren't you hungry after your long journey?'

He was sure he recognised the voice.

'Is that you, Gobann?'

But there was no answer.

'Gobann?'

In the instant when the doubt crept in to Caoimhin's

thoughts he remembered that he'd been standing on the battlements fighting off three Redcaps only a few moments earlier. He remembered his wound. He recalled falling off the wall, his tunic torn open and his body badly wounded. He looked down at his chest. He was wearing an undyed tunic woven of a very fine material he did not recognise. And the remarkable thing was it didn't have any seams at all.

Caoimhin was still frowning at that when the voice called up to him again.

'Hurry up, lad! I'm not waiting my breakfast all day on your account.'

Without another moment of indecision Caoimhin set off down into the cellars. Thirty steps down he came to the cobbled polished floor of the corridor and he had to stop and look in wonder at the scene before him.

A great celebration was taking place. Tables were laid with every kind of food and drink imaginable. There were three fires where wildfowl were roasting on spits. Huge fat candles and silver lamps lit the interior of the chamber with the most beautiful light. It was such a gorgeous glow that our lad gasped with the beauty of it.

But that wasn't the most astounding thing of all. Everyone he knew and everyone he had ever known was there. There were even some folk he'd not yet met. Nevertheless he had an uncanny feeling he would meet them one day and that they'd be quite close friends with him.

'What's going on here?' he asked.

As soon as he posed the question Mawn stepped out from the crowd to raise a cup high above his head.

'He's here! Be quiet everyone!'

But the gathered people were entirely consumed with chatting away noisily, laughing boisterously and downing cups of fine mead. Mawn cleared himself a space on one of the tables. Then he jumped up to stand where everyone could see him.

'Can I have your attention please!'

Mawn cleared his throat, waiting for the quiet to spread through the gathering. Then he spoke.

'Caoimhin has just entered the hall!'

Everyone spun round to look toward our lad. Then they put their cups down and applauded him loudly. A few folk cheered. Some whistled loudly and one fellow started chanting his name in the manner of the Sen Erainn warriors.

Caoimhin blushed deeply, unsure what was going on. The attention seemed a bit too prolonged and he became un-comfortable. He felt compelled to bow to the folk who were cheering, clapping and calling out to him. He'd hoped that would settle them down but it only encouraged them.

Srón was there among the throng and she pushed her way forward to smile at him with sparkling eyes filled with tears of pride. Mawn was already calling for silence as she ran up to our lad. As soon as she got close enough she grabbed him with her hands on either side of his cheeks and she kissed him full and hard on the lips.

That, of course, set the crowd off again. They went wild with cheering, screaming and laughing.

'Kay-vin! Kay-vin! Kay-vin!'

Despite the fact that he was certainly enjoying the kiss, Caoimhin tried to push away from Srón. But she wouldn't let him and that started the cheers again. Finally he managed to extricate himself from her but she stared at him with a worried look.

'What's wrong?' There was a hint of hurt in her voice. 'Don't you like what we've done for you?'

Our lad frowned with confusion.

'What *have* you done?'

'This hall. We've adorned it for you. We've cleared the rubble and cleaned out the ash. Then we brought in tables and set the roasting spits turning. Don't you like it?'

'It's marvellous! But I don't understand what happened. How did this place come to be like this? The great hall is in ruins.'

Srón's face drained of colour as he said those words. She held up her hand to the people gathered behind her in a silent plea for them to be quiet.

'What's become of the gatehouses?' Caoimhin went on. 'And the walls of the rath are overgrown with grass. How did that come about?'

There were whispers among the assembled guests and many folk looked to the floor as their mood was dampened.

'Caoimhin, my darling!' said Srón with a hint of discomfort as she hugged him close then brushed her fingers over his forehead. 'Come and sit down. Have something to drink.'

'What's going on?'

Srón took him by the hand to lead him to the tables but he resisted her.

'I won't do anything till someone explains what all these people are doing here. What's happened to Rath Killibegs.'

'Don't you remember, my dear?' Srón asked, a tear welling her eye.

'Where's Clemens? He'll tell me what's going on.'

'Clemens is dead,' Mawn cut in.

The immortal strode across to where Caoimhin was standing. 'Don't you remember?'

Our lad started to shake his head but Mawn touched a finger under his chin to stop the movement. He looked deep into Caoimhin's eyes.

'What's wrong?' Srón asked nervously. 'Is he having another lapse?'

'Lapse?' Caoimhin repeated and there was near outrage in his voice. 'What do you mean by that?'

'She doesn't mean anything, my friend,' Mawn soothed. 'Calm down and don't be so snappy.'

The immortal turned to Srón and whispered. 'I'll take him up for a breath of fresh air. He'll be fine after we've had a chat. Don't worry.'

'I'm standing right here beside you,' Caoimhin said. 'Why are you talking about me as if I'm not here?'

Mawn looked embarrassed.

'You're right. Let's go up into the sunlight. You'll feel much better when you've cleared your head. Then we'll come back downstairs again and get on with the celebration.'

Mawn touched Srón on the shoulder.

'Don't worry, I'll look after him.'

Caoimhin allowed himself to be led up to where the sun was streaming down on to the top of the deserted rath. As soon as he was out of the staircase he turned to confront the immortal.

'Are you going to tell me what's going on?'

Mawn opened his mouth to reply but he didn't get the opportunity to speak. Before he could say a single word he was interrupted. It was Gobann who spoke.

'I'll tell you if you want to know,' the Druid said harshly. 'But you'd better speak to me with a bit more respect than you did to your friends.'

Caoimhin turned round in surprise.

'Where did you spring from? You weren't here a minute ago.'

'Of course I was!' the Druid laughed. 'Wherever you are, I'm not far off. Of that you may be certain.'

Gobann strode forward, holding Caoimhin's walking stick out before him.

'Didn't I tell you to carry this with you at all times? What's the point in owning a staff with an enchantment of protection attached to it if you don't carry it around with you wherever you go?'

'I must have left it somewhere,' Caoimhin shrugged. 'I didn't even realise I'd lost it.'

'Do you want to know what's happening?' the Druid pressed.

'Yes.'

'You've made a terrible mistake.'

'What do you mean?'

Gobann traced a shape in the air with the stick.

'Do you know what that is?'

Caoimhin shook his head.

Before Caoimhin's eyes the design Gobann had traced in the air appeared carved deeply into a ruined wall of the battlements.

'Is that clearer?'

The pattern was a triple spiral. As a scribe Caoimhin had seen many of them adorning the pages of the great manuscripts. But this one was unlike any other he'd ever laid eyes on. It was bold with three outward pointing arms that ended in points. And at the centre, where there should have been a single convergence of lines, there were three convergences which crossed together and were woven into one pattern.

'What is it?' Caoimhin asked.

'That is the Mystery,' Gobann replied.

And what did he mean by that? Perhaps I can give you a few clues. According to the Culdees and the Druids who were in Ireland before them, every mortal is made up of three parts, none of which is first or foremost above the others.

The soul is our identity and the passenger on the soul-voyage. The body is the vessel in which we undertake the journey through life. And the mind is the navigator, the observer and the crew all rolled into one.

When we are brought to birth, body, mind and soul are melded together to form a single entity of three parts. So the triple spiral also represents the time when we are born and the birth canal which mixes the three separate parts together so that when we emerge from the womb we are one. Some great teachers describe the spiral as a view from the womb as our three parts merge. We come from this spiral which is known to the mystics as the Well of Incarnation. That is the superficial meaning of the triple spiral.

But it has deeper meaning. For in this life there are three main initiations which anyone may undertake. The Christians call these initiations baptisms but they've forgotten the true meaning of the word. They think that baptism only takes place in water. Well of course it doesn't.

The first baptism we each and every one of us undertakes in this life is the baptism of Earth. We are born of the clay and thrust out from our mother's wombs to experience the world of material things and the realm of the senses. This initiation is a prerequisite for living among the mortal and immortal kind alike. None who draws breath can escape it.

The next initiation we may choose to undertake is the baptism of water. That represents a spiritual cleansing, a washing away of fear and an opening of awareness to the spiritual aspects of life which compliment the material. Many people believe this is the last initiation one ever need take in this life. But we Culdees think differently.

It is all well and good to aspire to living a spiritual life but a mere awareness of those aspects of life is not enough. Everyone who takes the initiation of cleansing by water must eventually one day accept the baptism of air. This involves more than a simple following of the rules of religious teachers or moral advisors. It requires more than a simple awareness of the spirit or a desire to know God. This baptism opens a person not only to knowledge of the One but also to direct experience and conscious relationship with the One.

Those are the three great baptisms of this mortal life and they are represented in the triple spiral which Caoimhin saw carved into the ruined wall. There is a fourth initiation of course.

However, not many mortals ever undergo the baptism of fire

which entails return to the One. For that is the only true immortality that anyone can hope to achieve. The Ever-Living Ones are denied that initiation. To undergo it one must quit the material world altogether and that is rare for the immortal kind.

The sign of the triple spiral doesn't refer to them anyway. It only relates to those of us who are either trapped within the circle of rebirth and death or to those who have ceased to be reborn through the acquisition of immortality of the body.

'What has all that got to do with me?' Caoimhin asked. 'Why won't you tell me what's going on?'

'I am telling you!' Gobann shouted. 'You stupid boy. Why won't you listen to me?'

'Now I know what you're on about. You're upset with me for kissing Srón.'

He stepped forward and pointed at the Druid in emphasis.

'Well I enjoyed it! And you can't stop me enjoying it either.'

Gobann pointed the walking stick at his other self.

'Yes I can. I could force you to suffer guilt and shame. I could make your life a real living hell in the most skin-crawling sense.'

Caoimhin snatched the stick away.

'I'm going back down to join the celebration. And you can't stop me.'

He turned round and stormed off toward the stairs, using the walking stick to lash out at the flowers scattered around the grassy hilltop. But as he reached the hole in the ground where the stairs emerged he thought of something and turned to ask Gobann a question.

'Is the battle over?'

'Not yet.'

'Is the rath destroyed?'

Gobann held his arms wide.

'Can you not see for yourself?'

'Is this a vision?'

'Don't you know?'

Caoimhin swung the stick around in the air in frustration.

'I hate the way you do that!'

'Do what?'

'I hate the way you avoid my questions!'

'A wise man asks another question before he answers one.'

'You infuriate me!'

At that moment Mawn stepped past the Druid and stood between them.

'Don't take any notice of him. It's all just a game to him. Like the Brandubh. And you are one of the pieces in that game.'

'But he's a part of me! Are you saying that I'm manipulating myself like a piece on the Brandubh board?'

'Of course you are,' Mawn nodded. 'That's it exactly.'

'Why would he do that to me? Why would he do that to himself? Why would I do that to me?'

'He's confused and a little bitter that things aren't turning out exactly the way he wanted them to. He's an impatient old bugger.'

'Well I've had a gut full of his impatience,' Caoimhin replied sternly. 'I wish he'd leave me alone and let me get on with my life.'

'If only I could!' Gobann despaired as he threw his arms into the air and rolled his eyes skyward. 'But you simply won't let go of me.'

'Rubbish!' Caoimhin spat.

He turned around and made his way down the stairs again. But he was no more than halfway to the bottom when he realised something was amiss. The lights were subdued and where there had been many voices chatting excitedly there was now no other sound but the slow steady drip of water echoing inside the chambers.

At the bottom of the stairs he could see the cellars were abandoned except for a small fire that was burning at the far end of the corridor. Confused about where everyone could have disappeared to so quickly, Caoimhin made his way cautiously toward the fire.

When he reached it he was surprised to find that he was very cold indeed. All the warmth he'd gained from the sun outside was gone from his body. His fingers ached from the freezing air inside the cellars, and his breath steamed out before him as he exhaled.

He knelt down to the fire and spread his fingers out before it. And as he did so he looked deeply into the flames. He was immediately intrigued by this strange blaze which seemed to burn without consuming any of the wood piled on to it. Indeed, the flames didn't even scorch or char the timber.

'This is the tomb of Lazarus,' Gobann said in a melancholy voice and Caoimhin nearly jumped out of his skin with shock.

'Why are you always sneaking up on me like that?'

'I've told you before. We are never separated. When will you understand that?'

Caoimhin stood up from the fire to confront his other self.

'Why do always talk in riddles?'

'It keeps me entertained and helps pass the time.'

'Just tell me what you're on about, will you?'

'The tomb of Lazarus is where all those who are embodied trap themselves.'

Once again Gobann was quoting a belief which was common among the Culdee folk. For I was taught that the story of Christ raising Lazarus from the dead was a symbolic one. Lazarus wasn't really dead. He was locked within the tomb which is this material existence.

What Jesus did when he raised Lazarus was to free him from the eternal round of birth and death by granting him the baptism of air. That's why the story says that the tomb of

Lazarus had a terrible stench about it which Christ banished when he made the air fresh.

Well, if you understand that this is the Culdee interpretation of the tale you might realise that Gobann was revealing a deeper truth to Caoimhin. He was saying that our lad was trapped in the tomb of the body by virtue of his immortality. But when that point didn't get through to him the Druid decided to speak plainly.

'You took the Quicken Brew. You will not suffer death or disease ever again. But that also means you are stuck here in the material world. You may journey across to the Otherworld as so many of your kind do. And the Otherworld may grant you some peace from your affliction. But you will weary of both worlds one day. You will seek rest in sleep. And when that does not satisfy you, your soul will cry out for liberation.'

'Are you trying to tell me that I'm an immortal?' Caoimhin asked with growing scepticism.

As he spoke these words he felt a terrible pain in his chest. He closed his eyes with the sudden agony of it and when he opened them again he was lying on his back looking up at the wall where Srón had been standing.

It was night, the air was freezing and the ground was hard under him. He sat up straightaway, wondering what on Earth could have happened to him. Then in little flashes he began to recall the fight with the Redcaps. He looked around him. To his relief the fortress was still intact. Nearby the corpses of the three enemy warriors were piled against the wall, their severed heads bundled on top of the stack.

He shook his head to clear his thoughts then tentatively touched the spot on his chest where he remembered he'd been cut by the Redcap sickle. His mail was rent apart and his tunic torn but there wasn't a mark on him. All that remained of his terrible wound was a mild itchiness along the line of the cut.

Caoimhin scratched the invisible scar as he struggled to get to his feet. And as he did so he heard the terrible scream of a woman. He looked around to see Srón, ashen-faced, staring at him. Scodán stood beside her with his mouth wide open.

'He is a bloody immortal,' the warrior murmured in awe. 'I told you so.'

FIRES OF SAMHAIN

S codán had just spoken when the blast of a war trumpet sounded out across the rath. All eyes turned toward the great hall. On the battlement roof a warrior stood with a great circular trumpet held to his lips. He blew another long blast, followed by three short sharp notes at a very high pitch.

Almost immediately Caoimhin noticed he could see the reflected light of flames through the narrow window slits of the hall. Then he caught a glimpse of smoke.

'It's the hall!' he shouted. 'Clemens has set fire to the hall!'

He ran up to Srón and they fell into a tearful, joyous embrace.

'I thought you were dead,' she sobbed.

But there was no time for rejoicing. There were still Redcaps at large within the rath and they had to be dealt with.

'Light torches!' Caoimhin commanded of the Sen Erainn warriors. 'Search the buildings for the enemy.'

He, Srón and Scodán made their way through the chaotic melee of the wounded and distraught to the doors of the great hall. A huge log had been jammed across the entrance from the outside to prevent it being opened. And smoke was already pouring from the gap under the doors.

'He's trapped the Redcaps inside the hall!' Caoimhin exclaimed.

And of course that is exactly what the old priest had done. It had been his desperate plan all along to draw the Redcaps into the hall then set fire to it to block their escape. He was well aware of the rumour that immortals may be brought to their mortality by flame. Haven't I told you all about the baptism of fire which is the initiation that sends a soul back to God?

Well, it so happened that the Redcaps were terribly afraid of fire on such a grand scale. No one had expected they'd go into such a panic when confronted by it, not even Clemens.

As soon as all the enemy had been drawn into the hall William and Old Guy had run downstairs to pass on the word to Alan and the rest of us. Rónán Og and his archers had waited by the stairs leading down into the cellars. There they'd kept up a steady flow of arrows at the Redcaps who were marked out as targets by the torches they carried. When the enemy had taken the bait Rónán and his warriors withdrew down the stairs to the basement level.

All the while they kept shooting up at the Redcaps as they tried to descend the stairs. Nearly one hundred and fifty Redcaps were in the hall when Clemens and his wife slammed the doors shut.

The old priest lit two torches. One he gave to his wife. By way of farewell she kissed him passionately on the lips then wasted not a moment more taking the torch upstairs to set those chambers alight. The Redcaps were so intent on attacking Rónán and his men they didn't even notice her moving around behind them.

Clemens lifted the second torch and calmly carried it to various places around the hall where oil had been spilled. He touched the flames at those spots and waited till the fire had caught hold. Soon enough the whole of the feasting chamber was alight. Tapestries, furniture and roof timbers erupted into a ferocious fire that threatened to engulf the whole building very quickly.

The Redcaps didn't take long to become aware of the danger. But their way was blocked by the spreading flames. Certain that he'd done all he could to create an inferno to the hall, Clemens took up the axe he'd left by the doors. Then he waited for the first of the Redcaps to make his way in his direction, seeking an escape from the ferocious blaze.

I can't tell you for certain whether he was calm to the last or not. I can't tell you whether there was regret in his heart, or anger either. But I'm sure he stood there until his strength failed him and he succumbed to smoke, heat or the Redcap sickles. I knew the stubborn old bugger. I'm sure that's how he would have done things.

All we will ever know for certain is that before he expired he brought down six Redcaps. Not bad for an old boy! Six hard warriors of the ancient Fir Bolg fell before him. Though I have to concede they were probably panicked and disoriented at the time. Nevertheless it was a mighty achievement.

That is all I can tell you of what happened to my father. I felt no loss when I heard about his passing. I don't feel as if he ever left me. But then again I'm a Culdee. I'm bound to think that way. And you may recall that I was distracted by a love potion at the time.

Of Derbaíl I only know she perished on the rooftop battlements of the hall. The strange thing was there was no trace of her left behind after the fire which brought down the building.

Once the flames had caught hold it did not take long for them to spread. In a very short while the whole of the upper part of the building was ablaze. Screams of Redcaps consumed by the fire could be heard in every part of the rath. Their awful cries will echo in my memory until my dying day. And the smoky stench of burning leather will always haunt the back of my throat.

Rónán Og and his warriors retreated in good order and with

no losses down to the level above the storage chambers. There they had prepared a maze of barrels, immense wine jars and spilled oil behind which they could conceal themselves from the enemy and set traps of fire whenever they got the chance. But they must have known, all of them, that their chances of survival were not good, even if the audacious plan went entirely their way.

As it was, Clemens trap did work to a certain extent. Of the hundred and fifty or so Redcaps who'd charged into the hall, perhaps half that number perished in the upper floors. But that left seventy or more desperate warriors whose escape was blocked and for whom there was only one way out. And that was to press ahead into the depths of the storage cellars. That was a far greater number than Rónán and his dozen bowmen had imagined they'd be up against.

Martin was among Rónán's men and he fought with courage, I am told. But he took one too many risks and was caught in the sweep of a Redcap sickle. Rónán had to leave him wounded on the stairs as the enemy surged down at his men.

The bowmen struggled to keep the Redcaps back with oil-soaked fire traps and constant bowshot. But of course arrows have very little effect on the immortals. They thought of them as little more than bee stings. It wasn't long before Rónán realised he would have to sacrifice his life and the lives of his men if this force of Redcaps was to be defeated. He knew that the victory relied on him. If he made the wrong decision the courage of Derbáil and Clemens would have been in vain. So he took a terrible decision.

A line of oil had been spilled across the wooden floor of the chamber to mark a line of last hope. From behind that line, with the stairs to the cellar at his back, Rónán Og sent a pitch-soaked arrow of fire into the oil. It exploded into flames as tall as a man and easily sufficient to hold the Redcaps back for a while.

The chieftain called his archers to him and told them that all hope was lost. He told them that any one of them who chose to escape through the cellars would be accounted blameless and their bravery never questioned. Then he released them all from his service.

To their credit they all elected to stay with him to the end. But Rónán wouldn't have that. He commanded the youngest of them to retreat down into the cellars to pass the word of what had become of them at the last. They might have all made it out, I suppose. But Rónán didn't want to take the chance. He decided to hold them there as best he could to ensure as many of them were caught in the flames as possible. Every one that perished in the fire would be one less for us down below to deal with.

By then the flames had taken to the upper timbers of the ceiling which was also the floor of the great hall. Sections of it were creaking, threatening to collapse at any moment. The youngest of the bowmen left them to descend the stairs into the cellars and the bowmen of Rónán Og prepared to meet their doom. No one knows how they fared, except to say that not one among them lived to tell of what happened after.

We could hear the terrible din of the Redcaps charging into the hall above us. They were screaming with battle rage and fear. They were tossing tables and cauldrons and all manner of household articles this way and that.

Then we heard the screaming. Stronghold turned to me and I clasped his hand tightly in mine.

'Clemens has set fire to the hall,' I whispered.

'Be quiet!' Alan hissed under his breath. 'You'll give the game away!'

My throat was dry with fear and apprehension so I took off the skin I had hung over my shoulder. I uncorked it and took a swig. Then I handed it to Stronghold. He took a deep draught of the broth then handed it back to me with a nod of thanks.

It was at that moment I realised this was the broth tainted with the love potion. What had I done? I called myself an eedyit under my breath, I did. To have made this mistake once was foolish. But to have blundered again was plain idiocy.

'Stronghold,' I whispered urgently.

'Shut up!' Alan insisted. 'If you won't be quiet I'll slit your throat myself. You're putting all our lives in danger.'

I scowled but kept silent. Then I took the stopper out of the skin of broth and poured the bloody lot out on to the cobbles.

Alan stared wide-eyed at me, clearly frustrated that I was behaving so strangely. But I shook my head and waved my hands to show I wasn't going to make any more noise. He seemed satisfied at that and turned his attention back to the corridor beyond the barrels we'd stacked up.

It was in that moment William and Old Guy appeared to us on the stairs. They'd been up in the hall defending the stairs until the smoke had got so thick they couldn't breathe. They'd been separated from Rónán in the confusion. How they'd missed him is anyone's guess. But not having a clear idea whether Rónán had retreated they decided to make their way down to the storage chambers where their weapons might make a real difference.

Behind them on the stairs. the young archer was struggling down. He'd been injured. Will ran on to reach us, desperate to pass on the news of the fire and have us ready for the attack.

But Old Guy saw the wounded archer and went back up the stairs to where the smoke was already thick. He had an axe in his hand and he meant to use it.

Lord Will turned round to help the young man into the

safety of the corridor behind the gap we'd narrowed for ourselves. Once the lad was safe he told Mirim to take him to one of the empty rooms.

'The Redcaps may not see him if he's hidden well,' he told her.

William turned his attention back to the stairs. Old Guy had already cut down two Redcaps and he was taunting another to try to take him on.

'Come back here, you fool!' William cried out. 'There's no sense in risking your life that way!'

But Old Guy had realised that the longer he held the Redcaps on the stairs, the more would die by the flames or be weakened and blinded by the smoke. So he stood his ground. And his great-grandson watched from the door as he relieved two more Redcaps of their heads.

By then the old man was starting to weaken. The smoke was pouring down from above and burning embers spilled about him on every side. He suddenly turned round and looked his great-grandson in the eye, then he ran on up the stairs and out of view.

I looked up at Stronghold and could see he was awed by the old man's courage. A few seconds later Guy the Elder retreated back down the steps to where we could see him again. But now his head was cut and he was drenched in blood. Whether it was his own or that of the Redcaps he had slain, we never knew. For as we watched, Old Guy d'Alville slipped on the stairs, fell down and when he reached the bottom he did not move again.

Stronghold made a move to run out to the old man, but Alan restrained him.

'Stand your ground!' he ordered. 'I'll have need of your sword arm soon. I can't afford to lose two of you this night.'

As Stronghold stepped back away from the door, we all heard the Redcaps screaming as they ran down from the hall above. The first one was squealing as he leaped down the stairs with his back on fire. The little blaze lit the whole chamber with a bloody red glow. He struggled to pat out the flames but he couldn't manage to reach round behind far enough.

He ran on as if he could get away from the fire that had caught hold of his tunic. At the bottom of the stairs he quickly searched this way and that till he noticed the gap at the end of the corridor. Then he ran straight towards us.

Stronghold pushed me aside, drew his blade and the chamber filled with the odd luminescence of the Frightener spirit called Eterscél. The Redcap ran on toward the gap, heedless of the fate which awaited him.

Stronghold readied his weapon for the blow. Another couple of breaths passed and then the enemy warrior had barged through the gap between the barrels. Stronghold's blade came down with a crunch and it was all over.

The stench of burning cloth, leather and flesh made me gag. I could hardly breathe. Mirim brought out a torch from behind the barrels and I saw my first dead Redcap up close. His head had rolled aside to sit staring at us with shock. But the body lay where it had fallen, burned and bloody.

I felt my knees weaken as if I were about to faint. My vision blurred and I felt the floor move under me. Stronghold cast aside his sword in an instant to catch me before I fell. Then he swept me up and carried me out of the way. As he set me down on the cobbles I looked up into his eyes and sure enough I got another kick from that bloody love potion and nearly swooned again to have him so close to me.

He brushed the hair from my eyes and smiled at me with adoration.

'Stay here, my love,' he whispered. 'I'll watch over you. And while there's strength in my body no harm will come to you.'

Then he was up on his feet to retrieve his weapon before I could wet myself with joy at what he'd said.

I still call myself an eedyit, even to this day. But at that moment I didn't have either the time or the inclination to call myself anything. A dozen more Redcaps had fled down the stairs from the hall above. The smell of burning timber was drifting down ahead of the smoke. The whole hall must have been ablaze.

Alan readied his bow a pitch-soaked arrow. Mirim stood back with her torch behind the barrels where the enemy wouldn't be able to glimpse the flames. She was waiting for the word from her husband to light the tip of his arrow.

But Alan held off. Three Redcaps made it to the gap and passed through one at a time. The first two were frantic and confused. They'd dropped their sickles in the rush to escape the burning hall. So when they found themselves faced with a Frightener sword and the two axes of Gusán and John, they froze with fear.

Stronghold waited till the third one had got through the gap before he hacked the head off the first Redcap. Then he moved on to the next one, wielding his blade with ease and confidence. The third slipped in the blood of his comrades and was set upon by Gusán, who managed to strike off the head after two botched attempts.

I sat against the wall in abject horror. I couldn't believe what I was witnessing. It was not a pretty sight, I can tell you.

'Twenty more coming in!' Alan reported.

'We'll have to hold them!' Stronghold cried. 'There's not enough of them down in the cellars to light the oil.'

Without a pause for breath he stepped out into the corridor beyond, which was quickly filling with panicked Redcaps. I screamed out to him but he didn't hear me. Before I knew what I was doing I'd forgotten my queasiness and I was up after him.

Mirim caught a glimpse of me running for the gap. She stepped out in front of me, waving the torch around wildly to keep me back.

'Stay where you are, you stupid girl! It's certain death for you out there!'

But I wasn't going to let my Stronghold face those foul creatures alone. I was determined to stand by his side and fight them off him.

Mirim kept me at bay, all the while glancing over her shoulder into the corridor beyond to keep an eye on the advancing enemy.

'Stay back!' she warned me. 'I'll burn you. I swear I will. You're putting us all in danger!'

Out in the dark corridor Stronghold had Eterscél raised up above his head. An awesome fiery glow surrounded the blade so the Redcap warriors stood back from him, fearful to advance.

By now the stairs were crowded with the enemy. And the first of them with bows stood up on the stairs. They put a few arrows into Old Guy's body to make sure he was dead. I heard the deadly whistle of the shafts falling from above and I straightaway moved forward to try to get a glimpse of what was happening.

'Stand back!' Mirim shrieked. 'I won't warn you again.'

She glanced over her shoulder in time to glimpse her husband stepping out into the gap to see whether Stronghold needed any help. Alan must have been visible to the Redcap archers for no more than a split second but it was long enough for one of them to take his mark.

An arrow cut through the air. Its black feather fletching seemed to leave an invisible trail of darkness. I saw it hit Alan. I saw him drop his own bow as the arrow struck him hard in the chest. I saw his face pale to grey and his knees buckle under him.

John grabbed the torch from Mirim's hands and Gusán took up the bow. In seconds they'd lit the pitch-soaked arrow and the flaming missile was sailing across the corridor to scutter along the floor against the stairs.

In an instant the corridor beyond exploded in flames. Gusán

THE WELL OF MANY BLESSINGS

Gelt and John were already dragging Alan back into the depths of the cellars with Mirim leaning over him trying to discern whether or not the wound was fatal.

Stronghold leaped through the gap, immediately followed by two Redcaps. He dispatched them both with no more effort than he might have given to a pair of buzzing insects. Then he grabbed me by the hand and dragged me on after him down into the darker parts of the storage cellars.

I must have been in deep shock by then. I don't recall in any detail anything else that happened for a long while after. All I can remember is that there was a steady stream of Redcaps pushing their way into the cellars from the burning corridor. Many of them were on fire and most of them were terrified.

Not one of them managed to put up more than token resistance to William, Stronghold, Gusán and John. But all through the fighting against the Redcaps Mirim was quiet. She sat close beside her husband who was propped against the wall. And while the awful battle raged about us she bathed his head with cool water. As for me? I was certain none of us would ever get out of that place alive.

BELATED THANKS

I lost count of the number of Redcaps who charged into our little corridor. Their bodies were strewn across the cellar cobbles. Their heads rolled round underfoot. And more than once I felt my stomach churn in rebellion at the terrible sight.

After a while I stopped looking at them. I kept my gaze upon the faces of my companions. Their expressions were grim and desperate but at least they were familiar and alive.

Gusán was a rough woodsman with a knotted beard and tattered clothes. But his eyes were bright with determination. William FitzWilliam stood proud where most men his age would have been stooped with the burden of their winters. I had known him three years but I'd never seen him like this. The axe in his hand was stained with blood and his tunic was scorched and torn. But he shone like a saint to my eyes.

Mirim, that proud woman of the desert, had turned all her attention to her husband. He gazed up into her eyes as she tended him, looking as if he could have been leaning up against a tree out in the peaceful forest. Mirim's eyes were as dark as her complexion. I'd never seen such a beauty as her in my life before. And as I watched them, catching snippets of their conversation, I determined that one day I would travel to the Holy Land where the folk are all like Mirim.

'I remember everything,' Alan told her. 'I recall the place

where I was born and the family who nurtured me. I can bring to mind the face of my mother and all my kindred.'

'The waters of the Well of Many Blessings have worked the wonder of their healing upon you, my love,' Mirim soothed. 'You have been given a great gift.'

'Indeed, it is true. But do you know something?'

'What's that?'

'The dearest memory I have is of the moment I first caught a glimpse of you.'

Mirim choked back a tear.

'Do you really recall our first meeting?'

'Of course I do,' he smiled. 'You were walking up towards the well where I had knelt down to take a drink. At first I thought you were the Blessèd Virgin Mary herself by the way you were dressed and the light that shone about you. Then I remembered a chapel I'd visited. I can't recall whether it was in Marseilles or Acre.'

He laughed a little.

'So the Well of Many Blessings has not restored my memory completely!'

She smiled at him in adoration. I felt a tear in my own eye that he could joke with her while it seemed his life was ebbing out of him.

'In that chapel, wherever it was, I saw a statue of the Madonna. Her skin was dark like yours. So when you stepped up from the valley of Shali to tend to me I was sure you were the Black Madonna come to usher me into Heaven!'

She laughed.

'You were very confused!'

'I'd just walked in from the desert.'

'Not many men can honestly say that. For once the desert gets a hold of a man she does not let him go without a fight.'

'You did usher me into Heaven,' he told her. 'For the time I spent at the Oasis of Shali was the happiest time of my life.

314

Your people treated me as if I were one of them. I will never forget that.'

'You came to us from the desert. My people have learned that when the desert gives a gift, which she rarely does, then truly it must be a precious one. You are one of us. Your home is at the Oasis of Shali. And when the time comes you will return there to spend the remainder of your days in peace surrounded by those who consider you a gift.'

'I'm dying,' Alan whispered.

Mirim swallowed her emotion, unwilling to accept that he perhaps spoke the truth.

'I don't think so,' she replied eventually. 'I will take care of you.'

'Will the desert people come to take me when the time comes?'

'You are one of my clan now. My ancestors will take care of you. They will come when the time is nigh. And they will guide you on your journey.'

That seemed to give Alan a great sense of peace. He breathed easier. I turned my attention away from them then. I couldn't bear to hear another word.

I remember wishing that the Redcaps would break through the fires to attack. All this sitting around waiting for the stragglers to appear was starting to give me the jitters. The quiet was getting me thinking. And I didn't want to be thinking too much just then.

I looked across at John Toothache who was resting up against the wall with an axe on his lap. He was a big ugly man scarred by battle and, I suspect, a propensity for the drink. How he'd changed since I had knocked his tooth out. Despite the fact that we were trapped in the cellars with little hope of making it out alive, he was smiling broadly. His eyes were closed and his head thrown back in absolute bliss.

I had to smile to look at him. And it was hard for me to recall that he'd slipped that poison into the cup of the sacrament. That's how Caoimhin came to be so ill. That's how I came to lose my temper with the brute and knock his tooth out. Now he was here with the rest of us and he'd fought bravely too.

John must have sensed I was looking at him. His eyes snapped open and he turned to stare at me. Then he dragged his weary body up and made his way across the corridor to kneel down beside me.

'I reckon there's not much chance any of us will get out of here alive,' he began. 'So I just wanted to thank you for taking away my pain and allowing some room for joy again. If, by some miracle, we are delivered from this danger, I hope I can do something in return for you.'

He took my hand and laid a gentle kiss upon it. He smiled again, then went to sit beside Mawn at the opposite wall.

Mawn's outlandish clothes marked him as a foreigner, yet I'd heard him speak in the poetic Gaelic language of the old days. He was no foreigner. Of course I knew he was a Fánaí but I didn't feel comfortable around him as I did around Sianan. His large dark eyes were downcast. Even when John spoke with him, he didn't look up.

I was just wondering how Sianan was getting along when Stronghold appeared at my side.

'What did he want?' my knight asked.

'He wanted to thank me for knocking his tooth out,' I replied.

'Oh.'

Stronghold leaned in close to me to speak so that no one else would hear.

'William doesn't think we have much of a chance against all those Redcaps. But if we do survive I want you to marry me and be the lady of my hearth and heart.'

I must have beamed back at him so beautifully that I didn't need to answer him with mere words.

'I'm so glad,' he told me when he saw the smile on my face. 'You see, I have a secret. I've never told anyone about it.'

'Go on,' I gushed.

I love secrets.

'Before I met you, before I ever came to Ireland, I spoke with a soothsayer. It was in the Holy Land. I went to her hoping to find out what course my life would take.'

'What did she say?'

'She told me that my life would be consumed with hatred and vengeance. She told me that I would lose everything I held dear, and only after I'd lost everything would I realise what a fool I'd been.'

'Is that all?'

'No, there was more,' he whispered. 'She told me I would come to Ireland seeking to satisfy a great yearning in my heart. She told me I would discover it here in the place I least expected to find it. And it's true. I came to Ireland with a longing for vengeance on Robert FitzWilliam. But there was another older, deeper yearning in my heart. And that has been satisfied since we met.'

I looked into his eyes and I could see he was sincere. But how could I let him believe that he had fallen in love with me without more than a little help from the love potion of Ortha?

'I was misguided,' he said. 'I was without love. And lacking love I acted selfishly.'

'But the love you feel for me is not real,' I cut in.

I confessed everything then. I informed him that I'd taken the love philtre by mistake just before I set eyes on him at the bridge in the Otherworld. I told him our love for one another was false. It was based on nothing more than a silly concoction that had turned our eyes to one another without our mutual consent. I told him I'd mixed it up for Caoimhin, not for him. And I admitted I hadn't thought very highly of Guy d'Alville when I'd first encountered him. I told him he'd just had a sup of the love potion himself.

He thought about all I'd said for a little while. Then he smiled.

'I am no longer Guy d'Alville. Our love was meant to be. And so everything has turned out for the best.'

'What do you mean?'

'If you and Caoimhin had been meant for one another, the love potion would have worked on him.'

'But it did!'

'But he has an eye for that woman of the Sen Erainn.'

'Caoimhin drank from the Well of Many Blessings. That must have annulled the effects of the love philtre he had at my hand.'

'So you see!' Stronghold beamed. 'Our love was meant to be. The love potion just helped things along, that's all. And what's more, now that we're both under the effects of it we should take full advantage of the situation.'

I couldn't fault his reasoning. And, truth to tell, I didn't want to either. I took his hand and held it up to my lips.

'The soothsayer told me something else before I left her company,' Stronghold said. 'I have often wondered at the meaning of her words. But now I think I understand.'

'What was it she said?'

'The three strongest forces in this world are the force of water, the force of fire and the force of hatred. Yet one who wields the first two guided by the force of love may be a one to be reckoned with.'

As he spoke there was a terrible rumbling in the Earth; it seemed to be coming from all around us. The floor shook as the ceiling shed dust in great clouds.

'What's happening?' Gusán shouted. 'What's causing that terrible noise? Is it the Redcaps come to tear us apart?'

Mawn stood up. He put his ear against the wall to listen. Then he stood back and his face was pale.

'That's not the Redcaps.'

'Thank goodness!' Gusán sighed with relief.

'It's something far worse,' Mawn went on. 'It's a menace older than anyone or anything I know. And if there were only one of them we would never be able to defeat it even if there were a hundred of us.'

'What do mean?' Gusán sputtered in terror. 'How many are there? What manner of monster is it?'

'There are two of them,' Mawn replied. 'They are Nathairaí. And their names are Lochie and Isleen.'

'Is there nothing we can do to hold them off?' William asked. 'Is there no way to defeat them?'

'They are immortals,' Mawn shrugged. 'So I suppose you could try cutting off their heads. But that won't be an easy thing. They both have necks as wide as the girth of four horses.'

William lifted his axe, preparing for the fight.

'Stand close together,' he commanded. 'Don't allow yourselves to be scattered or separated. Our only hope is if we stay together.'

As soon as he spoke those words the wall behind him collapsed in a great rush of falling rock and dust. Behind it there was a deep growling laugh and a voice so dæmonic that it could have issued forth from Satan himself.

'They're in here, Isleen! I've found them.'

LULLABY

R obert stirred and slowly blinked open his eyes. He was slumped face down over the corpse of an oak-knight who'd fallen in the first attack. His throat was dry and his tongue was swollen. His head was spinning with a terrible pulsing headache.

As he lay there he touched his tongue to the roof of his mouth and remembered the leather-covered water bottle Aoife had given him. You might recall that by some Faerie trickery or other it always replenished itself once it was empty.

Rob reached round to fetch it from the pouch pocket of the book satchel. He hadn't moved his arm far when he flinched with agony. There was an arrow sticking out from his shoulder.

With great effort he rolled on to his back, sweating with pain even though the air was icy. At last he managed to find the bottle, and with his good hand he somehow removed the stopper and drank the contents. He was instantly refreshed. And to his surprise he found the pain was eased.

He coughed then and covered his mouth. There was blood backing the palm of his hand. Robert stared at it for a long time, refusing to believe what he saw.

When you've seen as many battle wounds as our Rob you come to be an expert on whether a man will survive his misfortune. Robert knew from the vermilion red of the blood and the fact that he had no feeling in his left shoulder or arm that his wound was a bad one.

He coughed again and this time his palm was spattered with bright red spots. Well, that was enough for him. He wasn't afraid of death, mind you. It was just that he hadn't expected it to end so soon. There were so many dreams he wanted to pursue. So many unfulfilled wishes he longed to fulfil. And he'd only just begun to dream or wish in earnest.

He closed his eyes for a moment, trying to accept his fate, and when he opened them again he was not alone.

A hand was being held out to him.

'Can I help you to your feet?' Órán offered. 'You've still got some work to do.'

'I'm dying. I'll wager you hadn't counted on that!'

Then he laughed a little, though it obviously caused him a great deal of pain.

'What are you going to do now? How will you get by without me?'

'I won't have to,' the Frightener told him. 'You're not going to die.'

Robert struggled to sit up by himself, refusing the assistance of the spirit. When at last he was seated upright, leaning against the corpse, he put the water bottle to his lips and had another drink.

'Don't have too much of that,' Órán warned. 'We don't want you getting drunk, do we? It wouldn't do for Aoife's consort to be tiddly while he's overseeing his first great victory. '

'My wound is mortal. I'll be dead before sunrise.'

The self-satisfied smile fell away from Órán's face as he stepped closer to inspect the wound. He poked his fingers around where the arrow had struck then moved the missile a little from side to side. Robert cried out then grabbed the spirit by the hand.

'Would you mind not doing that?' he said through gritted teeth. 'It's bloody painful.'

'Pain is a liar,' the Frightener chirped up cheerily. 'Didn't your father teach you that?'

'Didn't you teach *him* that?'

'Of course. I taught him a great many things.'

The spirit put a hand on Rob's forehead to judge whether he was suffering a fever. He lifted the knight's eyelids to observe the whites of his eyes, then he grabbed Robert under the chin.

'Open your mouth and stick out your tongue,' he demanded.

Robert did what he was told. The Frightener had a good look at the inside of his mouth, humming to himself all the while.

When his observations were complete, Órán stepped back. 'Well, you're certainly very pale. And I don't like the look of that festering round the arrow wound. I think you may have copped a missile that was tipped with something nasty.'

'Are you suggesting I've been poisoned?'

'Possibly.'

'Gaelic warriors don't commit such barbaric acts.'

'Perhaps this is a Norman arrow. It certainly looks more like a piece of their work than those crude missiles the Irish make.'

'Ollo,' Robert whispered. 'I should have guessed.'

The spirit stepped forward again and grasped the arrow firmly by the shaft. Naturally Robert screamed and tried to shift back out of the way. But there was a corpse behind him, and anyway he didn't have much strength left to him.

'What are you doing?' the knight shrieked. 'Are you trying to kill me?'

'You've done a good enough job of that yourself. No. I'm trying to save your life. If this arrow stays in your body too long, you'll certainly die. And we wouldn't want that, would we?'

'I might. It's certainly an alternative to the life you have planned for me.'

The Frightener sighed with regret as he prepared to withdraw the missile.

'I'm truly sorry it has come to this. And I'm just as sorry for the pain I'm about to inflict on you. But you must understand you've brought it on yourself.'

With that Órán pulled the arrow straight out of Robert's shoulder. It came out smoothly though there was a lot of blood. Rob fell back in agony and his face turned very pale indeed.

'God!' he moaned. 'Why are you punishing me?'

'He's not punishing you. I am.'

The Frightener tossed the bloody arrow aside after quickly inspecting the barb.

'You're lucky,' he noted. 'You may recover.'

'What do you mean?'

'If you're a good lad and you do as you're told, you'll get better.'

'What have I done to deserve this?'

'You're stubborn.'

'I know all about you and Aoife,' Robert hissed. 'I know what you have planned for me.'

'What are you talking about, you delirious fool?'

'I know you made a treaty with her. I know you agreed to pass me over to her in exchange for a feeding frenzy from the fear I could bring.'

Órán frowned.

'Where did you get that idea? Did Aoife tell you this?'

'She didn't have to,' Robert smiled through the haze of sweat and pain. 'I worked it out for myself.'

'What a clever lad you are,' the Frightener declared sarcastically. 'What other conclusions have you come to?'

'That you are more frightened of Aoife than anyone has ever been of you.'

Órán laughed but it was a hollow sound and Robert knew he'd struck close to the truth.

'I don't know what makes you think I'd be frightened of Aoife,' the spirit declared.

'Well let's see. The way you tried to convince me that you were God himself after you left me in the caverns of Aoife's halls seemed a little too desperate for a start. Then that confrontation on the stairs in the tower of glass was too contrived to be genuine.'

'You are very clever,' Órán conceded. 'I did impersonate your God before Aoife's feast. It was the only way I could see of convincing you to go through with the attack on Flidais. And you have to admit I took you in.'

Robert laughed, even though it was very painful to do so.

'I didn't believe that was the voice of God. It was a ridiculous impersonation of the Almighty.'

'Rubbish. You were so convinced I was the God of floods and fiery chariots that you knelt down in fear and promised you do whatever I told you to do.'

'I did not!' Rob countered. But the truth was he didn't want to admit he'd been taken in.

'Then why did you go ahead and murder Flidais?'

'Because I have glimpsed a greater view of the world. I've come to understand that my part in this life is not to live according to the rules of others but to follow my own heart. And since I am a good person at heart I will always strive not to harm anyone.'

'But you killed Flidais!'

'I prevented Flidais from murdering Aoife,' Robert countered. 'I saved her life. So perhaps I wasn't behaving that badly after all.'

'That's not good enough,' Órán scoffed. 'You cannot take a life for a life. You must have believed I was God.'

Robert couldn't deny it any longer. He had been taken in by the Frightener. He'd truly believed it was God speaking to him, commanding him to act.

'All right. You've made your point and you're very clever. I hope you're well pleased with yourself. What difference does it make? Flidais is dead. Aoife lives. And soon I'll be dead too. Perhaps I'm paying for my crime by relinquishing my life.'

'You're a fool. You can't escape your destiny that easily. Aoife and I have been around for a long, long time. We don't often find ourselves outwitted by a mortal such as yourself. Indeed, I can't recall the last time one of your kind got the better of me.'

'Well I have,' Robert said. 'I'm not going to be your High-King. I'm not going to live long enough.'

'Yes you will,' a woman's voice interrupted. 'I've waited a long while for someone of your calibre to come along. And I'll not just sit by and watch you expire.'

Robert turned his head to where the voice had come from. And sure enough there stood Aoife with her hands on her hips, staring defiantly at him.

'I wondered when you'd turn up,' Robert said. 'Please excuse me. I hope you don't think me rude. But it is rather difficult for me to bow to you just at present.'

'Don't be impudent! It ill becomes you.'

Robert coughed up blood before he spoke.

'We wouldn't want that, would we?' His voice was filled with bitterness, perhaps as much because his life was coming to an end as for the countless times he'd slavishly followed the edicts and orders of others 'We couldn't have the famous, gallant Robert FitzWilliam being impudent, could we?'

'Be careful, young man,' Aoife warned. 'I could make things most uncomfortable for you.'

'I'm dying. How could it possibly get any worse?'

'You have no idea,' the queen said. 'Do you?'

She stepped closer to where he was sitting propped against the dead oak-warrior. As she knelt down Robert thought she was going to reach out a hand to touch him, but instead she placed her palm on the oak-knight instead.

Instantly the corpse shuddered. Then it shook. In the next

breath the body moved and rolled over. The dead warrior was alive. He pushed Robert off him with fear written deep in the lines of his face.

'What have you done to me!' the warrior screamed at Aoife. 'When will this torture end? When will you let me rest?'

'Go now,' the queen commanded.

The oak-warrior struggled to his feet then stumbled off down the hill, constantly looking back over his shoulder at Aoife until at last he passed out of sight. Robert watched him every step of the way. And he knew what the queen was trying to say to him. That she would not grant him death until she was good and ready.

Sianan was concentrating hard. To wake Danu, she would have to travel back to the Otherworld to the grove wherein the goddess had been sleeping undisturbed for so long. But she didn't have time to traipse all the way back to the doorway at the forest entrance. Besides, that the road was swarming with enemies. No. She had to open a doorway in this storage room. And for that she'd need to sing the song of opening.

As chance would have it, among all the books that had been in the keeping of the people of the Killibegs, one page in particular had been rescued and passed safely on to Sianan. On one side of the page was an incantation capable of opening the doorway to the Otherworld. On the other side was scribed a song which would lull Enticer spirits and Frighteners alike into sleep.

Sianan had correctly discerned that she would have to put aside Aoife's Enticer and Frightener before she'd be able to make contact with the goddess Danu. For those spirits had a great deal to lose by Danu coming to wakefulness and ending Aoife's ambitions. After all, they'd been the ones who'd set her on her path to becoming a goddess.

By the light of one candle, our Sianan set about her task. I have to tell you that the singing of an enchantment of the Draoi kind is not unlike the singing of any other song. There are important differences, though, which the aspiring practitioner of the Draoi should bear in mind.

A song of enchantment involves a great deal of concentration of the most focused variety. There must be no chance of distraction at any time or the results may be disastrous. When you play with enchantment you are taking your life into your own hands.

Fortunately for Sianan the raising of a Draoi song was not such a difficult matter. She'd spent much of her long life in meditation and the practice of solitude. So she was able to quite easily invoke a sense of peace and determined, dedicated focus on the object of her desires. She knew that this was all that was required if one intended to bring one's deepest desires to fruit.

You may recall that both Caoimhin and the jester Mugwort had indulged in the practice of sigil magic. This is a method of distilling one's wishes into a tincture of intent by writing the wish down and then transforming it into a symbol which represents the wish.

Sianan didn't need to do all that work. All she had to do was concentrate with all her being.

The trouble was, she'd never tried it before. That's because she really believed that it was wrong to exercise such power over the world around her. And that just goes to prove that even someone as wise as our Sianan can get it wrong sometimes.

So there she was, seated on the cobbled floor of the storage chamber with the candle placed in front of her and her eyes focused on the flame. Her legs were crossed under her in the position she'd always adopted in her meditations.

For a long, long while she concentrated on nothing more than the gentle inward-outward movement of her breath. She listened to the rhythm of her own body, to the steady beat of her heart in her ears, to the subtle hum of the blood pulsing through her head.

Eventually she became aware of a deeper sound which coursed up through the floor beneath her and set every part of her body to trembling. It was that noise which most of us do not hear because we are bathed in it every day of our lives. It is a sound you may hear if you attune your senses to it, but unless you do you'll never hear it clearly.

It was known to Sianan and to the Culdee folk as the Song of the Earth. It is the hum, the gentle breath of the ground beneath us. And any who hear it instantly realise that they are insignificant in this world. You will know, when you hear it, that you are part of something much bigger than you could have imagined. You will understand that you are not just the body that you call yourself.

With that consciousness it is possible to attain great knowledge or to experience wonders beyond description or, in the case of the practitioner of the Draoi-craft, to work wondrous enchantments. So as Sianan fell into that state she started to sing the song she'd read on the page of the manuscript.

It wasn't a long song. Nor was it particularly poetic. I don't know exactly what was written on the page and even if I did I'd be cautious about letting you know. For this song was a lullaby. It was the most powerful lullaby known in the ancient days. It was the sleep song of the Frighteners and the slumber melody of the Enticers.

Our Sianan must have been chanting that song verse for a long while before she noticed a change come about in the air all around her. Then she heard an almighty crash and in that instant when the first burning timbers of the hall above her collapsed, she opened her eyes.

I have to say that she was startled at what she saw. Before her on a throne of gold sat a woman dressed in a long black raven-feather cloak. She leaned back in her chair with her eyes closed and her hands crossed over in her lap. And she had the most peaceful expression on her face.

Sianan recognised the woman immediately.

'What are you doing here?'

The woman opened her eyes to yawn.

'I came to listen to your singing. You have a marvellous voice.'

'Why are you here, Sorcha?'

'Don't you know?'

'If you've come to ask me to take on the office of Morrigán when you retire, then you should know this is a very inconvenient time. I have to concentrate on opening the doorway to the Otherworld so I can go and seek out Danu.'

'Why would you want to do that?'

'She is the only one who can put a stop to Aoife and save the Culdees of the Killibegs from slaughter.'

'You're too attached to these mortals,' Sorcha chided. 'You really should try to step back a little from them and allow them to decide their own destinies.'

'You mean I should abandon them to their fates without raising a hand in their defence!'

Sorcha shrugged.

'I suppose that's one way of putting it.'

'Well I won't! I know it's your job to cull the mortal kind, so I don't expect you to understand.'

'Cull is such an ugly term!' Sorcha said with obvious distaste. 'I prefer to look upon my duty as the control of a nasty infection.'

'I was a mortal once, you know. And not so long ago that I've forgotten what it means to be in pain or in fear of death.'

'Do you think it is easier to forget as time goes by?' the

Morrigán asked. 'Well it isn't. I was mortal too until I took the Quicken Brew. But now I am immortal. And immortality carries with it the weight of some certain responsibilities.'

Sorcha was speaking about the responsibility all immortals feel about caring for the Earth. I've spoken of this to you before. It's not so much that they feel an obligation to the Earth itself; they're mostly interested in their own wellbeing. If the Earth labours under the burden of too many short-sighted mortals then life will eventually become quite uncomfortable for the Ever-Living Ones. You see, mortals may kill themselves off through wars or through stripping the land of its goodness. But the immortals will live on.

In this world they'll have to suffer the consequences of having to put up with poor food in small quantities and war-ravaged lands that have been burned black by the barbarity of the mortals. Can you imagine what it must be like to have to live in the same body for all time? Now try to imagine what it would be like to be hungry for the rest of eternity. That's a thought that sends shudders down the spine of any immortal.

'Mortals will kill each other anyway. All I do is clean up the battlefield.'

'You spur them on!'

'Now and then,' the Morrigán admitted. 'But for the most part they don't need that much encouragement.'

'I could never do what you do,' Sianan vowed. 'I'm not callous like you. I have too much compassion for the mortal kind.'

'My dear!' Sorcha laughed. 'It is compassion which drives me on to do my duty. Imagine what the world would be like without me!

'In any case you'll find out all about that when you become my apprentice,' Sorcha said. 'You have a year to learn everything that has to be learned. Do you think you're up to it?'

'I refuse your offer,' Sianan replied with a hint of venom in her tone. 'The people of the Killibegs are relying on me to raise Danu. I must concentrate on that task. So if you will excuse me, I'd like to be left alone.'

'Congratulations,' the Morrigán went on as if Sianan hadn't said a thing. 'Any woman who aspires to the office of Morrigán has to be able to neutralise Enticers and Frighteners. A Morrigán must be entirely unbiased. You can't risk being influenced by feeding spirits. Imagine what would happen!'

'I told you I'm not going to be the Morrigán.'

'I thought you were a very intelligent young elder.' Sorcha shook her head. 'I was certain you'd have worked it out by now.'

'Worked what out?'

'Lulling the spirits into sleep was a test of your suitability. And you've done a brilliant job. Congratulations. You'll make a fine apprentice and an even better Morrigán of the Battlefield.'

'I must go in search of Danu,' Sianan said flatly. 'Leave me alone.'

'You won't find her,' Sorcha shrugged. 'She's in hiding.'

'I'll find her.'

'Not before it's too late. Once Aoife has been made a goddess no one, not even Danu, will be able to strip her of the title. And the Redcaps will have destroyed this rath before you've found where the old girl has concealed herself.'

Above them there was a terrible crash as another part of the great hall collapsed in the inferno. Of course Sianan had no way of knowing what was going on. So the cataclysmic noise unsettled her deeply. She assumed the Redcaps must have embarked on a rampage of destruction.

'I'll find Danu,' she promised, looking Sorcha directly in the eye.

'Even if you do locate the Goddess of the Flowing Waters, you won't be able to wake her. You don't know which song to

331

sing to rouse her. Just as there is a lullaby for the feeder spirits, there is also an awakening song for Danu.'

'You know that song.' Sianan sighed as she realised what was going to be demanded of her. 'You'll sing it if I promise to become your apprentice.'

'That's right!' the Morrigán clapped. 'You *are* as intelligent as I thought after all. You'll make a great Morrigán. You will.'

Above them there was another tremendous crash. Sianan looked up to the ceiling and noticed there was dust filtering down from above.

'Do you promise to bring Danu here immediately?' she asked.

'I do. I'll bring her here so fast your head will spin. But you must make three promises.'

'What would they be?'

'You must first swear to undertake to become my apprentice.'

'I promise.'

'Second you must promise to take full responsibility for waking the old girl. She can be mighty unsettled when she's been woken up. I don't want to have to bear the brunt of her temper if it gets the better of her.'

'I promise I'll take full responsibility. I'll say I begged you to wake her if you like.'

'No need to go that far. It's best to tell her the truth wherever possible.'

'What's the last promise?' Sianan asked wearily.

'You must solemnly vow to take on the office of Morrigán after your one year in training.'

Sianan hesitated. Her imagination was fired up by every sound of destruction coming from the hall above. And the pictures conjured up in her head were not pretty ones. She was about to tell Sorcha she wouldn't become Morrigán. She was going to say she'd rather take her chances trying to track Danu down for herself. But then there were shouts in the corridor outside where Alan and the others were stationed to defend the stores. The clash of steel could be plainly discerned. Sianan closed her eyes and swallowed hard, unwilling to make this commitment yet certain now there was no time to waste.

'Will you promise?' Sorcha pressed.

'Yes.'

'Say it.'

'I promise I will take the office of Morrigán from you at the end of my one year as an apprentice.'

Sianan opened her eyes to look at the raven queen. But to her shock and disappointment Sorcha was gone.

So there we were in the storage cellars of Rath Killibegs. And there was a terrible commotion taking place the like of which I shall never forget. The walls, floor and ceiling were shaking up a terrible storm of dirt, dust and crushed rocks. My ears were stinging with the din. And worst of all, the corridor in which we were sheltering was filled with an overpowering, indescribable stench.

'Isleen!' a great booming voice called out from somewhere within the hole in the wall that had opened to let the stink in. 'Where are you, woman?'

'Keep your ugly skin on! I'm coming! Couldn't you have made this tunnel a little wider?'

'I would have had to make it a great deal wider than it is to comfortably accommodate you, my dear. And that would have taken me twice as long to dig.'

'Just wait till I catch up with you, Lochie. You'll regret those words.'

William, Stronghold and the rest of us gathered in front of

the spot where Alan was resting against the wall. We had each silently determined to protect him to the last against whatever dæmons were about to assail us.

'What's that lovely aroma?' one of the worms asked the other.

'Isleen my darling, don't you know the smell of supper when it reaches your nostrils?'

'There's some tasty-smelling morsels up there in that cellar,' she replied enthusiastically. 'By my reckoning there's two women and an immortal. This will be a fine feast.'

'I've caught the scent of a few Norman warriors as well.'

'You can have them. I like my meat well washed. Those Normans we ate a few days ago are still playing havoc with my bowels.'

As if to emphasise the point there was a massive, earth-shattering sound of wind breaking.

'Do you feel better, my dear?' Lochie asked.

'I do. But there's more where that came from. So you better take the warriors. If I eat them there'll be no stilling my backside this side of Judgement Day.'

'Very well.'

In the next breath, and believe me when I tell you it was a cautious one, a great bulbous grey-black blob slid out of the hole in the wall. It was huge. Four horses could have been concealed behind it. But not for long of course. Nathairaí have voracious appetites.

There was a giant wet black lump which rolled about to one side of the blob. It took me a few seconds to realise this was an eye. And it was looking directly at me.

'Perhaps I could just taste one of the females,' Lochie whispered to himself. 'Isleen would never know.'

Stronghold stepped forward then, outraged that this creature could have been considering me as a meal. He drew his sword with a great flourish. But to his astonishment no change came over him. Eterscél did not emerge.

'Where are you, you damned Frightener?' Stronghold yelled at the sword. 'Just when I need you most you desert me.'

He had no way of knowing that Sianan had sung the lullaby of the feeding spirits. Eterscél was fast asleep and would probably remain that way for a long while.

'Eterscél!' my knight bellowed.

'Stop that yelling!' Lochie demanded. 'It's a frightful noise. You'll give me a terrible headache. And what's more you'll give her a headache as well. And believe me you don't want to do that.'

'We've met before,' Stronghold informed the worm.

Lochie took a few moments to observe the knight.

'I don't think I've had the pleasure,' he countered.

'You're friends of Aoife. I met you in the forest after you'd eaten my foot soldiers.'

'Were they yours?'

Stronghold nodded.

'Then I'd make myself scarce if I were you. Isleen has had a terrible case of wind ever since she devoured those men. And she'd love to have someone to blame.'

'I'm not afraid of either of you!' Stronghold stated.

Then he strode forward with his blade lifted high. As he came close to the worm's eye he slashed the sword down across the great black lump, cutting a deep gash into the eye. Dark grey ooze trickled out from the wound. I suppose it was what a Nathair would call blood.

'Steady on!' the worm shrieked. 'I haven't got myself out of this hole yet. At least wait until we can have a fair fight. What sort of a stoush would it be if I can't defend myself?'

'An easy one!' William answered and struck the creature with his axe.

The blade cut even deeper than the sword had done and a great gush of fluid spurted forth all over both William and Stronghold. The creature screamed in agony as Gusán and

John lent their hands to the attack. I picked up the bow Gusán had been using earlier and shot a few arrows into the beast as it squirmed about trying to extricate itself from the hole.

'You'll be sorry you started this!' Lochie cried. 'Things will go very bad for you now. I won't just eat you. I'll eat you slowly!'

'Not if we put an end to your appetite,' William retorted.

'You can't do that! I'm immortal.'

'Then we'll cut your head off like we did with all these Redcaps.'

Lochie froze as his eye scanned the corridor; there were indeed many dead headless Redcaps strewn about. This seemed to result in a complete change of heart, if it could be said that a Nathair had a heart.

'Don't hurt me!' the worm pleaded. 'I won't eat you! I'm only doing what Aoife told me to do. I don't really want to do you any harm.'

'Come out from that hole,' William demanded.

As the worm was squirming its way into the corridor Lord William marched up to the creature and shoved the flaming torch in its eye.

'I swear to you you'll burn if you try any tricks on us,' he threatened.

William turned to us.

'Fetch the oil.'

It was to our good fortune there was still a barrel of oil remaining. Gusán and John rolled it out and set about pouring it over the floor in front of the creature. Then William found a big ladle. He used this to pour oil all over the Nathair.

'Now let's see if we get a fair fight,' he laughed. 'You will behave yourself or we'll set you on fire and that'll be the end of you.'

'No! Don't do that! I've been a worm for centuries. I just want my old self back. You wouldn't set me on fire, would you?

336

Just wait till Aoife makes me a man again. Then you can try what you like.'

'What's all that bloody noise about?' Isleen cried out. 'What's going on up there?'

Lochie cast a slobbering eye back in her direction.

'Why don't you answer her?' William asked.

'That wouldn't be a wise thing to do. She's got a terrible temper. She won't take too kindly to all this.'

'Won't she?' William cupped his hand around his mouth and yelled into the tunnel. 'We have your husband hostage. If you don't behave yourself when you emerge we'll set fire to both of you. Do you understand?'

There was a long pause.

'That was a terrible mistake,' Lochie sighed eventually. 'You shouldn't have said that. Now she'll be really mad.'

'He's not my husband!' Isleen bellowed and I swear the very walls of the cellar shook with the reverberations of her rage.

In a very short Isleen's bulbous head emerged out of the hole. The first person she set eyes on was Stronghold.

'You!' she shrieked. 'I thought Aoife had dealt with you! I thought she'd changed you into a tree.'

'I've been changed. But it was none of Aoife's doing.'

'Wait till she finds out you're here! She'll tear you to pieces. No one escapes the Queen of the Night and lives to tell the tale.'

'Then perhaps you should fetch her,' William suggested. 'Go! Bring Aoife to us. And if you haven't returned in an hour we'll set fire to your husband.'

'How many times have I got to tell you? He's not my bloody husband! He's just the bastard I've had to spend the last several thousand summers with. I wouldn't marry him if we were the last giant worms on Earth.'

'Which we are,' Lochie pointed out.

'Shut up, you fool!' she screamed. 'What's Aoife going to

say? She's not going to be too happy that you've been outwitted by a handful of mortals.'

'I know,' Lochie sobbed. 'And everything was going so well. But you won't let them set fire to me, will you?'

'Of course I won't. Stop your blubbing! If there's anything I can't stand it's blubbing. I'll go and find Aoife. She can sort this mess out. We've done as she asked us. We've lived up to our part of the bargain. She should be happy with us.'

Isleen rolled her huge body toward the stairs which led up to the main gate.

'I won't be long,' she called back. 'Aoife can't be far away. Don't set him on fire while I'm gone. I'm sure we can sort this whole thing out amicably.'

I can remember leaning against the wall of the cellar and wondering how in the name of Saint Michael's Vomity Beard we managed to avoid that disaster.

ALL WILL BE REVEALED SHORTLY

I t would be true to say that Aoife, Queen of the Night, Sovereign Lady of the Redcaps, was a woman who rarely showed any true emotion. Sure she swaggered about dishing out verbal drubbings to anyone who got in her way, but that sort of thing doesn't replace real feelings. She'd grown more bitter with each passing winter and had long ago lost a connection with others.

I know you're going to think it a little strange but I can't help but feel compassion for her plight. You see, I know what it was that set her off on this wild, ill-advised attempt to attain the rank of goddess.

It all began not long after Aoife and her brothers had taken the Quicken Brew. She'd been in love with a Danaan prince by the name of Mahon. Now this Mahon was a simple fellow who was utterly devoted to his Aoife. But her father, King Brocan of the Fir Bolg, didn't approve of the match one bit.

The fact was his own wife, Aoife's mother, was said to have been regularly flattening the bed feathers with Mahon's father. So old Brocan wasn't too keen to have his daughter doing the same with another of that house.

That's why Brocan arranged a marriage of alliance between Aoife and King Eber Finn of the Gaels. Our Aoife wasn't too happy about that at first. That is until she caught sight of young Eber. He was a fine specimen of manhood it is said. And besides, she noticed how upset the whole business had got Mahon. She got it into her head to milk the situation for a bit of attention.

She was like that in her youth: self-centred and quite uncontrollable. Well it was bound to happen that Mahon decided to rescue her from the clutches of Eber Finn, who until recently had been an enemy of the Danaans and the Fir Bolg. Of course she pretended she didn't want to go, and there was a terrible mess that resulted in Aoife going off to take the long sleep which immortals are wont to do at times.

Thus she never saw her beloved Mahon again. By the time she'd woken up from her prolonged rest of several hundred years he'd left Ireland and headed off for sunnier climes. And who can blame him? He'd been spurned by his true love and he wasn't feeling too jolly about it, I can tell you. The trouble was that all that sleep had brought our Aoife to her senses, in a manner of speaking. She woke up and the first thought that entered her head was: where's that lad who used to follow me round and treat me like a goddess?

And that's where the problems started. She searched high and low for Mahon. Then she searched low and high. For good measure she looked wide, narrow, high and deep. But he was well gone by that time. She concluded that he was probably off in the mysterious east flattening mysterious eastern bed feathers with a mysterious eastern feather-flattener of the female kind. For the beds of the east are as well feathered as they are mysterious. I can surely attest to that.

But back to Aoife. She'd woken up expecting Mahon to have spent a goodly while pining for her company. She wanted to be treated like a goddess, she did. So she got it into her head that she'd become a goddess. Not just in the mind of some spotty lad with a weakness for poetry and an overinflated impression of his effect on women either.

She wanted to be a *real* goddess. The kind that folks bow down to and worship. The kind of goddess they carve beautiful sensuous statues of so they can present flowers and fruits to her at sunrise every morning.

She wanted to be just like Danu had been. Not only respected and worshipped but placed above all other creatures in the affections of the people. No, I'm not saying that was an unreasonable ambition. She was an immortal after all. And if there's one thing a goddess really has to be if she's going to leave a lasting impression, it's immortal. Few mortals have been accorded that honour in their lifetime. Those that have are mostly princesses and the like. They're halfway to deity status anyway but they're soon forgotten once the funeral is finished with.

No. I can't blame Aoife for having that particular aspiration. If I had the time on my hands and an eternity to while away I'd probably have a go at becoming a goddess myself. I may even have a go at it yet. I'm only ninety and that's considered young for a goddess.

But as I was saying, it's not her ambition I have a quibble with. It's the way she went about it. Aoife spent many, many years gathering to her the support of the Redcaps and the ravens. Now, the Redcaps were her father's people. They were Fir Bolg who had taken the Quicken Brew. So they accorded her some degree of loyalty already. As for the ravens, her brothers arranged that alliance for her.

Down through the centuries Aoife studied the Draoi-craft as she should have done when she was younger and had been apprenticed to the Druid profession. Better late than never, I suppose. Along the way she learned shape-shifting and many other enchantments, so that by the time Órán came to her with a candidate for a consort she was well and truly ready to take her chances at becoming a goddess.

Órán the Frightener had been attached to Lord William

FitzWilliam and had been grooming his son Robert as a possible High-King of Ireland. Of course when he heard that Aoife was after attaining a membership of the deity tribe he concluded they could work together.

As soon as she got a good look at Robert she heartily agreed. But it was her condition that he pass a few tests before she committed herself to him. The first of these tests was loyalty. Of course Robert being the man he was passed that one with a fanfare. He escorted Alan and Mirim on their long journey to Ireland and stood by them all the way.

The next test was of his fighting skill, which is why Aoife pitted him against Guy d'Alville. She even arranged for Guy to have a sword with a minor Frightener spirit inside. That was the one he had before Eterscél. And she stirred Guy up by convincing him she'd chosen him for her consort.

Of course she hadn't. She was just filling Guy full of foolish notions to get him put his best into the fight. Well our Rob beat him. That's another test he passed. The next one was a little more tricksy and it required quite a bit of subterfuge. Aoife had Órán lead Robert into the Otherworld to face the test of the moat maidens.

That's where Rob received his first initiation. That's where he was baptised with water when the maidens dragged him down into their depths. But he did not succumb to them. He escaped their clutches and went on to climb the Tower of Glass.

It was in the Tower of Glass that Robert was given the baptism of air when he climbed to the high battlements. And in accepting Aoife's quest he proved that he had an adventurous heart and ambition enough to attain the High-Kingship.

The murder of Flidais was yet another test. But by that time Aoife was pretty impressed with her man. That's when she started to give him more responsibility. She sent him off at the head of the oak-warriors to attack Rath Killibegs. She even arranged a suitable enemy for him to confront.

342

Yes, my dear. It was Aoife's doing that led the Sen Erainn to the Killibegs, though it may have seemed it was due to the intervention of Caoimhin. That was the way our Aoife used to do things in those days. It was she who brought Caoimhin to the place where Srón and Scodán were trapped in the form of wooden idols. And it was she who allowed him to find and rescue the hosts of the Sen Erainn. And once they were awakened from their enchantment Aoife led them out of the Otherworld as quickly as possible so they wouldn't be so much of a threat to her. She was a wily, cunning one that Aoife. And no one among us would have guessed it.

That is if Robert hadn't worked it out for himself. For when Aoife chose Rob to be her consort she picked a man who was her equal in all things but one. He was as quick-witted and ambitious as she was. He was as loyal and certainly as inquisitive. The only thing he lacked, which she had, was the gift of immortality.

'It's time we brought this adventure to an end,' Aoife sighed. 'It's time we went down to the cellars where the Culdees are about to make their last stand.'

'I'm sorry to disappoint you, my lady,' Robert replied. 'But I'm mortally wounded. The life is ebbing out of me. I cannot go with you.'

'Nonsense!' she laughed.

And in less time than it took for her to say that single word the wound in Robert's shoulder closed up. The colour returned to his face in an instant and he breathed easy without any pain whatsoever.

'What have you done to me?' he gasped.

'I haven't done anything you couldn't have done yourself. That is if you only understood you are in charge of your own destiny. You didn't have to take that arrow in the shoulder. You don't need to suffer pain. It is all a matter of choice.'

'I know what you're trying to say!' Robert sat forward and

rubbed his forehead, relieved the headache had dissipated. 'But you're wrong!'

'I'm right!' she laughed. 'Everything anyone encounters or accepts in this life is a matter of choice.'

Robert got carefully to his feet, wary lest the agony should suddenly return to assault his senses.

'It is not our choice. The choices are made by the One. We are merely instruments of the One. If you truly believe that you are an individual separated from the One and free to make choices, you are deluding yourself.'

Aoife frowned. If there was one thing she hated it was to be contradicted. For a moment she considered knocking Robert over in a fit of temper to teach him that her will was real. But then she smiled and shrugged as another thought came to her.

'We will go now. Lom Dubh! You will accompany us!'

In the next breath the air was filled with the buzzing hum of countless bees. Abruptly Robert felt his body engulfed by the humming creatures in the warm safe casing made up of their swarming bodies.

Then he lost sight of the battlefield as the bees blocked out all vision of the world. He felt himself lifted up off the ground and then he knew they were travelling high in the air over the battlement walls of Rath Killibegs. They had landed just inside the main gate before the doors which led down to the cellars. Robert shook himself, glad to feel the solid Earth beneath his feet, and the bees dispersed as quickly as they'd come.

Robert was appalled to see the great hall afire in a massive blaze which lit the entire rath like daylight. The heat was so powerful he had to shield his eyes from the burning intensity of it. Other outbuildings had also caught fire. He glimpsed Caoimhin directing folk to put out the flames and he wondered what had become of William, his father.

'Let's see what they're up to down there,' Aoife suggested. 'Don't worry. William FitzWilliam is still alive. He's waiting down in the storage rooms for us. Are you ready to come with me?'

'Take me to my father,' Robert demanded.

Aoife laughed and held out her hands over the double doors which sealed the cellars. In just a few brief seconds the doors began to rattle as if some horrendous beast was struggling to arise out of the depths. As indeed it was.

The doors suddenly flew off, splintering in every direction so that Robert cowered to protect his face from the flying shards of timber. When the dust had settled, the knight shuddered with disgust at what was revealed to him.

A great greyish-black creature as wide as four cows and covered in a thick putrid slime rose up out of the staircase. A huge monstrous black bulb rolled around at the foremost part of it. Then another. These two black pearls of malice moved around in the head of the creature until they caught sight of Aoife.

'Hello my dear,' a woman's voice said sweetly. 'I'm so glad you managed to get here in time. I've just come up to look for you. Lochie and I were about to start our meal when we were interrupted.'

'Isleen, my darling,' Aoife replied, wagging a finger in the air as if she were upbraiding a small child. 'We had an agreement. You promised you wouldn't eat anyone of importance to this plan.'

'I know. I know,' the Nathair sighed. 'But you can't blame me for wanting a little taste. I'm a giant flesh-eating worm with an appetite the size of a . . .'

She paused, trying to think of some creature that might have as great a capacity for hunger.

'The size of a giant flesh-eating worm?' Aoife offered.

'Quite.' Isleen shrugged, or as close to a shrug as one of those beasts can approximate. 'Lochie is waiting down below for you. He's managed to get himself into a bit of trouble with

345

a barrel of oil and a handful of torch-bearing mortals. He can be such a fool sometimes! Between you and me, I'll be glad when he gets his old body back. This worm business has been very damaging to his self-esteem. You should hear him blubbing!'

'And what about the Druid who calls herself an abbess? Has she called down Danu yet?'

'Possibly. She's locked up in one of the storage chambers where she can have some peace and quiet. We didn't want to disturb her.'

'Quite right too,' the queen agreed. 'We don't want her getting distracted, do we?'

Aoife turned to Robert.

'I'm sorry. I haven't introduced you. This ugly great lump of worm flesh is Isleen. Isleen, this is Robert FitzWilliam.'

'I know,' the worm replied. 'I met at your feast last night. Of course I was more elegantly attired on that occasion.'

Robert bowed, unsure of the polite manner in which to address a giant flesh-eating worm. In my experience it's best to douse them with oil and shove a torch under their noses to threaten them. But that's just my opinion.

Fortunately Robert's discomfort wasn't noticed by either Aoife nor Isleen. For at that moment Lom Dubh arrived in a great flurry of wings.

'What's happened?' he gasped. 'Have I missed anything?'

'Danu isn't here yet,' Aoife told him. 'Sianan is still busy trying to summon her.'

'I do hope she isn't going to fail us,' Isleen said.

'She won't!' Lom shot back. 'If anyone can do it then Sianan will. She's tough, that one, and she's got a good heart. Don't forget she's doing it to save the people of the Killibegs. I'm sure she'll have old Danu here in no time. Is the Morrigán still with her? Has Sianan made her promise yet?'

'She should have by now,' Aoife replied. 'We don't have

346

much longer to wait. All our plans are finally coming to a head. Everything we've hoped for will soon be ours.'

'What about Sárán?' Isleen cut in. 'What's happened to him?'

'He hasn't got a clue what we're up to,' Lom Dubh laughed. 'He's so caught up in his own petty little intrigues and bitter vengeances he never even guessed what we had in mind.'

'What did you have in mind?' Robert interrupted. 'What's going on here?'

The raven hopped over to where the knight was standing with a hand shielding his face from the heat of the fire. He cocked his head this way and that to get a good look at Robert then he turned to Aoife.

'Shouldn't you tell him?'

'In my own sweet time, dear brother. In my own sweet time.'

Isleen grunted.

'What are you waiting for? Tell him!'

'Not yet! I don't want to spoil things. Believe me, it'll be much better this way. There's one more little test I have for him. I want to see whether he's capable of getting really angry.'

'Will somebody please tell me what's going on?' Robert shouted.

'Do be quiet, my dear,' Aoife soothed. 'That's not what I meant at all. We don't want to attract any unwanted attention. All will be revealed soon enough. Trust me. You have nothing to fear.'

Lom Dubh raised his beak to the wind, catching a scent that made him shake his head with distaste.

'It's our brother. He's on his way. I can smell the downdraft of his wings on the breeze. Since he's started hanging round with the bark-splitting Norman bastards he's taken to their ways. He rarely washes. They're all filthy bloody heathens those foreigners.'

Then he remembered Robert was standing nearby.

'Present company excluded of course,' he added hastily. 'You're not like the rest of your people. You and your father are the finest of folk.'

'I demand to see my father,' Robert hissed. 'What have you done with him?'

'Keep your hair shirt on!' Lom answered. 'He's fine I'm sure.'

'Last time I saw him he was,' Isleen confirmed. 'Of course he's trapped down there with Lochie so anything could have happened to him. He's probably tearing his hair out by now with the agony of that ugly worm's company.'

'Take me to him!' Robert demanded. 'If you've harmed so much as a fingernail of my father's hand you'll suffer for it.'

All three guffawed.

'What are you laughing at, you fiendish creatures?' the knight spat. 'What have you done to my old man?'

'Calm yourself, Sir Robert,' Aoife said. 'He's perfectly safe. Believe me, of all the folk in Ireland we would like to visit our wrath upon, William FitzWilliam is not among them. We wouldn't dream of harming him. Your father is a firm friend to all of us, though he might not be aware of it. We couldn't have achieved our aims without him.'

'I don't understand.' Robert looked bemused.

There was another great fluttering and flapping of wings as a raven identical in every respect to Lom Dubh landed on the cobbles near to the gate. The bird stood with its head cocked to one side for a long while before it took a tentative step forward. Then it hopped a few paces.

Isleen, Aoife and Lom cast knowing glances at one another the whole time but they didn't look directly at the raven.

'Hello Sárán,' Aoife offered eventually.

'My name is Sciathan Cog!' the raven spat. 'When are you going to get that right?'

'Sorry!' Aoife held up the palms of her hands in a sign of her sincerity. 'I didn't mean to upset you.'

'So you're finally on the brink of becoming a goddess, are you?' Cog observed. 'I hope you're well pleased with yourself.'

Isleen stifled a laugh. Then Lom Dubh chuckled a little in the back of his throat. In the next breath Aoife was holding her hand in front of her mouth to stop herself from laughing. But it was all to no avail. All three of them broke out into loud fits of amusement.

'Oh you silly bird!' Aoife guffawed. 'You really have no idea, do you?'

The raven hopped forward, scowling deeply.

'What's going on here? I smell a rancid corpse and for the first time in centuries I don't like the aroma.'

At that very moment there was a great rumbling from deep below. Robert had to steady himself so he wouldn't fall over as the ground beneath him shook violently.

'She's here!' Isleen announced.

'Or she soon will be,' Aoife confirmed. 'It's time for us to adjourn downstairs.'

She turned to Sciathan Cog.

'You're welcome to join us if you like. Or you could wait up here till we're done and we'll tell you all about our meeting with Danu later.'

'I'll come with you,' Cog spat. 'I had a feeling you'd done something that could cost you dearly. Now I want to witness Danu's wrath at first hand.'

'Let's go then!' Isleen said. And she slithered, rolled and slid backwards down the stairs into the storage cellars.

Aoife took Robert by the arm to lead him down after the worm.

'Don't worry, my dear. You've nothing to fear. All will be revealed to you shortly.'

Sianan was beginning to despair that the Morrigán would keep her word when a great buzzing, as if of many bees, began to ring in her ears.

Sianan felt something in her hair and as she brushed the disturbance with the back of her hand she found a bee crawling on her finger. She flicked it away without a thought. Then she noticed another fly through the candlelight. In seconds thousands of the insects appeared in the chamber buzzing wildly. Sianan ducked for cover, fearing to be stung. She may have been immortal but that doesn't mean she didn't feel any pain. Then it struck her that perhaps this was Aoife's doing. Bees were her favourite way of announcing herself.

The candle flickered as it was swarmed by the insects and in the next breath it went out completely, plunging the chamber into darkness.

Sianan had no time to exclaim before a blinding flash of blue filled the room. It was so piercing that poor Sianan had to shield her eyes.

'You'd better be bloody careful what you say, young lady,' a stern matronly voice warned. 'I've come a long way to speak with you. And this business has interrupted a lovely dream I was having about the old days.'

Sianan looked up as the bright light subsided a little. She could make out the form of a woman standing with her hands on her hips. The light obscured her from view so she couldn't hope to glimpse her face. Another figure stepped forward to speak.

'Sianan? Are you all right?'

'Yes. But could you do something about the harsh lighting?'

'Don't be impudent, my dear,' the matronly voice snapped.

350

'This is the Goddess of the Flowing Waters who is standing before you. This is Danu.'

Sianan shielded her eyes and tried to stand up to bow. As she did so the light softened. Before her stood a little old grey-haired lady dressed in a long cloak with a tattered skirt of brown that dragged around her feet. Sorcha was standing behind her.

'Is that better?' the old woman asked in a gentle tone. 'I'm sorry if I startled you. Sometimes I don't know what comes over me. I forget how utterly awesome I am.'

'Danu?'

'Yes, my dear?'

'Is that really you?'

'Of course it bloody is! And people wonder why I don't manifest so often any more! Every time I put in an appearance someone questions my identity. Well what do you want? Proof? A miracle? What would satisfy you, you tiresome, faithless little excuse for a Fánaí?'

Danu stepped closer.

'I know all about you, my dear. You're supposed to have been a protector of the lore and law of your people. Well you're not much good at it, are you? You don't even recognise Danu of the Flowing Waters, Mother of All when you see her.'

'It's just you're not what I expected,' Sianan said hesitantly.

'Oh yes,' the goddess nodded. 'Here it comes. Just what were you expecting? A beautiful voluptuous young woman with impossibly large breasts and hips that could bring a horse into the world?'

Sianan swallowed, trying to choose her words carefully. But she didn't get the opportunity to speak.

'Or perhaps you were expecting me to have long red hair and a sensual wiggle to my walk?'

'No—'

'Of course you were. You Gaels have no imagination at all.

351

It's a wonder you ever overran this island in the first place. Perhaps if I hadn't left the defence of the country to the Danaans your lot might have stayed away. I'm sure I could have frightened your ancestors off. The roar of a lion here and there can have a devastating effect on a mortal.'

'Are you the lion that's been terrorising the countryside?' Sianan asked excitedly, thinking she'd solved a mystery.

'Of course not, you stupid girl!'

Then Danu turned to Sorcha.

'I thought you told me she was intelligent?'

'She is.'

'If she had half a measure of wits she'd know I'd be a lioness not a lion if I *was* going to masquerade as a large predatory cat.'

Danu turned her attention back to Sianan.

'So why have you summoned me? Sorcha tells me it couldn't wait another hundred summers.'

'It's Aoife. She's got aspirations to becoming a goddess and replacing you.'

'Has she?' Danu replied with interest. 'Go on.'

'She's sent a host of Redcaps against the Culdees of this rath and I fear they mean to slaughter its folk brutally.'

'And what do you want me to do about it?'

'I want you to stop her.'

Danu frowned. Then she stepped back a pace or two and placed a hand under her chin to. At last after a prolonged pause she replied, 'Why should I?'

'Because you are their only hope. Because you are the protector of the weak and the guardian of those who are enslaved.'

Danu waved her hand dismissively.

'Flatterer.'

'You're the Mother of All. Don't you care what happens to the Culdees? Doesn't it bother you that Aoife might be conspiring to usurp you?'

Sorcha stifled a laugh and Danu raised her eyebrows.

'Good luck to her,' the old woman replied. 'I'd like to see her try.'

'The Culdees are good people,' Sianan protested. 'Are you going to stand by and watch them butchered at the hands of Aoife?'

'Why are these people so important to you? You're immortal.'

'They are my people. They're Gaels.'

Danu's expression softened and she took a few steps closer to Sianan.

'How old are you, my dear?'

'Seven hundred and fifty summers or thereabouts.'

'Ah, I remember when I was a young innocent thing!' Danu sighed. 'I thought I could change the world, I did.'

She smiled indulgently at Sianan.

'Your people are not the Gaels. You are one of the immortals now. You must not spend so much time with those who suffer death. You'll only end up broken-hearted. They are dust. Only we endure.'

'But what about Aoife?'

'You're right,' Danu nodded and held out her hand. 'It's high time I dealt with Aoife. Shall we go?'

Sianan took her hand and in the next moment found herself hugging the old woman close as if she were a long-lost friend. Or her long-lost mother, which of course in one sense she was because Danu is the Mother of All. She wept then to feel so safe and cared for. She wept for the joy of that embrace. And she wept that she had denied herself this wondrous experience for so long.

'I hope you will spend more time among us now,' Danu soothed as they separated. 'Sorcha tells me you might be considering taking up the position of Morrigán.'

'She's promised,' Sorcha cut in.

'I'm so glad!' the old lady beamed. 'It'll do you good. And remember, if you ever need any advice, just come to me. I'll be only too happy to help.'

Then Danu yawned.

'Well, it really is time I was off to bed. I've got a lot of sleeping to catch up on. Good night, my dear. I'm glad we've sorted that all out.'

'But you were going to confront Aoife!'

'So I was!' The goddess laughed, amused at her own forgetfulness. 'I'll be losing track of my own name next! I'm getting terribly forgetful you know.'

She took Sianan's hand again and as she did so the doorway to the corridor was instantly clear of all the barrels and jars that had been stacked against it. In the corridor beyond lay the scorched, decapitated bodies of many Redcaps who'd fallen in their frantic attempt to escape the flames.

'What's all this then?' Danu asked Sorcha. 'Is there a battle going on?'

'Yes, my lady.'

'Well this has nothing to do with me. Battles are your responsibility.'

'I was hoping you'd put an end to this one,' the Morrigán admitted.

'There's a first! The Queen of the Ravens wants a battle to end! What is the world coming to?'

Danu stared down the corridor to where there was a clash of weapons taking place.

'I suppose we should just follow on after the din of battle?'

'That's right,' Sorcha nodded. 'Where there's conflict, Aoife won't be far off.'

The New Apprentice

Don't hurt me!' Lochie cried. 'You promised you wouldn't hurt me!'

'She's been gone a long while!' William raised his axe. 'What's she doing up there? I can hear her speaking with someone.'

'I'm not her keeper!' Lochie shrieked. 'You can't hold me responsible for her misconduct!'

Danu stood back to observe for a while.

'I suppose I'll have to take on some awe-inspiring form,' the old woman sighed. 'I do so hate having to resort to it. But most folk just wouldn't be very impressed if they saw me like this.'

With that Danu stepped away from Sianan and Sorcha.

'Wait here for a little bit,' she commanded them. 'After I've made my entrance you may come in after me.'

Then she tottered off like the little old lady she appeared to be. It was Gusán who noticed her first. But of course all he saw was an old biddy wandering about in the cellars. So his greeting wasn't all that polite.

'What do you think you're doing, you silly old badger? Can't you see there's a bloody great worm here fit to bite your head off if you come any closer? Are you blind as well as stupid?'

'My young man,' she began, shocked at his lack of respect, 'my name is Danu and I am Mother of All.'

'By Finbar's Leather Boat!' Gusán exclaimed with a laugh.

355

'What happened to you, my darling? Did you crack your skull? Or have you just limped out to lick the loony stick?'

'That's enough!' she shrieked.

In the next instant the entire cellar was filled with the same piercing blue light Sianan had seen when Danu first appeared to her. Then a terrible crash rocked the corridor, shaking the floor so that we were all knocked down to our knees.

The light intensified such that I had to cover my eyes and curl up on the floor. I was so frightened I nearly wet myself. Then as suddenly as the light had appeared it vanished, leaving the cellar lit only by the few torches we'd carried with us.

The little old lady was gone. In her place was a beautiful woman with long golden hair. She was wrapped in a long cloak of fine deep-blue wool edged in gold. All about her there was a glorious golden light that seemed to shine down upon her from above.

As she walked slowly closer to where Lochie was cowering I looked up and caught a glimpse of her eyes. At first I thought they were two huge sapphires, not eyes at all. They were like Sianan's and Mawn's eyes in some respects. But there was something else about them, a quality I cannot fully explain to you. It was as if when those eyes fell upon you she knew everything about you. Everything. Every dark secret. Every petty desire. Every fleeting indiscretion. Every dream. Nothing was hidden from her. Nothing was immune to her scrutiny. All folk were awed and ashamed in her presence.

There was something else about Danu I shall never forget. When she appeared the corridor filled with the sweet scent of honey and roses. I can still conjure to my mind a clear memory of that scent even to this day. And I recall that I breathed it in as if I was sipping a cup of the finest ancient mead. I may even have become a little drunk on it.

Gusán was kneeling down in awestruck terror before the goddess. She sauntered confidently over to where he was cowering, his eyes downcast. A few steps away from him she stopped. She threw back her cloak to reveal a tight tunic which wrapped around her upper body and outlined every contour of breasts and hips. Her skirt was long but it also fitted her closely.

'Young man,' she began, 'I want you to take a look at me.'

Gusán gulped loudly, certain he was about to have the most terrible punishment visited upon him. But he raised his eyes nevertheless. It doesn't do to disobey a goddess. His gaze followed up the length of her legs to her hips and then onward until he looked at the goddess eye to eye.

'Am I not beautiful?'

He was naturally speechless at her goddessy gorgeousness. So he nodded enthusiastically.

'Let this be a lesson to you. Always treat your elders with respect.'

Again he nodded.

Danu smiled and held her hand out to him. And as her palm spread out in the traditional attitude of blessing Gusán turned to dust. That's right, piece by piece he fell apart, falling to the ground in large portions of ash-like dust.

At first he was so shocked he couldn't cry out. By the time he did say something it was too late.

'I wish I'd kept my mouth shut,' he gasped.

Satisfied with the way she'd dealt with Gusán, Danu cast her attention about the corridor to see who else she might inflict some of her righteous outrage upon.

'I'm not in a very good mood this evening,' she warned everyone. 'I've been woken from a long sleep to come here and I'm not happy about it. So you'd all better treat me like the goddess I am or I'll fill this place to the rafters with dust.'

Everyone was perfectly silent, their eyes cast down, even Lochie. I'm sure you'll appreciate that was no easy thing for an ugly great worm.

'Well?' the goddess shrieked. 'What are we waiting for? Where's this Aoife? Why isn't she here?'

Danu's question was no sooner out than Isleen appeared sliding down from the stairs which led to the main gate. As soon as she saw the woman standing under the strange light she knew who she was looking at.

'All praise to you, Goddess of the Flowing Waters,' Isleen began. 'May the light of your countenance shine upon us this night and forever more.'

'That's more like it!' Danu smiled. 'That's how you greet a bloody goddess. Are you all listening? That was splendid. Now we're cracking.'

She turned her attention to Isleen.

'Don't I know you from somewhere?'

Isleen bowed as best she could considering the shape and expanse of her body.

'Oh Shining One of the Golden Radiance,' she gushed.

Danu held up her hand.

'No more toadying. If there's anything I can't stand it's excessive toadying. You got off to a good start but you ruined it with that slimy preamble. Just answer the question.'

'My name is Isleen. I am under punishment from you in your immense wisdom.'

Isleen bit her tongue, worried that last part might have sounded like she was laying it on thick.

'I remember you! I turned you into a worm for stirring up all that trouble between the Gaels and the Fir-Bolg. Weren't you a Fir-Bolg Druid who turned traitor, did a deal with Balor of the Evil Eye and then ended up imprisoned in spirit form?'

'Yes.'

'Didn't you have a husband who suffered the same fate?'

'He's not my husband,' the Nathair answered as politely as she could, trying not to show any hint of her frustration

358

that everyone kept assuming they were married. 'He's my companion.'

'I thought he was your husband.' Isleen got the impression the goddess was trying her patience. 'I don't know where I got that idea from. That was a long time ago, wasn't it?'

'It was, my lady.'

'I mean to say, it was a long, long time ago, wasn't it?'

'Indeed it was.'

'So have you learned your lesson?'

'I have, my lady.'

'All right then. You're free to go.'

'What did you say?'

'Your punishment is ended. You're free to go. I'll give you one mortal life to make up for the fact that it may have slipped my mind that you were trapped down in that awful well for so long. When you're done with that you can move on to be a feeder spirit if you like.'

'Thank you! Oh Mother of All! Thank you!'

'Yes, yes. That's quite enough of that.'

Danu raised her hand in exactly the same gesture she'd used to turn Gusán to dust. Lochie, who'd witnessed the demise of the unfortunate brigand, flinched. But Isleen closed her eyes in anticipation.

There was no flash of light, no magnificent spectacle. They both simply transformed. Instantly. It was remarkable. One moment there were two huge ugly worms sprawled there. The next there were two quite ordinary-looking people dressed in quite ordinary clothes. Nothing special.

But of course they were both overjoyed.

'We're free!' they shouted together as they danced around the cellar arm in arm. 'We don't have any unnatural powers either! We're just ordinary mortals. Hurrah!'

That would have gone on for some time but Danu lost patience with them. She told them to shut up. So they did.

Believe me, if you'd been stuck down a well in the shape of a worm for two thousand seven hundred summers, you'd sit up and take notice of the goddess who'd put you there.

Sianan and Sorcha walked down the corridor and stood behind the goddess as if they were ladies-in-waiting to a queen. But Danu was beginning to lose interest in the proceedings.

'Where's Aoife?' she yawned. 'I'm not hanging round till sunrise waiting for her. Tell her to get her arse down here now or she can forget about becoming any sort of a goddess this time round.'

'I'm here, my lady,' Aoife declared as she stepped down the last few stairs and into the corridor. Robert followed closely behind her, his head bowed. Lom Dubh and Sciathan Cog came along after.

'Who's the lad?' Danu inquired.

'This is Robert FitzWilliam,' Aoife replied.

William looked up at the mention of his son's name. There was such joy in his eyes to see his son alive again and to know he was safe. Stronghold looked up and the expression on his face was one of utter surprise.

'He's quite a dish of fish, isn't he?' Danu said. 'I like the white tunic. Nice touch.'

Aoife bowed.

'That's not exactly what I had in mind,' Danu said, turning her attention back to Aoife, 'but I'll take your word for it.'

It was at that very moment Robert caught sight of Stronghold. I don't know what came over him but it seemed to be nothing short of a violent rage. Rob strode past Aoife into the middle of the broad corridor. He drew his sword with a broad sweeping flourish as he went. When the blade was revealed Robert frowned. He must have been very surprised that Órán had not emerged.

'Where are you, Órán?' he called out. 'I have need of you!'

'What are you doing?' Sorcha cut in. 'Can't you see you're in the presence of Danu?'

'Let him be,' the goddess soothed. 'This should be interesting. By all accounts it's been coming to a head for a while.'

'Guy d'Alville!' Robert bellowed. 'Come out and meet your doom.'

My knight stepped forward.

'I'm not known by that name any longer. I'm called Stronghold.'

'I have a score to settle with you, d'Alville.'

'I have no quarrel with you, Robert. And I'm called Stronghold.'

'That's a strange name you've chosen for yourself. A stronghold built on a high fortified hill is not easy to assail. But it cannot be hidden either.'

He was quoting from the Gospel of Thomas. Our Rob had spent far too much of his life absorbed in books. It just wasn't healthy for a young man such as him.

He swung his sword around over his head, indicating that he would surely strike my knight down unless he defended himself. But Stronghold refused to draw his blade.

'Stand to me like a man!' Robert demanded. 'I will have your head as I should have done long ago.'

Stronghold drew his sword, more from habit than malice. He prepared to fight even though his heart wasn't in it. I suppose he didn't know any other way.

It was as well he did defend himself as it turned out. Robert swung at him with such ferocity their weapons rang out like bells in the corridor. Then they set upon one another with enthusiasm. The ringing of their blades was enough to set our teeth on edge. Every blow was a deadly one. Every parry put off death for one more moment.

'I'll kill you!' Robert screamed.

'I will not kill you.'

'You will die by my sword!'

'You will not die by mine.'

'You are my enemy!'

'I am not your enemy.'

Robert refused to listen to Stronghold's words of peace. He grunted like a creature made of pure malice. I could not stand back a moment longer. I ran out, flinging myself between the two of them.

'Leave him alone!' I screamed. 'Can't you see he means you no harm?'

But our Rob was whipped into a frenzy by then. He was so worked up he didn't see me at all. All he saw was someone who was standing between him and his enemy. He lifted his weapon to my throat and he held it there. I trembled, unable to make a sound. Everyone in the cellar gasped with shock.

Robert held me at the point of his sword but his eyes were on Stronghold.

'Yield to my blade!' Robert demanded. 'Or I will not answer for what happens next.'

I glanced at Stronghold. There were tiny beads of sweat at his brow and he was shaking slightly. Stronghold was frightened. And it wasn't the result of Eterscél's interference either. Eterscél was asleep.

In the next second Stronghold cast aside his sword, bowed down to his knees and offered his neck.

'I yield to you, Robert FitzWilliam.'

Robert forgot about me in an instant. He laughed as he raised Órán high to strike off his enemy's head. I screamed at him to hold back, begging him not to kill my knight.

Robert took no notice of me. He pushed me aside so that I tumbled over in the dust. His sword was ready. He gripped it with both hands. And just as he was about to bring it down he stopped.

He felt a hand at his shoulder and a familiar voice spoke to him soothingly.

'Thou shalt not kill,' Lord William told his son. 'This man

has fought alongside us tonight. He is your friend, not your enemy.'

Robert turned round.

'What has become of you, my son?' Will sobbed. 'What has become of you?'

Robert's eyes filled with tears and Órán slipped from his grasp. William kicked the sword away and held his son in an embrace that lasted for a long while.

Stronghold rose to his feet, picked up his sword, sheathed it and helped me to my feet. Then, our hands grasped tightly together, we retreated to our place at the wall.

'That was very exciting!' Danu whistled through her teeth. 'I haven't seen a display of passion like that since the days of Cuchulin. Magnificent!'

She turned her attention to my knight.

'That's what fear is really like, Master Stronghold. I'll wager you won't forget that experience in a hurry.'

My knight bowed his head before he grabbed me and held me for an age.

'Forgive me, my lady,' Robert apologised, breaking from his father's embrace.

'There's nothing to forgive. You've granted Stronghold a valuable gift and an incomparable lesson. You've taught him what it means to fear. I just hope you've got all that violence out of your system. You and Stronghold have a lot in common. I wouldn't be surprised if you became fast friends one day. Now go and stand with the Queen of the Night, there's a good lad.'

The goddess turned her attention back to Aoife.

'So have you completed the tasks I set you?'

'I have, my lady.'

'But have you completed them to my satisfaction?'

'I believe I have, my lady.'

'Let me see,' the goddess began, a hand to her chin as she

tried to recall each task in order. 'First of all you had to lure a suitable consort here from a far-off land.'

She pointed to Robert.

'He seems suitable. Is he?'

'He's loyal, courageous, dedicated and true to his word. He is of noble blood. He has undertaken the baptisms of water and of air. He followed my orders only to the point where they conflicted with his own sense of right and wrong. He's passionate, as you have witnessed. He undertook a quest to prove his worth to me and he fulfilled it completely and to my satisfaction.'

'What was that quest, if you don't mind me asking?'

'He cut the head off Flidais.'

'Flidais!' Danu whistled through her teeth again. 'I'm impressed. Still, she had it coming to her. She was a busy little bed-feather flattener that one. I'm not surprised she ended up with a blade at her throat.'

'That was my second task, my lady.'

'What was?'

'To bring about the death of another goddess without personally staining my hands with her blood,' Aoife reminded her.

'That's right! I remember now. There can only be so many goddesses, you know. We can't have everyone turning into a deity. The place would be overrun with them. That wouldn't do. It wouldn't do at all.'

You've guessed it by now I suppose. Danu had indeed been testing Aoife to see whether or not she had what it takes to be a deity. Almost everything that happened in my tale before Caoimhin came to Ireland and after was the result of some task Danu had set Aoife to complete. But now she was done with them all there was nothing left but for us to listen to her achievements.

Another of her tasks was to bring two foreign armies to war, which she did. The Hospitallers were foreigners, as were the oak-knights. Indeed, if you wanted to be picky you could have said that the Sen Erainn were foreigners too, for they came from Aran which is a good way off the coast of Ireland.

The full list of the tasks is quite long. I'll mention only a few of them here. To disrupt the ceremony of the Need-Fire at the Killibegs. Which she certainly did. To make a king out of a commoner. That was Caoimhin. To make a warrior out of a holy man. That was Clemens. To make a holy man out of a warrior. That was William.

To make an evil-hearted man into a loving soul. That was Stronghold. To make a mortal into an immortal. Caoimhin again. To free as many souls as possible who desired to be released from the enchantment of the Quicken Brew. That was the Redcaps who had volunteered to march on the Killibegs in Aoife's host. I know you're going to say they didn't go to their deaths willingly. But you'd be wrong. It's just that they decided they might as well take a few mortals with them. If you'd spent an eternity avoiding death perhaps you'd like to make something of it too when it finally happened to you.

What else was there? To help the Morrigán find a successor. That was Sianan. To make a jittery man into a courageous one. That was Lanfranc.

The list goes on. Indeed, there isn't a single transformation in this tale that wasn't a task set by the Mother of All for Aoife to complete. Now, you might say that it wasn't very nice of Danu to use us all as playing pieces in her game. You might say that Aoife had no right to manipulate us all the way she did. But try saying that to the Goddess of the Flowing Waters. See what she says.

I dare you.

Things didn't turn out too badly. Not really. But I'm jumping ahead of myself again.

'You've done quite well,' Danu conceded. 'I'm impressed with you.'

'Thank you, my lady.'

'I accept you as my apprentice. You will begin your training in earnest on the morrow.'

'Thank you, my lady.'

Then Aoife remembered something very important.

'My lady, may I ask a favour of you?'

'You can *ask*.'

'My brother Lom Dubh helped me to attain my goals. Would you be able to see your way clear to rewarding him in some way?'

'In what way?'

'He's been under an enchantment for a long while . . . You probably don't remember what happened.'

'Yes I do! He and his good-for-nothing twin brother murdered two ravens. The Morrigán who reigned before Sorcha demanded the stiffest penalty under the law. The pair of them were condemned to live out their lives as ravens.'

'That's true, my lady,' Aoife agreed. 'But that was a long time ago. Surely he's served out his sentence.'

'Is his life over?'

'It is not, my lady,' Lom Dubh chirped up.

'I wasn't asking you!' Danu shrieked.

She softened as she saw him hopping forward. He truly cut a pathetic figure considering he'd once been the king of his people.

'I can't just let you go,' the goddess said. 'If I release you I have to release your brother. And in any case, the imprisonment was for the term of your natural life. I admit that for an immortal the punishment is much harsher than if you'd been born to many lives. But there's nothing I can do about it.'

'Can you find no room for mercy in your heart, my lady?' Lom cried.

'Not if you continue addressing me without my leave!'

Then she relented again.

'This sort of thing doesn't happen every night, I suppose. I mean, Aoife has earned her apprenticeship. And it is Samhain Eve after all. So come here, Master Lom.'

Lom Dubh hopped excitedly over to stand before the goddess. He bowed as best he could, clacking his beak with excitement. Danu leaned down to whisper a few words in his ear. As she spoke his eyes widened and he took a sharp breath in shock.

When she stood up again the raven jumped back and cocked his head to one side.

'That's it! A geas? That's all you're going to give me? A bloody geas?'

'Don't be impolite. It's the best I can do under the circumstances. Be grateful for small mercies. I'd advise you not to divulge to anyone the details of this arrangement. '

The raven bowed again and hopped away, muttering, 'Geas' under his breath. In my opinion it was a fine thing Danu did for him. You see, a geas is a prohibition. And the whole mess Lom Dubh had got himself into was over a geas or two.

Well, Danu had arranged it so that this geas she'd given him only had to be broken for him to meet his death. In other words, Lom Dubh now had what most immortals would never have. He had the power to choose the moment and the manner of his own death. So in a sense he was no longer an immortal.

'What about me?' Sciathan Cog interrupted. 'You can't let him go and not release me!'

'Be quiet!' Danu touched her fingers to her forehead. 'I've just been struck by a terrible headache. And I hate the way everyone starts lining up for favours as soon as I dish them out to a few worthy folk.'

'I'm worthy!' Cog protested.

'That's enough! I'm off home. I refuse to be hounded by petitioners. If I'd wanted that sort of a life I'd be an absolute monarch with an empire at my feet.'

She turned to Aoife.

'That reminds me,' she said lowering her voice. 'Do you still intend to put that lad of yours on the throne?'

'No, my lady,' Aoife laughed. 'That was just a little something I told him to find out whether he'd put his ambition before his ideals.'

'How did he fare?'

'He refused the crown, my lady.'

Danu winked at the younger woman and whistled softly through her teeth.

'I think you may have done very well for yourself there,' she told her with a nudge of the elbow. 'I'd keep him if I were you.'

'I intend to, my lady.'

'Right!' Danu clapped of her hands. 'I'm off now. The Morrigán will attend on me. We have to organise a bit of a celebration for Aoife and Sianan. And there's the funeral for Flidais to be considered.'

'My lady,' another woman interrupted. 'Forgive me.'

Danu turned to look down upon the desert woman who was kneeling before her with tears in her eyes.

'What do you want, Mirim?' the goddess asked her gently.

The desert woman was a little surprised that Danu knew her name.

'I know everything. It's one of the tricks we deities learn early on in our careers.'

'Can you help my husband?' Mirim begged quietly. 'He's dying.'

Danu was clearly moved. She stepped forward and placed a hand on Mirim's shoulder

'Stand up, my dear.'

Mirim arose and no one who looked on her face could have been unmoved by her expression.

'You of all people have been blessed more than most,' the goddess told her. 'And I bless you now. I bless your husband also. Though you may not understand the form my blessing takes, I want you to keep faith that you have indeed been blessed. Don't ever forget it.'

'Thank you, my lady.'

'Now it might be a good idea to take him up to see the sunrise.' With that the Goddess of the Flowing Waters turned sharply on her heel and walked back down the corridor toward Sianan.

'You'll make a fine Morrigán,' she whispered as she passed the abbess. 'And Mawn should be your consort. It's time the two of you spent more time among your own kind.'

As she spoke those words Danu transformed completely into the old woman who'd first appeared to them. Her clothes were simple and her hair was grey.

'That's better!' she sighed. 'But there are two more things before I go.'

She pointed to William FitzWilliam.

'When you've said goodbye to your son and finished tidying up here, I want you to come to visit me. The Morrigán will fetch you when you're ready. I think we have a lot to discuss.'

She winked and cackled like the mischievous old woman that I am now. And then she vanished without another word or even the slightest hint of a hive of bees to see her off.

'She said there were two things left for her to settle,' Sianan whispered to Sorcha. 'Has she forgotten something?'

That's when the pile of dust that had been Gusán began to shift in the breeze. It swirled up and around in a spiral of dirt until it resembled the shape of a man. Then the colour darkened as the dust coagulated into the form of Gusán.

He took a deep breath, sneezed violently then shook the dust out of his hair.

'By the Holy Bearded Jowls of Saint Michael!' he exclaimed. 'Bless you, Lady Danu!'

In my opinion she let him off lightly, she did. I suppose

almost everything that took place in my tale was set in motion by Danu and not just because she's the source of all things. She'd set the tasks to Aoife and everything that happened afterwards was a measure of her suitability to become an apprentice to the Mother of All.

But of course that's not the end of my story. Not by a short distance anyway.

As soon as Danu had gone, Aoife took her leave also. She embraced Lochie and Isleen, promising that if ever they needed anything at all they only had to ask and she'd be there to help. Her gratitude was limitless, she said.

She told Robert he was an inspiration to the mortal kind, that he had earned the right to sit at her side. Then she invited him to join her at the Tower of Glass.

'This time do not dally at the moat,' she advised. 'Come straight up to the roof. I'll be waiting for you.'

Then she stood before Guy Stronghold and smiled.

'You've done well. Of all these folk you have perhaps journeyed the furthest and achieved the most. I'm sorry I led you on. I'm sorry I turned you into a tree.'

'I'm grateful for the experience.' He bowed graciously. 'It is one I will cherish for the rest of my days.'

'I grant you this fortress,' Aoife declared. 'I charge you to rebuild it and to make it a refuge for the Culdee folk. It will be a place where they can come to hear the stories of the old days and learn about the transformations which may change any of us at any time.'

She turned to me.

'When you tell this story, Binney, don't forget to mention

that you all thought I was an evil-hearted so-and-so and that it wasn't till Danu turned up that you discovered the truth. And since there are no Sen Erainn here, please pass on my apologies to them. It was a terrible thing for them to be trapped as wooden idols. Tell them I beg their forgiveness and I'll watch over them always. When you tell this story don't leave anything out. Not even the slightest detail. Don't forget.'

'I won't forget,' I promised. 'What about Caoimhin?'

She smiled.

'Still interested in him? Aren't you satisfied with Stronghold?'

I blushed.

'Of course I am.'

'Caoimhin will always be your fast friend. And perhaps one day you may earn the right to join him. Wait and see.'

She moved on to Mirim. No words passed between them but I could see that Aoife was distressed at what had become of Alan at the last. She placed a hand upon the desert woman's head and passed to her a silent blessing. And folks often said in later years, when Mirim's good fortune was considered remarkable, that Aoife herself had blessed her with a full life.

'I'm sorry,' Aoife told Lom.

'It's all right!' he cawed. 'At least I have a geas. That's better than nothing.'

'When I'm a fully fledged goddess, I'll release you,' Aoife promised in a whisper, just in case Danu was listening.

'What about me?' Sciathan Cog piped up.

'You have a lot of work to do if you're ever going to make it up to me for your evil-hearted treachery,' she replied sternly. 'Fortunately for you there's plenty of time. Indeed, you have the rest of eternity to make amends.'

Aoife raised her hands to the ceiling to call in her bees. They buzzed wildly down the staircase in a great swarm, sending everyone ducking for cover. As they were about to engulf her the apprentice goddess said one last thing.

371

'I won't forget any of you. You will all forever hold a special place in my affections. Call on me now and then. And do not forget what we have shared together.'

'Thank you for fixing my toothache!' John cried out.

She bowed her head to him as the swarm covered her. The bees lifted her off the ground and flew up the stairs, spiralling out into the open air. Then they were up and away over the battlements of Rath Killibegs, headed back to the forests of the Otherworld.

Once she was gone William, Stronghold, Gusán and John lifted Alan up as carefully as they could and carried him upstairs into the open air. Mirim was by her husband's side all the way, talking gently with him and mopping his brow. Not that he could hear her. He was unconscious as they laid him down on the cobbles at the top of the stairs and flung the main gates open.

I was able to get much closer then. I saw that the arrow was lodged deep in between the second and third ribs.

Caoimhin, Srón and Scodán ran over to us, excited that the Redcaps had been defeated. I learned later that the Sen Erainn warriors who'd come into the fortress with Caoimhin had been very busy. Under Scodán's leadership they'd spent most of their time rounding up the one or two Redcap stragglers who hadn't been caught in the hall. It may not sound much to you but two immortal warriors on the rampage can be more than enough to deal with.

Once they'd done that they made valiant but futile attempt to put out the fire in the great hall. Of course by that time they had no hope of doing so.

Caoimhin and Srón had busied themselves helping the wounded and distressed folk of the Killibegs and searching among the slain or injured for some sign of William FitzWilliam, Clemens and Derbáil.

They were relieved and happy to see us all alive. But their

mood turned sombre when they saw Alan laid out on the ground.

There wasn't much blood staining his brown tunic and for that we were all silently thankful. A quantity of blood would have been a sure sign that the wound was mortal. The desert woman cradled his head on her lap as she waited for Sianan to bring her healing knowledge to him. As Mirim brushed the hair out of his eyes he came to and looked up at her with tenderness and deep affection.

'What hit me?' He frowned like a little boy who has fallen out of a tree but can't explain where he put a foot wrong. 'I feel like I've just been butted over by a bull.'

Despite the seriousness of the situation Mirim laughed. She couldn't help herself. In part she was relieved he was awake and able to talk. I suppose, too, Danu's words had offered her some comfort.

Sianan was by his side then. She took his hand, looked into his eyes and checked his heartbeat.

'Was I butted over by a bull?' he asked her.

Sianan smiled at him but as her eyes met Mirim's her conclusion was clear. The abbess hardly moved her head. But it was enough for the desert woman to know the verdict.

'You've been hit by an arrow shaft, my love,' Mirim told him, and her eyes welled with tears.

Alan struggled to sit up so he could get a better look at the wound. His fingers found the shaft then he carefully touched it along its length to the point where it entered his body.

'It can't be too serious. I can't feel any pain at all.'

The desert woman's face drained of colour. She knew well enough what it meant that he could feel no pain.

'It can't be too serious,' she echoed, brushing the hair from his face again. 'It's nothing to worry about.'

'I must get up and go back to the fight. The enemy will be upon us in a few moments.'

'The enemy has been routed. The battle is over. Rest awhile here in my arms before you arise. There's no hurry for you to be going anywhere.'

Alan looked into her eyes again and smiled.

'I know who I am. I am Alan de Harcourt. I am of a noble family. I was a Templar knight once. I am husband to Mirim of the Shali Oasis who is my joy and my light.'

As he spoke he tried to get up but Mirim would not let him.

'You must lie perfectly still for a while, my love. Sianan has commanded it. She is a healer and she knows best. The sun is rising. Let us watch it together.'

'It's so dark!' he coughed. 'Surely sunrise is a long way off.'

The light of life in his eyes was already fading. We could all see that plainly enough. He blinked to clear his vision but it was no good. Mirim placed a leather water-skin at his mouth and poured a little liquid in. He swallowed it then smiled broadly.

'That's come from the Well of Many Blessings. I'll never forget the sweet flavour of that water.'

He coughed again. He seemed suddenly to understand that his life was ebbing out of him. He struggled to look at the arrow again. Then he collapsed back on to his wife's lap.

'Alas, but the well waters cannot help me now. I am too badly injured.'

'Don't speak so, my love,' she cried softly. 'All will be well. Danu has given us her blessing.'

'What will become of me?' he asked. 'Will I go to Hell for breaking my vows to the Temple?'

'You will go to Heaven for keeping your vows to me. And since you have married into my clan, my ancestors will come to fetch your spirit away to the Land of Bliss. Wait for me there. I'll be along when my time is done.'

Alan smiled again and closed his eyes.

'Sing to me,' he whispered. 'I want to hear you sing.'

Mirim choked back the tears. The only song she could think of was the love song that had been running through her thoughts since the night before. So she took his hands in hers and sang.

'While I am sleeping you carry off all my pain and suffering, in your beautiful hands, your beautiful hands. While I am weeping you carry me like fragrant rosewater, in your beautiful hands, your beautiful hands.'

Speech left her as the melody became a wordless lilt. Mournful it was and joyous too. This was her parting gift to him. This was their last farewell so she determined to sing one verse again.

'While I am sleeping you carry off all my pain and suffering, in your beautiful hands, your beautiful hands.'

As her voice trailed off she realised Alan had ceased his breathing. His eyes were shut and he was perfectly still. There was a little smile at the corners of his lips, almost as if he'd simply fallen asleep. So it was a few moments before Mirim realised he was gone.

She closed her eyes tightly to stem the tears and it was while they were shut she thought she heard the sound of a drum. Then she was sure she could discern the music of a lute plucking out a strange rhythmic melody. Hands began to clap in time with the tune. And as she opened her eyes again a strange sight was revealed to her.

There were people gathered round dressed in the manner of the desert folk of Shali. Their skin was dark like hers and their eyes were bright with joy. Their robes were white and their dance was a celebration.

The ghosts of her ancestors had come to take Alan home with them. She'd heard her grandmother describe them on her deathbed when they came to take her home.

The Shali ancestors formed a crescent around the spot where Alan had been laid. Among their number were lute players, drummers and many folk who simply added the sound of their clapping beat to the music. And every one among them was smiling with immeasurable ecstasy.

The desert woman sniffed back the sobs as an old woman stepped out from the crowd. She held a wooden flute in her aged fingers and she looked directly into Mirim's eyes. It was obvious now to Mirim what was happening. The flute had ever been the instrument ghostly guides used to summon the soul of a newly departed. The old woman placed the instrument to her lips and played a gentle, haunting, enticing melody such as Mirim had never heard before. It was a touch melancholy, yet it begged the listener to stand up and dance along with it.

Mirim was slightly startled to see the ethereal form of Alan rising gently out of his body. He floated up just enough to separate him from his corpse. Then he sat up slowly, all the while keeping his eyes firmly fixed on the old woman.

In a few moments he was standing. Then he was walking slowly toward the flautist in time with the music. A long silver cord connected his soul heart to his body heart. As Mirim watched, the silver cord unravelled like an old rope. In a few brief seconds it had fallen apart and broken in the very middle.

The old woman's melody dropped away and she played only long, slow, wailing notes. The clapping ceased too. But the music wasn't ended. It was merely calming.

At that very instant Alan turned around. There was a look on his ghostly face as if he'd forgotten something. He searched for Mirim. His vision of this world had dimmed. He was already walking in the world of souls.

When at last he caught her eye, he smiled again before he spoke.

'While I was sleeping you brought to me gifts of love in your beautiful hands.'

The old woman struck up the flute again. Alan turned regretfully toward her just as the rising sun peeped up into a cloudless morning sky. The old flautist guided him through the crowd of folk gathered behind her and into the sunlight.

Just as the old woman herself disappeared into the blinding sunrise Mirim finally recognised her as her very own grandmother. She knew then that Alan was in safe hands. He would be welcomed into the bosom of her clan as he was when he first arrived at the Shali Oasis. But most important of all, she knew he would be waiting for her when it was her turn to depart this life.

The desert woman could no longer hold back the flood of tears. Thoughts of hopelessness caught hold of her. What use had all their journeying been? In the end all their struggles together, all those years searching for an enchanted well, had been for nothing.

But our Mirim wasn't the kind to entertain such self-indulgent thoughts for very long. It hadn't all been for nothing, she admonished herself. It had been a wonderful journey and she had been blessed to share it with such a man as Alan.

She understood what Danu's blessing had meant and she was grateful for it.

She looked down at Alan's corpse and brushed the hair from his eyes again. This cold body was not her husband. He was gone. Her attention shifted to his lifeless fingers and she clasped them tightly in her own.

She remained there for a long time, lamenting the passing of her dear one. Lanfranc and his men had made their way up to the gates before she arose. They stood around with bowed heads to pay homage to Alan.

Lewyn and Overton emerged from the storage chambers where they'd been walled in. And Mirim was still there staring down. I clearly recall that all the folk gathered there were perfectly still as they showed their respect. Only the desert woman spoke. Every once in a while she'd whisper just two words.

'Beautiful hands.'

The Deepest Part of the Lough

aoimhin, Srón and Robert waited at the edge of the lapping waters of the lough as the holy Finbar rowed ever closer. The sainted one was in no hurry either. Why would any man be in a hurry to cross back and forth ceaselessly between the island and the shore?

The holy leather boat was still a long way off when Caoimhin noticed there was a single passenger seated in front of Finbar. The chill winds of Mi na Samhna, the month of Samhain, lifted up Caoimhin's cloak then. By the time he'd smoothed it down the passenger in the boat had turned around to look closely at the three of them gathered on the shore.

'Keep your head covered,' Caoimhin hissed. 'And don't speak a word or you'll give the game away. There's no women or headaches allowed on the holy Island of the Living.'

Srón nodded and wrapped the cloak tightly round her head, as much to keep out the cold as to abide by his instructions.

'Does he really know the answer to any question?' she asked in a whisper.

Caoimhin smiled.

'There isn't anything he doesn't think he knows.'

By that time Finbar's boat was less than ten oar strokes off from the pebbled beach.

The passenger stood up.

'Is that you, Caoimhin?' the old man shouted, waving wildly so his motion rocked the little vessel.

'Sit down, you bloody fool!' Finbar shouted. 'You'll drown us both!'

'If twenty years living on this ale-soaked island couldn't drown me, then a quick dip in the lough won't do it either,' the old man replied gruffly.

It was then Caoimhin recognised the passenger. It was Michael, who was of course renowned throughout Ireland in those days as Saint Michael of the Unkempt Beard.

'His beard doesn't look very unkempt to me,' Srón noted dryly. 'It's neatly combed and trimmed. Are you sure it's him?'

Before Caoimhin could reply, the leather boat scraped along the pebbles and came to a halt near to where the three of them were standing.

'Caoimhin my boy!' the saint cried as if he'd been reunited with a long-lost friend. 'I was just coming over to search for you. I had no idea you'd be returning to the island so soon.'

'Are you really leaving?' our young king asked.

'I am indeed,' Michael nodded enthusiastically. 'But you've saved me traipsing the whole country round searching for you.'

'You look much better than you did the first time we met.'

'Do you want to hear a story?'

The old boy didn't wait to find out the answer. He went straight on with his tale.

'I had spent two of those farthings you gave me on strong drink when I discovered I'd misplaced the third. I searched high and low for it, cursing and swearing like a man dispossessed. Which I certainly was. I cried for strong drink. I begged for it. I offered to barter the words of my wisdom for a jug, but I could not find the lost farthing.'

'That's why you're leaving?'

'No. You see, in the end I realised that farthing could have got me away from this island forever. I took a solemn vow not to get soused again. I haven't touched a drop since.'

Finbar coughed.

'Except for Samhain Eve,' the old man conceded. 'I did get myself pickled that night! After all, it is the night the gateway to the Otherworld is thrown wide open. I didn't want to be lured into that awful country to be enslaved by the dæmons who dwell there.'

'How would getting yourself drunk ensure you wouldn't be lured into the Otherworld?' Robert asked.

'Have you ever seen a fish take the bait on a hook?'

The knight nodded.

'What do you notice about such a fish as gets hooked by the aforesaid bait?'

Robert shrugged.

The old man winked. 'For a fish to take the bait it generally has to be conscious.'

There were frowns all round.

'How could I be lured into the Otherworld if I was dead drunk?' Michael sighed as if to say they were all stupid. 'So of course I had a drink on Samhain Eve.'

'You had a barrel of drink,' Finbar corrected him.

'And I don't remember a drop of it,' the old man stated proudly.

Then he recalled why he'd been so excited to see Caoimhin again.

'My boy!' he cried excitedly. 'My dear lad. Did you see the Book of Aontacht? Did that old bastard Clemens of the Killibegs let you read the sacred words within the mighty manuscript?'

Caoimhin shook his head, wondering how he was going to break the news to the old man. Very quickly he decided it was best to be direct.

'There is no Book of Aontacht. It's just a story the Culdees tell to distract the curious from the real treasures of their library. I'm sorry.'

The old man was crestfallen at the news. Clearly he'd been looking forward to finding an answer to his malady. For Michael, as you may recall, was afflicted with the visions as Caoimhin was.

'Never mind,' he sighed, but it was obvious the news had hit him hard.

Then a thought crossed the old man's mind.

'I don't suppose you found the answer to your question? Do you know how to overcome the visions?'

Caoimhin smiled.

'I have not. I have learned to live with them. I understand them as a blessing now, not a curse. For I have taken a sip from the waters of the Well of Many Blessings. And I've tasted of the Well of the Goddess also. Neither could quench my thirst and neither compares to the sacred waters sprung from the Well of Yearning.'

'You've been to the Otherworld then,' Michael nodded. 'So perhaps I must go there also to find the answer for myself.'

With that he clambered out of the boat to stand ankle-deep in the chilly waters.

'I haven't been away from that cursed island for twenty years. Now at last I'm free.'

'Where did you find the farthing to pay for your journey?' Caoimhin asked.

'I was washing out my beard for the first time in a long while. I decided I'd better clean myself up a bit. Suddenly, lo and behold, there it was in my hand, all sparkling and bright like the first cup of cider from the barrel.'

He thought for a moment.

'That's not all I found either. There was a key, a toasting rack, three small white pebbles and a treatise on heresy by Saint Augustine of Hippo. Very entertaining it was too. What a master comedian that fellow was in his day! I haven't laughed so much in years.'

The old man held out his hand to Caoimhin. He turned the palm up to reveal three white pebbles.

'Take them.'

The lad opened his hand to receive the tiny precious stones.

'That's not on!' Finbar protested. 'All pebbles have to pass through my hands!'

'They have passed through your hands,' Michael told him tersely. 'Where else would I have got hold of white pebbles in this godforsaken lough of the dark wet stones? I've just been saving these up for a while.'

A shadow passed over Finbar's expression.

'Very well. Let's push off for the island. Farewell old man. I hope you find whatever it is you're looking for out there in the wide world.'

'Or in the Otherworld,' Caoimhin added.

'I will,' Michael replied cheerfully. 'I will.'

With that he made his fond farewells and set off into the wilds. His soul-voyage had begun anew with a short trip in a leather boat.

Robert and Srón stepped into the vessel to take up their seats.

'Is that a sword you have there?' Finbar asked Robert.

'It is.'

'No swords allowed on the Island of the Living.'

'No women and no headaches,' Caoimhin cut in. 'That's the only rules I ever heard of. No one ever mentioned anything about swords.'

'Well I'm mentioning it now! No swords allowed on the Island of the Living.'

'Don't worry. I wouldn't dream of breaking the rules of your community.'

'Then leave the blade behind!'

'I won't get out on the other side with this sword in my possession,' Robert promised. 'You have my word on that.'

'I'll make sure you don't.' Finbar muttered under his breath. 'Bloody mystics.'

By then Caoimhin had stepped into the curragh and seated himself. The boatman pushed off and took up his position at the rear of the little vessel.

'Are we all ready to cross over to the holy isle?' he asked.

They nodded, so with a great downward thrust of his oar against the pebble beach the boatman set off.

'Is it your first time across then?' the boatman asked the two strangers, which was a bit of an unusual thing to ask when you think about it because he knew the answer. Finbar never forgot a face.

Both nodded silently.

'Are you a knight?' he asked Robert.

'Yes.'

'Are you a Norman?'

'Yes.'

The boatman pretended to concentrate on pushing his pole into the muddy bottom of the lough to propel them along. A good while passed in that fashion with no words passing between any of them; when they were halfway across the lough Finbar finally broke the quiet.

'Haven't any of you got any questions?' he snapped impatiently.

Caoimhin held out a white pebble.

'One white pebble.'

'One white pebble,' the boatman repeated as he took the stone in his hand. 'That entitles you to one question.'

'Why do you charge a white pebble for each question?'

The boatman stopped rowing to lean on his oar.

'That's a good question. I started doing this forty years ago. I had read the Gospel according to Thomas. And Jesus said, "Be passers-by."'

Finbar laughed at the memory before he went on.

'I took it to mean that I should pass through this world making as little impact on it as possible. Like the wake behind my boat I'll disappear completely when I pass over. And then I'll just be a memory.'

He coughed to bring himself out of his dreamy recollection.

'In those days no one else could be bothered ferrying pilgrims back and forth across the lough. My mother told me I was wasting my time. She reckoned I should take up a profession that would earn me a decent living.'

He paused for breath.

'I suppose I could have been a pig provider or even a turf merchant, if I'd set my mind to learning a trade, but those vocations didn't appeal to me. I wanted to travel.

'I suppose I have rowed a vast distance since I started,' he noted. 'My wife left me after the first year. That's when I took up the life of a holy hermit. Collecting pebbles for questions seemed the best way to get the money together to pay for my ale. I'm a bit of a souse, myself, I am.'

Caoimhin thrust another pebble forward but Finbar shook his head.

'I'll not answer another question from you, my lad. In all these forty years you're the first man to ask me why and wherefore I collect the white pebbles. So you've forfeited the right to ask me any more. If you please, it will be this gentleman's turn here.'

He turned to Robert.

'Sir knight, what would you ask?'

'Is there any way to rid oneself of a Frightener spirit?'

'Is that a personal Frightener or one who has attached himself to some article in your possession?'

'The latter.'

'Is the spirit awake?'

'It was lulled by a Draoi-song into sleep.'

'A good thing!'

Caoimhin handed over the pebble.

'The only sure way to rid oneself of a Frightener, or an Enticer for that matter, which has attached to some article, is to discard the said article in a place where it cannot be easily retrieved. For that purpose a deep cave or a mountaintop would suffice. But be it on your conscience if some poor soul in the future should come across that thing you've thrown away and then that spirit become the very bane of their existence.'

The boatman took a deep breath as he pushed against his oar once again.

'Of course it's much easier to cast aside a Frightener than it is an Enticer,' he added. 'Enticers are the very Devil to get rid of, you know.'

'So I've heard,' Robert replied.

'What about him?' Finbar asked, pointing to Srón. 'Does he have a question?'

Caoimhin frowned at his companion to show she should shake her head and stay silent.

'He's not a very inquisitive fellow,' he cut in quickly as Srón opened her mouth to speak.

'Why aren't women allowed on the Island of the Living?' she asked in an unnaturally deep voice that was obviously suspect.

Caoimhin covered his eyes, waiting for the boatman to lose his temper. After a few moments he looked up to see Finbar holding out his hand for the white pebble.

'Come on, give it to me!' he shouted. 'Do you want to hear the answer or not?'

Caoimhin handed over the stone, surprised Finbar hadn't noticed Srón was a woman.

'You are a young man,' the boatman began. 'I can hear that in the high-pitched tones of your voice. You have little understanding of women. So I will answer this question for you. And more.'

He paused with his pushing for a moment to consider what he was about to say.

'Women are among the most evil of all the things ever concocted in the dark depths of Satan's kingdom. They inspire poetry, which as we all know is the very seed of decadence. For as soon as one is exposed to poetry one is doomed to encounter metaphor. Right this minute I won't expound upon my thoughts with regard to that particular subject since our journey is but a short one.'

He leaned on his oar.

'Enough to say that metaphors are the very seeds of heresy waiting to sprout. Look what happened to the Romans as soon as they got involved with poetry. Metaphors sprung up on every street corner touting their wares. Next thing they knew they'd abolished the Republic and elected an emperor. It was a long downhill slide for them after that. We all know what happened after Constantine's Epicurean adventures.'

He pushed against the oar again and stared off into the distance as the boat glided forward.

'Women are to be avoided, my boy. When you're older you'll understand the reasons.'

'I wish to ask another question,' Robert interrupted, holding up a shining silver penny. 'Will four farthings buy it for me?'

'I don't sell questions!' Finbar snapped in an injured tone. 'I exchange them for pebbles. For a penny you may have four white stones and four questions.'

Robert handed over the penny. Finbar took it, immediately weighing it in his hand. Then he bit down hard on the silver coin to make certain it was genuine.

'There's a lot of pewter forgeries about these days. You can't be too careful.'

Then he rummaged about in his pouch for the pebbles. When he'd counted four he gave them to Robert who immediately handed one to Srón. Then he nodded his head to encourage her to ask another question. She protested for a few seconds then handed the pebble back to the boatman.

'Why is this place called the Island of the Living?'

The boatman's eyes lit up.

'At last! An intelligent question. The young master is very learned and wise for his age. I've no doubt about it.'

He stopped rowing and let the boat drift forward on the still waters.

'Look over there at the isle where I dwell. It is a fair place. But would you believe it was created by the hands of men? That's right. The monks who first came here found a lough but no island. So they decided to make one for themselves where they could live undisturbed by the world beyond.'

He pushed against the oar.

'That was hundreds of years ago in the time of the blesséd Patrick. They loaded their boats with soil and after many journeys back and forth gradually built up the island where it stands now.'

'You haven't answered my question,' Srón cut in.

'Be patient, young master,' Finbar snapped. 'It's a good story so it's worth telling properly. And with a tale like this it's best to be on your guard for metaphor. Metaphor can easily drag you down to break wind at the bottom-basting breakfast banquet of Beelzebub. So it pays to be vigilant.'

He shoved hard on the oar again and the curragh surged forward.

'In those days the Culdees who came here also allowed women among them as equals. But do not judge them harshly for that. They were pious and true nevertheless. Indeed, it is a measure of their piety that they put up with the incessant temptation the females dangled before them every day.

'Those folk who decided to dwell among the holy ones here on the island were known as the Perfecti. To become a Perfecti was not an easy matter. They had to have gone through the

388

baptisms of water, of air and be ready to undertake the baptism of fire which reunites the soul with the One.'

He took a sharp breath.

'I trust you understand what I'm on about.'

Finbar waited until Srón nodded. Then he continued.

'The Perfecti were also known as the Living Ones in those days. And that was because they had come to understand the meaning and purpose of God. They had moved beyond the desire to suffer death. They had come to know the truth of existence.'

The boatman paused for effect.

'So that's why this place is called the Island of the Living.'

Robert handed a pebble across.

'And what is the truth of existence?'

'That we are all immortal!' Finbar laughed as if that were obvious. 'Whether you've taken the Quicken Brew or not, there is no death. This world is but a dream wherein we play out our part in the story. However, few folk understand they have the power to compose the story for themselves. And fewer realise they can do or be anything their heart desires. For we are each a part of the One. And we are the One who is immortal, changeless, yet forever constantly transforming.'

He smiled, pleased with his explanation.

'The Island of the Living was a place where those who were ready to take the baptism of fire waited out their days until they returned to the One.'

He pushed down on the oar again before he went on.

'Of course that all changed with the coming of the Normans. Since the bark-splitters arrived it's become a refuge for folk wishing to avoid the terrible consequences of war, famine, plague and death. Not to mention the dreaded fifth horseman who takes the female guise. This is a place where men come to get drunk and forget the world beyond. It is a place where a man may have the time to contemplate the greater questions and serve his conscience without the constant nagging of a woman to distract him.'

Finbar smiled sweetly at Robert.

'Do you have another question? I see you have more pebbles.'

Without hesitation Rob handed over another stone.

'Can you show me the deepest part of the lough?'

Finbar frowned. 'I don't understand the philosophical implications of your question. You'll have to be more specific.'

Then a realisation struck the boatman and he recoiled from the knight.

'By Saint Michael's Bushy Chin! How dare you bring such a malodorous metaphor on to my boat? You mystical bastards are all the same! How dare you drag a man out into the middle of the lough and assail him with the very instruments of the Devil's own torture chamber? You cannot tempt me. Out!'

'What?' Robert smiled, trying to make sense of the boatman's rage.

'Get out! I won't take you any further. You, your sword and your clever storytelling device can get off my boat right now!'

'You've misunderstood me,' the knight protested. 'I really want to know where the deepest part of this lough is situated.'

Finbar frowned again, then swallowed hard with embarrassment. He pointed to the water.

'This lough?'

'This lough,' Robert confirmed gently.

'I see. Forgive me. One can never be too careful. You never know when Satan is going to lay a linguistic doo-lally in your lap. It pays to be on your guard.'

He pointed across to a dark patch of water.

'It's bottomless over there,' he whispered with dread. 'Or so folks say.'

'Take us to where the water is darkest,' Robert demanded. 'I want a closer look.'

'I will not! Too many folk have drowned in that part of the lough. Those are dark and treacherous waters. Some folk say the Queen of the Night lives within a cave underneath. I won't risk running into one such as her. Not for any man.'

Caoimhin and Srón stifled laughter at the ridiculous notion of Aoife living under this lough. Robert held up another shining coin.

'This is a brand-new King John penny. It's yours if you'll row over Aoife's cave.'

Once again Finbar swallowed hard. The penny sparkled with reflected sunlight as Robert rolled it around enticingly in his fingers.

'Very well.' The boatman snatched the coin from the knight. 'I'll take you. But you mustn't rock the boat about or we'll all be drowned.'

He pushed the oar down into the mud beneath the shallow waters and pushed off toward the deep part of the pool. It wasn't long before they were directly over the dark bottomless hole.

Robert noted that the water had grown darker hue and the boatman's oar no longer touched the mud on the bottom.

'This will do nicely,' he stated as he stood up in the boat.

The tiny vessel rocked this way and that as Robert's weight shifted in the boat.

'What are you doing?' Finbar screamed.

'Something I should have done when I first encountered this weapon,' Robert replied.

He raised the sword in its black leather scabbard and examined the finely wrought hilt one last time. Then he simply held the blade over the side of the boat and dropped it. It fell in with a splash and the weapon was instantly lost in the cold depths of the lough.

'Farewell Órán,' the knight whispered. 'May you never emerge into the light of day again. May you never tempt a mortal till the day of judgement. And may you be forgotten along with all of your kind.'

As he finished speaking a great roar rolled across the lough from the further shore where they'd met Finbar's boat.

'What was that?' Srón shrieked.

'Sit down, will you?' Finbar screamed, frantic now. 'Sit down!'

Robert did as he was told. Then he smiled as he passed the last pebble to the Sen Erainn warrior-woman.

Another roar thundered over the water.

'What was that?' Srón repeated as she passed the pebble across to the boatman.

'That was the lion,' the boatman nodded knowingly. 'Some folk say she was abandoned by some Norman lord years ago and trudges the country round, searching for suitable victims.'

'But you don't agree,' Srón stated, careful not to make her words sound like a question. She wanted to lead him on to tell her some more and they'd run out of pebbles.

'Others say she's the goddess Danu of the Flowing Waters who wanders round in the guise of a large predatory cat.'

'But that's not what you believe.'

'No I don't believe that's the truth of it at all. I don't reckon she's even a lion.'

'You mean she's a lioness then,' Caoimhin noted.

'In what sense?' the boatman asked, his head cocked to one side like a raven's.

'If it's a female lion then it would be a lioness.'

'Ah! But *is* she a lion?' Finbar countered. 'That's the question. As I said, I don't reckon she is.'

'I'm sure she's a fine lion.' Caoimhin realised grammatical points were lost on this fellow. He obviously had no experience of lions. Or lionesses either for that matter.

'I'd like to see this lion,' Srón giggled.

'Lioness,' Caoimhin sighed.

'As I said, I reckon that's no lion,' Finbar declared. 'She's something far worse than any beast who ever lived. She's a monster. An abomination. An evil-hearted, self-centred pit of delusion, manipulation and all-devouring greed.'

Robert, Caoimhin and Srón were all lost for words, drawn in by the sincerity of his explanation. They waited to hear what he was going to say next.

'The creature bellowing those calls is the ugliest, vilest, most contemptible, most treacherous, least compassionate and above all the bloodthirstiest of any being it has been my misfortune to describe during the all too brief span of my years.'

'Go on,' Caoimhin urged him.

'She's a Frightener spirit. That's what she is.'

Robert raised his eyebrows as Finbar went on.

'Think of it this way. If she was a man-eating lion she'd have been feeding off the flesh of poor Irish folk all these years. We would have heard some word about her. But all you ever hear is that bloody roar. She's a Frightener all right. She feeds off the fear she spreads with those roars of hers.'

Srón snuggled closer to Caoimhin. With all this talk of Frighteners and man-eating lions she was beginning to get the jitters. Then, without thinking, she fondly traced the fingers of one hand across Caoimhin's knee.

'You may be right,' Srón agreed. 'A lion would have left some trace of her presence somewhere.'

'Lioness,' Caoimhin corrected with a roll of his eyes.

But Finbar wasn't listening to a word they said. He was staring in disbelief at the close proximity between the two of them and he was clearly shocked.

'Bloody mystics,' he muttered under his breath as he tried to concentrate on rowing. 'They're all the bloody same.'

Then he dipped his oar to cut through the water, propelling the little curragh off towards the Island of the Living. But they didn't get out when the curragh struck the stony shore. They bought three more pebbles and got Finbar to row them back to the other side again. And just for a bit of a laugh they asked him three quite searching but rather silly questions about lions to pass the time.

WELLSPRINGS

I don't know if I believe there ever was a lion or lioness, whatever the case may be. I've never been convinced of its existence. But I promised Aoife I wouldn't leave anything out. So there you have it. All that's left to tell is what happened to everyone after that Samhain.

Lewyn and Overton, the two monks who'd accompanied Caoimhin to the Killibegs, went on to travel the whole of Ireland and write a wonderful guidebook for pilgrims. I've read it. It was a breath-taking account of this country in the early years of the reign of King John. Some critics called it a tongue-in-cheek rebuttal of the works of Giraldus Cambrensis but that would be oversimplifying the monks' achievement.

Fifty years ago they went off on an expedition into the Otherworld, intent on compiling a travellers' guide to that country. They have not, as yet, returned. But I can't wait to read their manuscript when they do. It's bound to be a hoot!

Lanfranc escorted Mirim back to Wexford town and he was a true gentleman to her. Her grief was great but he was a true friend through it all. In the end she didn't take ship to her own country. She stayed and later married him. They had three fine daughters.

Tóraí Tairngire became good friends with Mawn and Sianan. They taught him the harp and he fathered a family of gifted musicians. He's well thought of by his descendants. And yes, they're all red-haired and gifted with an unusually sharp sense of smell and of fun.

Sianan was enthroned as Morrigán the next year at Samhain and Mawn was declared her consort. I haven't seen much of them lately. They've been quite busy since the English Crown got interested in Ireland again. Lom Dubh and Sciathan Cog settled their differences to some degree and sit at Sianan's right hand, or so I am told.

Lochie and Isleen took up the wandering life. They travelled east to the lands of mystery and were not heard of again. No one knows how they fared or what roads they journeyed at the end of their lives. But I'm sure when their mortal existences were done they ended up as Frighteners or Enticers as Danu promised.

No trace was ever found of Clemens or his wife Derbaíl. Their bodies were reduced to ashes in the inferno of the great hall. In that way they became a part of everything that was rebuilt after. Likewise the remains of Rónán Og were never found. Nor were those of any of his bowmen who'd perished in the defence of our people.

William FitzWilliam stayed at the Killibegs long enough to tell me some marvellous tales of his youthful adventures. If you ask me nicely I might share them with you one day. He took to the life of a hermit again at Beltinne the next year as soon as the weather improved. Then one day before Samhain someone noticed his hut had been deserted for a long time. I guess he accepted Danu's invitation.

The warriors of the Sen Erainn went home to Inis Mór and may they never stand to war again. May peace engulf their island. And may the English pass it by whenever they sail their warships through those waters.

Robert FitzWilliam made his peace with Stronghold and together they rebuilt the Killibegs. It was a fine fortress and a fine monument to an unlikely friendship. Culdees still go there to pay homage to those two men and all they achieved in later life. In the end Robert went off to be with Aoife in the Tower of Glass. And for all I know he dwells there still. I like to imagine he got everything he'd hoped for from life. I suspect he probably did.

Stronghold built a tomb for his great-grandfather in the cellars where the old man fell. There was also a monument to Clemens, Derbaíl, Rónán Og and all the folk who died defending the rath. And on the night it was dedicated Stronghold sat vigil through the dark hours in remembrance of the chivalrous knight whose name was Guy d'Alville.

The next year on Samhain Eve, the anniversary of the battle, Stronghold sat the vigil again on his knees before the tomb with his sword, Eterscél, point down upon the stones. The old Frightener never woke up. He's sleeping still. An altar was erected the year after. And by the third Samhain several other knights joined Stronghold at his vigil. Year by year more warriors made their pilgrimage to that tomb to pledge their lives to chivalry. And in the end, among the many flattering titles that were accorded to my knight, his favourite was Stronghold of the Silent Vigil.

Gusán and John became fast friends indeed. They went into service. In fact Gusán became the Chancellor of the Killibegs and John became the Chamberlain. They both married Culdee girls and settled down to lives well lived among their loved ones.

Caoimhin never went back to the monastery. He studied the harp under Mawn's tutelage. Eventually, after many years, he wed Srón and they were very happy. Though young Caoimhin often came to stay with us at the Killibegs and I have to admit I succumbed to bouts of illicit tickling with him on many occasions. The temptation was too great to resist. I loved my Stronghold dearly but there wasn't a man alive who could flatten the bed feathers like Caoimhin.

As I grew older he spent more time with Srón and visited me less and less. No children came of that union for he was an immortal and it is rare they ever have any offspring. Together they collected stories. I've told you Caoimhin wrote down Lom Dubh's story in the tale of the Watchers. He also wrote down Mawn's story in the manuscript known as the Wanderers. He related Robert and Guy's meeting in the Tale of the Tilecutter's Penny. But there were many other stories he put to parchment also. A treatise on sigil magic is probably his most famous, though he also compiled his own version of the Book of Destiny.

Srón collected fish poetry. She died some twenty summers ago with Caoimhin cradling her in his arms as they looked westward out to sea from her island home. Then he withdrew into the Otherworld and has not been heard of since.

I married Stronghold. I'm sure you guessed that by now. We had three sons and two daughters. And this tale represents but a small part of the adventures we shared. We presided over the rebuilding of the Killibegs and were treated like royalty by anyone who didn't know us too well.

My knight passed over last Samhain while he kneeled at his vigil. And no one knew he'd gone until the next morning when they tried to rouse him to his breakfast. He is entombed beside his ancestor and will be remembered as a fair man by many and just another bough-splitting bastard by some.

As for me, I'm ninety winters' worth. And I've a trick or two yet to play if I have my way. I've often wondered what my life would have been like if I hadn't gone off into the Otherworld chasing after Caoimhin. And I've wondered whether he and I would've been happy together if we'd tied the knot.

I can't say whether I believe all that rubbish about us being lovers in another life. But I have to admit I'm curious. I still have a portion of those herbs my friend Ortha gave me. I could mix up the love potion one last time.

If I go off to the Otherworld perhaps Caoimhin will give me a taste of the Quicken Brew and I'll be granted my chance to get to know him again. It's a lovely thought, isn't it?

The life of each and every mortal is filled to the very brim with unquenchable longing. Some folk long for peace from the spirits of fear that haunt the dark places of their soul. Others are consumed by the desire for material comforts to ease their passage through life. Most of us are instilled with an undeniable longing for love.

And every soul-traveller is searching. We all have our private quests. You see, before we come into this world all the Earthborn bathe in the sacred spring of the Well of Yearning.

An old Norman named William FitzWilliam first told me about these things. I'm not sure whether he truly understood them himself for there was some talk that he was mad. And it's likely my ears weren't quite ready to listen to him at that time either. But I reckon the truth passed through him to me.

Lord Will had been a knight once. He'd been a hero of the crusades. And a lord. He'd seen many terrible battles and much hardship during his lifetime. He'd also known his fair share of joy. In his later years he became a monk and decided to live in seclusion from society. That's how he came to be with my people.

When I was a lass of twenty-one winters I'd visit him with his daily bread. I used to walk all the way out to where he had his shelter. It was a respectable distance from everyone else.

His bread was always fresh and hot, wrapped in a linen cloth. It was difficult for me to resist the urge to taste it. I never did though. The old lord needed every morsel of food for his survival. Even ascetics must eat to keep the body alive. How could I, well fed and watered, consider thieving from such as he who had devoted the remains of his life to God?

I would place the bread on the doorstep of his dwelling. Sometimes when I arrived he'd be waiting to talk to me. But most times old Will simply stayed inside. He liked his solitude. So I'd leave the bread for him, wondering how he'd fared since the last time we'd spoken.

My companions whispered that a wizard from the land of Lochlann had captured the old man's heart in a bottle. A man without a heart finds no discomfort in solitude, they said. That's why William had turned his mind to meditation and reserved his sighs for himself.

I don't know whether they were right about Will. I can only tell you that on a cold night at the start of his third winter with us, William FitzWilliam fell into the dreaming of a powerful dream. And as the old tales tell, my dear, nothing is more powerful than a dream. Except the truth, of course. So don't get the idea this whole story was nothing more than a silly dream invented by a witless old warrior.

The story you've been told concerns the secret of the Well of Many Blessings, which is as real as anything can be. A draught from that spring causes our deepest dreams to become reality, even if we aren't aware they were our dreams to begin with.

Wellsprings are everywhere. You don't need a divining rod to find them. You don't need a golden Grail Cup to drink from them. You don't have to feel guilty if you take more than your fill. I've never forgotten what the soothsayer told my Stronghold when he was a young knight in the Holy Land.

The three strongest forces in this world are the force of water, the force of fire and the force of hatred. Yet one who wields the first two guided by the force of love may be a one to be reckoned with.

**POCKET
BOOKS**

Also by Caiseal Mor

The Well of Yearning

Book One of the Wellspring Trilogy

Guy d'Alville had been a Knight of the Hospital before he was expelled from the prestigious military order for failing in his duties. He blames the loss of his fortune on one man: a Templar knight named Robert Fitzwilliam.

But in his quest for vengeance, Guy discovers ancient forces afoot. The mysterious Otherworld is astir with rumours of war. The beautiful and terrible Aoife, Queen of the Night is gathering her armies to assault the realm of mortals. Recognising a shadowed soul when She sees one, She promises Guy the High-Kingshop of Ireland in exchange for his help. And, in time, the crown of England.

But Guy has unwittingly unleashed the frightening fury of the Nathairai, whom some call the Watchers. Imprisoned for centuries within the Well of Dun Gur, once these malevolent creatures are free, their rampage will know no bounds.

ISBN 0 7434 6856 2
PRICE £6.99

**POCKET
BOOKS**

Also by Caiseal Mor

The Well of the Goddess

Book Two of the Wellspring Trilogy

Guy d'Alville has already faced the terrible Nathairai –
and tasted humiliating defeat. But all is not lost. He has
taken possession of the sacred books of the holy community of Kellibegs. These heretical works are much
sought after by the officers of the Holy Inquisition.
D'Alville resolves to take the manuscripts to Rome in
the hope of restoring his reputation, title and lands.

But in making his escape from the Killibegs, Guy
commits a serious blunder. In his haste to leave the
heretics, he passes through a doorway to the
Otherworld, finding himself trudging through the
strange landscape of myth, spirits and mischief
beyond the magical barrier separating the two
worlds. Pursued by the elders of the Killibegs, led by
Robert FitzWilliam, Guy is faced with a remarkable
opportunity as his life takes an unexpected turn. He
discovers a friend in the most unlikely of men. And
all of this comes to pass the very moment he takes a
sip of the waters of the Well of the Goddess.

ISBN 0 7434 6858 9
PRICE £6.99

**POCKET
BOOKS**

This book and other **Pocket Books** titles are available from your local
bookshop or can be ordered direct from the publisher.

Please send cheque or postal order for the value of the book,
free postage and packing within the UK, to
SIMON & SCHUSTER CASH SALES
PO Box 29, Douglas, Isle of Man, IM99 1BQ
Tel: 01624 677237, Fax: 01624 670923
E-mail: bookshop@enterprise.net
www.bookpost.co.uk

Please allow 14 days for delivery.
Prices and availability subject to change without notice.